Prof. Suzanne J. Flynn
Department of English
Gettysburg College

D1255973

NEW PERSPECTIVES ON THOMAS HARDY

THE THOMAS HARDY SOCIETY

(President: **The Earl of Stockton**)

The Society welcomes anyone interested in Hardy's writings, his life and his times, and it takes pride in the way in which at its meetings people come together in a harmony which would have delighted Hardy himself. Among its members are many distinguished literary and academic figures, and many more who love and enjoy Hardy's work sufficiently to wish to meet fellow enthusiasts and develop their appreciation of it.

Members receive copies of *The Thomas Hardy Journal* which is published three times a year and is regarded as the leading source of Hardy studies. Lectures, guided tours and walks in Hardy's Wessex, and other events take place throughout the year, and there is a biennial conference in Dorchester which brings together students from all over the world.

For information about the Society please write to:

The Thomas Hardy Society
P. O. Box 1438
Dorchester
Dorset DT1 1YH

New Perspectives on Thomas Hardy

Edited by

Charles P. C. Pettit

St. Martin's Press

First published in Great Britain 1994 by
THE MACMILLAN PRESS LTD
Houndmills, Basingstoke, Hampshire RG21 2XS
and London
Companies and representatives
throughout the world

A catalogue record for this book is available
from the British Library.

ISBN 0–333–60660–4

Printed in Great Britain by
Ipswich Book Co Ltd
Ipswich, Suffolk

First published in the United States of America 1994 by
Scholarly and Reference Division,
ST. MARTIN'S PRESS, INC.,
175 Fifth Avenue,
New York, N.Y. 10010

ISBN 0–312–12036–2

Library of Congress Cataloging-in-Publication Data
New perspectives on Thomas Hardy / edited by Charles P. C. Pettit.
p.   cm.
Includes index.
ISBN 0–312–12036–2
1. Hardy, Thomas, 1840–1928—Criticism and interpretation.
I. Pettit, Charles P. C.
PR4754.N47   1994
823'.8—dc20
                                                            93–36998
                                                            CIP

For Judith

Contents

Contents

Preface

The 'appreciative readers, male and female' whom Hardy regretted being unable to 'shake ... by the hand' in his Preface to the Fifth Edition of *Tess of the d'Urbervilles* might be somewhat bemused by much current literary criticism. All too often, the use of unfamiliar jargon and the introduction of abstruse linguistic and critical concepts produce work which seems to speak only to a handful of fellow specialists and which seems impenetrable to the non-academic reader of literature. The *New Perspectives* contained in this volume avoid this kind of critical élitism. For all their variety of subject and approach, and despite a high level of critical sophistication, all the contributors share one vital and fundamental quality: the ability to convey their insights in a language which can be understood equally by academics and by the literary enthusiast, the modern representative of Hardy's 'appreciative reader'.

This quality stems directly from the origin of these papers, which were first presented at the Tenth International Thomas Hardy Conference, organised by the Thomas Hardy Society and held in Dorchester in 1992. The underlying reason for the continuing success of these conferences over some twenty years has been the creation of a programme which successfully brings together Hardy enthusiasts and academics in a week of shared enjoyment and mutual understanding. As Director of the Tenth Conference, therefore, my most fundamental principle when deciding which speakers to invite from among those of the world's leading Hardy scholars who had not spoken at the previous conference, was that they would be able to communicate their ideas effectively to all the participants. The universally enthusiastic reaction to the lectures by conference participants, coming from many parts of the world and bearing many different levels of critical expertise, demonstrates that the avoidance of critical élitism does not imply an unexciting or regressive critical stance. Far from it. This is no cosy coterie of Hardy worshippers: stringent and searching analyses, wide-ranging references to other writers and critical methods, a full awareness of current critical developments, debate, disagreement and controversy will all be found in the papers in this volume. The key is that the language of debate is accessible to all.

Apart from this fundamental quality of accessibility, the keynote of the volume is variety. Even without the two conference papers that we have regrettably been unable to include, the reader will find here examples of many different critical approaches, which range over the greater part of Hardy's *oeuvre*. The collection includes papers on both poetry and prose, considerations of individual works in detail and of themes running through many works, biographical enquiry, analysis of Hardy's language, assessments of his thought, his creative methods, his relationships with other writers and his reading, and a postmodernist's view of both Hardy and of critical approaches to him. Even this brief summary, while it does emphasise the variety of the book's contents, fails to do justice to their critical sophistication, for the detailed analyses of particular texts are among the most wide-ranging in their references, while the relationship between Hardy's life and his creativity which is explored in more than one paper transcends neat categorisation.

The majority of the critics are Hardy scholars of many years' standing, but it is a particular pleasure to include work by writers such as Craig Raine and Michael Slater who are turning their attention to Hardy after having made their reputations in other fields. The papers are presented in the order in which they appeared at the Conference, an order which emphasises their variety. My own paper was the reserve lecture for the Conference, and has been inserted in the sequence in the place originally occupied by one of the two missing lectures. Framing the volume at either end are papers by two scholars who also lectured at the very first Hardy Conference (then a 'Summer School') in 1973 and who have contributed so much to the wider world of Hardy studies as well as to the Thomas Hardy Society, namely James Gibson and F. B. Pinion.

'Amazingly high quality', 'excellent quality of material' and 'very varied topics' – these were some typical comments about the lecture programme made by conference participants in an end-of-course questionnaire. On reading through the papers I find that the variety, vitality and sheer quality of the lectures come across as effectively on the printed page as they did in the conference hall, enabling them to be shared by many other academics, students and Hardy enthusiasts. Above all, these thought-provoking essays send the reader back with new insights to Hardy's texts themselves.

CHARLES P. C. PETTIT

Notes on the Contributors

Lance St John Butler is Senior Lecturer in English Studies at the University of Stirling. His publications include: *Thomas Hardy after Fifty Years* (edited), *Thomas Hardy, Samuel Beckett and the Meaning of Being, Studying Thomas Hardy, Alternative Hardy* (edited) and *Victorian Doubt*.

Peter J. Casagrande is Professor of English and Associate Dean for the Humanities at the University of Kansas in Lawrence, Kansas. His major publications include *Unity in Hardy's Novels: 'Repetitive Symmetries', Hardy's Influence on the Modern Novel* and *'Tess of the d'Urbervilles': Unorthodox Beauty*. He is currently working on a study of Hardy's originality.

Raymond Chapman is Professor Emeritus of English in the University of London, and Lecturer and Academic Adviser at the London Centre of the Institute of European Studies. He has written a number of books on Victorian literature and the language of literature, including *The Victorian Debate* (1968), *Faith and Revolt: Studies in the Literature of the Oxford Movement* (1970), *The Sense of the Past in Victorian Literature* (1986), *The Language of Thomas Hardy* (1990), *Forms of Speech in Victorian Fiction* (forthcoming), and was an associate editor and contributor to the *Oxford Companion to the English Language* (1992).

James Gibson is an Honorary Vice President of the Thomas Hardy Society, of which he is currently Chairman; as creator and first editor of *The Thomas Hardy Journal* and Academic Director of two of the Society's Conferences he has played a leading role in Society affairs. He was formerly Principal Lecturer in English at Christ Church College, Canterbury. He has written or edited some fifty books, with total sales of some two million copies; his major Hardy works include his editions of *The Complete Poems* and *The Variorum Edition of the Complete Poems,* and various Hardy novels. He is editor of *A Casebook: The Poems of Thomas Hardy* (with Trevor Johnson) and both *Chosen Poems* and *Chosen Short Stories*. He is currently working on a short life of Hardy in the Macmillan 'Literary Lives' series and a volume of interviews and recollections of Hardy.

Timothy Hands is a Housemaster at King's School, Canterbury, and is the author of the George Eliot and Hardy volumes in the Macmillan 'Chronology' series, and of *Thomas Hardy: Distracted Preacher?* He has recently written a companion to the Stinsford Church Guide entitled *Thomas Hardy and Stinsford Church*, and is presently working on the Hardy volume in the 'Writers in their Times' series to be published by Macmillan, for which the current paper formed part of his preparation.

Trevor Johnson is the former Head of the Department of Language and Literature at Manchester College of Higher Education, and currently lectures on the part-time degree course at Manchester University and for the WEA. He is author of *Thomas Hardy, Thomas Hardy: An Annotated Reading List, 'Joseph Andrews' by Henry Fielding: A Critical Guide* and *A Critical Introduction to the Poems of Thomas Hardy.* He is editor of the Folio Society's selection of Hardy's poems, and has written the introductions for three novels in the Folio's collected Hardy. He edited (with James Gibson) *A Casebook: The Poems of Thomas Hardy,* and has written many articles on Hardy. He is currently engaged (with Alan Shelston) in a reprint in near facsimile form of the eight separate volumes of Hardy's verse, with substantial critical introductions.

Charles P. C. Pettit is a librarian, and manages libraries and a museum in west Oxfordshire as a Client Services Manager in Oxfordshire County Council's Department of Leisure and Arts. He has been a member of the Council of Management of the Thomas Hardy Society for over ten years, and has directed three of the Society's ten conferences, including the 1992 Tenth International Conference which has contributed the material for this volume. While working for Dorset County Library he compiled *A Catalogue of the Works of Thomas Hardy in Dorchester Reference Library.* He has contributed articles on Hardy to a number of periodicals, has lectured and reviewed for the Thomas Hardy Society, and has written a short guide *St Juliot Church and Thomas Hardy.*

F. B. Pinion is the author of the standard reference work *A Hardy Companion,* and has followed this up with other volumes in the

'Companion' series on writers as diverse as Jane Austen, Words-worth and T. S. Eliot. He has edited many Hardy novels and short stories, and his many other books include *A Commentary on the Poems of Thomas Hardy*, *Thomas Hardy: Art and Thought*, *A Thomas Hardy Dictionary* and *Hardy the Writer*. His latest book is *Thomas Hardy: His Life and Friends*. Formerly Reader in English Studies and a Sub-Dean at the University of Sheffield, he has been for many years an Honorary Vice-President of the Thomas Hardy Society, for which he has done much work, including editing *The Thomas Hardy Society Review* for the ten years of its life.

Craig Raine, formerly poetry editor at Faber & Faber, is now Fellow of New College, Oxford. His publications are: *The Onion, Memory* (1978), *A Martian Sends a Postcard Home* (1979), *Rich* (1984), *The Electrification of the Soviet Union* (1986), *'1953'* (1990) and a collection of essays *Haydn and the Valve Trumpet* (1990).

Michael Slater is Professor of Victorian Literature at Birkbeck College, University of London, a former editor of *The Dickensian* and a past President of the Dickens Fellowship. His publications include various editions of works by Dickens, also *Dickens on America and the Americans* and *Dickens and Women*. More recently, he has written a number of introductions for the new Everyman's Library series, including one on *Far from the Madding Crowd*. He is currently engaged on a four-volume edition of Dickens's journalism.

Peter Widdowson is Professor of Literature and Head of School of Historical and Critical Studies at the University of Brighton. Amongst his publications are: *E. M. Forster's 'Howards End': Fiction as History* (1977), his edited collection *Re-Reading English* (1982), *Hardy in History: A Study in Literary Sociology* (1989), a 'Critical Reader' on D. H. Lawrence (1992), a 'New Casebook' on *Tess of the d'Urbervilles* (1993, to which a version of the present paper is the introduction), and the revised third edition, on behalf of the late Raman Selden, of *A Reader's Guide to Contemporary Literary Theory* (1993). He is currently in the process of editing a selection of Hardy's poetry and non-fictional prose for Routledge's 'English Texts' series.

1

'The Characteristic of all Great Poetry – The General Perfectly Reduced in the Particular': Thomas Hardy

JAMES GIBSON

It is a fallacy that Hardy's old age was spent in a recluse-like existence at Max Gate. Celebrities, friends and relations came through its gates in such numbers that it is surprising how much work he still managed to do. One such visitor was a young army officer who was stationed near Dorchester at the end of the Great War and was welcomed by Hardy to Max Gate on several occasions in 1918 and 1919. Lt. Elliott Felkin came bearing an introduction from Lowes Dickinson and kept a full record of their discussions.[1] They make interesting reading. The earliest is dated 21 October 1918 when he had tea with the Hardys and he found Hardy 'amazingly lively, interested and interesting'. After discussing the novel and Hardy's assertion that 'all imaginative work was events seen through a temperament', Hardy, described as 'extraordinarily active', went for a walk with Felkin during which they discussed how much of a person's private life should be revealed by a biographer. He thought that George Eliot should be ranked with Goethe and Kant rather than Shakespeare and Sophocles, and that she was a neglected writer. When Felkin left, Hardy accompanied him for a walk and turned his money in his pocket at the sight of the new moon just 'in case'. At another meeting, on 21 July 1919, Hardy described how he often used to meet Browning, and how much he liked Browning's poem 'The Statue and the Bust' because 'it has the characteristic of all great poetry – the general perfectly reduced in the particular. "Procrastination, that's what it is, and there's nothing to be said about procrastination that is not in that poem." '

1

There are indications that the *Encounter* article in which these discussions were published in April 1962 was badly proof-read and it may not be accurate when it quotes Hardy's actual words, the more so as Felkin must have written them down some time after the meetings. Hardy would never have allowed him to take notes of the talks together while they were taking place. Hardy seldom uses 'general' in a literary critical context and it seems probable that he said 'universal' not 'general'. If he did say 'general' it is almost certain that he used it in the sense of 'universal' which is one of its possible meanings. This would make what he said: 'The characteristic of all great poetry: the universal perfectly reduced in the particular', and as this accords with other statements of Hardy it is in this sense that I shall take it. If I am wrong, I must hope that Hardy and Felkin, wherever they may now be – in heaven 'or some such place' – will forgive me.

The quotation is worth looking at in some detail because it was made towards the end of his life by one of our greatest poets, and it tells us a good deal about his own poetry and his own readings of life. In that remarkable but sadly neglected masterpiece of his, *The Life of Thomas Hardy*, now available for the first time in its unexpurgated text in Michael Millgate's edition entitled *The Life of Thomas Hardy by Thomas Hardy*, there are among the basic facts of his life fascinating insights into Hardy's way of looking at life and his ability to see the universal in the particular. Here is an entry for 1882:

> In the same month the Hardys attended Ambulance-Society lectures.... He makes a note concerning a particular lecture: 'A skeleton – the one used in these lectures – is hung up inside the window. We face it as we sit. Outside the band is playing, and the children are dancing. I can see their little figures through the window past the skeleton dangling in front.'[2]

Here Hardy is doing what Goethe in 1825 recommended when he said 'The Poet should seize the particular and he should if there be anything in it, thus represent the universal.' We are given the particulars – the Ambulance Society lectures, the skeleton, the band and the children playing – and these particulars lead us to the universal: the closeness of life and death, the child in the skeleton and the skeleton in the child. Past, present and future are as one to him and, like Webster, he is always aware of 'the skull beneath the skin'.

This universalising gift is seen, too, in the novels from which the harvest of the poetry was later to grow. In this following passage from *Far from the Madding Crowd*, Joseph Poorgrass is bringing back Fanny Robin's body in its 'plain elm coffin' and the universal sadness of death is emphasised by the particularity of the observed detail – 'flowering laurustinus', 'high trees', 'heavy particle', 'smart rap', the fog saturating the trees, 'beaded with the mist', and 'rusty-red leaves':

Joseph Poorgrass looked round upon his sad burden as it loomed faintly through the flowering laurustinus, then at the unfathomable gloom amid the high trees on each hand, indistinct, shadowless, and spectre-like in their monochrome of grey…. Stopping the horse he listened. Not a footstep or wheel was audible anywhere around, and the dead silence was broken only by a heavy particle falling from a tree through the evergreens and alighting with a smart rap upon the coffin of poor Fanny. The fog had by this time saturated the trees, and this was the first dropping of water from the overbrimming leaves. The hollow echo of its fall reminded the waggoner painfully of the grim Leveller. Then hard by came down another drop, then two or three. Presently there was a continual tapping of these heavy drops upon the dead leaves, the road, and the travellers. The nearer boughs were beaded with the mist to the greyness of aged men, and the rusty-red leaves of the beeches were hung with similar drops, like diamonds on auburn hair.[3]

As so often in Hardy's prose and verse, the pathetic mood is made more plangent by the sounds and sights of autumn, the season of melancholy, and the symbolism becomes part of the universal experience, the bell tolls not just for Fanny but for us. Hardy's words in a letter of 31 October 1903 to Sir George Douglas are revealing here: 'As you say, his [Hugo's] misérables are not so real as Dickens's, but they show, to my mind, one great superiority, that of universality, while those of Dickens express the particular only. Dickens in his details of things is, however, without a fellow, so special is his view.'[4]

It is necessary here to define one's terms and for a definition of 'universality', I go to *The Penguin Dictionary of Literary Terms* where it is described as 'That quality in a work of art which enables it to transcend the limits of the particular situation, place, time, person and incident in such a way that it may be of interest, pleasure and profit ... to mankind at any time, in any place. The writer who aspires to universality, therefore, concerns himself with, primarily, aspects of human nature and behaviour which seldom or never change.' The universal, one could say, is concerned with the mystery of things, with questionings of immortality, with those moments of vision which cause us to see through the glass less darkly and perceive the vanity of human wishes, and with the reality behind reality which comes, for example, from the death of someone near to us. This concern with the universal links poetry and religion as Hardy pointed out in his 'Apology' to his 1922 book of verse, *Late Lyrics and Earlier* where he writes:

> In any event poetry, pure literature in general, religion – I include religion, in its essential and undogmatic sense, because poetry and religion touch each other, or rather modulate into each other; are, indeed, often but different names for the same thing – these, I say, the visible signs of mental and emotional life, must like all other things keep moving, becoming ...

From the beginning, there had been something religious about Hardy's approach to poetry. Growing up in the wake of the great Romantic poets, he saw poetry as 'having a supreme place in literature', and in it was 'concentrated the essence of all imaginative and emotional literature'. He turned to novel-writing only because he could not earn a living as a poet, and in the 1890s he abandoned the novel with obvious delight and returned to his first love, poetry. During the next thirty years he was to write many poems whose greatness arises from the combination of universality and particularity which had contributed to the greatness of the novels. Just as religion should be available to all, so Hardy thought that poetry, because of its ability to move our hearts, should be as available to the poor man at his gate as to the rich man in his castle, and it was the universality which made it universally available. There is something very touching, and informative, in Hardy's request to his publishers that his complete poetical works should be available 'at a reasonable price so as to be within the reach of poorer readers'.

Hardy's universality results from a combination of qualities of which the most important are:

a. His passionate concern with truth, with which is associated a complete honesty and integrity. We see this in many of his poems, a particularly fine example being 'Surview'.

b. His courage in his search for truth in that he refused to shut his eyes to what was unwelcome, hypocritical, cruel and false. This led, of course, to cries of 'pessimist' and 'miserable old man' from those who wanted to believe that all was for the best in the best of all possible worlds. But, as he so often said, he was a realist rather than a pessimist, and his realist view of Victorian society has now been shown to be far more accurate than that of those who attacked him. Some of the bitterest of those attacks came from the nineteenth-century Church, and Hardy would have appreciated the irony that today's Church is now hurrying to see Hardy as a prophet before his time, someone who had the courage to expose the cruelty of its dogmatic, out-of-date tenets. The Bishops who burnt *Jude* in 1896, praise it today.

c. His sensitivity to what he called the 'on-going ... of the world', that is, life's transience. Always at his back he heard 'Time's wingèd chariot hurrying near'. This strong sense of time passing away, of a thousand ages in his sight being as yesterday, and his ability to see a world in a grain of sand meant that he was continually aware of universality, always asking – to use his own words – 'the eternal question of what Life was, And why we were there'. When in a poem like 'I look into my glass, / And view my wasting skin' Hardy uses the pronoun 'I' we sense that he not only speaks for himself but for the whole human race. Here, there is a strong feeling of solidarity with mankind, an appreciation of the oneness of humanity in its emotional life, that results in the greatest of all qualities a writer can possess.

d. That quality is compassion, and it was until the twentieth century nearly always regarded as an indispensable component of great writing. Sadly, it is no longer so. It led George Eliot to say that 'If art does nothing to enlarge men's sympathies, it does nothing morally' and Hardy to say 'What are my books but one plea against "man's inhumanity to man"?'[5] Compassion manifests itself in feelings of sympathy and the ability to empathise. In creating Tess Hardy became her and suffered with her, and we feel pity for her. Sympathy is a powerfully felt emotion in many of his poems. It suffuses poems like 'To an Unborn Pauper Child' and is manifest in its paternal tenderness:

> Fain would I, dear, find some shut plot
> Of earth's wide wold for thee, where not
>   One tear, one qualm,
>   Should break the calm.
> But I am weak as thou and bare;
> No man can change the common lot to rare.[6]

The words 'common lot' convey Hardy's feeling that we live in a flawed world, dominated by a witless and heartless Nature, in which survival is the most powerful force, a world in which Nature's plan is anything but 'holy' and mankind's worst vices can to a large extent be attributed to Nature at work within us. This sympathy for individuals and his compassion for all of Nature's creatures (and his sympathy for animals is everywhere present) result from the universality of his vision. We live on a blighted world but we are all on it together, and, for Hardy, our only hope is that loving-kindness – a word he uses again and again – would spread among the peoples of the world and that we would realise that we are all members of one family, one community. 'Evolutionary meliorism', as he called it, depended upon this.

But what about the second part of the quotation – 'perfectly reduced in the particular'? By this I take Hardy to mean the physical, material, concrete details which are the vehicle for the universality but he may also be thinking of the technical aspects of the poem which are a vital part of it – or were until the arrival of 'free verse', whatever that may mean. Hardy, 'the man with the watching eye', the 'man who used to notice such things' is particularly good at the particular. The raindrop ploughing its way down the carved names on the gravestones, the thin smoke without flames from the heaps of couch-grass, the May month flapping its 'glad green leaves like wings, / Delicate-filmed as new-spun silk', the auctioneer in 'A Sheep Fair' wringing out his beard and with a 'Going-going!' consigning the sheep to the abattoir, all these descriptions, and so many more, are brilliantly chosen metaphors of universality. It is his astonishing ability to select the particular particularity which suggests the universal which characterises his work. It is as if he could only see the particular in terms of the universal and the universal in terms of the particular, and the synthesis he expresses is remarkable in its richness. This gift for choosing the significant detail is manifest in 'In Time of "The Breaking of Nations" ':

I

Only a man harrowing clods
      In a slow silent walk
With an old horse that stumbles and nods
      Half asleep as they stalk.

II

Only thin smoke without flame
      From the heaps of couch-grass;
Yet this will go onward the same
      Though Dynasties pass.

III

Yonder a maid and her wight
      Come whispering by:
War's annals will cloud into night
      Ere their story die.[7]

1915

In the *Life* (p. 81) Hardy tells us that on the day that the battle of Gravelotte was fought in 1870 he was in the rectory garden at St Juliot in Cornwall and that

he was struck by the incident of the old horse harrowing the arable field in the valley below, which, when in far later years it was recalled to him by a still bloodier war, he made into the little poem of three verses entitled 'In Time of "The Breaking of Nations" '.

Later, referring to the same incident, he remarks that 'I believe it would be said by people who knew me well that I have a faculty (possibly not uncommon) for burying an emotion in my heart or brain for forty years, and exhuming it at the end of that time as fresh as when interred.' He then mentions the same 'agricultural incident'

(p. 408). It is worth noting here the quality of the retentive memory (not nearly so common as Hardy modestly suggests) and Hardy's ability to select subconsciously for retention an archetypal image of considerable emotional power. By means of three such images – the first drawing attention to the need to labour in the fields to produce the food we need to live, the second showing the fight against the weeds which would destroy our sustenance, and the third of love between men and women which will survive as part of Nature's plan in spite of dynastic wars – Hardy makes us aware of certain archetypal truths. The particular in this poem is economic indeed – a man and a horse harrowing clods, smoke from heaps of couch-grass, and a maid and her lover – but a universal truth has never been more movingly and memorably stated. And other particulars such as the use of the archaic word 'wight' which takes the poem back into the past and the '1915' which locates its moment of utterance as during one of the bloodiest wars of all time, contribute to the total effect on the reader.

Nearly all of Hardy's finest poems make use of this contrast between the past and the present with its emphasis on life and death and the transience of human lives, and they are all marked by a superb choice of detail. There is an intense particularity in the observation and what Professor Hynes refers to as his 'uncompromising fidelity to fact and detail'. Here is 'The Five Students':

> The sparrow dips in his wheel-rut bath,
>   The sun grows passionate-eyed,
> And boils the dew to smoke by the paddock-path;
>   As strenuously we stride, –
> Five of us; dark He, fair He, dark She, fair She, I,
>   All beating by.
>
> The air is shaken, the high-road hot,
>   Shadowless swoons the day,
> The greens are sobered and cattle at rest; but not
>   We on our urgent way, –
> Four of us; fair She, dark She, fair He, I, are there,
>   But one – elsewhere.
>
> Autumn moulds the hard fruit mellow,
>   And forward still we press

Through moors, briar-meshed plantations, clay-pits yellow,
    As in the spring hours – yes,
Three of us; fair He, fair She, I, as heretofore,
    But – fallen one more.

    The leaf drops: earthworms draw it in
    At night-time noiselessly,
The fingers of birch and beech are skeleton-thin,
    And yet on the beat are we, –
Two of us; fair She, I. But no more left to go
    The track we know.

    Icicles tag the church-aisle leads,
    The flag-rope gibbers hoarse,
The home-bound foot-folk wrap their snow-flaked heads,
    Yet I still stalk the course –
One of us ... Dark and fair He, dark and fair She, gone:
    The rest – anon.[8]

The universal theme is the transience of life and the sadness of the passing-away of friends, the tears of things. This is vintage Hardy, published by him in 1917 when he was seventy-seven. The evocativeness of the details is immediately obvious: the sparrow *dips*, the dew *smokes* (originally Hardy wrote 'fumes' but 'smokes' is far more visually effective), the air shakes with heat, the leaf is silently drawn in by the worm, and the flag-rope *gibbers*. Visual, auditory and kinaesthetic imagery are used in such a way that the very richness of the imagery contrasts with the refrainlike last two lines of each stanza which baldly and simply mark off the deaths of the 'He's and 'She's. These deaths are made more universal by the use of pronouns rather than proper nouns to describe those who have died. A feature of Hardy's verse is its significant and recurrent use of pronouns – 'They sing their dearest songs', 'She sat here in her chair', 'Why did you give no hint that night', 'He does not think that I haunt here nightly', and so many more. If Hardy had written 'Horace, Henry, Emma, Tryphena and I' his poem would have lost part of its universality, quite apart from the fact that many research workers would have been robbed of the opportunity of investigating who these 'pronouns' really were. Hardy was a Victorian in his upbringing and he did not regard the intimate particularities of his own life as anyone's business but his own. But, as one of the most autobiographical of poets, he drew heavily upon his own life for his material, distancing it in a number of ways including this use of pronouns.

Although the sparrow, the cattle, the fruit and the earthworm have lives so short that they make human lives seem long, the poem leaves the reader with an impression of the permanence, and indifference, of Nature and the transience of our lives, a transience which is emphasised by the 'Five of us . . .', 'Four of us . . .', 'Three of us . . .', 'Two of us . . .', 'One of us . . .'. It is significant, too, that the poem graphically takes the reader through seasons of the year, from the beginnings of life in the spring, through summer and autumn, to the coldness and deadness of winter, and in doing so again emphasises time passing. The carefully observed details in themselves give both a material authenticity and a powerful abstract feeling of life's 'on-goingness' and there is a perfect marriage between the universal and the particular. The leaf dropping is, of course, an obvious and frequently used image of life passing but it is made far more powerful by the earthworm drawing it in and consuming it 'at night-time noiselessly', while 'The flag-rope gibbers hoarse' is not only a strikingly evocative literal description but in sound and metaphorical undertones it suggests the senseless inarticulacy of old age and death. Possibly, too, Hardy was remembering the lines from *Hamlet* where 'The graves stood tenantless and the sheeted dead / Did squeak and gibber in the Roman streets.' There is here the exactness to be expected from a photograph and the emotional power of a great painting.

The next two poems, 'The Haunter' and 'The Voice', both appear in Hardy's 1914 volume of verse *Satires of Circumstance*, both come under the subheading of 'Poems of 1912–13', the poems Hardy wrote after the death of his first wife, Emma, in 1912, and, following each other in the sequence, they are clearly a linked pair:

'The Haunter'

He does not think that I haunt here nightly:
    How shall I let him know
That whither his fancy sets him wandering
    I, too, alertly go? –
Hover and hover a few feet from him
    Just as I used to do,
But cannot answer the words he lifts me –
    Only listen thereto!

When I could answer he did not say them:
   When I could let him know
How I would like to join in his journeys
   Seldom he wished to go.
Now that he goes and wants me with him
   More than he used to do,
Never he sees my faithful phantom
   Though he speaks thereto.

Yes, I companion him to places
   Only dreamers know,
Where the shy hares print long paces,
   Where the night rooks go;
Into old aisles where the past is all to him,
   Close as his shade can do,
Always lacking the power to call to him,
   Near as I reach thereto!

What a good haunter I am, O tell him!
   Quickly make him know
If he but sigh since my loss befell him
   Straight to his side I go.
Tell him a faithful one is doing
   All that love can do
Still that his path may be worth pursuing,
   And to bring peace thereto.[9]

'The Voice'

Woman much missed, how you call to me, call to me,
Saying that now you are not as you were
When you had changed from the one who was all to me,
But as at first, when our day was fair.

Can it be you that I hear? Let me view you, then,
Standing as when I drew near to the town
Where you would wait for me: yes, as I knew you then,
Even to the original air-blue gown!

Or is it only the breeze, in its listlessness
Travelling across the wet mead to me here,
You being ever dissolved to wan wistlessness,
Heard no more again far or near?

        Thus I; faltering forward,
        Leaves around me falling,
Wind oozing thin through the thorn from norward,
        And the woman calling.[10]

December 1912

Both these poems are concerned with the universal – with death, loss, regret, sadness and loneliness. Loneliness suffuses all the 1912–13 poems. No matter what coolness there may have been in the relationship with Emma, her death after thirty-eight years together must have left him a very lonely man. Particularities abound in these poems because they are concerned with a never-to-be-forgotten past: he will no longer see her 'At the end of the alley of bending boughs / Where so often at dusk you used to be'; or seeking 'With a child's eager glance / The shy snowdrops brought / By the new year's advance'. Loneliness is a recurring theme in almost all of Hardy's novels – Henchard dies a lonely death, Tess knew the loneliness of desertion by one she loved, and Jude's loneliness is too terrible to bear.

Hardy is not as successful in portraying Emma's feelings as he is in portraying his own. There is much to admire in 'The Haunter' – the tenderness and wistfulness, the sadness of their inability to communicate in death any more than they did in life, the ballad-like rhythms and repetitions – but the over-fancifulness of the situation, the awkwardness of some of the rhymes, particularly the legalistic 'thereto', and the lack of any real detail except in the description of the 'shy hares' may indicate that Hardy's creative imagination is not fully involved. It could, however, be argued that there is a particularity of experience to be found here that contributes to some extent to its universal appeal. Hardy draws so powerfully and authentically on his own experience that a personal incident in *his* life becomes part of *ours*. This partly explains why the cottage in which he was born, the family church at Stinsford, Beeny Cliff and Max Gate have acquired a metaphorical meaning for so many of Hardy's readers.

The difference in Hardy's approach to the two poems may be seen in the variant readings. Those in 'The Haunter' are revisions which replace awkward phrases by rather less awkward phrases. Thus, the stilted 'his words addressed me' is replaced by the better but still slack 'the words he lifts me'. In 'The Voice' the revisions sharpen the feeling by increasing the particularity. The first line, for example, was changed from

> O woman weird, how you call to me, call to me,

to

> Woman much missed, how you call to me, call to me,

For those not aware of the Cornish and archaic associations 'weird' would be taken to mean 'strange', 'queer', rather than 'enchanting' which Hardy almost certainly intended.

> Even to the original air-blue gown!

was first

> Even to the original hat and gown!

As we know that Emma did wear a blue gown in 1870 when Hardy was courting her, we have particularity of experience and, far more important, the image of the loved one becomes strongly visual and brings with it overtones of lightness and happiness because air-blue brings the picture of blue skies, yet another archetypal image. And there are more. The blue skies give way to the breeze blowing across a wet field, yet more falling leaves, a wind oozing thin from norward and the thorn tree, always for Hardy a symbol of hard and difficult times. When in Hardy's poetry we meet such striking particularity and it is combined with a technical achievement of a high order as it is in 'The Voice' Hardy's own personal involvement with his subject is manifest. He is writing here of the appalling oblivion of death, the suffering caused by loss of those near to us, and the loneliness which comes with bereavement. In Middleton Murry's words, Hardy has given 'to personal emotion what is called the impersonality of great poetry',[11] and as Irving Howe so nicely puts it, 'an obscure private hurt ends with the common wound of experience'.[12]

Hardy had no blood descendants but he had several literary children of whom Philip Larkin was one of the finest. Larkin's poem, 'Church Going' perfectly illustrates Hardy's dictum which is the subject of this paper. At the beginning of his poem Larkin in the Hardy tradition selects a number of natural but powerfully evocative details which establish very realistically both the atmosphere of the church and his attitude towards it. This then leads on to the universal – mankind's hunger for something to believe in, and the meaning of life itself, of birth, marriage and death. Hardy would have approved – it is a serious poem about serious things. Poetry for Hardy had a religious significance for at its best it was concerned, like religion, with universal matters, with the human heart, and with the exploration and questioning of human behaviour. Thinking and feeling as he did, he might easily have written poetry that was remote and esoteric. But – and this is a measure of his greatness – he wrote about the most ordinary things and situations and endowed them with a profundity which alters our perception of them. It takes a great writer to find a universal significance in the meeting of a longlegs, a moth, a bumble-bee and a sleepy fly one August midnight on the pages of his writing. For him the commonest objects may bring back thoughts, associations and memories too deep for tears. Talking about Hardy, his friend, J. M. Barrie, said, 'The man could not look out of a window without seeing something that had never been seen before.' Such a quality is evidence of his outstanding awareness of and sensitivity to the particulars and the universal aspects of life.

Notes

1. E. Felkin, 'Days with Thomas Hardy', *Encounter*, xviii (April 1962) pp. 27–33.
2. *The Life and Work of Thomas Hardy, by Thomas Hardy*, ed. Michael Millgate (London, 1984) p. 163. (Subsequently cited as *Life* in text, followed by page number.)
3. *Far from the Madding Crowd* (New Wessex Edition, paperback, London, 1985) Ch. 42, p. 248.
4. R. L. Purdy and M. Millgate (eds), *The Collected Letters of Thomas Hardy*, vol. 3 (Oxford, 1982) p. 81.
5. William Archer, *Real Conversations* (London, 1904) p. 46/7.
6. *The Complete Poems of Thomas Hardy*, ed. James Gibson (London, 1976) Poem no. 91.

7.   Ibid., no. 500.
8.   Ibid., no. 439.
9.   Ibid., no. 284.
10. Ibid., no. 285
11. James Gibson and Trevor Johnson (eds), *A Casebook: Thomas Hardy: Poems* (London, 1979) p. 85. Middleton Murry's essay first published as 'The Poetry of Mr Hardy', in *The Athenaeum*, November 1919.
12. Irving Howe, *Thomas Hardy* (London, 1967) p. 183.

2

'Something More to be Said': Hardy's Creative Process and the Case of *Tess* and *Jude*

PETER J. CASAGRANDE

What has been written cannot be blotted. Each new style of novel must be the old with added ideas, not an ignoring and avoidance of the old. And so of religion, and a good many other things![1]

I INTRODUCTION

The publication since the middle 1970s of scholarly editions of Hardy's letters, notebooks, and autobiography, as well as of critical editions of his poems and certain of his novels, makes possible a closer look than before into Hardy's day-to-day life as a working writer, particularly his sense of his readers and the effect of their responses on his writing.[2] For the student of Hardy's creative process, these documents reveal three important shifts in his sixty years of professional writing. Each shift was a clear response to readers' tastes and opinions, and each marked a turning point in his career as novelist and poet. Furthermore, each revealed Hardy's continuing need to mediate between two kinds of novelty: what in 1868 he termed 'novelty of *position* and *view* in relation to a known subject' and 'absolute novelty of subject'.[3]

Hardy's creative career was an attempt to mediate between relative and absolute originality of expression in the face of sharply defined, rigidly enforced constraints and conventions.

16

1. The first of these three shifts was his struggle, between 1867 and 1874, to break into print and establish himself as a serial novelist. This began with the rejection of *The Poor Man and the Lady* and the earliest poems, and continued, after strenuous efforts to learn publishers' and readers' tastes, through the publication of *Desperate Remedies, Under the Greenwood Tree, A Pair of Blue Eyes,* and the highly successful pastoral romance, *Far from the Madding Crowd.*

2. The second of these shifts was Hardy's break, between 1875 and 1878, from the pastoral mode of *Madding Crowd,* and from readers' expectations that pastoral was to be his favoured medium. Hardy made this break first by writing comedy of manners in *The Hand of Ethelberta* and then by writing romantic tragedy in *The Return of the Native. Ethelberta* was a failure, but a most instructive one, for it turned Hardy toward tragedy; in tragedy Hardy found his distinctive voice as a writer of fiction. The tragic *Return* established for him that circle of serious readers – not always sympathetic – that followed him through the 1890s, and beyond.

3. Finally, there is Hardy's major phase, the two decades after 1888, in which he wrote *Tess, Jude,* and *The Well-Beloved,* and turned from fiction writing to the writing of poetry of astonishing metrical variety. He published two volumes of poems (*Wessex Poems* and *Poems of the Past and the Present*), brought out three volumes of short stories (*Wessex Tales, A Group of Noble Dames, Life's Little Ironies*), completed *The Dynasts* (some 13,000 lines in length), and while in the white heat of this creative effort wrote, among other things, two discerning critical essays dealing explicitly with the reader and the reading of fiction. He wrote these essays between 1888 and 1890 largely because in the late 1880s and the 1890s he was at odds as never before with certain of his most influential readers.[4]

In each of these three creative turning points, Hardy's search for an acceptable novelty, that is, for a 'novelty of *position* and *view* in relation to a known subject', was paramount. In what follows, I will describe one moment in the third phase, the highly original interplay Hardy constructed between *Tess* and *Jude,* between the sexual violation of a woman and the sexual violation of a man. But before going into *Tess* and *Jude,* I would like to describe briefly Hardy's particular views of literary creating.

II   GENIUS VS. CULTURE

Hardy's rise to literary prominence between 1867 and 1874 illustrates nicely what today is our most cogent hypothesis about literary creating. I refer to the idea held by students of the sciences and the arts, as well as by students of the human mind, that creativity is 'divergence from the already-existing', or to put it more simply, that creativity involves the altering of conventions and other paradigms rather than the invention of new ones. Because Hardy instinctively wrote against the grain, his writing challenged precedent, tradition, convention, and custom – the already-existing in all its forms – in ways that the writing of contemporaries such as Dickens, Meredith, the Brontës, and even Eliot and Butler did not. Actually, as Hardy himself saw it, his battle with the literary authorities was more like Swinburne's, among his contemporaries, than like anyone else's. In fact, Hardy came to regard himself in his struggle with critics and reviewers, with Swinburne's approval, as Swinburne's continuator. To nearly the end of his days, Hardy was fond of quoting a remark that first appeared in a Scots paper: 'Swinburne planteth, Hardy watereth, and Satan giveth the increase' (*Life and Work*, pp. 349, 373).

Hardy's intellectual and emotional contrariness, rooted in a social and emotional if not a political radicalism, shaped decisively his use of precursors. Hardy had the ability of every original thinker and artist to embrace the already-existing and at the same time to diverge from it, and in doing so to create the illusion of novelty. As he himself remarked:

> What has been written cannot be blotted. Each new style of novel must be the old with added ideas, not an ignoring and avoidance of the old. And so of religion, and a good many other things!   (*Life and Work*, p. 227)

What Hardy is speaking of here is improvisatory skill. He demonstrated such skill to the highest degree, as we shall see, in the writing of *Tess* and *Jude*, and he acquired it, in so far as one acquires such a thing, from at least two sources:

1.   from his early experiences as a restorer of Gothic architecture, a practice that required that he learn to accommodate ancient

forms to modern tastes and needs in a publicly acceptable way, and required as well that he blend new architectural materials and designs with old ones;

2. from his having come of literary age at that moment in the nineteenth century when Romanticism's notion that creativity is the work of a uniquely gifted individual called a genius was collapsing under the weight of the idea that creativity is the work of culture and tradition. We can associate the first view with Kant, Shelley, Carlyle, Emerson, and other Romantics, the second with Arnold and Ruskin, as well as with Taine, Zola, and Tolstoy. One might characterize this important shift as a change from the notion of the writer as creator to the notion of the writer as creature.

Since about 1870, the notion that creativity is the work of collective rather than individual agency, of creators who are also creatures, has advanced on several broad fronts:

1. amongst both Marxists and Structuralists, who in different but equally powerful ways subordinate the individual mind to trans-individual forces of production;
2. among Formalists, who view the literary artefact as a force in its own making because in certain ways a law unto itself;
3. among historians of the arts and particularly of the sciences who view 'new' science and 'new' art as the unavoidable reworking of existing paradigms and conventions;
4. and among revisionary psychologists who question the very concept of the human ego or subject as an autonomous originative agency.[5]

Hardy's voracious reading enabled him to discern his own century's shift in thinking about human creativity at the very time he was beginning to write poetry and fiction in the late 1860s. Because he was both a sympathetic student of Romantic views of the artist and a sympathetic reader of mid-century doubts about those Romantic views, Hardy could not have inherited an established view of creativity or of the artist. He had to distrust what came before him on the matter of human creating, and so he had to shape his own views of creativity; and his notebooks show this quite clearly. It is quite clear that Hardy had to forge a view of creativity for himself, out of his work as a restorer of Gothic, out of his study of the thought of his age, and out of his contact with mentors such as Horace Moule and Leslie Stephen. Most of all, he had to forge a creative practice and theory out of an urgent need to adapt his private views and tastes to the severe constraints he encountered as a writer of serial fiction – constraints moral, social, and political, as well as aesthetic. By any measure, this was for him a daunting task, and it is worth our closest attention. Hardy is, after all, the greatest poet-novelist, or novelist-poet, in English. We can scarcely know too much about his creative habits.

I say these things with some confidence because we now can see that in the middle 1870s Hardy – at the suggestion of Leslie Stephen – was reading Matthew Arnold's criticism very attentively, and as we know from Hardy's literary notebooks, very retentively, for he copied out lengthy passages from Arnold, particularly from the essays 'Heinrich Heine' and 'The Function of Criticism at the Present Time'. He was also reading Carlyle, Disraeli, and a number of lesser lights. These notes, from the spring of 1876 on, reveal Hardy in search of an answer to a fundamental question about literary creating: is it the work of individual genius, on the one hand, or is it the product of extra-individual agency on the other? Or, put in more familiar terms, what is the point of intersection of tradition and individual talent?

On the side of the idea of individual genius, Hardy noted, for example, Carlyle's observation that 'Genius consists in an immense capacity for taking trouble' (*Literary Notes*, I, p. 108). He copied from an article on discovery in science the remark that 'great scientific effort demands ... the imaginative audacity to soar above the level of routine & prejudice' (*Literary Notes*, I, p. 51). He copied out Disraeli's observation that because 'that great pumice stone, Society, smooths down the edges of [one's] thoughts & manners', original thought 'is a labour to which few are competent; & truth requires for its development as much courage as acuteness' (*Literary Notes*, I, p. 125).

On the side of the idea of a cultural creativity, he was in 1876 reading biographies of the painters Raffaello and Michaelangelo and noting that 'a true artist's method of appropriation' is to amalgamate 'the style of several masters' (*Literary Notes*, I, p. 22). In 1880, reading Auguste Comte's *Theory of the Future of Man*, he noted the French thinker's warning against judging 'too harshly the writer who, compelled to work out new conceptions in the old language, can hardly avoid defects in composition' (*Literary Notes*, I, pp. 137–

8). In 1882, we find him sympathising with the view that the poet Gray was 'a spirit of gigantic proportions imprisoned in the sealed jar of 18th cent[ury] convention', and complaining that 'that ogre Gentility' was raising 'his head again in our time as boldly as ever' (*Literary Notes*, I, p. 154). One can see why Hardy would have copied out the observation that Goethe, like Milton, 'had the august arrogance of a supreme poet who is conscious that he confers immortality on a thought by stealing it, & that what is stolen leaves his lips so glorified in expression that it has become a new thing'. (*Literary Notes*, I, pp. 111–12). One can see as well why he responded to the charge that he had plagiarized from A. B. Longstreet's *Georgia Scenes* in *The Trumpet-Major* by asking what 'the concocters of the parallel columns [would] say if they knew that columns & columns from North's Plutarch are copied almost verbatim into Shakespeare's Roman & Greek plays'. 'Plagiarism in a work of invention', he insisted, is 'confined to the appropriation of another's inventions' (*Collected Letters*, I, pp. 103–4).

In short, Hardy found two messages about human creativity in the thought of his time: one that it was the product of individual genius, the other that it was the product of that ongoing collective effort of mind Matthew Arnold called culture. Hardy's great need in the 1870s and 1880s was to understand and put into practice the truth that creativity is the product of the difficult-to-define interchange between a writer and her or his culture, between what Arnold called the man and the moment. And so Hardy was preoccupied between age thirty and forty, in part as a result of his growing frustration with restraints imposed on him by the editors and reviewers of his first five novels, with what he termed 'the irritating necessity of conforming to rules which in themselves have no virtue' (*Life and Works*, p. 114). Literary genius, Hardy wished to believe, should and could exercise its will in defiance of tradition and its rules; but *his* own genius, he was coming to learn, he had to subject to powerful rules and conventions if he wished to sell the novels he was writing, gain a following as a writer, and achieve social respectability.

It was while in this highly receptive state of mind that in the middle 1870s Hardy read Arnold's 'Heine' and 'The Function of Criticism at the Present Time'. Arnold provided Hardy with two paths out of his dilemma: first, by holding up (in 'Heine') the example of Goethe as a great modern artist who, in Arnold's words, 'puts the standard ... inside every man instead of outside him' (*Literary Notes*, I, p. 109); and, second, by defining (in 'Function of Criticism') that interchange between writer and society necessary for successful creativity, that interchange between the 'man and ... the moment', as he there termed it.[6] As Arnold saw it, the job of the critic was to provide a climate of sound ideas on which the creative artist might draw. Arnold's notion of the critic as provider for and nurturer of the creative writer, was one Hardy never relinquished. To the end of his life, he sought such support from his reader. When he found it, as he did from Leslie Stephen, Edmund Gosse, Kegan Paul, and a few others, his confidence rose, and with it his productivity. When he did not find it, his confidence could be shaken, but his productivity held steady, and, as in the case of *Tess* and *Jude*, he not only held steady but went on the offensive.[7] One of Hardy's most admirable qualities as a writer is his toughness of mind, his refusal to be radically discouraged, his Goethean determination to place the standard of judgement within himself.

There is much more to be said about Hardy's debt to Arnold (and to others) in the 1870s, and after. However, more important than what Hardy borrowed from Arnold is the way he diverged from Arnold in the very act of borrowing. Hardy's creative style is emphatically not the style of the mere borrower. Because he instinctively wrote against the political, moral, and therefore the aesthetic grain, his style is that of the imitator, that is, of the artist who borrows and at the same time departs from his sources in tradition, in convention, in the already-existing in all its forms. It is no exaggeration to say that Hardy's style at its best resembles the confident, if not arrogant, manner, mentioned above, of a Milton or a Goethe: 'conscious that he confers immortality on a thought by stealing it'. The appeal of this idea for Hardy is suggested in the fact that he copied out and underlined, the following three sentences from Arnold's 'Heine':

Modern times find themselves with an immense system of institutions established facts, accredited dogmas, customs, rules which have come to them from times not modern. In this system their life has to be carried forward; yet they [modern times] have a sense that this system is not of their own creation, that it by no means corresponds exactly with the wants of their actual life, that, for them it is customary, not rational. The awakening of this sense is the awakening of the modern spirit. (*Literary Notes*, pp. 109–10)

Now how does a writer engage her or his cultural heritage so as both to exhibit originality and at the same time speak resonantly to readers? How does one preserve the capacity for original expression and at the same time not alienate one's readers? This was the key question for Hardy in his thinking about his own creativity: how to mediate between what he termed 'novelty of *position* and *view* in relation to a known subject' and 'absolute novelty of subject' (*Collected Letters*, I, p. 8). To study Hardy's pursuit of an answer casts light on his creative life. In the case of *Tess* and *Jude*, as we shall see, his answer was notably angry, sardonic, and darkly humorous.

III *TESS* AND *JUDE*

Hardy wrote out of the assumption that the already-written cannot be erased, that the writer of the 'new style of novel' must be prepared to write 'the old with added ideas' rather than ignore or avoid the old. The creative act, the act productive of useful and appealing originality, was not for him an act of 'starting from scratch', but rather an act of searching for and shaping something more to be said about the already-inscribed, as in the case of Shakespeare's use of Plutarch. Hardy applied this creative principle not just to his extensive use of texts and ideas belonging to other authors, but also to his use – more extensive than has been realised – with his own already-written texts. We know, for example, of the striking resemblances among *Under the Greenwood Tree*, *The Return of the Native*, and *The Woodlanders*, novels written over a span of nearly twenty years, each a story of homecoming, and each strikingly different, the first a comic, the second a tragic, the third an ironic story of the return of a native.[8]

It is with this habit of self-imitation in mind that we can profitably read *Tess* and *Jude*, for it seems quite clear that Hardy wrote *Jude* as the 'something more' he had to say about *Tess*. The relationships between the two illustrate the observation of that reviewer for the *Westminster Review* who in 1883 praised Hardy as a 'writer of distinct genius' who 'moves within a limited range, but is yet capable of producing many variations within that range'.[9] Hardy found so appealing the idea that, in a phrase from the *Literary Notes*, 'a true explanation describes the previously unknown in terms of the known', that he made it the germ of his most frequently quoted remark on literary creating:

> [T]he seer should watch that pattern among general things which his idiosyncrasy moves him to observe, and describe that alone. This is … a going to Nature; yet the result is no mere photograph, but purely the product of the writer's own mind. (*Life and Works*, p. 158)

If reviewers censured Hardy for not conforming to convention, then Hardy defended himself by appealing to a higher convention, a loftier already-existing model, Nature itself, 'that pattern among general things', but only to that part of that Nature pattern that his 'idiosyncrasy', i.e., his unique and individual consciousness, or genius, moved him to select for description. Hardy's two major efforts at criticism, 'The Profitable Reading of Fiction' (1888) and 'Candour in English Fiction' (1890) – both written at the time he was writing *Tess* – are the result of his ongoing attempt to obey and at the same time to break the laws governing the writing of fiction in England in the nineteenth century. On the one hand, he recognised that 'in fiction there can be no intrinsically new thing at this stage of the world's history'.[10] On the other, he insisted that 'the great imaginations … create and transform', that is, produce intrinsically new things (*Personal Writings*, p. 119). On the one hand, he urges that

> A writer who is not a mere imitator [i.e., copier] looks upon the world with his personal eyes, and in his peculiar moods; thence grows up his style, in the full sense of the term. (*Personal Writings*, p. 122)

On the other hand he writes that

> Even imagination is the slave of stolid circumstance; and the unending flow of inventiveness which finds expression in the literature of Fiction is no exception to the general law. It [inventiveness] is conditioned by its surroundings like a river-stream.[11]

By 1890, with *Tess* under way and the germ of *Jude* in his notebook, Hardy had been working for some twenty years at what he called his trade as writer of serial novels. But in *Tess*, and then in

Jude, Hardy challenged convention in a way he never had before. And readers responded accordingly, with epithets such as 'Tess-imism' on the one hand, and 'Jude the Obscene' and 'Hardy the Degenerate' on the other. What had Hardy written to provoke such outcries? There had been murmurings against certain episodes in *Return of the Native*, *Two on a Tower*, and *The Woodlanders*, but nothing like the howls and screeches over *Tess* and *Jude*.

In *Tess*, he chose to rewrite one of the most resonant of nineteenth-century fables, the story of the ruin of female innocence, and he treated the fable in ways that shocked many readers. Mainly, he startled readers by insisting on Tess's innocence, both of sexual complicity and of murder. Then, having shown Tess's sexual and spiritual ruin by two men, he turned *Tess* roundabout and told in *Jude* the story of the sexual and spiritual ruin of a man by two women.

He almost certainly found the idea for this reversal in reviews of *Tess* by Richard le Gallienne and Andrew Lang. Here is le Gallienne in December 1891:

> Mr. Hardy has heretofore been more inclined to champion man the faithful against woman the coquette, but in *Tess* he very definitely espouses 'the cause of woman', and devotes himself to show how often in this world ... when men and women break a law 'the woman pays.' Of course it is a special pleading, because a novel might be as readily written to show how often a man pays too. Indeed, was not *Middlemarch* such a novel?[12]

Now here is Andrew Lang in February 1892:

> Mr. Hardy's story [*Tess*] ... is a rural tragedy of the last century – reversed. In a little book on *The Quantocks*, by Mr. W. L. Nichols ... may be read the history of 'Poor Jack Walford'. Wordsworth wrote a poem on it in the Spenserian measure, but he felt that his work was a failure, and it remains unpublished. Reverse the *rôles* of the man and woman in this old and true tale, add a good deal of fantastic though not impossible matters about the D'Urbervilles, and you have the elements of *Tess*.   (*Critical Heritage*, p. 195)

Hardy was sufficiently interested in Lang's remarks to go to the British Museum to read Nichols's volume, only to decide there was no significant resemblance between *The Quantocks* and his own *Tess* after all.[13] But there is little doubt that Lang and le Gallienne – by naming possible precursors (by naming Hardy's Plutarchs, so to speak) – spurred Hardy's creative process, practised as that process already was in improvisation. Le Gallienne and Lang showed Hardy that there was something more to be said about sexual ruin. In truth, they showed him that the something more to be said had already been said.

So by December 1892, when Hardy was writing *Jude* in outline form, he knew of the possibility that a 'male' version of *Tess* might be written, a novel of sexual ruin in which the man pays. And in fact in his 1895 revision of *Tess*, made after he had published *Jude*, Hardy hinted that a male *Tess* had been written. In the Osgood edition of *Tess*, at the end of Chapter 11, where Hardy's narrator reflects in memorable terms on the rape of Tess, Hardy added five highly revealing words. Pre-1895 editions of *Tess* had read as follows:

> [W]hy so often the coarse appropriates the finer thus, the wrong man the woman, many thousand years of analytical philosophy have failed to explain to our sense of order. (Grindle & Gatrell's *Tess*, Ch. 11, p. 103n)

In the 1895 version of *Tess*, with *Jude* already in print, Hardy added the five words, creating that passage now so familiar to us:

> [W]hy so often the coarse appropriates the finer thus, the wrong man the woman, *the wrong woman the man*, many thousand years of analytical philosophy have failed to explain to our sense of order. (*Ibid.*; my italics)

In this comment on the violation of Tess Durbeyfield by Alec d'Urberville, Hardy is drawing on the violation of Jude Fawley by Arabella Donn. Arabella's appropriation of Jude is here commenting on Alec's appropriation of Tess. If Hardy has set aside chronology, it is because in his mind, in 1895, and before, *Tess* and *Jude* were not separate narratives, but were rather a Siamese twin of a narrative, a diptych in words, a kind of continuous narrative, a *Tess–Jude* rather than a *Tess* and a *Jude*. As D. H. Lawrence was the first to note, in his *Study of Thomas Hardy*, '*Jude* is only *Tess* turned roundabout.' What Lawrence did not know, since he did not have the benefit of Juliet Grindle and Simon Gatrell's edition of *Tess*, was that Hardy had hinted at this very turnabout in Chapter 11 of his 1895 revision of *Tess*.

Readers of *Jude*, however, do not often think of it as *Tess*'s counter-part, perhaps because there is a word, 'rape', for what Hardy termed Alec's appropriation of Tess; but no equally precise term for Arabel-la's appropriation of Jude. 'Seduction' or 'enticement', perhaps, but neither is 'rape', for neither involves violent intrusion. In spite of this, and with seemingly conscious deliberateness, Hardy transmuted the terms of Tess's sexual ruin into the terms of Jude's sexual ruin. Now what exactly did Hardy make of the violation of Tess by rewriting her story in the form of the story of the violation of Jude?

Tess, as we know, is Hardy's exhibition of the violation of an inno-cent girl of sixteen. Tess, a girl of intelligence, feeling, and remark-able beauty, suffers repeated affront. Her ruin – emotional and spiritual, as well as physical – begins with her parents' neglect and exploitation of her. Almost conspiratorially, they send her to work for a supposed relative of wealth who rapes and impregnates her. These parents are dismayed, but not overly, for they hope to enrich themselves by thus renewing kinship with a well-to-do member of the family, a man who is, of course, not a member of the family at all. Tess bears her child out of wedlock, watches it sicken and die, baptises it herself because her tipsy father will not permit the village clergyman to enter the cottage to confer the sacrament, then is refused permission by the same clergyman to bury the child (its name is Sorrow) in consecrated ground.

Having weathered these outrages without losing her will to live, Tess starts life anew by leaving home to work on a dairy farm. There she falls deeply in love with and is offered marriage by a gentle-manly apprentice-farmer who knows nothing of her past, and who, on the night of their wedding, upon learning of that past from Tess, abandons her. He does this in virtually the same breath in which he confesses to her a similar indiscretion.

Here a digression is in order. Some years ago, one of my favourite undergraduate professors – the woman with whom I first studied nineteenth-century British fiction, including Hardy's *Tess* – called this unforgiving and priggish husband of Tess 'the great donkey of English literature'. I remember her remark so well because she enshrined it in a question about Angel Clare on our final exam: 'Who is the great donkey of Victorian fiction? Explain fully.' I once spent an hour and fifteen minutes on the topic of 'Angel Clare as great donkey'. I thought I was very clever in the way I went about it writing an answer. I compared Clare to Thackeray's Jos Sedley and Dickens's Thomas Gradgrind. I made the mistake, however, of thinking Clare less a donkey than either Sedley or Gradgrind. Professor Pickering marked me down for this. She clearly believed Clare had no peer as a donkey.

Professor Olive Pickering meant this, no doubt, in aesthetic as well as in human terms, for Angel Clare is not one of Hardy's successes in characterisation; rather than becoming someone complexly human in the course of the novel, Clare simply comes to stand for something vaguely and incompletely human. Moreover, he never escapes his author's contempt. He hovers between plausibility and something else. I dwell on Clare's shortcomings here, with the help of Professor Pickering's picturesque phrase, because Hardy's failure with Clare is of crucial importance to understanding Hardy's improvisatory creativity in *Jude*; for in writing *Jude* Hardy invented a fascinating female counterpart to Clare, a woman (Sue Bridehead) critics find as interesting as they find Angel Clare dull, a woman, moreover, whose pained mental and emotional life becomes the most interesting thing in a novel titled after its male protagonist, a woman, finally, who enjoys her author's sympathy in a way her brother Angel never does.

But back to *Tess*. Driven to desperation and want by love for a husband blind to her virtue, Tess takes up with Alec, the man who raped her, becomes his kept woman in exchange for support for her impoverished family, and is nearly insane with self-hate and shame when Angel Clare reappears, seeking to make amends. In a fury of despair, Tess stabs Alec to death and flees with Angel to enjoy a few happy weeks as his wife before she is taken by the authorities, tried, and hanged for her crime. In short, the 'pure' Tess finds little love and less mercy. This grim conclusion produced one of the more memorable closing sentences in the history of the British novel: '"Justice" was done, and the President of the Immortals (in Aeschylean phrase) had ended his sport with Tess.' Tess's husband, that great donkey of Victorian fiction, a greater donkey than even Jos Sedley or Thomas Gradgrind, wanders off hand in hand with Tess's sister, Liza-Lu.

But even before he had completed *Tess*, Hardy – aware that there was something more to be said about sexual ruin, confident in his creative capacity for achieving 'novelty of *position* and *view* in relation to a known subject' – conceived the story of Jude Fawley. In fact, Hardy was reconceiving the ruin of Tess in male terms while still writing *Tess*; and within four years of publishing *Tess*, he published *Jude*.

In *Jude* Hardy transmuted his story of the neglected, sexually violated peasant girl into the story of an orphaned, sexually victimised boy of the rural working classes: a boy whose doom lies not in the beauty of his face but in the beauty of his aspirations, particularly his instinctive charity and passionate love of learning. When we first meet Jude Fawley, he is saying goodbye to a beloved teacher, his great hero and chief hope for advancement in the world. When we next meet him, he is being held aloft and beaten by an angry farmer. It seems the farmer had hired Jude to keep birds from a newly seeded field. The tenderhearted Jude had decided, however, that hungry birds should eat, a sentiment the farmer vigorously rejects. Later we will find Jude walking gingerly, virtually on tiptoe, across the evening damp of a meadow, so as not to disturb the breeding of earthworms. Always, Jude is too loving for the harsh world he inhabits, especially the world of sexual struggle. Like Tess, Jude is a victim of lust, but of his own lust as well as that of another person.

Jude dreams, with all the poignancy of a dreamer of impossible dreams, of becoming a man of learning, a university don, perhaps a clergyman, and he sets for himself the Herculean task of self-instruction, which he carries on, with touching dedication, while driving a delivery cart around the countryside. Jude's dream comes to a steamy end when he meets a young woman of his own age who sees in him a sexual conquest and a means thereby to security in marriage. Her name is Arabella Donn, daughter of a pig-farmer, 'a complete and substantial female animal – no more, no less', as Hardy describes her.[14] She first sights Jude while she is at work rendering a hog carcass at her father's establishment. She gains Jude's attention by pelting him on the cheek with 'a piece of flesh' that Hardy decorously calls 'the characteristic part of a barrow-pig', that is, the penis of a castrated boar (*Jude*, Pt First, Ch. 6, p. 58). This violent, if indirect, sexual summons astonishes the studious Jude, especially since, at the moment he is struck by this piece of pig flesh, he is taking mental inventory of his reading in the classics. He responds fatally, and in Hardy's view predictably, to Arabella's invitation to mate.

As Hardy sees it, Jude has no choice. He *must* obey 'unconsciously' received 'conjunctive orders from headquarters' (*Jude*, p. 59). Arabella's bizarre appropriation of Jude on the road to Marygreen is the counterpart – the equivalent, as Hardy would have it – of Alec's appropriation of Tess in The Chase. Though physical union between Arabella and Jude does not occur here, this moment of contact between the cheek of an innocent Jude and a pig's penis hurled by Arabella is, metonymically, the rape of Jude. Hardy's language leaves little doubt that he had this in mind:

> The unvoiced call of woman to man, which was uttered very distinctly by Arabella's personality, held Jude to the spot against his intention – almost against his will, and in a way new to his experience. (*Jude*, p. 60)

Making up for her biological lack by borrowing the bit of pig flesh, Arabella deflowers the innocent Jude by wakening his dormant sexuality. She gratifies her lust by striking him in this way, then speaking seductively to him, then enticing him into sexual union, then feigning pregnancy and demanding marriage. Of course she eventually abandons him because she finds him bookish, unexciting, and a poor earner. These events constitute the 'rape', or to use Hardy's word from Chapter 11 of *Tess*, the 'appropriation' of Jude Fawley, figurative to be sure, but as Hardy sees it, every bit as deadly to body and soul as Alec's actual rape of Tess. But one notes immediately that Hardy denied Jude the saving epitaph he granted Tess: Jude is no 'pure man' in the sense that Tess is a 'pure woman', i.e., pure in intention if not in act. The wrong woman can appropriate the wrong man just as surely as the wrong man can appropriate the wrong woman, but as Hardy would have it, a man violated by a woman is more culpable. Alec's actual rape of Tess and Arabella's virtual rape of Jude are, for Hardy, closely comparable but not identical.

Arabella's wakening of Jude's sexuality and the marriage she exacts of him destroys Jude's dream of a university education. To support his wife and supposed child he must – out of humane principle – set aside his books and go to work as a stonemason. Then Arabella deserts him, and he turns to hard drinking and seems on the brink of suicide when he falls in love once more, though this time with a woman of superior education and station, a woman, Sue Bridehead, fully capable of sharing and even of guiding Jude's dream of learning. Hardy gives Jude, as he had given Tess, a second chance in love, and in life. Christminster is Jude's Talbothays, Sue is Jude's Angel. Jude and Sue form a common law union, beget several children, and all seems well; but then Sue acts on what she has always known, that she has neither taste nor talent for the enforced intimacies of marriage. Sue shares with Angel a sexual reserve whose effect on a robust spouse is devastating. Angel's horror of marrying a woman with sexual experience is, for Hardy, the equivalent of Sue's horror of being, in her memorable phrase, 'licensed to be loved on the premises' (*Jude*, Pt Fifth, Ch. 1, p. 278).

Now this interesting and sympathetic Sue, this character readers continue to find original, eloquent, and challenging, is the counterpart of and derives from Angel Clare, that man of limited human and dramatic interest, that hollow man, that great donkey of Victorian fiction. So Sue is a powerful example of what Hardy meant – when speaking of originality in fiction – by 'the old with [something] added'. Sue is an example of his genius for creating novelty of '*position* and *view* in relation to a known subject'. Hardy's success with Sue springs from his decision to constrain himself in *Jude the Obscure* to the narrative terms of *Tess of the d'Urbervilles*, but at the same time to diverge, in this case by inverting sexual roles.

Sue is a female Angel, Jude a male Tess, Arabella a female Alec. But what does this mean for criticism of the novel? We can know at the same time we cannot. Part of the fascination of thinking of *Tess* and *Jude* in this way, is precisely this uncertainty, this invitation to agnosticism on the question of the meaning of female versus male experience. But more about this in just a bit.

The unhappy Jude and Sue are driven to despair, then near madness, when their eldest child, Little Father Time, unhappy cousin to Tess's infant Sorrow, out of anguish with his parents' harried lives, hangs himself after first hanging his brothers and sisters. This episode – this savage, if not bloodthirsty, counterpart to the quiet if agonising death of Tess's child – particularly outraged Hardy's readers. An Anglican bishop informed the *Yorkshire Post* he found *Jude* so insolent and indecent, such garbage, that he had burned his copy of it. Such violent reader reaction, more violent even than the reaction to *Tess*, is evidence for the originality of this in many ways 'unoriginal' book. To be sure, reviewers had grumbled over what they termed the indecency and the pessimism of *Tess*, but *Jude* they found obscene because grossly repugnant. Even Emma Hardy seems to have joined the fray: she sought to have *Jude* suppressed.[15] What had Hardy wrought in *Jude* to make it so offensively original?

In *Jude*, as in *Tess*, Hardy exhibits the ruin of an innocent by flanking his victim with a sexually aggressive lover and a sexually timid one. He had to contrive for Jude an equivalent to Tess's rape by Alec, the act that changed the course of her entire life, and led indirectly to her death. There being no exact physiological

equivalent, he shaped a psychic one consisting of Arabella's enticement and deception of Jude, and Jude's self-destructive compliance.
As Hardy saw it then, Alec's physical assault on Tess finds equiva-
lence in Arabella's psychic assault on Jude, turning Jude's sexual ruin
into self-ruin. In some sense, Jude is a victim of self-rape. Since his
response to Arabella is both 'unconscious' and conscious, he cannot
be a 'pure man' in the way that for Hardy, Tess can be a 'pure
woman'. There is of course no word for this semi-conscious compliance on Jude's part. All one can say is that Hardy chose to view the
two sexual assaults – Alec's on Tess, Arabella's on Jude – as equally
deadly. I can't here enter into the justice of the equivalency Hardy created, though it constitutes an intriguing question, or an intriguing
way to pose the question of what we might call 'sexual equity'. I can
say, from experience of teaching *Tess* and *Jude* as *Tess–Jude*, as an
extended meditation on what Hardy, in his 'Preface' to *The Woodlanders*, called the 'immortal puzzle' of finding a basis for the 'sexual
relation' between men and women, that readers generally suspect
that *Jude* is a male apologetic, a defensive and sexist *tu quoque* directed
at women. I hope, however, that I have made clear how Hardy's
inventiveness in *Jude* sprang from his decision to imitate, that is, copy
and at the same time diverge from, the already-existing in *Tess*.

IV   CONCLUSION

This brings us to a conclusion on some important differences between
Tess and *Jude*. And these differences matter greatly because in them
one sees most clearly the fruits of Hardy's improvisatory artistry.
Though there are several important differences, space permits me to
speak about only one of them, and that the most encompassing: Hardy's attempt to empower women in *Jude*. Hardy knew well that ever
since the agony of Virgil's Dido at the hand of Aeneas, Western writers of narrative – among them Samuel Richardson, Henry Fielding,
Sir Walter Scott, Charles Dickens, George Eliot, and Nathaniel Haw-
thorne – had told, and retold, the story of a woman's sexual ruin. For
Hardy to retell that story in *Tess*, then retell Tess's story from the point
of view of the male as victim in *Jude*, was to improvise startlingly
upon what by the 1890s amounted to cultural myth, the idea of
woman as sexual victim – a stock figure of the Victorian stage and of
Victorian painting as well as of Victorian fiction.[16]

Now what, mainly, does Hardy's divergent creativity consist of in *Jude*? It consists largely of placing power – physical, intellectual, and moral power – in the hands of the women of his novel. The most striking originality of the highly derivative *Jude* is that its men are virtually powerless. This, of course, had been the case to some degree in Hardy's novels from the beginning, but never before in the context of the story of sexual struggle. In the context of that story, Hardy had almost always placed the power with the male. Think not just of Alec's power over Tess, but of Henry Knight's over Elfride Swancourt in *A Pair of Blue Eyes*, of Sergeant Troy's over Fanny Robin in *Far from the Madding Crowd*, of Damon Wildeve's over Thomasin Yeobright in *The Return of the Native*, of Michael Henchard's over Lucetta Le Sueur in *The Mayor of Casterbridge*, of Edred Fitzpiers's over Grace Melbury in *The Woodlanders*. His departure from the stock notion of the female as sexual victim was, in great part, the reason Hardy's reviewers found *Jude* obscene rather than merely indecent.

Novelist Margaret Oliphant pronounced on this in her angry review of *Jude* for *Blackwood's* in January 1896. Having observed by way of beginning that she had never read a book from the hand of a master artist 'more disgusting, more impious as regards human nature, more foul in detail', and having vented her indignation on that 'human pig' Arabella and that 'fantastic *raisonneuse*' Sue, Oliphant complained that

> It is the women who are the active agents in all this unsavoury imbroglio: the story is carried on,0 0and life is represented as carried on, entirely by their [the women's] means. The men are passive, suffering, rather good than otherwise, victims of these and of fate. Not only do they [the men] never dominate, but they are quite incapable of holding their own against these remorseless ministers of destiny, these determined operators, [these women] managing all the machinery of life so as to secure their own way. This is one of the most curious developments of recent fiction.... In the books of the younger men, it is now the woman who seduces – it is no longer the man. (*Critical Heritage*, pp. 257, 259–60)

Hardy himself had hinted that this revision of male–female relations was not new in his choice of an epigraph for Part First of *Jude*, which he took from the Old Testament Book of Esdras:

'Yea, many there be that have run out of their wits for women, and become servants for their sakes. Many also have perished, have erred, and sinned, for women.... . O ye men, how can it be but women should be strong, seeing they do thus?'   (*Jude*, p. 27)

Such an opening might seem to signal misogyny, but that seems to be only part of the case.

As already noted, Arabella, in her way of appropriating Jude's innocence, is a strong character: passionate, cunning, relentless in her determination to have her way with men in a world she knows men dominate. And she remains strong and dominant throughout the novel, eventually winning back Jude, then deserting him again when he's near death and she sees another man beckoning. Hardy gave to Arabella the closing words of the novel, a scathing rejection of Sue's hopeless love for the dead Jude. Her words deserve to be set alongside the 'President of the Immortals' passage from *Tess*:

'She may swear that [she's found peace] on her knees to the holy cross upon her necklace till she's hoarse, but it won't be true! ... She's never found peace since she left his arms, and never will again till she's as he is now!'   (*Jude*, Pt Sixth, Ch. 11, p. 428)

If the President of the Immortals has the last word in *Tess*, Arabella Donn has the last word in *Jude* – so emphatically and convincingly that one can only call her the 'President of the Mortals'. In this regard, it is important to note that though Hardy allowed Tess to take revenge on the man who ruined her, he granted no such rudimentary justice to Jude. Jude, even more than Tess, is the helpless victim; and Arabella, even more than Alec, is the relentless predator. Alec dies at the hand of Tess after a clumsy attempt at atonement; Arabella lives on, robust, designing, eager to get her hands on Physician Vilbert, uninterested in atonement. Tess kills Alec, Jude is abandoned on his deathbed by Arabella.

More interesting than the strength and cunning Hardy grants Arabella is the intellectual vitality with which he endows Sue. If Sue is sexually diffident, intellectually she is superior to all others in the novel; and Hardy is interested enough in the quality of her intellect to make her intellect superior in strength and power to Jude's. In *Tess*, Angel's intellect comes off a drab second to Tess's capacity for feeling. In *Jude*, Sue's intellect is superior to Jude's. In fact, the rhythms, tonalities, and other energies of Sue's voice, when expressive of her energy of intellect, are unlike any other in Hardy's fiction. In creating this vitally intellectual woman out of the colourless, diffident, intellectually stale Angel Clare, Hardy created for the first time in his fiction a female voice struggling to articulate a woman's right to freedom and equality with men, a right to think openly and critically. Out of the great donkey of Victorian fiction Hardy fashioned one of the most striking and eloquent female protagonists of British fiction. Here is Sue telling Jude of the extent of her learning.

> 'You called me a creature of civilization, or something, didn't you?' she said... . 'It was very odd you should have done that.'
> 'Why?' [Jude asked]
> 'Well, because it is provokingly wrong. I am a sort of negation of [civilization].'
> 'You are very philosophical. "A negation" is profound talking.'
> 'Is it? Do I strike you as being learned?' she asked, with a touch of raillery.
> 'No – not learned. Only you don't talk quite like a girl – well, a girl who has had no advantages.'
> 'I have had advantages. I don't know Latin and Greek, though I know the grammars of those tongues. But I know most of the Greek and Latin classics through translations, and other books too. I read Lemprière, Catullus, Martial, Juvenal, Lucian, Beaumont and Fletcher, Boccaccio, Scarron, De Brantôme, Sterne, De Foe, Smollett, Fielding, Shakespeare, the Bible, and other such; and found that all interest in the unwholesome part of those books ended with its mystery.'
> 'You have read more than I,' he said with a sigh. 'How came you to read some of those queerer ones?'
> 'Well,' she said thoughtfully, 'it was by accident. My life has been entirely shaped by what people call a peculiarity in me. I have no fear of men, as such, nor of their books.' (*Jude*, Pt Third, Ch. 4, p. 167)

Here is that same Sue, but now defiant and mocking as she persuades Phillotson, her husband of just a few months, to permit her to live with Jude as his lover:

> 'Richard,' ... 'would you mind my living away from you?'

'Away from me? Why, that's what you were doing when I married you. What then was the meaning of marrying at all?'

'You wouldn't like me any the better for telling you.' ...

'Domestic laws should be made according to temperaments, which should be classified. If people are at all peculiar in character they have to suffer from the very rules that produce comfort in others! ... Will you let me?'

'But we married –'

'What is the use of thinking of laws and ordinances,' she burst out, 'if they make you miserable when you know you are committing no sin?'

'But you are committing a sin in not liking me.'

'I *do* like you! But I didn't reflect it would be – that it would be so much more than that.... For a man and woman to live on intimate terms when one feels as I do is adultery, in any circumstances, however legal. There – I've said it! ... [Now] [w]ill you let me [live away from you] Richard?' (*Jude*, Pt Fourth, Ch. 3, pp. 242–3)

As we know, Richard Phillotson permits Sue to live with her lover; and not only that, he is so swayed by her argument that he defends in public her right to be unfaithful to him, and as a result loses his position as a schoolmaster. Such, in Hardy's view, is the power of Sue's logic, such is the power of her right as a woman to liberty, that her husband can ruin his career that she may live with a lover. This of course will change: Sue will give way to pressures that drive her back into marriage to Phillotson. Jude will assume the alienated position that Sue has vacated. But Hardy's achievement in Sue remains intact.

Sue continues to fascinate readers because in her Hardy shaped not the wholly liberated or enfranchised woman, but the woman struggling, even though finally without success, toward personal and intellectual freedom; in this, he allows her to be the exact counterpart of her lover, the doomed Jude. Hardy allows their equality, their sex notwithstanding, in their unsuccessful struggle against a repressive society; they are equal in failure. Sue's intellect collapses, just as Jude's does, under the massive resistance – from church, society, and conscience – that rises up against their experiment in loving and living. But Jude and Sue do not go down as equals – Hardy depicts Jude as failed dreamer to be the inferior of Sue as failed thinker. And in Sue's superiority is the striking originality

Hardy achieves in *Jude*, a novel so derivative, and yet so unprecedented *because* so derivative. Sue's and Jude's counterparts in *Tess* – Angel and Tess respectively – know no such parity of aspiration and fate.

There is much more to be said about *Jude* as improvisation upon *Tess*. For example, I have said little about the differences between Alec and Arabella, nothing about the presence in *Jude* of Phillotson, a major character without a counterpart in *Tess*. There is more to be said about the question of what I call 'sexual equity', about whether the male victim of sexual exploitation pays as high a price as the female. Finally, I have said nothing about the different uses of setting in the two, and nothing about the differing modalities. Time permits only brief comment on this last by way of conclusion.

Jude's originality is measurable in part by criticism's continuing inability to categorise it. One can be satisfied that *Tess* is tragedy, a moving exhibition of the paradoxical beauty of irreparable loss. About *Jude's* modality it is more difficult to agree. One might term it an 'irony', an exhibition of the discrepancy between things as they appear to be and things as they really are. Or one might call it an 'agony', a display of meaningless human suffering. No doubt Hardy's contemporaries' angry view of it as an obscenity was a response to its anomalousness: they cursed where they could not categorise. I prefer to think of *Jude* as a parody of *Tess*.

But arriving at an exact designation for *Jude* is less important than seeing that by imitating *Tess* in *Jude*, Hardy moved beyond familiar modalities into something else, something indefinable apart from the kinships of the two. One can believe Hardy would have approved of an attempt to read *Jude* as the something more to be said about *Tess*, for he himself described his ideal reader as one willing to

> exercise ... a generous imaginativeness, which shall find in a tale not only all that was put there by the author ... but which shall find there what was never inserted by him, never foreseen, never contemplated.

Sometimes, he added,

> these additions which are woven around a work of fiction by the intensitive power of the reader's own imagination are the finest parts of the scenery. (*Personal Writings*, p. 112)

Notes

1. Thomas Hardy, *The Life and Work of Thomas Hardy*, ed. Michael Mill-
    gate (London: Macmillan, 1984; Athens, Georgia: The University of
    Georgia Press, 1985) p. 227 [cited hereafter in my text as *Life and Work*].
    I am indebted to the General Research Fund of the University of Kan-
    sas for support enabling me to prepare this essay, also to the office of
    the Dean of International Study at the University of Kansas for travel
    support.
2. I refer particularly to the following important works of editorial
    scholarship: Hardy's *Life and Work*, 'an edition on new principles' of
    Hardy's *Early Life* and *Later Years; The Literary Notes of Thomas Hardy*,
    ed. Lennart A. Björk (Göteborg, Sweden: Acta Universitatis Gotho-
    burgensis, 1974) [cited hereafter as *Literary Notes*]; *The Collected Letters
    of Thomas Hardy*, 7 vols, ed. Richard Little Purdy and Michael Millgate
    (Oxford: Clarendon Press, 1978–88) [cited hereafter as *Collected Let-
    ters*]; *The Personal Notebooks of Thomas Hardy*, ed. Richard H. Taylor
    (London: Macmillan, 1978; New York: Columbia University Press,
    1979); and Juliet Grindle and Simon Gatrell's edition of *Tess of the
    d'Urbervilles* (Oxford: Clarendon Press, 1983) [cited hereafter as
    Grindle & Gatrell's *Tess*].
3. *Collected Letters*, I, p. 8. Hardy made this remark in a letter to
    Alexander Macmillan about the never-published *The Poor Man and the
    Lady*, explaining the various 'considerations' behind the novel.
4. I refer to reviewers' complaints about *Two on a Tower, The Mayor of
    Casterbridge*, and *The Woodlanders*, which produced in Hardy the
    anguish expressed in a letter to Edmund Gosse in October 1886: 'I
    have suffered terribly at times from reviews – pecuniarily, & still more
    mentally, & the crown of my bitterness has been my sense of unfair-
    ness in such impersonal means of attack, wh[ich] conveys to an
    unthinking public the idea of an immense weight of opinion behind,
    to which you can only oppose your own little solitary personality:
    when the truth is that there is only another little solitary personality
    against yours all the time' (*Collected Letters*, I, p. 154). Richard Holt
    Hutton, writing for the *Spectator*, was the most eloquent, and most
    prominent, among Hardy's detractors.
5. For the Marxist/Structuralist position, see Louis Althusser, 'Ideology
    and Ideological State Apparatuses' [1970], trans. Ben Brewster, in *Crit-
    ical Theory since 1965*, ed. Hazard Adams and Leroy Searle
    (Tallahassee: Florida State University Press, 1986) pp. 239–50. For the
    Formalist view, see Monroe C. Beardsley, 'On the Creation of Art',
    Journal of Aesthetic and Art Criticism, 23 (1965) pp. 291–304. For history
    of science, see Thomas S. Kuhn, *The Structure of Scientific Revolutions*
    [1962], 2nd enlarged edn (Chicago: University of Chicago Press, 1970).
    For revision of the notion of the autonomous creative self, see among
    others Roland Barthes, 'The Death of the Author' [1968], trans.
    Stephen Heath in *Image Music Text* (New York: Hill & Wang, 1977)
    pp. 142–8; Michel Foucault, 'What is an Author?' [1969], trans. Donald
    F. Bouchard and Sherry Simon in *Language, Counter-Memory, Practice*,

ed. Donald F. Bouchard (Ithaca: Cornell University Press, 1977) pp. 113–38; and Jacques Lacan, *Ecrits: A Selection*, trans. A. Sheridan (London: Tavistock, 1977).

6. Though Hardy did not copy it out, the key passage from Arnold is as follows: 'Now, in literature ... the elements with which the creative power works are ideas; the best ideas, on every matter which literature touches, current at the time.... Creative literary genius does not principally show itself in discovering new ideas.... But it must have the atmosphere, it must find itself amidst the order of ideas, in order to work freely.... This is why great creative epochs in literature are so rare, this is why there is so much that is unsatisfactory in the productions of many men of real genius; because for the creation of a masterwork of literature two powers must concur, the power of the man and the power of the moment, and the man is not enough without the moment; the creative power has, for its happy exercise, appointed elements, and those elements are not in its own control'; in Matthew Arnold, *Lectures & Essays in Criticism*, ed. R. H. Super (Ann Arbor: The University of Michigan Press, 1962) pp. 260–1.

7. See Hardy's letter of 18 April 1881 to C. Kegan Paul: 'Nothing tends to draw out a writer's best work like the consciousness of a kindly feeling in his critics: & the worst work I have ever done has been written under the influence of stupidly adverse criticism – not just criticism of the adverse sort, which of course does good when deserved, as it often has been in my case' (*Collected Letters*, I, p. 89). Hardy was responding to Paul's appreciative survey of Hardy's novels in the *British Quarterly Review*.

8. For a more complete account of structural and thematic kinships among Hardy's novels, see Peter J. Casagrande, *Unity in Hardy's Novels: 'Repetitive Symmetries'* (London: Macmillan, 1982), especially pp. 199ff.

9. The writer was Havelock Ellis, in 'Thomas Hardy's Novels', *Westminster Review* (April 1883), in *Thomas Hardy: The Critical Heritage*, ed. R. G. Cox (London: Routledge & Kegan Paul; New York: Barnes & Noble, 1970) p. 116 [cited hereafter in my text as *Critical Heritage*].

10. 'The Profitable Reading of Fiction' [1888], in *Thomas Hardy's Personal Writings*, ed. Harold Orel (Lawrence, Kansas: University of Kansas Press, 1966; London: Macmillan, 1967) p. 114 [cited hereafter in my text as *Personal Writings*].

11. 'Candour in English Fiction' [1890], in *Personal Writings*, p. 125.

12. Le Gallienne's review appeared in the *Star* (23 December 1891), in *Critical Heritage*, p. 180. His reference to Eliot's *Middlemarch* is doubtlessly to Rosamund Vincy's undoing of her husband, Dr Tertius Lydgate.

13. In a remark dated 2 May 1892 deleted from the typescript of the *Life*, Hardy's exasperation with Lang is palpable: 'Wasted time in the B. Museum in hunting up a book that contains a tragedy, according to Lang in the New Review, of which "Tess" is a plagiarism. Discovered there was no resemblance, it being about an idiot.' *Life and Work*, p. 261.

14. *Jude the Obscure* [1895], The New Wessex Edition, ed. P. N. Furbank
     (London: Macmillan, 1974, paperback) Pt First, Ch. 6, p. 59. Sub-
     sequent references to *Jude* in my text are to the New Wessex Edition.
15. For a detailed account of the writing and reception of *Jude* see Michael
     Millgate, *Thomas Hardy: A Biography* (Oxford and New York: Oxford
     University Press, 1982) pp. 345–84.
16. See Nina Auerbach, 'The Rise of the Fallen Woman', *Nineteenth
     century Fiction*, 35 (1980) pp. 29–52. Also, Hardy in a letter of 31
     December 1891: 'Ever since I began to write – certainly ever since I
     wrote "Two on a Tower" in 1881 – I have felt that the doll of English
     fiction must be demolished, if England is to have a school of fiction at
     all: & I think great honour is due to the D: Chronicle for frankly
     recognizing that the development of a more virile type of novel is not
     incompatible with sound morality' (*Collected Letters*, I, p. 250).

3

Hardy and the City

MICHAEL SLATER

Hardy might have preferred this essay to be entitled 'Hardy the Londoner'. All his life he seems to have taken a particular pride in the way in which he had mastered the city during the years (1862–7) that he was employed there as a budding architect. In *The Life of Thomas Hardy*[1] (referred to hereafter as the *Life*) he notes that 'the most important scenes' of his first novel, *The Poor Man and the Lady*,

> were laid in London, of which city Hardy had just had between five and six years' constant and varied experience – as only a young man in the metropolis can get it – knowing every street and alley west of St. Paul's like a born Londoner, which he was often supposed to be; an experience quite ignored by the reviewers of his later books, who, if he only touched on London in his pages, promptly reminded him not to write of a place he was unacquainted with, but to get back to his sheepfolds.   (63–4)

Later he notes that at the time of his first visit to St Juliot he was not at all like the youthful, sanguine Stephen Smith of *A Pair of Blue Eyes* but 'a thoughtful man of twenty-nine, with years of London buffeting' behind him (76), much more like Knight in that novel. And in the later chapters of the *Life* he lays great emphasis upon the expertise with which he and Emma 'did' the London season every year, more, it would seem, as a matter of grim duty rather than pleasure. They were glad to escape from the season's 'artificial gaities' back to what he disarmingly calls 'primitive rustic life' in Dorset (257).

Whatever Hardy's attitude to the London Season may have been, readers of the *Life* soon become aware of the power the city exercised over his imagination as an ancient cultural capital, the former haunt of great figures from the past. Describing his first visit to the capital, with his mother when he was about nine or ten, he notes that the Clerkenwell inn where they stayed was the one at which

Shelley and Mary Godwin had met at weekends and was unchanged from that time; the Hardys might even have stayed in the very same room 'as that occupied by our most marvellous lyrist' (22). Later, London provided him with a liberal education. During his years working in Arthur Blomfield's drawing-office he frequented the National Gallery, the British Museum, the opera and the theatre, particularly Samuel Phelps's Shakespeare productions at Drury Lane which he always attended with 'a good edition' of the relevant play in his hand (54).

The British Museum seems to have occupied a special place in Hardy's consciousness as the place where he and others could be put in actual tactile contact with past greatness. There is, for example, the poem 'In the British Museum' about the man staring transfixed at a stone from the Areopagus, a stone that 'has echoed / The voice of Paul', or the episode in the Museum in *The Hand of Ethelberta* (Ch. 24) in which Faith Julian tries to convey to her brother just why an Assyrian relief excites her so much:

> ... this person is really Sennacherib, sitting on his throne... Only just think that this is not imagined of Assyria, but done in Assyrian times by Assyrian hands. Don't you feel as if you were actually in Nineveh .. ?

In the light of such passages as these we can easily understand Hardy's indignation at what he saw on another visit to the Museum one wet day in 1891:

> Crowds parading and gaily traipsing round the mummies, think- ing to-day is for ever, and the girls casting sly glances at young men across the swathed dust of Mycerinus [?]. They pass with flippant comments the illuminated MSS. – the labour of years and stand under Rameses the Great, joking.... when these people are our masters it will lead to more of this contempt, and possibly the utter ruin of art and literature! ... Looking, when I came out at the Oxford Music Hall, an hour before the time of opening there was already a queue. (247)

Always, it is the ancientness of London that fascinates Hardy. He notes in 1892 that the end of September 'is the time to realize London as an old city, all the pulsing excitements of May being absent' (264). He looks for continuities as in the old tavern where 'theatrical affairs are discussed neither from the point of view of the audience, nor of the actors, but from a third point – that of the recaller of past appearances', and 'old-fashioned country couples also come in, their fathers having recommended the tavern from recollections of the early part of the century' (250).

All this relates to what we might call the 'city of the mind' aspect of London for Hardy and we might compare it with other cities of the mind that appear in his work – Jude's Christminster, for example, in which he feels the living presence of the illustrious dead as he takes his first nocturnal ramble in its streets, or the even more purely imaginary city that is Eustacia Vye's Paris, eagerly constructed from her prompting of Clym Yeobright ('And Versailles – the King's Gallery is some such gorgeous room, is it not?')[2]. Another city-imaginer is the speaker in the poem 'From Her in the Country' (written while Hardy was still working in London):

> I thought and thought of thy crass clanging town
> To folly, till convinced such dreams were ill,
> I held my heart in bond, and tethered down
> Fancy to where I was, by force of will.
>
> I said: How beautiful are these flowers, this wood,
> One little bud is far more sweet to me
> Than all man's urban shows; and then I stood
> Urging new zest for bird, and bush, and tree;
>
> And strove to feel my nature brought it forth
> Of instinct, or no rural maid was I;
> But it was vain; for I could not see worth
> Enough around to charm a midge or fly,
>
> And mused again on city din and sin,
> Longing to madness I might move therein!
>
> *16 W.P.V., 1866*

'City of din and sin'. It is clear that the erotic aspect of London also exercised a powerful effect on Hardy's imagination. The 1860s London that he experienced as a young man was still, he reminds us in the *Life* (43–5), the raffish London of Dickens and Thackeray; such famous haunts of dissipation as Evans's supper-rooms in Covent

Garden, the Cider Cellars and the Coal Hole with its lubricious 'Judge and Jury' mock trials were still going strong, as were those 'gallant resorts', Cremorne Gardens and the Argyll Rooms, recalled in the poem 'Reminiscences of a Dancing Man' with its startlingly vindictive ending:

> Whither have danced those damsels now!
> Is Death the partner who doth moue
>   Their wormy chaps and bare?
> Do their spectres spin like sparks within
> The smoky halls of the Prince of Sin
>   To a thunderous Jullien air?[3]

The brutally Gothic image of smooth young female cheeks turned to 'wormy chaps' suggests the degree to which he was disturbed by watching the Cremorne and Argyll 'damsels' (and he seems to have been more spectator than participant – 'he did not dance there much himself, if at all' [45]). Many years later, viewing the cancan dancers at the Moulin Rouge in Paris, perhaps the most intense expression of female sexiness produced by any city in the nineteenth century, Hardy discovered a 'bizarre' ready-made image linking the women with death. The Moulin Rouge

> was close to the cemetery of Montmartre ... and as he stood somewhere in the building looking down at the young women dancing the *cancan*, and grimacing at the men, it appears that he could see through some back windows over their heads to the last resting-place of so many similar gay Parisians silent under the moonlight. (240)

Back in the London of Hardy's youth, sexually provocative females were hard to avoid as the streets were thronged with prostitutes, many very young as Dostoevsky noted in his horrified description of Haymarket in 1862.[4] Hardy was amused that the noble street named after the Prince Regent was a favourite promenade for such women: 'One can imagine *his shade* stalking up and down every night, smiling approvingly' (217). He recalls a girl holding a long-stemmed narcissus to his nose as he passed her in Piccadilly as well as his glimpse of *poules de luxe* at the Criterion supper-rooms:

where, first going to the second floor, he stumbled into a room whence proceeded 'low laughter and murmurs, the light of lamps with pink shades; where the men were all in evening clothes, ringed and studded, and the women much uncovered in the neck and heavily jewelled, their glazed and lamp-blacked eyes wandering'. He descended and had his supper in the grill-room.   (236)

There is a very Hardyan note of wistfulness about that last sentence, I think, responsive to the sinister allure of the scene. But it is the 'Noble Dames', the beautiful Society women whose initials stud the later pages of the *Life*, that really stir him. In their case, however, the erotic fascination is complicated by the class anxiety that they clearly provoked. This relates very directly to the poor-man-and-lady topos that lies at the heart of so much of Hardy's work – nowhere more so, of course, than in his London novel *The Hand of Ethelberta*. We might recall that he tells us the 'most important scenes' of *The Poor Man and the Lady* were set in London and also that an episode from the book is preserved in a similarly-titled poem, set in a Mayfair church. In this the 'poor man' remembers how class eventually proved stronger than the love he and the lady had secretly pledged to each other:

> I was a striver with deeds to do,
> And little enough to do them with,
> And a comely woman of noble kith,
> With a courtly match to make, were you;
> And we both were young; and though sterling-true
> You had proved to our pledge under previous strains,
> Our 'union', as we called it, grew
> Less grave to your eyes in your town campaigns.

The class-related anxiety that Hardy feels in connection with beautiful London Society women frequently expresses itself in aggressive fancies comparable to the death and hell imagery attending his contemplation of *demi-mondaines* or cancan dancers:

March 15. With E. to a crush at the Jeunes'.... Met Mrs. T. and her great eyes in a corner of the rooms, as if washed up by the surging crowd. The most beautiful woman present.... But these women! If put into rough wrappers in a turnip-field, where would their beauty be?   (234–5)

Perhaps the most striking of these Fancies is the really astonishingly aggressive (and curiously voyeuristic) one about an elaborately dressed upper-class young woman Hardy observes in her carriage:

> 19 July. Note the weight of a landau and pair, the coachman in his grey great-coat, footman ditto. All this mass of matter is moved along with brute force and clatter through a street congested and obstructed, to bear the *petite* figure of the owner's young wife in violet velvet and silver trimming, slim, small; who could be easily carried under a man's arm, and who, if held up by the hair and slipped out of her clothes, carriage, etc., etc., aforesaid, would not be much larger than a skinned rabbit, and of less use.   (249)

The nearest one gets to anything like this in the novels – and it is a long way indeed from the ferocity of the skinned-rabbit image – is Mrs Swancourt's satirising of the appearance of the noble ladies taking their carriage exercise in Hyde Park (*A Pair of Blue Eyes*, Ch. 14).

There is one passage in the *Life* where the two groups of London women that Hardy is so concerned with, the flaunting prostitutes and the great Society ladies, are brought into interesting juxta-position. He attends a soirée at the beautiful Countess of Yarbor-ough's, and finds her fearful lest the rain should keep her guests away. They turn up, however, and she touches Hardy joyfully on the shoulder telling him 'You've conjured them!' Leaving the party, he takes an open-top bus to return home, there being no cabs:

> No sooner was I up there than the rain began again. A girl who had scrambled up after me asked for the shelter of my umbrella, and I gave it, – when she startled me by holding on tight to my arm and bestowing on me many kisses for the trivial kindness. She told me she had been to 'The Pav', and was tired, and was going home. She had not been drinking. I descended at the South Kensington Station and watched the 'bus bearing her away. An affectionate nature wasted on the streets! It was a strange contrast to the scene I had just left.   (281)

It is as though the potentially erotic element in Hardy's contact with the great lady who almost pets him is safely displaced into the encounter with the street-girl where he is the class superior and has all the power (to say nothing of the umbrella).

But London induced in Hardy an even deeper anxiety than the one relating to class and sex. In the crowded city the individual could lose his or her identity, the very sense of selfhood. This might be a matter of sheer social conformity: 'Our great fault', Mrs Procter wrote to Hardy when she heard he was coming to live in what she called 'stony-hearted London', 'is that we are all alike.... We press so closely against each other that any small shoots are cut off at once, and the young tree grows in shape like the old one' (103–4). People fall into a kind of enchantment or somnambulism as they go through various social rituals such as viewing pictures at the Royal Academy or praying in church. Their 'real life' is elsewhere and only tenuously connected with what their bodies are doing. And the individual who has not become absorbed into such rituals but is a mere wanderer in the city, as Jude is at first in Christminster, can even begin to feel actually disembodied, spectral:

> Knowing not a human being here, Jude began to be impressed with the isolation of his own personality, as with a self-spectre, the sensation being that of one who walked but could not make himself seen or heard.   (*Jude*, Part Second, Ch. 1)

The city induces a sense of temporal dislocation because, Hardy notes, 'There is no consciousness here of where anything comes from or goes to – only that it is present' (215). Wordsworth records a similar impression in his famous description of how London eroded his sense of personal identity as he goes forward with the crowd in 'the overflowing streets' until he seems to be moving in a dream:

> And all the ballast of familiar life,
> The present, and the past; hope, fear; all stays,
> All laws of acting, thinking, speaking man
> Went from me, neither knowing me, nor known.
>   (*The Prelude*, 1805, Book VII, ll. 603–6)

Hardy goes beyond Wordsworth in that he seems to see London as consuming people both body and soul:

> March 9. British Museum Reading Room. Souls are gliding about here in a sort of dream – screened somewhat by their bodies, but

imaginable behind them. Dissolution is gnawing at them all, slightly hampered by renovations....

March 28. On returning to London after an absence I find the people of my acquaintance abraded, their hair disappearing; also their flesh, by degrees.   (215)

And the diners at all those fashionable dinners during the Season are themselves consumed: 'London, that *hot-plate* of humanity, on which we first sing, then simmer, then boil, then dry away to dust and ashes!' (260).

London is sometimes strikingly totalised in the *Life* as a monstrous, threatening organism as when, for example, he records stopping at Swiss Cottage with his mother on that first visit to look back at 'the *outside* of London creeping towards them across green fields' (22). During his suburban years at Tooting (1878–81) he found himself unable to sleep one night

> partly on account of an eerie feeling which sometimes haunted him, a horror at lying down in close proximity to 'a monster whose body had four million heads and eight million eyes'.   (141)

His most horrific vision of this 'monster' occurred when he and Emma were watching the 1879 Lord Mayor's Show from an office window on Ludgate Hill. To Emma the crowd in the streets below looked like 'a boiling cauldron of porridge', a lively but hardly menacing image; Hardy, however, noticing the way in which individuals became lost in the mass, was visited by darker imaginings:

> as the crowd grows denser it loses its character of an aggregate of countless units, and becomes an organic whole, a molluscous black creature having nothing in common with humanity, that takes the shape of the streets along which it has lain itself, and throws out horrid excrescences and limbs into neighbouring alleys; a creature whose voice exudes from its scaly coat, and who has an eye in every pore of its body. The balconies, stands, and railway-bridge are occupied by small detached shapes of the same tissue, but of gentler motion, as if they were the spawn of the monster in their midst.   (134)

A crowd scene such as the one Hardy was contemplating here may provide the most dramatic manifestation possible of the city's power to obliterate individuality but there are other, less sensational, ways in which this happens – classification, for example. Stephen Smith's father in *A Pair of Blue Eyes* has, like most 'rural mechanics'

> too much individuality to be a typical 'working-man' – a resultant of that beach-pebble attrition with his kind only to be experienced in large towns, which metamorphoses the unit Self into a fraction of the unit Class.   (Ch. 10)

In *The Hand of Ethelberta* the heroine's brothers Sol and Dan resist such 'attrition', preserve their individual rural selves, with a comic contrast being provided by their younger brother Joey who becomes preposterously citified in his role as Ethelberta's page. Ethelberta herself, of course, is seeking to cheat the city through her art, to prevent the discovery that she is 'working class' and assert her individuality in an extreme way, i.e., as a unique kind of artist.

The tentacles of the kind of de-individualising metropolitan culture that Ethelberta is emphatically not a part of, reach out all over the country. Observing the first Avice on the remote Isle of Slingers, Pierston sees

> that every aim of those who had brought her up had been to get her away mentally as far as possible from her natural and individual life as an inhabitant of a peculiar island: to make her an exact copy of tens of thousands of other people, in whose circumstances there was nothing special, distinctive, or picturesque.   (*The Well-Beloved*, Part First, Ch. 2)

It is significant that the protagonists of Hardy's two London novels, *Ethelberta* and *The Well-Beloved*, are both artists. Despite all the anxieties it provokes in him, Hardy recognises that the city is the place where art is validated, where the artist must go to achieve recognition.[5] The problem for the artist is how to survive this process without losing his or her individuality and becoming a mere 'mechanical' performer or producer. Ethelberta avoids this because of the extraordinary nature of her social position and the uniqueness of her art. Pierston, although he 'prospers without effort', becomes an ARA, and so on, is nevertheless always distanced from Society and protected from corruption by his obsessive idealism.

Hardy himself, told by Thackeray's daughter that 'a novelist must necessarily like society' (107), seems to have felt he had to live in or near London while he was establishing himself but returned to Dorset as soon as he could:

> both for reasons of health and for mental inspiration, Hardy finding, or thinking he found, that residence in or near a city tended to force mechanical and ordinary productions from his pen, concerning ordinary society-life and habits.   (154)

So far we have been considering the city as the focus for a number of anxieties on Hardy's part – social anxieties, particularly in relation to women, anxieties about loss of personal identity, and anxiety about his work as an artist. But we should also note a number of passages, particularly in the novels, that show his imagination responding in a more detached way to the visual stimulus provided by city sights. In Chapter 13 of *A Pair of Blue Eyes*, for example, Hardy explicitly invokes a great painter in seeking to convey a particular city scene, the market-alley seen from the back window of Knight's chambers in Bede's Inn at dusk:

> Crowds – mostly of women – were surging, bustling, and pacing up and down. Gaslights glared from butchers' stalls, illuminating the lumps of flesh to splotches of orange and vermilion, like the wild colouring of Turner's later pictures, whilst the purl and babble of tongues of every pitch and mood was to this human wild-wood what the ripple of a brook is to the natural forest.[6]

And the urban paintings of Atkinson Grimshaw (1836–93) could have provided a pictorial equivalent to the following description of autumnal London from *The Well-Beloved* (Part Third, Ch. 5).

> It was one of those ripe and mellow afternoons that sometimes colour London with their golden light at this time of year, and produce those marvellous sunset effects which, if they were not known to be made up of kitchen coal-smoke and animal exhalations, would be rapturously applauded. Behind the perpendicular, oblique, zigzagged, and curved zinc 'tall-boys', that formed a grey pattern not unlike early Gothic numerals against

the sky, the men and women on the tops of the omnibuses saw an irradiation of topaz hues, darkened here and there into richest russet.

But in the following passage from *The Hand of Ethelberta* (Ch. 18) it is surely Wordsworth's famous sonnet rather than the work of any painter that Hardy is intending the reader to recall:

Picotee arrived in town late on a cold February afternoon.... She crossed Westminster Bridge on foot, just after dusk, and saw a luminous haze hanging over each well-lighted street as it withdrew into distance behind the nearer houses, showing its direction as a train of morning mist shows the course of a distant stream when the stream itself is hidden. The lights along the riverside towards Charing Cross sent an inverted palisade of gleaming swords down into the shaking water, and the pavement ticked to the touch of pedestrians' feet, most of whom tripped along as if walking only to practise a favourite quick step, and held handkerchiefs to their mouths to strain off the river mist from their lungs.

Instead of the city lying 'all bright and glittering in the smokeless air' of the early morning it is enveloped in a 'luminous haze' of gaslight, light which seems both to parody and attack the natural world; instead of Wordsworth's beneficent river 'glid[ing]' at its own sweet will' here the 'shaking water' is a source of apprehension for passers-by; and instead of the 'calm so deep' savoured by Wordsworth there is the incessant 'ticking' of pedestrians' feet as they scurry along with their half-covered faces.

Such 'cityscapes' as this are rare in Hardy's work and this is not surprising since, apart from Jude's Christminster, it is only in the two artist-novels, *The Hand of Ethelberta* and *The Well-Beloved*, that the city figures as a character, so to speak, hence one would not expect such passages in the other novels. In some of them, however, a city does figure as a powerful off-stage presence – Paris in *The Return of the Native*, for example, or London in *Tess*.

In *Tess*, London is the place where Angel was 'ensnared' (again, we notice the city's erotic significance for Hardy) and the mere thought of it is curiously disturbing to Tess herself. It is something deeply alien to her as Hardy conveys in the juxtaposition of her and the London-bound train in Ch. 30: 'No object could have looked

more foreign to the gleaming cranks and wheels than this unsophisticated girl'. In the midst of her intense struggle with herself over
Angel's increasingly pressing courtship she is suddenly made
aware of the total indifference to her and Angel of all those legions
of Londoners, 'strange people that we have never seen.... Noble
men and noble women, ambassadors and centurions, ladies and
tradeswomen, and babies who have never seen a cow.' Later, when
Angel is pressing her still harder and she is on the point of yielding
to his importunity, the 'multitudinous intonation' of the natural
sounds of the valley they are standing looking down on 'forced
upon their fancy that a great city lay below them, and that the mur-
mur was the vociferation of its populace'. To Tess these city voices
speak only of discord and suffering:

> It seems like tens of thousands of them ... holding public-
> meetings in their market-places, arguing, preaching, quarrelling,
> sobbing, groaning, praying, and cursing.   (Ch. 32)

And she continues to fear and avoid towns after Angel has left her
and she has to look for work:

> She refrained from seeking an indoor occupation; fearing towns,
> large houses, people of means and social sophistication and of
> manners other than rural. From that direction of gentility Black
> Care had come ...   (Ch. 41)

But the city gets her in the end – not London indeed but what Hardy
calls the 'pleasure city' of Sandbourne. Everything outside Sandbourne, situated as it is on the edge of the Egdon Waste, is prehis-
toric but 'the exotic had grown here, suddenly as the prophet's
gourd; and had drawn hither Tess' (Ch. 55).
   The combination of woman and city usually leads to tragic results
in Hardy, the big exception to the rule being Ethelberta in his 'comedy in chapters'. Paris draws Eustacia Vye to her death and the city
and city values gradually kill Sophy in the short story 'The Son's
Veto' as she pines away with longing for her forbidden rural lover.
A mere glimpse of London from the train window is enough to fill
Elfride in *A Pair of Blue Eyes* with dread and distress:

> She peered out ... and saw only the lamps, which had just been
> lit, blinking in the wet atmosphere, and rows of hideous zinc

chimney-pipes in dim relief against the sky. She writhed uneasily, as when a thought is swelling in the mind which must cause much pain at its deliverance in words. Elfride had known no more about the stings of evil report than the native wild-fowl knew of the effects of Crusoe's first shot. Now she saw a little further, and a little further still.   (Ch. 12)

The utterly unsophisticated second Avice in *The Well-Beloved* (Part Second, Ch. 12) has no notion of the danger she is exposing herself to when she wanders about the fashionable streets of London to gratify her curiosity, and admires all the charming gentlemen she sees. 'They were dressed in the latest fashion', she tells the horrified Pierston, 'and would have scorned to do me any harm; and as to their love-making, I never heard anything so polite before.' A little longer in the streets and Avice could well have become another 'ruined maid':

> 'O 'Melia, my dear, this does everything crown!
> Who could have supposed I should meet you in Town?
> And whence such fair garments, such prosperi-ty?'–
> 'O didn't you know I'd been ruined?' said she.

The comic urban voices of 'Melia and her friend might prompt thoughts of that greatest master of such voices, Dickens (not that he would ever have presented a fallen woman as a comic figure[7]) and I want to conclude this discussion of Hardy and the city by noting the remarkable paucity of Hardy's references to Dickens, and the strangely grudging nature of those that do exist. I would suggest that we have here a clear Bloomian case of the 'anxiety of influence'.

Apparently Hardy told his fellow architectural apprentices in the 1860s that 'he would not have the reputation of Dickens for anything' yet, consciously or unconsciously, he would seem to have been under Dickens's influence – the strongly Dickensian traits present in the young Hardy's 'How I built myself a house' have been noted by Robert Gittings, for example.[8] Hardy tells us that he frequented Dickens's public readings but makes no comment on them whatsoever (54). Similarly tight-lipped is his mention of Dickens's death: 'Crossing Hyde Park one morning in June he saw the announcement of Dickens's death' (79). At this very time he was working on *Desperate Remedies*, the complicated plotting of which surely owes something to the Dickens/Wilkie Collins school and which also contains some very Dickensian touches, as in this description of a poor London household:

> Mrs. Higgins was the wife of a carpenter who from want of employment one winter had decided to marry. Afterwards they both took to drink, and sank into desperate circumstances. A few chairs and a table were the chief articles of furniture in the third-floor back room which they occupied. A roll of baby-linen lay on the floor; beside it a pap-clogged spoon and an overturned tin pap-cup. Against the wall a Dutch clock was fixed out of level, and ticked wildly in longs and shorts, its entrails hanging down beneath its white face and wiry hands, like the faeces of a Harpy ('foedissima ventris proluvies, uncaeque manus, et pallida semper ora'). A baby was crying against every chair-leg, the whole family of six or seven being small enough to be covered by a washing-tub.   (Ch. 16, Section 4)

The detailism here, and the grotesque animism used in the description of the clock, strongly recall Dickens, though the faeces image and the parenthetical quotation from Virgil are very *un*-Dickensian indeed.

It may be significant that it is only after Dickens's death that Hardy comes into his literary own with *Under the Greenwood Tree* (1872), almost as though the disappearance of the bestriding colossus of the contemporary novel was a kind of release for him (even though he still had the majestic presence of George Eliot to contend with). When in the Dickens centenary year of 1912, *The Bookman* asked him and other notables about Dickens's effect on their imaginations, Hardy replied that his own literary efforts did not owe much to Dickens's influence, but added the grudging-sounding rider, 'No doubt they owed something unconsciously, since everybody's did in those days.'[9] It is difficult to believe, however, that Dickens was not a continuing presence in Hardy's writing whenever he touched on the city. We might instance the 1891 description of the old waiter in the London theatrical tavern:

> He has whiskers of the rare old mutton-chop pattern, and a manner of confidence. He has shaved so many years that his face is of a bluish soap-colour, and if wetted and rubbed would raise a lather of itself.   (249)

And it is certainly hard to believe that the famous opening of *Bleak House*, describing London fog, does not lie somewhere behind this passage:

[Hardy] was also in London a part of the month, where he saw 'what is called sunshine up here – a red-hot bullet hanging in a livid atmosphere – reflected from window-panes in the form of bleared copper eyes, and inflaming the sheets of plate-glass with smears of gory light. A drab snow mingled itself with liquid horsedung and in the river puddings of ice moved slowly on. The steamers were moored, with snow on their gangways. A captain, in sad solitude, smoked his pipe against the bulk-head of the cabin stairs. (243)

But Hardy's essential vision of London, city of 'Four million forlorn hopes!' (227), is a tragic one, except in *The Hand of Ethelberta*, whereas Dickens's is comic/satiric, based firmly on an underlying belief 'that life in society can be lived successfully, and that moral judgement is the guide to this'.[10] Where Hardy often seems closest to Dickens in treating the city is in certain poems in which he picks out a face from the crowd and tells its story as in 'An East-End Curate' with its description of the man's dreary daily round and his lodgings with its 'bleached pianoforte' and framed 'Laws of Heaven for Earth' on the wall, or in 'A Beauty's Soliloquy during her Honeymoon' (signed 'In a London Hotel, 1892') in which the woman begins to think that in her rustic ignorance she threw herself away on a 'poor plain man' when she might have had a dazzling choice of suitors in town. Hardy's urban 'snapshots' have always a harsher edge to them than Dickens's, however. Dickens ends his description of the deprived lifestyle of the shabby city clerk he sees in St James's Park as follows:

Poor, harmless creatures such men are; contented but not happy; broken-spirited and humbled, they may feel no pain, but they never know pleasure. (*Sketches by Boz*, 'Thoughts About People')

A good deal bleaker is the ending of Hardy's 'Coming Up Oxford Street: Evening' as the sun

    dazzles the pupils of one who walks west,
A city-clerk, with eyesight not of the best,
Who sees no escape to the very verge of his days

From the rut of Oxford Street into open ways;
And he goes along with head and eyes flagging forlorn,
Empty of interest in things, and wondering why he was born.

(The signature reads 'As seen 4 July 1872'.)

Nor is it only the human victims of the city that attract Hardy's attention. Whereas Dickens's urban animals are matter for comedy (e.g., the dogs and birds in 'Shy Neighbourhoods' in *The Uncommercial Traveller*) we find this journal entry in Hardy's *Life*:

13 July [1888]. After being in the street: – What was it on the faces of those horses? – Resignation. Their eyes looked at me, haunted me. The absoluteness of their resignation was terrible. When afterwards I heard their tramp as I lay in bed, the ghosts of their eyes came in to me, saying, 'Where is your justice, O man and ruler?' (220)

For Dickens, on the other hand, the horses he sees at a hackney coach stand are forlorn indeed but grotesquely comic too:

The horses, with drooping heads, and each with a mane and tail as scanty and straggling as those of a worn-out rocking-horse are standing patiently on some damp straw, occasionally wincing and rattling the harness; and now and then one of them lifts his mouth to the ear of his companion, as if he were saying, in a whisper, that he should like to assassinate the coachman. (*Sketches by Boz*, Ch. 7, 'Hackney-coach Stands')

It is, then, Hardy's tragic vision that finally distinguishes his response to the city so fundamentally from Dickens's and nowhere is that vision more clearly expressed than in a journal entry for 28 May 1885, my concluding quotation from the *Life*:

Waiting at the Marble Arch while Em called a little way further on to enquire after —'s children…. This hum of the wheel – the roar of London! What is it composed of? Hurry, speech, laughters, moans, cries of little children. The people in this tragedy laugh, sing, smoke, toss off wines, etc, make love to girls in drawing-rooms and areas; and yet are playing their parts in the tragedy just the same. Some wear jewels and feathers, some wear rags. All are caged birds; the only difference lies in the size of the cage. This too is part of the tragedy. (178)

Notes

1. All quotations from the *Life* are drawn from the rescension by Michael Millgate, published under the title of *The Life and Work of Thomas Hardy* (Macmillan, 1984); page references are given in parenthesis following quotations. The texts of all Hardy poems quoted have been taken from *The Variorum Edition of the Complete Poems of Thomas Hardy,* ed. James Gibson (Macmillan, 1979). Quotations from Hardy's novels and short stories have been taken from Macmillan's New Wessex Edition (1974–7); chapter references are given in parenthesis following quotations.

2. *Jude the Obscure*, Part Second, Ch. 1; *The Return of the Native*, Book III, Ch. 4.

3. Jullien was the musical conductor Louis Antoine Jullien (1812–60) who gave concerts at Drury Lane in the 1840s and 1850s and was the composer of many popular quadrilles.

4. Dostoevsky, *Winter Notes on Summer Impressions* (1863), trans. D. Patterson (Northwestern University Press, 1988) p. 39f. In his *Young Thomas Hardy* (Penguin, 1978) Robert Gittings quotes (p. 92) Mayhew's estimate that 'there were no less than 80,000 prostitutes in London, many of them children' and Arthur Munby's recording in his diary of the various sexual services on offer in the streets.

5. My attention was drawn to this point by my colleague, Mr Michael Baron, to whom I am also generally grateful for very helpful discussions on the topic of Hardy and the city.

6. Hardy is describing Clare Market, behind Lincoln's Inn. Compare this with the description given by Charles Dickens, Jr, in his *Dickens's Dictionary of London* (1879): 'To see Clare Market at its best, it is needful to go there on Saturday evening: then the narrow lanes are crowded, then the butchers' shops are ablaze with gas-lights flaring in the air, and the shouting of the salesman and costermonger is at its loudest.... The greater portion of those who are passing through the crowd to make their purchases for to-morrow's dinner are women, and of them many have children in their arms.... The din and bustle last till midnight, and it is a strange phase of life to study the faces and listen to the conversation of people bargain-hunting in this market'.

7. The only exception I can think of is the initial description of Nancy in *Oliver Twist* (Ch. 9) but Dickens quickly changes those notes to tragic.

8. Robert Gittings, *Young Thomas Hardy*, p. 116.

9. Harold Orel (ed.), *Thomas Hardy's Personal Writings* (Macmillan, 1967) p. 246.

10. P. N. Furbank, Introduction to the New Wessex Edition of *Tess of the d'Urbervilles* (1974/5) pp. 12–13. (hardback).

4

'Thoroughfares of Stones': Hardy's 'Other' Love Poetry

TREVOR JOHNSON

All lovers of Hardy owe the late Professor Carl Weber a sizeable debt – his best memorial is the splendid Colby College Hardy collection – but, by one of life's little posthumous ironies, the last of his many books has, I fear, done his hero a grave disservice. His *Hardy's Love Poems*, published in 1963 and often reprinted, though it does, as he says, contain 'some of the finest ... love poems in English' has a most misleading title. For its contents are rigidly restricted to poems about Emma Hardy, rearranged to make a quasi-narrative by Weber; and the ingenious or ingenuous blurb-writer for the very recent paperback makes matters worse by saying 'this unique collection brings together *all* Hardy's love poetry'. If that were so we should have the remarkable spectacle of a poet's not only confining his amatory verse to his wife but also waiting until after her death and his attainment of the age of seventy-two before embarking on it, which would surely take self-abnegation beyond belief.

Of course, Weber did not mean to propound such an absurdity, though his lengthy introduction contains no disclaimer. Even so, his anthology gave and still gives wide currency to the bizarre critical shibboleth that the elegies for Emma are the *only* love poems by Hardy that really matter.

Yet Hardy's tribute to what Dr Johnson, no sentimentalist, called 'a passion which he who never felt never was happy, and he who laughs at never deserves to feel'[1] amounts to over a third of his total output, while that part of it which is neither about Emma, nor 'dramatic and personative' yields over a hundred poems which at least seem to express Hardy's personal responses to love. Moreover, even Weber's inventory includes four poems which are most

58

certainly *not* about Emma and a further twenty odd which are, to varying degrees, questionably so ascribed.[2]

But, though I regret that new readers of Hardy may meet him on so arbitrarily restricted a front, I am far more concerned that Weber's drastic narrowing of the field typifies an ongoing critical consensus. And close investigation of nearly twenty books and critical symposia devoted to Hardy's poetry bears out my gloomiest forebodings. With honourable exceptions like Tom Paulin and Dennis Taylor,[3] the scope most commentators allow Hardy's 'other' love poems is negligible. Typically, the early lyrics from the 1860s will be skated over as *juvenilia* with a polite bob to 'Neutral Tones'. A handful from the 1890s will receive muted approval and then it is full speed ahead for 1912 and the elegies to Emma.

Some of these 'other' love poems merit their obscurity of course. 'I Said and Sang Her Excellence (Fickle Lover's Song)' lives up to its inauspicious subtitle with the refrain 'Have your way my heart O!'; the 'art of sinking' is well exemplified in lines like 'She is the God-created norm / Of perfect woman-kind ', and Hardy's variation on the well-known song 'Dashing Away with a Smoothing-Iron',[4] with its fifth verse: 'On Friday it was with a thrill / In gazing towards your distant vill [sic] / I owned you were my dear one still' is markedly less entertaining than the Flanders and Swann variant beginning ''Twas on a Monday morning / The gasman came to call'. Yet the most cursory survey of Hardy's eight successive volumes of verse will show how few, of the dozen or so 'other' love poems which each contains, fail to live up to Philip Larkin's perception that, at least, each has 'a little spinal cord of thought and ... a little tune of its own ... something you can say of very few poets.'[5]

You may feel that my own judgement, which is that at least a third of those poems I am here concerned with are comparable with all but the very best of those to Emma, savours of the *parti-pris*. If so, I invite you to consider that Hardy included no less than 48 of his 'other' love poems in his last selection from his own verse, *Chosen Poems* of 1929, besides 24 about Emma, from a total of 161. If he valued them so much more than most of his critics, ought we not, in Cromwell's famous words, to consider it possible we may be mistaken?[6]

Hardy dated more than half these poems which helps us to assess his artistic development. Nearly thirty, written in the 1860s, were unpublished until 1898, in *Wessex Poems*, or later. Though Hardy says that the 'middle period ... of his novel-writing' produced 'very few [poems]' he adds that in the 1890s they were 'added to with great rapidity',[7] and these largely appeared in the 1902 and 1909 volumes – *The Dynasts* filling the interval – with some additions in *Satires of Circumstance* in 1914. Subsequently, in Hardy's last four volumes, though other love poems continue to appear, they tend to be overshadowed by his elegiac tributes and 'expiations' to Emma.

So we are left with three more or less discrete groups: thirty poems or so from Hardy's twenties, and before he met Emma, nearly as many again from his fifties or thereabouts, when his marriage was in the doldrums, and a rather larger miscellaneous batch mostly from his later years, often retrospective and generally undated. I intend to look largely at the first two, beginning with those from the 1860s.

Hardy supplies some useful information about the circumstances in which he wrote them.[8] Between 1862 and 1869 he worked as an assistant architect, at first in London, living in bachelor digs, mostly in Westbourne Park Villas, Paddington, then, briefly, in Weymouth when ill health prompted him to quit London. Outside working hours he was reading, with passionate enthusiasm, primarily in English poetry. Indeed, he tells us that in 1866–7 'for nearly or quite two years [I] did not read a word of prose except ... daily newspapers and weekly reviews'.[9] A well-thumbed, heavily annotated copy of Palgrave's *Golden Treasury* was what Dennis Taylor terms his 'primary poetic manual'[10]: many of his early poems employ verse-forms common in Palgrave.

At some time in 1865, he says, he embarked on the enterprise with which he hoped to make his name as a poet, and we may envisage him, sitting up by lamplight as was his lifelong habit, far into the night; penning in his strong, clear draftsman's hand his first sustained attempts to secure what his admired Shelley had summed up in the line 'Poet's food is love and fame.'[11]

Much of what he wrote then has vanished; later Hardy 'fancied he had destroyed too many'[12] of his prentice efforts. But the residual evidence allows a reasoned conjecture which also points to Hardy's conception as bold and original. We know from his ambitious – if soon abandoned – attempt to versify the Book of Ecclesiastes into 'Spenserian stanzas'[13] that he was already drawn to the kind of large-scale poetic endeavour which finally emerged as *The Dynasts*. Hardy himself stated that the four surviving 'She to Him' sonnets originally formed 'part of a much larger number which perished'.[14] His fascination with the quatorzain form is attested by nearly half his early poems, but only 'She to Him III' follows the 'Shakespearian' sonnet form with a final rhyming couplet; the others show his readiness to experiment with blends of the Spenserian and Petrarchan modes, while his remarks in his short story *An Imaginative Woman*[15] about 'sonnets in the loosely rhymed Elizabethan fashion', show his acquaintance with other exemplars as well as his awareness that the term 'sonnet' was much more loosely employed then. The story tells us of a young poet, Robert Trewe, whose style was 'luxuriant rather than finished', a 'pessimist in so far as that character applies to a man who looks at the worst contingencies as well as the best in the human condition' and who is 'little attracted by excellencies of form and rhythm apart from content'. His 'loosely rhymed sonnets' were condemned by 'every right-minded reviewer'. It is hard to resist the thought that here in Trewe we have Hardy's portrait of himself when a young aspirant in poetry.

Then there are the titles. Of these, eleven dated in the 1860s include the word 'She' or 'Her' indicating a woman 'narrator' a feature shared by 'The Musing Maiden' of 1866, not printed until 1928, while both 'Neutral Tones' and '1967', though usually ascribed to a man, could equally well be spoken by a woman.

We know Hardy wrote at least a substantial part of a sequence. We know he did not confine himself to a single sonnet form. We know he was familiar with Elizabethan sequences which avail themselves of interspersed short lyrics. We have at least twelve poems with the eponymous 'She' as their narrator, all displaying strong thematic affinities. It does not seem to me that a vast imaginative leap is required to take all these poems as part of a full-blown sequence which deployed several differing forms of sonnet together with other short lyric forms to give variety. If we further bear in mind that the sonnet sequence or series was immensely popular in the nineteenth century – over five hundred are recorded – we can readily appreciate how an unknown young poet might hope to make his mark in this way. It was a well-trodden path, after all.

However, in one important aspect Hardy chose not to tread it, for to make a betrayed and deserted woman his protagonist, to speak with her imagined, anguished voice, was surely to invite rejection from periodical editors to whom he seems to have submitted samples. Even a man like Leslie Stephen could be remarkably prudish about such matters, as his shilly-shallying about *The Return of the Native* reveals.[16]

In consequence of their rejection by those who, as Hardy later grumbled 'did not know good poetry from bad',[17] a good deal of his

early verse was lost. Some, as he confessed, was actually recycled
into prose, notably in *Desperate Remedies*,[18] whose heroine
Cytherea's plight significantly resembles that of the eponymous
'She' in the sequence. But that was avowedly fictitious; was the original conception of the sequence based, however tangentially, on
fact? Michael Millgate suggests that it was, that it derived from
Hardy's putative engagement during the period 1863 to 1867.[19]
Although his evidence for this seems pretty tenuous, besides
involving Hardy casting himself as the villain of the piece and Eliza
Nicholls as the tragic protagonist, his suggestion is not incompatible
with my hypothesis, which merely requires Hardy's narrative thread
to be at a greater remove from actuality, a far from unlikely contingency. Sonnet sequences like Meredith's recent *Modern Love*,[20]
which almost certainly served Hardy as an inspirational example,
traditionally adopted an oblique approach to actuality.

Fictitious or not, I suggest Hardy's *schema* can be summarised as
follows. His narrator has fallen passionately in love with a man who
is her social superior. Initially he reciprocates her feelings; they are,
Hardy says, 'fused from [life's] separateness by ecstasy' a phrase
which states what was to become a *leitmotif* of Hardy's love poetry.
But, spurred by ambition for 'Fame's far summits' he deserts her for
London's opportunities; which would, as far as it goes, fit Millgate's
theory. The remaining 'She to Him' sonnets would then express her
bereft state of mind, summed up in the famous trope where she
speaks of herself as 'Numb as a vane that cankers on its point, /
True to the wind that kissed ere canker came', a state of despairing
inanition markedly resembling that of 'Neutral Tones' which, if it is
accepted into the sequence, would record the lovers' last, hopeless
assignation. His impending marriage, by implication loveless but
self-serving, moves her to anger and jealousy 'I can but maledict
her, pray her dead,' she says. But he falls ill of consumption and, in
'Her Dilemma' they meet for the last time. He knows he is dying but
pleads for reassurance that she loves him still and she, torn by the
knowledge that she has no right to do so, nevertheless gives him the
assurance he craves feeling, '"Twas worth her soul to be a moment
kind'. The last scene is enacted in 'She at his Funeral' which she
attends as an anonymous spectator. To her the official mourners'
grief appears conventional while 'My regret consumes like fire!'

I willingly concede that other arrangements are feasible, but it
does seem to me that to view the remains of Hardy's sequence as a
whole allows us to see more clearly how original and daring his

overall conception was. For so young and inexperienced a poet to venture on such a large-scale exposure of the darker face of Eros, and for him not only to treat of betrayal, frustration, jealousy and despair but also to present them through the *persona* of a woman was a truly remarkable departure from the norm of mid-Victorian love poetry when Elizabeth Barrett Browning's *Sonnets from the Portuguese* were widely regarded as the apogee of lyrical intensity. It was the period of which Meredith wrote to his friend Maxse, with sardonic emphasis, in 1869 '[Tennyson] the foremost poet of the age goes on fluting of creatures who have not a breath of vital humanity in them ... doling us out the curate's moral sentiments [with] the British matron's and her daughter's purity'.[21] In 1862 Meredith in his sequence 'Modern Love' had so nakedly revealed the biitterness and suffering which had ensued from his wife's unfaithfulness, that he had brought down upon his head howls of execration about 'prurient meddling'.

If, as he later said, Hardy had followed the 'royal road'[22] to publication, he would, instead of emulating Meredith, have added to the catalogue of 'Airy, Fairy Lilian', 'Eileen Aroon', 'Dark Rosaleen', 'Ever-varying Madeline' and those other euphonious objects of Victorian male adulation who adorn the pages of the original *Oxford Book of Victorian Verse*. But, whether or not he admired them, he chose to do otherwise; to defy the unwritten convention which restricted love poetry to lyrical celebration on the one hand and to melancholy sublimation on the other.

Hardy, in terms of both theme and treatment, had other aims to pursue: it is time to consider how far he achieved them. In so far as diction is concerned, the potent influence of Shakespeare's magniloquent style in his *Sonnets* is at once apparent in the opening of 'She to Him I', 'When you shall see me in the toils of Time, / My lauded beauties carried off from me', and in 'Her Definition' with its extended simile 'As common chests encasing wares of price / Are borne with tenderness through halls of state'. This over-aureate manner can decline into clichés like 'Time that tyrant fell', 'Lovelorn wooer' and 'Immortal light illumes the lay', while sometimes 'alliteration's artful aid' is over-liberally invoked, as in 'Her Definition' with 'Debarred from due description then did I / Perceive the indefinite phrase could yet define'. Yet even this early in his career Hardy's authentic accent can be heard. The octave of 'She to Him I', in the high Elizabethan manner, 'recalls the excellencies I once enshrined'. But by line 10 the traditional figure of Time has been transmogrified from the old gentleman with a scythe into a Victorian gamekeeper who 'but rears his brood to kill'. To be sure, lovers have been likened to many birds: swans, doves and nightingales among them ... but partridges?

Again, who else in 1867 had not only read John Donne – incidentally, the one poet whose direct influence Hardy twice acknowledges[23] – but was willing to emulate his manner as directly as Hardy's '1967' does? Perhaps he was too sanguine in his declared belief that 'in [our] live century's vivid view' we might find 'A scope above this blinkered time'. But Hardy's conclusion has a macabre intensity which derives, as Edward Thomas shrewdly pointed out, from its metaphysical mingling of unexpected elements.[24] The amenities of life in 1967 are dismissed with contempt

> – Yet what to me how far above?
> For I would only ask thereof
> That thy worm should be my worm, Love!

Mrs Browning was prepared to postpone, for her husband Robert, 'My near sweet view of heaven, for earth with thee',[25] and the two conclusions neatly encapsulate the difference between Hardy's and Victorian love poetry generally. To the unbeliever, love is not a fore-taste of either heaven or hell but an end in itself, and whenever Hardy first read Arnold's 'Dover Beach' – first published in 1867 – he must have experienced an extraordinary sense of *déjà vu*. 'Neutral Tones' for all its whiff of Dante Gabriel Rossetti, not only offers a uniquely arid and colourless winter landscape but makes it the objective cor-relative not of despair – which fell within the permissible range of emotion – but of apathy; of love not so much spurned as listlessly relinquished by lovers dumb to tell what has sundered them; a sharp, original perception, which one is tempted to call amazingly 'modern'.

'She at His Funeral' would have marked one of the climactic points of Hardy's sequence. Succinct, direct and written in one of the simple quatrain forms known as 'common metre' it begins innocuously enough,

> They bear him to his resting-place –
> In slow procession sweeping by;
> I follow at a stranger's space;

but then leaps into three dramatic contrasts with

His kindred they, his sweetheart I.

Unchanged my gown of garish dye,
Though sable-sad is their attire;
But they stand round with griefless eye,
Whilst my regret consumes like fire!

The choice of 'kindred' and 'sweetheart' already shows Hardy's sensitivity to the nuances of language; the epithets 'garish' and 'sable-sad' not only imply difference of class but also convey the gulf between convention and true feeling, while the last lines give the poem its reverberant impact, its impassioned poignancy. It is not unlike early Yeats.

Similar qualities are to be found in 'Her Dilemma' which was originally cast in the first person with the woman speaking again. Whether Hardy's later change to a more detached tone was well-judged is debatable. The form, though heroic quatrains are a common hymn-metre, probably derives from Gray's *Elegy*, one of Hardy's favourite poems. Later he tended to avoid the iambic pentameter line; here its insistent rhythms help suggest the 'clock's dull monotones' and frame the mood. The setting, one familiar to the young architect, is of a 'sunless church' with 'mildewed walls', symbolising the inadequacy of religion to the 'dilemma'. The once-beautiful 'carvings' epitomising medieval faith, are now 'wasted' which neatly implies both 'decayed' and 'irrelevant'. Even an antiquarian will find nothing to detain him here where 'nothing broke the clock's dull monotones'. 'Dull' is another apt ambiguity here for both sound and association. The atmosphere of dank ecclesiastical inertia is carried over by 'wormy poppy-head', a phrase which brilliantly compresses suggestions of decay, drugs and death, reinforced by the alliterated epithets 'wormy', 'wan' and 'worn'; identifying the man's much more rapid decay with the slow crumbling of the pew-ends, of the whole church indeed, with all that implies.

The man has become his own *memento mori*; his death sentence – a mere parenthesis – is followed by his anguished entreaty, on which the moral crux hinges with what, in a sonnet, would be the formal 'turn': 'Tell me you love me!'

In a sense this poem expresses Hardy's own dilemma as a poet. If he had been primarily concerned with publication how easy it would have been to slip into pious rectitude, to write perhaps – instead of what we have –

> But could not lie, her heart persuaded throughly
> 'Twould *cost* her soul to be a moment kind.

But that was not his way, then or ever. Like Dr Samuel Johnson, he could only 'repose on the stability of truth'. And if the third stanza confounds conventional expectations, the fourth, in its defiant hopelessness, its refusal to offer any escape, looks forward to poems like Wilfred Owen's 'Futility' with its anguished entreaty 'O what made fatuous sunbeams toil / To break earth's sleep at all?', and backward to John Clare's insistence that 'Real poets must be truly honest men / Tied to no mongrel laws on flattery's page'.[26] Regrettably, the chance for readers to judge whether Hardy was a 'true poet' or not had to wait another thirty years until 1898.

However, in 1883 Hardy wrote a remarkable poem, entitled 'He Abjures Love'. Not only is it the single firmly-dated love poem we possess from the 1880s, but it also forms a peculiarly appropriate bridge between Hardy's youthful love lyrics and those he wrote in middle age. His title is significant in itself; the unusual verb 'to abjure', meaning 'to renounce upon oath' was once more or less confined to the formal declaration made by a repentant heretic. Here – as is plain from the tenor of the whole poem – the religion is Love, and the heretic, it seems, Hardy, who declares 'At last I put off love', though 'put off' is interestingly ambiguous. By implication he has worshipped at the shrine of Eros (hence 'give *him* glory' and '*his* wiles') since he was twenty-three, just after he came to London, in fact.

The poem's verse structure is original; even the indefatigable Dennis Taylor has not found an analogue for it.[27] It is written in octaval stanzas, intricately rhymed ABCD/ABCD. However, its flavour is unmistakably traditional with its strong rhythms, impeccable rhymes and marked use of alliteration. Sir Thomas Wyatt, whose verse Hardy admired,[28] could command exactly this kind of smooth, elegant musicality, masking but not concealing great depth of feeling, as he does in his lute songs. And the resemblance is unsurprising because Hardy's theme is that archetypal *topos* of Courtly Love, the Lover's Complaint, in the version which protests at his 'heart-enslavement', not to his mistress but to the God himself. At first glance nothing could be more traditional; such turns of phrase as 'kith and kind', 'fatuous fires' and 'comelier hue' reinforce the resemblance to Renaissance examples, and even Hardy's emendations show him expunging diction of the kind we have come to see as characteristically Hardeian (line 37, for example, originally read, rather oddly, 'The creak a jealous cry'). Nor do we commonly find in Hardy, lines which display the cool, classical poise of

> But lo, Love beckoned me,
>   And I was bare,
> And poor, and starved, and dry,
>   And fever-stricken.

So the first four stanzas chronicle the Lover's descent into enthralment; it is with the fifth that the critics and biographers who take it at face value, as the apotheosis of disillusion, part company from me.

> No more will now rate I
>   The common rare,
> The midnight drizzle dew,
>   The gray hour golden,
> The wind a yearning cry,
>   The faulty fair,
> Things dreamt, of comelier hue
> Than things beholden! ...

The denotative meaning is plain enough, but what connotative weight does that 'No more' – itself a phrase implying regret – retain as against the incandescently romantic images which follow. It is more than a piece of Hardy's clandestine irony, the triple periods at the end imply uncertainty, placed as they are immediately after the emphatic point of exclamation. To me Hardy says, 'Love to be sure may be an illusion: do we really desire to live without illusions as potent as this?' It is a volte-face or paradox of the kind Donne employed. In the act of abjuring love's 'fatuous fires', 'desolations', and 'wiles', Hardy, by the intensity with which he evokes them, seems to cry out for their recurrence. And, knowing what we know about Hardy's distrust of 'convictions' as opposed to 'impressions',[29] doesn't his icily ratiocinative boast to have attained 'clear views and certain' arouse suspicions which are clinched by that leaden stress on 'But' followed by three of the most desolate and desolating lines in English poetry. I think this is a neglected masterpiece and am gratified to find Gilbert Murray before me. He wrote to Hardy in 1909: 'The poem that really delights me most is "He Abjures Love". Perhaps it is the classical scholar [in me] that likes it specially. It is so like Horace, the thought, the severity and clearness of form, and the fine stinging rhythm.'[30] In the eighty-three years since he wrote, shamefully few critics have either echoed or even dissented from Murray's judgement.

Nevertheless, even if as I have suggested, 'He Abjures Love' should not be taken *au pied de la lettre*, it does more than imply a rift in the Hardys' matrimonial lute, a rift which had by 1909 grown so wide that he no longer cared to conceal it from his readers. Another poem, perhaps retrospective, entitled 'Alike and Unlike' treats of an incident which occurred when, in May 1893, the Hardys took a drive around Great Orme's Head, near Llandudno,[31] when they were en route to Dublin where they were to meet Mrs Florence Henniker for the first time. She was certainly to become the subject, so far as Hardy was concerned, of renewed and possibly 'fatuous fires'. We have arrived at a point in Hardy's emotional life where, as 'Alike and Unlike' puts it, his and Emma's views, symbolised by their reactions to the landscape, had irrevocably diverged, 'Tending to sever us thenceforth alway'. He remained loyal to Emma but his loyalty did not stretch to a wholesale renunciation of sympathetic feminine company and he found that in Mrs Henniker, whom he immediately categorised as 'charming' and *'intuitive'*[32] and with whom, after an initial spell when he hoped they might become 'more than friends', which she brought briskly to an end, he maintained what the French so delightfully call an 'amitié amoureuse' for the rest of her life. She was a handsome, well-read, on occasion witty woman, married to an amicable philistine of a soldier husband, and herself a writer of no small talent who maintained something of a salon at her London home. Several good poems undoubtedly refer to her, all of them probably dating from 1893 to the time in 1896 when Hardy wrote 'Wessex Heights', in which Mrs Henniker is the 'rare fair woman' in whose mind Hardy is now 'but a thought', never having realised his 'love for her in its fulness', so that he feels 'now I can let her go'. Of these, I think those with the most secure provenance are also the best. Florence Hardy stated that 'A Broken Appointment' and 'A Thunderstorm in Town' were both about Mrs Henniker. 'At an Inn' has strong circumstantial backing; Mrs Henniker actually quoted two stanzas of 'The Division' in her own novel *Second Fiddle*[33] and both 'In Death Divided' and 'Last Love-Word' are dated, with deliberate inexactness 189–. Moreover, all these poems except 'A Thunderstorm in Town' were included by Hardy in his *Selected Poems* a copy of which he sent to Mrs Henniker. There are several other, more speculative, ascriptions.[34]

'At an Inn' was the first to see print in 1898. It takes off from that very kind of cruel 'Satire of Circumstance' which Hardy was so quick to notice. When he met Mrs Henniker for lunch at The George Inn, Winchester, the staff, supposing them husband and wife, showed them both into a bedroom to wash their hands.[35] Hardy dramatises the incident slightly, implying that the staff took the meeting for a lovers' assignation, that they 'had all resigned / For love's dear ends'. But their 'ministers' 'imputed wish, 'Ah, God, that bliss like theirs / Would flush our day' – and what an apt verb 'flush' is here – introduces the pattern of irony so familiar to readers of Hardy, who now conveys with sombre exactitude the 'one-sidedness' of their relationship, as he put it in his letters to Mrs Henniker. It is precisely this benign misapprehension that they are 'Love's own pair' which 'chilled the breath / Of afternoon, / And palsied into death / The pane-fly's tune'. That singularly acute touch of observation – who else would have made a bluebottle in a window-pane at once lyrical and portentous? – illuminates the whole poem, injects it with actuality and sustains it to the eloquent, painful conclusion, which displays that stark, succinct directness that marks the mature Hardy.

> O severing sea and land,
> O laws of men,
> Ere death, once let us stand
> As we stood then!

Hardy had come a long way since the 1860s; there is a bone-bare tautness about those lines which resembles the best of Housman.

'A Broken Appointment' has been highly praised by several critics, who perhaps approved of what Douglas Brown disliked in it as being too much in 'the grand manner'[36]. Certainly the diction is, for Hardy, high-faluting. 'High compassion', 'pure lovingkindness', 'human deeds divine' might have been aimed at Mrs Henniker's 'ecclesiasticism', as he rather tartly called it in one of his letters. Nevertheless, the opening and closing linked images: 'You did not come, / And marching Time drew on and wore me numb', so tellingly linked with 'Once you, a woman, came / To soothe a time-torn man' do give the poem a satisfying unity of effect, the more so if we know that the phrase which really prints itself on the memory 'a time-torn man', was the product of a marvellous emendation from the MS 'soul-sad'. It is perhaps a pity that Hardy did not similarly tone down some other expressions of an over-effulgent kind.

'The Division' is written in the folk-song measure Robert Burns used for his 'O My Luve's Like a Red, Red Rose' and it is possible Hardy took a hint from Burns's lines 'I will come again, my luve / Though 'twere ten thousand mile' for his own fourth line, 'And a hundred miles between!' But though Hardy gives us a songlike grace and flow, the same smooth alliteration which somewhat dilutes the sombre implications of the first two stanzas with their implicit entreaty is just what points up, with bitter emphasis, the last stanza's total reversal of mood. The leaden emphases, the all-but-thumping stresses on 'thwart thing', 'betwixt us twain', and 'nothing cleaves or clears' establish hopeless acceptance, only faintly alleviated by the yearning emphasis on 'Dear'[37] a word that always, in Hardy, seems to connote profound feeling. And the collusion of the wind, the rain and the years looks forward to Hardy's masterpiece, 'During Wind and Rain'.

Nothing could be much more different from 'A Thunderstorm in Town', rare among Hardy's love poems for its London setting, appropriately urbane in mood and elegantly controlled in form. The first stanza sets the tone economically with its glancing hint of the artificial world of fashionable society in 'terra-cotta dress', and there is a sly humour in the mention of the 'hansom' a form of cab whose driver could not see his passengers because he was perched up on the roof above them, conveniently for some! The 'pelting storm' and 'downpour' suggest a sudden irruption of feeling; the 'snug and warm' interior is subtly sensual. It is as if the outside world of polite convention is momentarily suspended; as if time, like the horse, were motionless; a not uncommon occurrence in the 'Poems of 1912–13'.

Here it is only a momentary illusion. In the second stanza a deftly chosen sequence of verbs – 'ceased', 'flew up' and 'out she sprang' – shatters the fragile equipoise; an effect which Hardy's change to 'sharp, sad pain' from his MS 'lasting pain' accentuates. The flurry of action ceases, to leave Hardy sitting alone with his regret. But, like a clip from a film, it would be unwise to read too much into this. There is irony here and a wry self-mockery too. Though not without undertones of sadness for a 'road not taken',[38] a favourite theme of his, it remains a dry, delicate, poised performance. One hopes Mrs

Henniker, who had a sense of humour, appreciated it, since it is hard to imagine it better done.

'In Death Divided' is quite different again; Hardy's command of variety is, in these 1890s poems, manifestly far greater than in those from the 1860s. It is another example, I suggest, of Donne's influence. The abrupt, shocking, opening 'I shall rot here' must have raised many polite eyebrows at a time when it was usual to 'pass away' more discreetly. And the invisible 'eternal tie which binds us twain in one' is very reminiscent of Donne's 'eye-beams twisted ... upon one double string'.[39] The second stanza's epigraphic intensity all but allows it to stand on its own:

> No shade of pinnacle or tree or tower,
> > While earth endures,
> Will fall on my mound and within the hour
> > Steal on to yours;
> One robin never haunt our two green covertures.

The simple words 'While earth endures' have a Wordsworthian gravitas, the silent, ineluctable passing of time in 'shade', 'steal' and haunt', the poignant vignette of the robin with the slow, stately march of the verse all yield a marmoreal resonance, give the effect, as Dennis Taylor says, of a 'lapidary inscription.'[40] No question then that this is a fine poem: nevertheless questions have been raised about its subject. To whom does it refer?

Knowing what passionate divergencies about her role in the life and work of Hardy may lurk beneath your polite regard, it is with some trepidation that I introduce the name of Tryphena Sparks. So I shall make my position clear at once: I subscribe to C. S. Lewis's opinion, in his debate with Professor Tillyard,[41] that, if invited to view a splendid prospect, it is perverse to waste time examining the window that frames it: all truly great poetry is impervious to anonymity. None the less, besides the one indisputable attribution, there are several poems which can, plausibly, if not certainly, be attributed to Hardy's relationship with Tryphena. The fact that they are retrospective is no sort of obstacle, since he wrote three love poems about Louisa Harding on a far more tenuous acquaintance.[42] The glance backward is the structural lynchpin of nearly all his love poetry, after all.

'Thoughts of Phena at News of Her Death' was, Hardy said, 'a curious instance of sympathetic telepathy',[43] which he began 'in

the train' only six days before her death and unaware she was ill
Dated 1890, this is an early instance of Hardy's poetic renascence
a complex poem in which lightness and vivacity of movement ac
as counterpoise to the elegiac mood. It has also that meditative
cast of mind common to much of the later love poetry, a quality
rarely found in the 1860s verse, which can be shrill on occasion
This is what Hardy termed a 'reverie', and one of its most strik
ing qualities is the way it suggests the poet musing on mutability
rejecting the sentimental escape route of 'an aureate nimb' just as
he long ago discarded Tryphena's letters and a lock of her hair
He works his way to the tentative conclusion, quite at odds with
conventional expectations, that 'haply the best of her' is what he
has 'fined in [his] brain'. He can envisage his 'lost prize' more
clearly precisely *because* he no longer possesses anything tangible
of her. She has become, as Emma was to become, a 'phantom', a
'loved ghost'. The way in which the last stanza concludes with a
subtle, technically assured variation on the first is a good exam
ple of the skill and individuality Hardy could now command
Here is a poet able to write a graceful, gentle farewell in 'calm o
mind, all passion spent'.[44]

In the face of the 1890 date and the firm provenance provided by
Hardy's *Wessex Poems* illustration,[45] it is hard to ascribe 'In a
Eweleaze near Weatherbury' to anyone other than Hardy's girl nex
door – even if next door was Puddletown. The theme, love versus
time, is an age-old *topos*, but Hardy's treatment is attractively
quirky, with its wry Donne-like image of 'never-napping Time's
'little chisel', and its polka-like rhythms. Only with the last three
lines does it modulate into a muted regret, a sad acceptance.

In this it differs from 'A Spot' which, however, I would associate
with the same 'eweleaze', where Hardy took the composer Rutland
Boughton[46] when he was seeking lyrics to incorporate into his opera
based on Hardy's play *The Queen of Cornwall*. It does not seem unfair
to suppose that Boughton's inclusion of his setting of 'A Spot', as a
choral epilogue, derived from this visit to its location, while the div
inatory powers of the shepherds in verse three are a part of Dorse
folklore.[47] The unusual verse-form probably derives from Tate and
Brady's version of Psalm 148. It gives a stately, sombre resonance to
the verse which is echoed by its gnomic bareness of utterance. There
is a fleeting allusion to Time who has 'defaced' the years, which
Hardy implicitly compares to the pages of a book. The charac
teristically Hardeian phrases, 'wilted world' and 'Scared momently

By gaingivings' combine to suggest 'the world well lost' with the extreme fragility and vulnerability of young love. The scenario of 'hoping things/That could not be... ' would certainly fit what we know of Hardy's and Tryphena's circumstances and yet how little identification ultimately matters when we confront the second stanza and 'the general perfectly reduced in the particular'[48] by its superb economy of statement. First we have the empty landscape, the sense of vacancy, of the utter insignificance of man and his ephemeral passions as against the inexorable, indifferent procession of the seasons and the weather, until gradually the 'spot' – in time as in its physical setting – is lost to 'gust and gale', as once more wind and rain symbolically assert themselves.

> Of love and us no trace
> Abides upon the place;
> The sun and shadows wheel,
> Season and season sereward steal;
> Foul days and fair
> Here, too, prevail,
> And gust and gale
> As everywhere

It might have ended there, but Hardy with an unexpected Keats-like fancy, turns the poem back to the summery scenes of its beginning and makes the point, though here it is only lightly stressed, that the very intensity of love can make it immutable to time, at least 'Till Earth outwears' – a wonderful line – foreshadowing one of the great recurrent themes of the 'Poems of 1912–13'.

Yet the residual sense is of deprivation, and Hardy's love poetry is largely, of course, not that of Eros assured and triumphant, but of Eros dismayed and defeated. Pre-eminently he treats of loneliness, loss, regret, missed opportunities, and frustration; all seen, as if through the wrong end of a telescope, from an immense distance yet with extreme clarity. Hardy's stance is not unusual; C. Day Lewis rightly said 'Love remembered and regretted is the [English] poet's most fruitful theme'.[49] Even Donne, who gives us perhaps the most incandescent celebrations of the sensual here-and-now we have, is far more commonly cynical or despairing in his *Songs and Sonnets*. It is partly his lifelong aversion to what he called 'mellifluous preciosity'[50] in verse; his lifelong attachment to the principle that 'the truth shall make you free' that prompts Hardy never to evade or prettify.

But he convinces no one, not even himself, when he demands 'Shut Out That Moon' in the 1904 poem of that title. For once, here, ostensibly, his counsel, to 'draw the blind', to 'step not forth' to 'stay in', is icily prudential. But what he imparts, with images thick with romantic associations – 'the dew-dashed lawn', 'immense Orion's glittering form', and 'midnight scents / That come forth lingeringly' urges us rather to scatter prudence to the winds. It is this continual tension between the arithmetic of thought and the music of feeling which constitutes another hallmark of Hardy's mature love poetry.

'Shut Out That Moon', dated 1904, loses nothing by being unattributable; indeed it is a bone of critical contention whether it is a love poem at all! But to know about whom a poem is written, or not written, *can* preserve us from critical as well as factual misconceptions, which returns me to my starting-point.

For Weber included in his 'Emma' poems one which he associates with an 'episode' at Windsor[51] when Emma took the last seat in a carriage, leaving her ageing husband to walk behind. But, as his poem 'Epeisodia' makes clear, Hardy was well aware that the root Greek meaning of episode is not that of a mere 'happening' as we might say, but of a self-contained part of a larger scheme or interlude. Per contra, Deacon and Coleman assert that, because Boughton used this poem also in his opera, after being shown the 'eweleaze' of 'A Spot', it too must refer to Tryphena.[52] Now, as it happens, there is an intriguing verbal link, hitherto unnoticed, between this poem and 'A Spot'.

Thus, in 'A Spot' we have 'Of love and us no trace / Abides' while in 'The End of the Episode' we have the close parallel 'There shall remain no trace / Of what so closely tied us' which inclines me to think that the two poems are connected; both too seem set in the Dorset countryside. But then Deacon and Coleman call this 'a bitter poem of parting' which it manifestly is not. Their biographical preconceptions distract us from what Hardy is saying, which is the more to be regretted when the poem is, as I believe it to be, a neglected masterpiece, included in only three of the sixteen selections from Hardy's verse I have collated, and almost unnoticed by the critics; one contemporary reviewer actually said of it that 'Hardy ... congratulates himself for his forbearance'. That indeed is what Hardy sardonically called 'judg[ing] the landscape ... with a flash-lantern'.[53]

The form of the simple quatrains is reminiscent of folk-song, but I can find no analogue for the feminine rhymes in the internal couplets and this verse-pattern is one of Dennis Taylor's rare omissions in the invaluable Metrical Appendix to his book.[54] Victorian poets shunned the feminine rhyme, perhaps because it had been over-worked in light verse, but such considerations rarely bothered a poet notably resistant to the voice of the age. Here, together with a pervasive but subtly varied alliteration, rhymes like 'pastime'/'last time', prevent the spondaic stress-pattern from becoming mono-tonous. The diction is all but homespun; only in the inverted com-pound 'sweet-bitter', (where we expect 'bitter-sweet' which would give a false stress), and in the faintly archaic 'stilly' perhaps, (though it was good enough for Shakespeare and Coleridge) do we catch Hardy's voice. Again, though each verse has an epigrammatic pun-gency, none is superfluous; what Hardy called 'poetic veneer' is wholly absent.

So far from being 'bitter' or 'self-congratulatory' the mood is gentle, the tone entirely free from rancour or recrimination. The detachment which some have objected to vanishes with the single, stressed word 'Dear'; an amendment of genius made as late as 1923, from the original 'Sweet' which gives off the faintest whiff of sentimentality, in a poem that is in no way soft-centred. The middle stanzas destroy any consolatory illusions: the pathetic fallacy is knocked briskly on its head. The lovers' time is up; none can prevail over that implacable but here masked adversary, whose malign presence is suggested by Hardy's brilliant pun on the two senses of 'measure' as 'dance' and 'allocated share'.

Yet the iron honesty is offset by the pastoral images of the 'dumb-les' the 'flowers and thymy air', while the fourth stanza, with its richness and warmth of diction, in particular the beautifully judged stress on 'Bliss', imparts the frisson of lost ecstasy in preparation for the chilling conclusion, signalled by the implications of 'sentence', changed from the MS's innocuous 'ending' to suggest the verdict of a hanging judge.

And then if you will allow me to quote from myself, we have the last stanza:

If Hardy wrote better poems, he wrote no better lines than these. How easy it seems, yet how difficult it is, that heroic plainness of diction. Like nearly all the finest love poetry, this lies only a hairsbreadth away from the banal: it says nothing new, nothing we might not have thought of ourselves.

As for the last two lines they have that simple, proverbial ring that persuades us something has been said once and for all, like Shakespeare's 'Youth's a stuff will not endure'. Nevertheless, the lasting impression is not one of love as ultimately futile and transitory but of a mind capable of re-entering the past with joy while still able to view it dispassionately. Here again is that equipoise between cool head and warm heart which gives Hardy's love poetry its peculiar intensity.[55]

There are so many more poems I should dearly like, if time allowed, to touch on. Hardy gives us the charm and delicacy of 'To Lizbie Brown', the pure lyricism of 'I Need Not Go', the tart insight of 'The Conformers', the irreverent post-mortem on love of 'One Ralph Blossom Soliloquizes', the lost chance of 'Faintheart in a Railway Train', the hilarious defiance of Mrs Grundy in 'The Dark-Eyed Gentleman' as he draws his unrivalled, intricate map of love. But I want to end with 'To Meet, Or Otherwise', partly because he wrote it for and indeed to Florence Emily Dugdale in 1913, partly because he told Edward Thomas that it particularly well exemplified his 'idiosyncrasy … [as a] writer',[56] and partly because, as well as being a fine poem – and don't we all wish we could write one half as good at seventy-three? – it may be said to embody Hardy's final verdict on human love.

He begins jauntily, with a colloquial-seeming mixture of long and short lines, but soon turns to the intractable question of love and time. The traditional riposte of '*carpe diem*' or 'seize the moment' dwindles into a bleak acceptance that our world – like Homer's country of the blind – is a 'brake / Cimmerian', perhaps an allusion to Dante's all-but-impenetrable dark wood.[57] The last line draggingly emphasises how 'frail' and 'faltering' our struggles must be to find meaning in life. The first two stanzas are, deliberately, muted and hesitant. Their contrast could not be greater with the third which immediately, in its rhythms as well as its diction, strikes a deep, reverberating cadence that resounds through Hardy's later love poetry as a whole.

> By briefest meeting something sure is won;
>   It will have been:
> Nor God nor Demon can undo the done,
>   Unsight the seen,

There are allusions here to both Horace and Milton,[58] pagan and Christian analogues, but the thunderous insistence of 'It will have been' is more than a mere defiance of the dust. Hardy always sought for some assurance of human continuity and significance in a scheme of things increasingly dominated by the grey vision of scientific materialism. Dryden's version of Horace runs, magniloquently, indeed,

> Not Heav'n itself upon the past has pow'r
> But what has been, has been, and I have had my hour.

To this assertion Hardy adds, in the last stanza, a recent scientific perception which paradoxically contradicts the nihilism of Victorian physics. If every word we utter has continuity in space, however 'small and untraced', if – this is implicit – they may one day again be audible, then our love will not be annihilated by time, will have some continuance with our successors, while Earth endures, at least.

It may not be a very reassuring prospect, but it is better than nothing to feel as Proust, who so much admired Hardy said, that 'Love is space and time made directly perceptible to the heart',[59] a sentence which sums up what Hardy's love poetry, at its best, continues to give us – a touch of infinity one might say, in an ephemeral world.

Notes

Quotations from Hardy's poems are taken from *The Complete Poems of Thomas Hardy*, ed. James Gibson (Macmillan, 1976), and variant readings from the same editor's *The Variorum Edition of the Complete Poems of Thomas Hardy* (Macmillan, 1979).

1. *Johnsonian Miscellanies*, ed. G. Birkbeck Hill (1897) vol. I, p. 290.
2. I list these by their *Complete Poems* serial numbers. 169 is agreed to refer to Mrs Henniker, 313 to Florence Emily Dugdale, 178 is *most* unlikely to refer to Emma, 400 is irrelevant. Of those that follow, I have bracketed the ones that seem 'probables' to me; the remainder range from possible to unlikely. (538), 312, 677, 579, 485, 135, 52, 150, (463), 272, (397), (529), (395), 819, 689, 488, (481), 480, 671. The gravest objection that can be made to Weber's arrangement is the way in which it scatters the 21 'Poems of 1912–13' – deliberately grouped and ordered by Hardy – through its pages piecemeal, to fit its 'programme'.

3. T. Paulin, *Thomas Hardy: The Poetry of Perception* (1975); D. Taylor, *Hardy's Poetry 1860–1928* (1981).
4. 'A Week'.
5. Philip Larkin, 'The Poetry of Hardy', in his *Required Writing: Miscellaneous Pieces 1955–82* (1983).
6. Oliver Cromwell, 'Letter to the General Assembly of the Church of Scotland', 3 August 1650: 'I beseech you, in the bowels of Christ, think it possible you may be mistaken.'
7. F. E. Hardy, *The Life of Thomas Hardy 1840–1928* (1962) p. 292. Hereafter cited as *Life*.
8. *Life*, pp. 48–50.
9. Ibid., p. 49.
10. D. Taylor, *Hardy's Metres and Victorian Prosody* (1988) p. 56.
11. P. B. Shelley, 'An Exhortation'.
12. *Life*, p. 49.
13. Ibid., p. 47.
14. Ibid., p. 54.
15. In *Pall Mall Magazine* (1894) and, finally, in 1912 edition of *Life's Little Ironies*.
16. F. W. Maitland, *The Life and Letters of Leslie Stephen* (1906) pp. 276–7.
17. *Life*, p. 48.
18. See 1912 Preface to *Desperate Remedies*.
19. M. Millgate, *Thomas Hardy: A Biography* (1982) pp. 85–6.
20. George Meredith, *Modern Love*, 1st edn 1862 (not reissued until 1892).
21. *The Letters of George Meredith* (1912) vol. I, p. 169.
22. See *The Personal Notebooks of Thomas Hardy*, ed. R. H. Taylor (1978) p. 252.
23. *Life*, p. 49, and note in Hardy's copy of S. Chew, *Hardy: Poet and Novelist* (1921). Hardy says 'it is curious that the influence of Donne is not noted' [i.e., in Chew's text].
24. E. Thomas, 'Three Wessex Poets', in his *In Pursuit of Spring* (1914), reprinted in *The Thomas Hardy Yearbook*, 5 (1976).
25. E. Barrett Browning, *Sonnets from the Portuguese* (1850) Sonnet 23.
26. John Clare, *Child Harold*, Canto I (unpublished in Clare's lifetime).
27. D. Taylor, *Hardy's Metres and Victorian Prosody* (1988) gives no instance of octave stanzas rhymed ABCD/ABCD: see his Metrical Appendix, pp. 245–51.
28. See *The Hand of Ethelberta* (Ch. 2), *A Pair of Blue Eyes* (Ch. 35 – epigraph) and *The Well-Beloved* (1897 – epigraph to Part Second).
29. See Hardy's 'General Preface to the Novels and Poems' in Macmillan's Wessex Edition (1912), and his restatement in his 'Apology' to *Late Lyrics and Earlier* (1922).
30. Murray's letter to Hardy of 11 December 1909 is in the Dorset County Museum.
31. *Life*, p. 254 (entry for 18 May 1893).
32. *Life*, p. 254. A fuller paragraph on Mrs Henniker, stating that 'some of [Hardy's] best short poems were inspired by her' was written by Florence Hardy but not included. See M. Millgate (ed.), *The Life and Work of Thomas Hardy* by Thomas Hardy (1984) p. 537.

33. Besides *Second Fiddle* (1912), Mrs Henniker published other fiction etc. Her *In Scarlet and Grey* (1896) included 'The Spectre of the Real' on which Hardy collaborated.
34. These include 'Come Not; Yet Come!', 'He Wonders About Himself', 'The Month's Calendar', 'The Coming of the End' (unlikely in view of drafts of first verse, see *The Variorum Edition of the Complete Poems of Thomas Hardy*, ed. J. Gibson, 1979) and, in my opinion, 'Between Us Now'.
35. M. Millgate, *Thomas Hardy: A Biography* (1982) p. 340.
36. D. Brown, *Thomas Hardy* (1954) p. 178.
37. Note: 'Dear' is used three times in Burns's poem.
38. The phrase is from Robert Frost's famous poem, but the idea is Hardy's.
39. John Donne, 'The Ecstasy'.
40. D. Taylor, *Hardy's Metres and Victorian Prosody* (1988) p. 173.
41. E. M. W. Tillyard and C. S. Lewis, *The Personal Heresy: A Controversy* (1939).
42. Namely, 'The Passer-By', 'Louie' and 'To Louisa in the Lane'.
43. *Life*, p. 224.
44. Milton, conclusion of *Samson Agonistes*.
45. Hardy's drawing appears opposite the poem in *Wessex Poems* (1898).
46. See R. L. Purdy and M. Millgate (eds), *The Collected Letters of Thomas Hardy*, vols VI (1987) and VII (1988) *passim*. Hereafter cited as *Collected Letters*.
47. See R. Firor, *Folkways in Thomas Hardy* (1931) p. 70.
48. E. Felkin, 'Days with Thomas Hardy', *Encounter*, XVIII (April 1962) pp. 27–33.
49. C. Day Lewis, *A Lasting Joy* (1974) p. 70.
50. Letter to Edmund Gosse, see *Collected Letters*, vol. II (1980) p. 208.
51. *Hardy's Love Poems*, ed. C. Weber (1963) p. 57.
52. L. Deacon and T. Coleman, *Providence and Mr Hardy* (1966) p. 83.
53. Hardy's 'Apology' to *Late Lyrics and Earlier* (1922) p. xv.
54. D. Taylor, *Hardy's Metres and Victorian Prosody* (1988) pp. 207–66.
55. T. Johnson, *A Critical Introduction to the Poems of Thomas Hardy* (1991) pp. 197–8.
56. *Collected Letters*, vol. V (1985) p. 87.
57. Dante, *The Divina Commedia*, opening of *The Inferno*.
58. See Horace, *Odes III*, 29, viii; Milton, *Paradise Lost*, IX, ll. 925–6.
59. Cited in W. H. Auden and L. Kronenberger (eds), *The Faber Book of Aphorisms* (1962) p. 185.

5

'Moments of Vision': Postmodernising *Tess of the d'Urbervilles*; or,

Tess of the d'Urbervilles Faithfully Presented by

PETER WIDDOWSON

Anyone who has read *Tess of the d'Urbervilles* (and certainly any modern criticism about it) will be in no doubt that the novel is emphatically visual in many of its effects. There are those famous set-piece 'descriptions' of rural Wessex (not quite Dorset, let us remember); the inescapably scenic moments, such as the May-dance at Marlott as the novel opens or sunrise at Stonehenge towards the end, which render talk about Hardy's proto-cinematic techniques more than merely chic; and the narrative's obsessive voyeuristic gazing at Tess herself (especially that famous 'mobile peony mouth'[1]) which has made so many readers *wonder* a little about Thomas Hardy. But there is also a great deal of visual imagery in the novel of a rather more self-reflexive sort – a kind of metadiscourse about looking, seeing, perception, representation, imaging.

This is not new or unique to *Tess of the d'Urbervilles*, of course: it is everywhere apparent in Hardy's fiction – from the subtitling of *Under the Greenwood Tree* as 'A Rural Painting of the Dutch School' to the presence (betimes) of a photographer in *A Laodicean*; from the staged artificiality of the tableaux vivants in *The Hand of Ethelberta* to the blindness of Clym in *The Return of the Native*; from the astronomer's telescope in *Two on a Tower* to striking 'moments of vision' (a phrase I shall return to) such as that in *Desperate Remedies* (Hardy's first published novel) where Cytherea Graye, watching her father and some masons at the top of a church spire – 'it was an *illuminated miniature, framed in* by the dark *margin* of the window' (my italics) – suddenly sees him fall to his death: 'he reeled off into the air, immediately disappearing downwards'.[2] And there are the typographical signs and devices scattered throughout the text of *Jude the Obscure* – a novel significantly characterised by its author in his preface to the first edition (1895) as 'a series of seemings, or personal impressions'.[3]

But self-conscious techniques of visualisation are particularly insistent in *Tess*, a novel also prefatorily described by Hardy as 'an impression'[4] – a significant word, perhaps, given his fascination with the late 'impressionist' paintings of J. M. W. Turner.[5] Chapter 2, for example, opens with a reference to a 'landscape-painter', and from there on – as J. B. Bullen has pointed out – the novel abounds with overt or covert references to pictures.[6] There is also the complex ambiguity of the narrator's point of view or stance – towards Tess in particular. For instance:

> As she walked along to-day, for all her *bouncing handsome woman-liness, you* could sometimes *see* her twelfth year in her cheeks, or her ninth *sparkling from her eyes;* and even her fifth would flit over the *curves of her mouth* now and then.
>
> Yet *few* knew, and *still fewer* considered this. *A small minority,* mainly strangers, would *look long at her* in casually passing by, and grow momentarily fascinated by her freshness, and wonder if *they* would ever *see* her again: but *to almost everybody* she was a *fine and picturesque* country girl, and no more.   (Ch. 2, p. 52)

My italics draw attention to the voyeurism of the passage, but the uncertainty of focus ('you ... few ... still fewer ... a small minority ... almost everybody') and the peculiar logic of the syntax in the second paragraph ('Yet ... but ... and no more') make it very difficult to say who sees her like this and whether the narrative is attempting to distance itself from the erotic imaging the passage in fact delivers or is fully complicit in it. Furthermore, there is the continual presentation of Tess in terms of the way she is 'seen' by others – most especially, of course, Alec and Angel – until her 'character' seems to be composed entirely of other people's images of her (a point I will return to later). And there are the many other instances where the narrative deploys strikingly visual devices and motifs, from the filmic long-shots (the farm-girls picking swedes at Flintcomb-Ash) and close-ups (Tess's mouth), to the final scene where Angel and Liza Lu, 'their eyes rivetted' to the gaol's flag-pole, watch the 'black flag' unfurl which denotes that Tess has been hanged (notice how, at this point, a novel which has fetishised Tess's visual presence throughout now signals its absence by her displacement into a black flag).

It is quite possible to think, therefore, that *Tess of the d'Urbervilles* is actually in some way *about* seeing and representation. After all, Hardy himself describes it in the preface to the first edition – although we can never really trust that wary old ironist and least self-revealing of writers – as 'an *attempt to give artistic form* to a true sequence of things' (my italics). And he also claims, by way of the novel's hugely contentious subtitle ('appended', he would have us believe in a prefatory postscript of 1912, 'at the last moment' and with no premeditation), that his 'Pure Woman' is '*faithfully presented by Thomas Hardy*' (my italics). Does the phrasing here suggest just how ironically conscious he was of representation as a potent source, precisely, of *mis*representation? Had the image, as we all now know in these post-modern times, already substantively replaced 'the thing itself' for Hardy? Was he already discrediting the notion that there is an ultimate reality, or true essence, outside of history and discourse – such as 'human nature', for example, or even perhaps: *pure woman*? But a discussion of this key term in Hardy's disingenuous subtitle – and a central theme of critical commentary on *Tess* – must wait for a moment, although, as we shall see the 'pure woman' and her attendant debate in fact focuses the issues of seeing and representation which I have suggested the novel so insistently raises. Certainly a good deal of recent criticism emphasises these issues as crucial terms in discussing *Tess of the d'Urbervilles* – an emphasis which derives principally from two very contemporary critical sources: feminism and post-structuralism. In order to explain what I mean here, I need to reflect briefly on the general state of the last two decades of Hardy criticism, before returning to the problems of 'seeing', (mis)representation and pure women.

While selecting work from the past twenty years for the Macmillan *New Casebook* on *Tess*, I found that with a few honourable exceptions, all the really interesting material came after 1980. It appeared that work from the 1970s, even that of high quality and sophisticated in its own terms, somehow 'belonged' to an earlier critical phase[7] – rather like those automobiles which are still being made new and still function adequately, but which, when you lift the bonnet, clearly betray a prior generation of technology. I do not mean to be gratuitously dismissive, nor to foster a 'whig' view of literary-critical history as continually 'progressive', nor do I wish to be wilfully partial and partisan, but so much critical writing on *Tess* in the 1970s, with its emphases on plot, 'poetic structure', character, 'ideas' and imagery (sometimes symbolism), *does* now seem passé, beside the point, going nowhere – except over well-trodden (some might say exhausted) ground.

What gradually becomes apparent, despite an obsessive inno-vativeness and self-presentation of *difference*, is that by far the greatest proportion of criticism on Hardy's fiction in the 1970s was held within the (by then) traditional parameters of critical intelligibility.[8] These were fundamentally humanist-realist in origin, promoting notions of a unified human subject ('the indi-vidual', 'character') at the centre of the general scheme of things – metaphysical, natural and social ('environment') – and of the artist's prime responsibility and achievement as being to repre-sent this relationship with veracity (or with 'realism'). This, in turn, implies, on the one hand, the existence of an external reality to be copied – a given 'real world' and 'characters' both know-able and describable – and, on the other, the possibility of deploying a language which could accurately *describe* – not mediate – that reality, one which had a precise referentiality and would 'tell things as they really are'. What lies at the heart of such an essentialist world-view is a belief that everything has an ultimate ontological reality, an irreducible essence, quite outside its material, historical or discursive circumstances (things as they *really* are). The commonest (and most ideologically potent) expression of this is the notion of 'Human Nature' – the pro-position that whatever the circumstances, and with the best will in the world, human beings cannot change their basic nature, or have it changed for them: that they are, as it were, trapped by their own very human-ness. But it is, of course, this 'essential' human nature which artists are most praised for depicting, and their 'realism' is, paradoxically, at once their ability to represent the contingent reality of everyday life, *and*, by way of this, the essential unchanging reality of 'human nature' itself. In its attempt to render this essence visible by describing it in referential language, realism too is essentialist.

Hardy, against the grain of much of his writing, has, from the earliest reviews, been hauled into consonance with such a world-view and such an aesthetic. Borrowing his own phrase, 'Novels of Character and Environment',[9] to praise what are generally regarded as his 'major' novels, critics have characteristically seen Hardy, 'at his best', as the tragic humanist-realist of Wessex, finding essential human nature in the lives of his rural protagonists (and in his 'rustic chorus') pitted in conflict with 'Fate' or 'Nature' (much less often with 'Society'). This, together with his descriptions of nature and his evocation of a 'passing' rural community, has been regarded as his major achievement, and accounts for the elevation into canonic texts of about eight out of his fourteen novels (the six 'minor novels' fail in various ways to fit this mould[10]). Even so, Hardy presents problems, and it is noteworthy how much damage-limitation criticism has had to go in for in order to wrench this 'flawed genius' into the canon and tradition. Hardy's 'faults' are said to be: his tendency to 'melodrama'; the excessive use of chance and coincidence in his plots; his 'pessimism'; his parading of 'ill-digested' ideas; his at times pedantic, awkward, mannered style; and, over and above all these – indeed subsuming them – his tendency to 'improbability' and 'implausibility'; in other words, his failure to be 'realistic', or, to put it yet another way, to represent 'essential reality' accurately. These 'faults' and 'flaws' bedevil even his major works, where they have to be ignored or explained away, but they are the principal cause of his 'failure' in the 'minor novels'.

All too often, and however sophisticated the particular inflexions of critical inquiry in the 1970s, many of these governing co-ordinates remained unchallenged. Certainly there were innovative approaches, with a kind of high-powered humanistic formalism (emphasising imagery, symbolism, 'poetic structure' and so forth) replacing the older 'character'/'Fate'/Tragedy/rural-elegy nexus, but fundamentally similar underlying assumptions (about Hardy's humanism, about his 'flaws', and especially about his 'uneasy' relation to realism) continued to determine the critical positions taken up. There was little attempt, for example, to rethink the tendency to reject large chunks of Hardy's texts simply as bad writing; little sense that viewing them through a realist lens might result in them appearing 'improbable', and that perhaps the lens was wrong; little inquiry into the nature and function of Hardy's language (except perhaps its 'poetics'); little inquiry into his 'inadequate' characterisation (because 'character' itself remains an unproblematic concept) or his contingent plotting; little thought that perhaps Hardy was an *anti*-realist, challenging and demystifying the limits and conventions of realism and humanist essentialism. But the fundamental inadequacy of most of the 1970s criticism which I have been generalising about is not so much its residual subscription to the conventional critical stereotypes of Hardy's fiction, but rather its failure to admit, disguised by grandiloquent evaluations and judgements, that it was inadequate to the task of dealing with the *entire textuality* of the literary works it had in hand. All novels, but Hardy's especially so, are riddled with contradictory discourses, are inscribed throughout with fault-lines thrown up by the clash of competing discursive 'plates' just below the text's surface, and it is surely the job of criticism, not to reject them as 'failures of taste', but to explore and explain the significance of the work *as a whole*. It is instructive to compare criticism from the seventies with the many eighties essays[11] which focus on the dynamically unstable textuality of Hardy's fictional writing: its plural discourses and competing styles, its irony, mannerism and self-deconstructing artificiality, its self-conscious vocabulary and modes of address, its language of tension. But the perception of these features is the reflex, I have suggested particularly, of feminist and post-structuralist initiatives and it is to these that we will return in a moment.

However, there is one impressive piece of scholarship from the 1970s which should first be acknowledged as fundamentally influential in the contemporary redirecting of attention to Hardy's textuality in relation to *Tess*: J. T. Laird's *The Shaping of Tess of the d'Urbervilles* (1975), a book which traces the evolution of the novel from its earliest stages of manuscript composition, through various editions and revisions, to the 'quasi-definitive' version of the Wessex Edition of 1912. Despite a rather unnerving self-contradiction when Laird seems to suggest, *contra* his own exhaustive proof of the instability of the text, that 'studying the author's creative processes ... eventually leads to a surer and deeper understanding of the meaning of *the definitive text*' (my italics),[12] his work nevertheless reveals the extent and significance of Hardy's revisions and emendations, how conscious their effects were, and how a detailed examination of the textuality of *Tess* reinforces the sense that 'representation' and notions of a 'pure woman' are bedrock issues in the novel. Much criticism since 1975 has been deeply beholden to Laird in its pursuit of textual *cruces* to explain the signifying effects of *Tess*, and his work has been taken further since – most particularly in the monumental Oxford edition of the novel edited by Juliet Grindle and Simon Gatrell[13] –

and in the latter's *Hardy the Creator*, whose critical method its author calls 'textual biography' and which establishes how extensively and radically Hardy revised his texts in a subversive, experimental practice of writing, a practice which, as Terry Eagleton has put it, shows a 'novelist whose work ... is always on the point of breaking through its own containing forms'.[14]

But it is with the intervention of feminism and post-structuralism that Hardy criticism significantly begins to retool. From the start of his novel-writing career, of course, critics noticed and focused upon 'Hardy's Heroines', and there are many essays entitled thus (or alternatively 'Hardy's Women'), most of which reproduce, not surprisingly, the sexual stereotyping of dominant gender ideology.[15] *Feminist* criticism, conversely, aims to decode the sexual/ textual politics of literary texts, and has therefore been especially concerned with the *representation* of women; with the whole construction of gender in discourse; and with the notion of the 'male gaze', its consumption of women and its tendency to reproduce its own images and fantasies as female sexuality. In this respect, Hardy's novels are an ideal site on which to explore such issues – and not by any means necessarily from a position of hostility to his representation of women, but rather from a recognition of the complexity and innovativeness of what he seems to be doing.

Alternatively, post-structuralist criticism, most obviously in Deconstruction, has re-emphasised textuality as the primary concern of criticism – though not as evidence of the integrated wholeness of the text as great work of art so beloved of New Criticism, but on the contrary, as a fissured, riven, deranged, unstable linguistic terrain. In this case, too, Hardy's texts – and in particular their evident artificiality, self-reflexiveness about modes of perception and reproduction, and their contradictory constituent discourses – offer themselves as fertile ground for analysis.

A seminal early essay,[16] in the contexts of both textuality and gender, is one by John Goode called 'Woman and the Literary Text' (1976), in which he suggests that we can only see the 'political implications' of a work by attending to its 'formal identity', and that in relation to *Tess* what we witness (and are implicated in) is 'the objectification of Tess by the narrator', especially by way of making her 'the object of consumption' of Alec and Angel (and then of us as voyeuristic readers consuming with our eyes both the text and, hence, Tess herself). The effect is to make us 'the subject of her, and thus guilty of the object images whose contradictions she is subject to'. In other words, Tess is composed of all the 'object images' the novel defines her as, primarily deriving from male lookers and including the narrator/Hardy and us as readers in our collusion with those images: nubile country-girl, plump arms, erotic mouth, etc. Goode comments that this is why, 'whatever Hardy's own ideological commitment, no frame will hold his novel in place', or, to put it another way, why the text's discourses *have to be* accepted as contradictory. These themes are extended in Goode's later (1979) essay, 'Sue Bridehead and the New Woman', where he suggests that Sue is an 'exposing image' in the 'taking of reality apart' which *Jude the Obscure* effects – most particularly of the mystifications inherent in conventional notions of love and marriage.[17] More recently, Goode's pioneering and radical recognition of the textual/sexual politics and subversive anti-realism of Hardy's fiction have received sustained expression in his *Thomas Hardy: the Offensive Truth*, a book described by Terry Eagleton as 'alert to Hardy's fiction ... as transformative practice, disruption, intervention, texts which ... often enough meditate on the act of writing as a metaphor of their preoccupations, [and which show] astonishing ... radicalism of gender as well as class'.[18]

What is happening to Hardy, as a reflex of his new critical reproduction in the 1980s and 1990s is that he is in the process of being post-modernised. The foregrounding of sexual politics in *Tess*, and of the tensions incident on a late-nineteenth-century male novelist writing so ambiguously about his 'pure woman' heroine, about the destructive maleness of his two heroes' relations with her (especially the – apparent – ambiguity of seduction and rape), and about marriage, separation, bigamy, extra-marital sex and childbirth, all imply a writer whose 'consciousness' is in some sense being recast in the mould of feminist thinking about sexuality and patriarchy.

More obviously post-structuralist in its variously stylistic, semiotic and deconstructive analyses of the complex, riven, heteroglossic textuality of *Tess*, equal amounts of contemporary criticism all point to the unstable play of the signifier as the nodal experience of the novel. In other words, we have a text which has indeed become a disruptive 'series of seemings', one which, in its destabilising formal dynamics 'disproportions' (Hardy's own word – see below, p. 92) reality by revealing how slippery language is, how 'meaning' (and hence ideology) is constructed within discourse, and, precisely therefore, how representation becomes *mis*representation. By disturbing and displacing 'reality' (together with its servant, Realism) in the defamiliarising discourse of his own texts, Hardy exposes (or, more exactly, as a creature of post-modernism *is made to* expose) the mystifications, naturalisations and (mis)representations by which the dominant ideology and culture sentence us all to lives of false being.

However, before I alchemise Hardy once and for all as a postmodernist (and throw away the stone), let me more properly register – so that I can bring it into sharper focus in the following section – that in his own historical period, and certainly when he was publishing his poetry, Hardy was indeed a contemporary of the Modernists. It may be that the critical industry, already in his lifetime busily at work on him as both poet and novelist (combined, let us admit, with not a little self-fashioning[19]), had so constructed him as the great proto-Georgian poet, as the humanist-realist rural-tragedian, as Grand Old Man of English Letters, that the *modernist* in Hardy could not then or later easily be perceived. Of course, it is a critical truism to say that he is a 'transitional' writer, but I wonder now just *how* transitional, or whether Hardy was not in fact already *there*, already a Modernist. D. H. Lawrence recognised it in the *Study of Thomas Hardy* (1914), written as he launched into the work which was to become *The Rainbow* and *Women in Love*, and Ezra Pound hailed him as a contemporary poet; but still, it is only with hindsight and the clearing of the critical trees that the innovative anti-realism and self-conscious modernity of much of Hardy's fictional *oeuvre* comes into view. Which is why, I suggest, it has been so simple for recent criticism to find the ingredients in him for a transmogrification into post-modernist.

Well, you might say, who would have thought it: 'good little Thomas Hardy', the poet of Wessex and the English countryside, the great humanist tragedian of the 'Novels of Character and Environment', the elegist of a passing rural tradition, etc., suddenly becoming subversively post-modern. But then, literary criticism never *could* quite handle Hardy: didn't make it to F. R. Leavis's Great Tradition; always 'flawed' by contingency, melodrama and improbability; neither securely 'Victorian' nor 'modern'; uncertain whether he is primarily novelist or poet. But in neither genre has Hardy ever really been made to *fit* (except by a lot of critical manhandling and dismissal of recalcitrant elements), which makes one think, doesn't it, that our disruptive post-modern Hardy may, after all, be nearer the mark. It is with this in mind that I now return to my two focal themes: 'seeing'/representation and the notion of Tess as '(a) pure woman'.

With characteristic ambiguity of utterance, Hardy entitled one of his later volumes of poetry *Moments of Vision* (1917). The ambiguity of the word 'vision' is readily apparent: at once the literal 'seeing/ sight' (as in '20/20 vision'), the metaphysical notion of imaginative revelation ('she had a vision'), and the proleptic ability to see through or beyond the immediately determinate ('he has vision', 'her vision of the future'). The ambiguity of the cluster of inflections around 'moments', however, is rather less obvious. Of course, 'moments' are brief fractions of time, usually implying stopped fragments in the temporal process (as in 'wait a moment', 'magic moments' or 'moment of truth'), and this is certainly the upper meaning in Hardy's title: particular instances of 'vision'. But there are two other senses which also haunt the fringes of the word: first, that of serious consequence ('momentous', 'matters of pith and moment'); second, and for my purposes here more significant, that within physics which means the measure of a turning effect (as in 'the moment of a force'). So Hardy's title may imply that the instants of 'vision' are important ('moments' of great 'moment'), but also that the vision is somehow itself in motion, turning, swinging round a point, pivoting.

If we think for a (dare I say) moment of the effect of a turning vision – in the most literal sense – then we must conceive of a 'seeing' which moves round its object (consider astronauts observing Earth from their circulating spacecraft), and which can theoretically move round it through 360 degrees in any direction, i.e., in three-dimensional mode. Move round your chair, *looking* at it, and you will, at various stages, see it from all sides and all angles (downwards, upwards, sideways, etc.). In other words you will be able to apprehend it as a totality, a three-dimensional object. But two things may strike you: one, if you 'stopped' the moment when you were theoretically looking straight up at it from below (chair suspended absolutely vertically above you), the 'image' from that 'moment of vision' would look remarkably unlike one's standard received image of a chair (think of the kind of trick-photography which takes familiar objects from unfamiliar angles: where a bucket, for example, taken from directly above, becomes no more than a set of concentric circles). Two, how on earth (and I use this phrase, here, not *merely* as a manner of speaking) would you represent, *in visual terms*, your total apprehension of the total, three-dimensional chair – the chair in all its chairness? How, indeed, would you 'see' it all, all in one moment? Two senses of 'moment' – turning and stopped instant of time – clash here in fundamental contradiction: one is, precisely, *in motion*, in time; the other, equally precisely, is still, 'stopped', out of time. Is there any way of resolving this physical impossibility? Well, yes – if we return to the other term in Hardy's title: 'vision'.

For vision, in what I have called its metaphysical senses, allows us (but especially the creative artist) to break out of the space/time trap of the third dimension, and enter that zone of relativity beyond the determinate factors of time and space. Put simply and crudely, 'vision' allows us to 'see' the future, or 'envisage' another world; it would also enable us to see, in one totalising 'moment' (in this case, *both* stopped instant *and* full circular movement) all of our chair at the same time. It is not without point, here, when approaching so visual an artist as Hardy (and indeed one who draws heavily on painting for both his terms of reference and his imagery[20]), to note that this liberation from space/time, this envisioned *simultaneity* of experience, was the principle on which the modernist painters, only a dozen years after *Jude the Obscure* (why don't we think of Hardy and Picasso as contemporaries? – Picasso was well into his 'Metamorphic' phase when Hardy died in 1928), based their dislocations of conventional (realist/mimetic) form. That is why one can see both profiles of a face simultaneously in Cubist portraits, or a violin dismantled with all its planes simultaneously displayed on the two-dimensional picture-surface of a modernist still life.

'Vision', then, both as momentary revelation (what James Joyce, only ten years after *Tess*, was to call an 'epiphany') and as 'turning' or destabilising perception, is a way of breaking out of the conventional, the normative, the familiar, the naturalised fictions of 'common sense'. Indeed it ruptures a (bourgeois) world constructed very largely by the cultural ideology of a Realism which 'tells things as they really are' and has a profound antipathy to the 'improbable' or 'implausible' – qualities which are themselves frequently the result of, precisely, 'vision' and 'the visionary'. For Hardy, vision in this binary sense ('double-vision'?) is a way of 'defamiliarising', of 'making strange' – and I strategically choose the formalists' terms to

signal once again his consanguinity with modernism – the naturalised world of conventional perceptual reality, of 'seeing things
as they really are'. It is subversive in many ways, and not least in its
anti-realist stance – which may help to explain the troubled history
of Hardy's place in the conventional canon of English fiction and the
difficulty many critics have had in comprehending the apparently
schizophrenic textuality of his novels. It is worth adding here that
Hardy himself was not just 'doing defamiliarisation' by chance – as
an automatic and unwilled reflex of his (unconscious) proto-
modernist mind. On the contrary, he was thinking about it throughout his writing life, but especially from the 1880s onwards; and his
last, highly self-reflexive and self-conscious work of fiction,
'Florence Emily Hardy's *The Life of Thomas Hardy*' (he composed it
himself, before his death, in the 1920s[21]), is full of concepts and
phrases which at once define 'vision' as what we would now call
'complex seeing' and which would, had they been written by a
twentieth-century cultural theorist, have equal currency with terms
like 'defamiliarisation' and 'baring the device' or the Brechtian
notion of 'alienation'.

Prior to the 1880s, Hardy's views show a more purely Romantic
conception of the visionary function of art: 'irradiating ... with "the
light that never was" ... a hitherto unperceived beauty ... seen to be
latent ... by the spiritual eye'.[22] But by 1886 Hardy is reflecting:
'novel-writing as an art cannot go backward. Having reached the
analytic stage it must transcend it by going still further in the same
direction. Why not by rendering as visible essences, spectres, etc.,
the abstract thoughts of the analytic school?' And later in the same
passage he proposes the use of 'abstract realisms', significantly stating that this project was actually carried out, not in a novel, but in
'the more appropriate medium' of his immense epic poetic-drama,
The Dynasts (p. 177). What is clear, if nothing else, is that Hardy was
being pressed against the limits of conventional realism. The following year, in expressing his admiration for the paintings of 'the
much-decried, mad, late-Turner', he rejects 'the original realities – as
optical effects, that is' in favour of the 'expression of ... abstract
imaginings' (p. 185). Taken in conjunction with his remarks about
'impressions' and 'seemings' in the prefaces to the novels of the
1890s referred to earlier, it is clear that notions of 'vision', and how
to realise it formally, were much on Hardy's mind. But it is in a
couple of memoranda from 1890 (while he was completing *Tess*) that
his most prophetically modernist utterances are made:

'Reflections on Art. Art is a changing of the actual proportions and order of things, so as to bring out more forcibly than might otherwise be done that feature in them which appeals most strongly to the idiosyncrasy of the artist.'

'Art is a disproportioning – (*i.e.* distorting, throwing out of proportion) – of realities, to show more clearly the features that matter in those realities, which, if merely copied or reported inventorially, might possibly be observed, but would more probably be overlooked. Hence "realism" is not Art.'   (pp. 228–9)

It is here, I think, that the core of Hardy's fictional aesthetic is to be found, and the informing frame of reference for a reading of *Tess*: art is a 'disproportioning' of reality – realism is not art. In other words, 'vision' (abstract imaginings), swinging round its 'moment', makes visible 'essences' (the notion of a 'pure woman', for example). But at the same time, vision 'distorts', 'disproportions', those representations of reality ('copied or reported inventorially') which are the naturalised (mis)representations of Realism, in order to expose essentialist misrepresentation for what it is (how can there, in fact, be 'a pure woman' or 'pure woman'?), and to illuminate another truth which those misrepresentations obscure: that 'reality' is only ever *discourse* – 'seemings', 'imaginings', 'impressions'.

'My art', Hardy wrote in 1886, 'is to intensify the expression of things ... so that the heart and inner meaning is made vividly visible' (p. 177). *Tess*, that most 'vividly visible' of novels, may be an example of Hardy 'intensifying the expression' in order to bring into view precisely that 'expression' – the discourses of representation themselves – for scrutiny and demystification in order to exemplify the fact that 'expression' is its own very 'heart and inner meaning', that the 'reality' of an image *is* the image itself, that its only reality is what it constructs through representation. 'Expression' does not copy 'things as they really are', it forges images in its artifice. Tess may indeed be 'a pure woman', but *only as she is imaged*, only as the 'artificial' construct of representation – and who knows whether this is true or false: except, unless we miss the irony (for Hardy knows full well the claim is nonsense), when she is '*faithfully* presented by Thomas Hardy'.

Let us now turn, at last, to that subtitle itself, and consider it as the pivot of a 'moment' around which *Tess of the d'Urbervilles* swings in exemplification of Hardy's disproportioning art discussed above.

The two main senses of the phrase 'a pure woman' are readily evident: the ethical/sexual (the use of which in relation to Tess as fornicator-murderess so incensed Hardy's Victorian critics), and the ontological/archetypal (in which she would be, were Bob Dylan her bard, 'just like a woman' in every respect). There is also the further related sense of the generic as 'ideal' – again, perhaps, in two inflexions: both prototypical and perfect. I am not primarily concerned here with the ethical sense, although for Hardy at the time it was clearly a strategic assault on the moral attitudes of his readers and *their perception* of purity. It is that other essentialist meaning that is of interest to me, and especially in relation to Hardy's concern with making 'visible essences' noted above. The novel is full of phrases which indicate that he was thoroughly conscious of this second sense and probably more interested in it than the contemporary moral issue. Let me start with the two most obvious examples: at Talbothays, in the early morning idyll with Angel, Tess is described as 'a visionary essence of woman – a whole sex condensed into one typical form' (Ch. 20, p. 187); and later, as she approaches Flintcomb-Ash, the narrative, in an odd shift of tense and focus, presents her in this way: 'Thus Tess walks on; a figure which is part of the landscape; a fieldwoman pure and simple, in winter guise' (Ch. 42, p. 355) – where the phrase 'pure and simple' *could* mean a pure, simple fieldwoman, but clearly actually implies the essential stereotype. (Much earlier, during the harvesting at Marlott, the narrative has already given us this generalisation: 'A field-man is a personality afield; a field-woman is a portion of the field; she has somehow *lost her own margin*, imbibed the *essence* of her surrounding, and assimilated herself with it' [Ch. 14, pp. 137–8, my italics] – so that Tess, too, the 'fieldwoman pure and simple', must also be subsumed within this characterisation – or rather, *de*-characterisation.) Further, as we have seen, when Tess is first introduced in Chapter 2 she is described as 'a fine and picturesque country girl, and no more' (p. 52, note that word 'picturesque' and the phrase 'and no more'), and later again, just after the generalisation about field-women above, she is called, in an oddly contradictive phrase, 'an almost standard woman' (Ch. 14, p. 141). Elsewhere, the narrative regularly generalises about women – for example, on Tess's 'rally' after the death of her child, it muses: 'Let the truth be told – women do as a rule live through such humiliations, and regain their spirits, and again look about them with an interested eye' (Ch. 16, p. 158) – a sentence remarkable both for its patriarchal patronising (do men – by implication of finer sensibility – not 'regain their spirits' then?) and for that revealing phrase 'an interested eye'. Again, in relation to the dairymaids' passion for Angel at Talbothays, we are told they are involuntarily overwhelmed by 'an emotion thrust on them by cruel Nature's law'; and, in an even more insulting instance of chauvinistic essentialism, 'the differences which distinguished them as individuals were abstracted by this passion, and each was but portion of one organism called sex' (Ch. 23, p. 204) – 'pure women' indeed, and just like the field-women who have lost their 'own margin'. For Angel, of course (and for the narrator too?), Tess is archetypally this 'organism' in the famously erotic passage when she has just awoken on a summer afternoon:

> She had not heard him enter, and hardly realized his presence there. She was yawning, and *he saw the red interior of her mouth* as if it had been a snake's. She had stretched one arm so high above her coiled-up cable of hair that he could see its satin delicacy above the sunburn; her face was flushed with sleep, and her eyelids hung heavy over their pupils. The brim-fulness of her nature breathed from her. It was a moment when *a woman's soul* is more incarnate than at any other time; when the most spiritual beauty bespeaks itself flesh; and sex takes the outside place in *the presentation.*   (Ch. 27, p. 231, my italics)

Is this what Hardy means by 'a pure woman' in his subtitle? But notice again, as in all these quotations, how he seems to be doing the very opposite of establishing Tess's 'character'; that, conversely, in rendering her as essence – 'a woman's soul' – he is making her an enigma, unknowable, subject only to speculation (rather as Hardy's later disciple, John Fowles, was to do with Sarah Woodruff in *The French Lieutenant's Woman*), and inimical, therefore, to the *raison d'être* of a fictional realism which finds its very heart in well-rounded 'character'.

But, of course, it is the continuous textual 'presentation' (notice Hardy's use of the word at the end of the last quotation above) of Tess that makes the obsessive (and usually erotic) imaging of her as something to *look at*, as something *seen*, as a visual *object*, so inescapable. Space prevents a full account of the number of occasions her mouth (again, see the above quotation) is fetishistically focused upon – for example, 'To a young man with the least fire in him that little upward lift in the middle of her red top lip was distracting, infatuating, maddening' (Ch. 24, p. 209). But her smile and her eyes also receive continual attention ('her rosy lips curved towards a smile' [Ch. 5, p. 79], 'a roguish curl coming upon her mouth' [Ch. 29, p. 247], 'her eyes enlarged, and she involuntarily smiled in his face' [Ch. 9, p. 103]), as do her neck, her arms, her hair and general deportment ('Tess stood there in her prettily tucked-up milking gown, her hair carelessly heaped upon her head' [Ch. 29, p. 247]). Equally heavily emphasised is the 'bouncing handsome womanliness' of her figure (see the quotation at the beginning of this paper); even Angel at his most idealising – in the passage where he sees her as the 'visionary essence of woman' (see above, p. 93) – is still aware that there weren't many women 'so well endowed in person as she was' (Ch. 20, p. 186); and for Alec she is of course the true *femme fatale* (not, by the by, necessarily a scheming woman or 'siren', merely 'irresistibly attractive'): 'She had an attribute which amounted to a disadvantage just now; and it was this that caused Alec d'Urberville's *eyes to rivet themselves upon her*. It was a luxuriance of aspect, a fulness of growth, which made her appear *more of a woman* than she *really* was' (Ch. 5, p. 82, my emphases; note both the male gaze and the physical essentialism implied by the phrases 'more of a woman' and 'really'.) And later it is this voluptuousness which starts the process of de-converting Alec as preacher: 'his eyes, falling casually upon the familiar countenance and form, remained contemplating her.... "Don't look at me like that!" he said abruptly' (Ch. 45, p. 388) – an inversion which must surely be the most brilliant evocation in fiction of male perfidy and the double standard, for who, after all, is doing the looking? It is further worth noticing in passing that it is not just Tess who is made into a sex-object by the text: Car Darch, just before Alec has sex with Tess, is described thus: 'she had bared her plump neck, shoulders, and arms to the moonshine, under which they looked as luminous and beautiful as some Praxitelean[23] creation, in their possession of the faultless rotundities of a lusty country girl' (Ch. 10, pp. 111–12).

In late twentieth-century terms, the above descriptions would surely amount to 'soft' pornography, or at least to accurate representations of the titillatory visual devices employed therein. And the text further emphasises this voyeuristic stance in its recurrent verbal and narrative objectification ('the presentation') of women in the novel. The 'club-walking' girls in Chapter 2, for instance, are taking part in 'their first *exhibition* of themselves' (p. 49, my italics here and below); the Clare brothers are 'on-lookers' at 'the *spectacle* of a bevy of girls dancing' (pp. 52–3); Tess, after her first visit to Trantridge, 'became aware of the *spectacle* she presented to [her fellow-travellers'] surprised vision: roses at her breast; roses in her hat; roses and strawberries in her basket to the brim' (Ch. 6, p. 84); Mrs Durbeyfield, 'bedecking' Tess for the sacrifice to Alec, is so proud of 'the girl's *appearance*' that she is led to 'step back, *like a painter from his easel*, and survey her work as a whole'; and in order to let Tess 'zee' herself, she hangs a large 'black cloak [surely the 'black flag' of Tess's hanging] outside the casement, and so made a large reflector of the panes' (Ch. 7, pp. 89–90). On other occasions the text pans back from Tess and reduces her (once again de-characterising her in the process) to an insignificant dot on the landscape: 'Tess stood still upon the hemmed expanse of verdant flatness, like a fly on a billiard-table of indefinite length, and of no more consequence to the surroundings than that fly' (Ch. 16, p. 159); 'the two girls crawl[ed] over the surface of [the 'desolate drab' field] like flies' (Ch. 43, p. 360).

Throughout the novel, then, Tess in particular is highly visualised as an object of 'vision' in the swinging 'moment' of the text's gaze. Only on two significant occasions does she disappear from view: once, when she is hanged, with Angel and Liza-Lu's eyes 'rivetted' (like Alec's on her body) to the gaol flag-pole, and she becomes merely 'a black flag' (Ch. 59, p. 489); the other when, in the old phrase precisely, Alec commits 'the act of darkness' with her: 'The obscurity was now so great that he could see absolutely nothing but a pale nebulousness at his feet, which represented the white muslin figure he had left upon the dead leaves. Everything else was blackness alike' (Ch. 11, pp. 118–19). It is as if, paradoxically and point-edly, the novel implies that the essence, the 'pure woman', can only be 'presented' as visualisations, only as she *appears*, but that the basic 'realities' of her existence (sex, death) are unknowable, unrepresentable – like those innermost secrets of 'character' that no one quite comprehends or can describe in other people, however well one knows them.

And let us be clear: we know almost nothing substantive about Tess's 'character', for the novel never attempts to penetrate her secret being. It may tell us things *about* her (she 'spoke two languages' [Ch. 3, p. 58]); give us her views (about the 'blighted star', for example); and show her spirited moments of mettle (to Alec's male cliché, '"that's what every woman says"', she retorts in implicit rejection of 'pure woman' essentialism: ' "Did it never strike your mind that what every woman says some women may feel?" ' [Ch. 12, p. 125], just as she tells Angel to 'call me Tess' when he insists, in the 'visionary essence' scene, on idealising her with names like Artemis and Demeter [Ch. 20, p. 187]). The novel may further appear to try and characterise her state of mind – 'she looked upon herself as a figure of Guilt intruding into the haunts of Innocence ... she fancied herself such an anomaly' (Ch. 13, p. 135) – but only, we note, at a detached psychologistic distance; it may try and explain her love for Angel ('its single-mindedness, its meekness; what long-suffering it guaranteed, what honesty, what endurance, what good faith' [Ch. 33, p. 279]), but the more the text produces phrase after defining phrase, the more a palpable sense of her love recedes – just as earlier, despite all its words, the narrative signally fails to describe her eyes: 'neither black nor blue nor gray nor violet; rather all those shades together, and a hundred others ... around pupils that had no bottom' (Ch. 14, pp. 140–1). For all this 'charac-terisation', then, we really 'know' Tess very little indeed – which is presumably why so much critical argument has raged over whether she is 'passive' or not, whether she is 'pure' or not, indeed whether she is a 'fully-rounded character' at all.

Which is, I would suggest in conclusion, to beg the question. For *Tess of the d'Urbervilles* is precisely *not* a novel attempting to offer us a 'knowable' character, but rather one which exposes *characterisation* itself as a humanist-realist mystification (producing 'visible essences') and which parades the *mis*representation that 'charac-terisation' involves by subjecting to irony the falsifying essentialism of 'faithfully presenting a pure woman'. In her excellent essay of 1982, 'Pure Tess: Hardy on Knowing a Woman',[24] Kathleen Blake remarks that the novel 'really scrutinizes the sexual typing that plays havoc with a woman's life', while George Wotton in his book *Thomas Hardy: Towards a Materialist Criticism*, in suggesting that we recognise 'class and gender conflicts ... as conflicts of perception in the multifarious acts of seeing of the characters who inhabit Wessex', points out that Hardy's 'production (writing) determines consumption (reading) by casting the reader in the role of seer'.[25] In other words, we may say that Hardy's 'moments of vision' dis-proportion characterisation and character so that we can 'see' how they function. Tess as a 'character' is no more than an amalgam – often destructively contradictory – of 'images' of her as perceived by individuals and by 'society': Angel idealises her, Alec sees her as sex-object, the narrative voice fetishises her, society regards her as prodigal, the novel 'faithfully presents' her as 'a pure woman' (with all the ironies that phrasing invokes). But Tess *has no character at all*: she is only what others (most especially the author) construct her as; and so she is herself merely a 'series of seemings' or 'impressions'. This, of course, gives the final ironic twist to the notion of her being '(a) pure woman', since there can be no such thing as 'essential character' when a woman is merely the construct of male socio-sexual images of her desired form (although my basic point here need not be limited to *gender*-stereotyping). Hardy's novel, then, well ahead of its time, seems to be dismantling the bourgeois-humanist (patriarchal and realist) notion of the unified and unitary human subject, and to be doing so by way of a discourse so self-reflexive and defamiliarising about representation, so unstable and dialogical, that it deconstructs itself even as it creates. Which is why, I believe, we can justly discover a contemporary post-modern text in *Tess of the d'Urbervilles*.

Notes

An amended version of this essay appeared as the editor's introduction to the *New Casebook* on *Tess of the d'Urbervilles* (London: Macmillan, 1993).

1. Thomas Hardy, *Tess of the d'Urbervilles* (1891), ed. David Skilton, with an Introduction by A. Alvarez, Penguin Classics Edition (Harmondsworth, [1978] 1987) Ch. 2, p. 51. All further references to the novel are to this edition, and appear in brackets in the text.

2. Thomas Hardy, *Desperate Remedies* (1871), ed. with Introduction by C. J. P. Beatty, New Wessex Edition (London, 1975) pp. 46–7 (pbk).

3. Thomas Hardy, *Jude the Obscure* (1896), ed. with Introduction by Terry Eagleton (and notes by P. N. Furbank), New Wessex Edition (London, 1974) p. 23 (pbk).

4. 'Author's Preface to the Fifth and Later Editions' (1892), *Tess*, p. 38. Hardy, in the same sentence here, also quotes Schiller on 'representation' and 'poetical representations'.

5. See Florence Emily Hardy, *The Life of Thomas Hardy 1840–1928* (London, [1962] 1975) p. 185, for a typical memorandum (Jan. 1887) on this subject during the period of the composition of *Tess*.

6. For extensive treatment of this subject, and of Turner in particular, see Chapter 8 especially, 'Patterns of Light and Dark in *Tess of the d'Urbervilles*', in J. B. Bullen, *The Expressive Eye: Fiction and Perception in the Work of Thomas Hardy* (Oxford, 1986).

7. This 'phase' is perhaps exemplified at its best by R. P. Draper's earlier Casebook, *Hardy: The Tragic Novels* (London, 1975), and by Albert J. LaValley's, *Twentieth-Century Interpretations of Tess of the d'Urbervilles* (Englewood Cliffs, N. J., 1969).

8. For an extended analysis of these by the present author, see Peter Widdowson, *Hardy in History: A Study in Literary Sociology* (London, 1989), especially Chapter 1, 'The Critical Constitution of "Thomas Hardy"'.

9. This singularly pre-emptive and subsequently ubiquitous phrase in Hardy criticism appears in Hardy's 'General Preface' to the Wessex Edition of his works in 1912 (which is reproduced in each volume of the Penguin and New Wessex editions of his novels). It occurs when he is 'classifying', and, in effect, hierarchically evaluating, his fictional *oeuvre* – with the ones so described clearly privileged.

10. Widdowson, *Hardy in History*, pp. 44–55 especially, for a discussion of critical treatment of the 'minor novels'.

11. With those, for example, collected in my Macmillan *New Casebook on 'Tess'*, and in recent volumes, such as Harold Bloom (ed.), *Modern Critical Interpretations of Thomas Hardy* (New York, 1987), and Lance St John Butler (ed.), *Alternative Hardy* (London, 1989).

12. J. T. Laird, *The Shaping of 'Tess of the d'Urbervilles'* (Oxford, 1975) p. 4. For a slightly fuller critique of Laird's stance, see my *Hardy in History*, pp. 30–1. There is a further essay by Laird on the textual development of *Tess*, 'New Light on the Evolution of *Tess of the d'Urbervilles*', in *Review of English Studies*, 31: 124 (Winter 1980) pp. 414–35.

13. Thomas Hardy, *Tess of the d'Urbervilles*, ed. Juliet Grindle and Simon Gatrell, the Clarendon Edition (Oxford, 1983).

14. In the Editor's Preface to John Goode, *Thomas Hardy: The Offensive Truth* (Oxford, 1988) p. vii.

15. For a fuller account and analysis of this, see in particular Chapter 13, 'The Production of Meaning: "Hardy's Women" and the Eternal Feminine', in George Wotton, *Thomas Hardy: Towards a Materialist Criticism* (Goldenbridge, 1985).

16. In Juliet Mitchell and Ann Oakley (eds), *The Rights and Wrongs of Women* (Harmondsworth, 1976). The following quotations, *passim*, are from pp. 255, 253, 254. Two other influential essays on the textuality/ sexuality nexus are: Mary Jacobus, 'Tess: The Making of a Pure Woman', in Susan Lipshitz (ed.), *Tearing the Veil: Essays on Femininity* (London, 1978) which first appeared in *Critical Quarterly*, 26 (October 1976); and J. Hillis Miller, 'Fiction and Repetition: *Tess of the d'Urbervilles*', in Alan Warren Friedman (ed.), *Forms of Modern British Fiction* (Austin, 1975). This was reprinted, in revised form, as the chapter, '*Tess of the d'Urbervilles*: Repetition as Immanent Design', in Hillis Miller's *Fiction and Repetition: Seven English Novels* (Cambridge, Mass., 1982), and again, with Jacobus above, in Bloom (ed.), *Modern Critical Interpretations*.

17. In Mary Jacobus (ed.), *Women's Writing and Writing about Women* (Beckenham, 1979). See especially, pp. 100, 107–8.

18. Editor's Preface to Goode, *Thomas Hardy*, p. vii.

19. I have already implied this in Note 9 above, in reference to Hardy's own categorisation of his novels in the General Preface of 1912. But we also have to remember that he himself, in fact, wrote Florence Emily Hardy's supposed biography of him, *The Life of Thomas Hardy 1840–1928*, in the years immediately preceding his death, and so effectively composed his own 'life' as he wished it to be perceived. An account of this characteristically self-protective subterfuge is to be found in the first chapter of Robert Gittings's *Young Thomas Hardy* (Harmondsworth, [1975] 1978).

20. See Bullen, *The Expressive Eye*, for full discussion of this.

21. See above, note 19.

22. *The Life of Thomas Hardy*, p. 114 (see note 5 above). All further references are given in the text.

23. Praxiteles was a fourth-century BC Greek sculptor whose work celebrated sensuality (for example, in depicting naked gods for the first time).

24. The essay appeared first in *Studies in English Literature*, 22: 4 (Autumn 1982) pp. 689–705, but has been reprinted in Bloom (ed.), Modern Critical Interpretations.

25. Wotton, *Thomas Hardy*, p. 4 .

6

'Bosh' or: Believing neither More nor Less – Hardy, George Eliot and God

LANCE ST JOHN BUTLER

The sources of Hardy's thought lie in his reading. It is often considered, especially by those who quote rather gleefully Hardy's own admission that he read, for instance, the leaders in *The Times* to improve his style, that he went to masters to learn the aesthetic or technical or formal tricks of the novelist's trade while his philosophy came to him as it were from the depths of his own mind or perhaps, by some process of intellectual osmosis, out of the Dorset air. A recent study of his philosophy, for instance, while mostly quite intellectually respectable, can drift off into this sort of misty speculation:

> Nature's apparently random cruelty to one creature meant prosperity for another – this lesson had been impressed upon him as a child – and so for Hardy this darkness of heart had edged into his soulscape long before he had read books which affirmed it.[1]

That this *is* only speculation is established by the consideration that Hardy did *not* have the cruelty of nature impressed on him any more strongly than any other child and that, in fact, he grew up, as his biographers make clear, secure in the powerful love of his mother and happy in the relaxed atmosphere of his father's rather passive personality.

It follows from this sort of projection onto Hardy of the critic's own expectations that he comes to be seen as learning how to turn a phrase from Gibbon or learning how to stage-manage a rustic chorus from Shakespeare while his actual thinking is taken as proceeding along a deep stream of rustic fatalism contributed to by a thinker such as Darwin only by way of confirmation. On this model

101

Hardy is seen as gifted with some sort of special insight into the Nature of Things; even his education is taken to be something natural – what is at first a 'lesson' quickly becomes 'darkness of heart'. The Bible, then, especially the pessimism of parts of the Old Testament, is taken as definitive of Hardy's cast of mind but in a way that emphasises it not so much as an element in Hardy's reading but as the old acquaintance of his many long hours in Stinsford church listening to the cadences of Job or of Esdras or Jeremiah. Surely, this style of thinking goes, Hardy saw life steadily and saw it whole without the benefit of much book – developments in nineteenth-century thought merely confirmed what he already knew.

And yet Hardy was not God, and perhaps would have preferred with a more than ordinary fervour not to be. His thought was not *sui generis* but was formed and *in*formed by the overall texture of his culture just as everybody else's is. Take for example the well-known episode in *Tess* where Tess and her brother are driving their father's cart by starlight and they start discussing the conditions of the universe. Here, if anywhere, we seem to be in the presence of homespun wisdom. Little Abraham asks Tess 'Did you say the stars were worlds, Tess?' – 'Yes'. – 'All like ours?' to which latter question he gets the answer

> I don't know; but I think so. They sometimes seem to be like the apples on our stubbard-tree. Most of them splendid and sound – a few blighted.

Tess tells her brother that we live on a blighted star which provokes from him the comment "Tis very unlucky that we didn't pitch on a sound one, when there were so many more of 'em!"[2]

But eight years before the publication of *Tess*, and therefore some six years before he first drafted this scene, Hardy noted in his *Literary Notes* something he had been reading in the *Spectator* of 11 August 1883. It was a review of Francis Galton's *Inquiries into Human Faculty and Development* published that year; Hardy excerpted, slightly inaccurately, a sentence of the reviewer's:

> We perceive around us a countless number of abortive seeds & germs; we find out of any group of a thousand men selected at random, some who are crippled, insane, idiotic, & otherwise

incurably imperfect in body or mind, & it is possible that this world may rank as one of these.[3]

Galton's application of Darwinian thought to the human species in the first part of this quotation is something we would expect Hardy to be interested in, but I suggest that most of us would have thought that the final part of the sentence, which applies the notion of Darwinian unfitness to worlds (here I think Galton has *planets* in mind) was characteristically Hardyan – that is, it could conceivably be an addition of Hardy's to the basic idea in Galton – but no, as we see, it is Galton himself who extends the speculation to the possibility of there being good and bad planets; Hardy reads this, quotes it in his notebook and it comes out artistically reworked in *Tess*. The thought comes from the reading.

I am at pains to establish this point because I want to situate Hardy more firmly in the intellectual life of his time than is sometimes thought necessary. Pursuing some of the ideas set out in my book on *Victorian Doubt*[4] I am concerned to assert the inescapability of culture, the inevitability of any writer employing only the discourse available to him, and the absolute intertextual interdependence of all moments of a culture sliced synchronically or traced diachronically. In particular, as those who have read my book on the topic will know, this is highly evident in the discourse of religion and doubt in the nineteenth century; the doubters employed the vocabulary of the believers and the believers found themselves willy-nilly involved in the questions and speculations of the doubters; as Tennyson put it, neatly tying up both ends of the paradox, 'There lives more faith in honest doubt, / Believe me, than in half the creeds' (I particularly like the 'believe me' and the careful 'half the creeds').

Thus when we turn to the neglected topic of Hardy's relationship with George Eliot we may find a greater number of intellectual similarities than has been appreciated and also that merely technical comparisons concerning subject-matter or style may be inadequate.

A little later in 1883 than the point at which he had been reading Galton's *Inquiries* Hardy was reading *Blackwood's Magazine* where an article on 'Shakespeare and George Eliot' excited the greatest indignation he manifested throughout the *Literary Notes*. He wrote 'bosh' against the following excerpt from the article (he headed his quotation 'Spiritual belief'):

There is no reason to believe that the state of half-belief in which we now exist will be permanent. Men will again, as in former ages, believe more than we, or they will push on to something like finality, & believe still less than we.[5]   [Hardy added: '*Blackwood* (& bosh)']

The first thing I want to point out about this is that it concerns not George Eliot's style or her handling of rustic characters but her *thought* and, typically, her thought as an agnostic on the matter of faith. In the *Life* Hardy refers to her as 'a great thinker – one of the greatest living' but 'not a born storyteller by any means' and he tried to distance himself from the received critical wisdom that put him into the same camp as George Eliot – that of the rural novelist. For a start, he did not even think of her as a true ruralist at all and, in the same passage from the *Life* where he is admiring the quality of her thought, he claims, correctly enough, that she 'had never touched the life of the fields' and that her country people were 'more like small townsfolk than rustics'. As Lennart Björk comments in his notes on the *Literary Notes*, 'while indicating appreciation of G. Eliot on ideological grounds ... Hardy was not willing to acknowledge any aesthetic influence'.[6]

So what exactly is it that Hardy dismisses as 'bosh' here? His comment indicates disagreement with the suggestion that the present state of half-belief will have to end or, more simply, he is asserting that we will never have either less or more faith than we do 'now' in the late nineteenth century. This is most interesting; it puts very well the delicacy of Hardy's position, that of the true agnostic in the Eliot mould, suspended between belief and unbelief rather than committed to either; it also demonstrates how, like Eliot, he was caught up in an absolutely specific moment of discourse when, as at all other moments of discourse, the horizons were filled with certain possibilities and not with others. This was the moment when it seemed as if there never could be grounds for moving beyond an agnostic uncertainty because, for instance, science was evidently never going to be able to prove or to disprove the existence of God and scientific proof had an authority in the structure of that discourse such that this seemed an insurmountable obstacle to any possible 'finality' or conclusion of the question.

To explore this a little further it might be worth considering Hardy and Eliot together on the assumption that when he refers to her as one of the greatest living thinkers he is hinting that some of her work influenced his own views (rather than merely his style) and that he is best seen together with her as representatives of a cultural moment that had them in its grip (rather than as free-standing geniuses who happened to coincide on some points).

Reading through the *Life*, through the biographies of Hardy, and through his essays, the presence of George Eliot is unmistakable. The *Life* reveals odd moments of Eliot connection of which I shall limit myself to one example; in May 1891 Hardy visited 'a large private lunatic asylum' with Clifford Allbutt, a Commissioner in Lunacy who, it was said, had been the model for Tertius Lydgate in *Middlemarch*.[7] It is a trivial connection but not, perhaps, in its imaginative power; it demonstrates at any rate that Hardy and Eliot inhabited the same intellectual world.

Among the biographers Michael Millgate, for instance, suggests that Felix Holt's 'Address to Working-Men' of January 1868 was echoed in *The Poor Man and the Lady*, completed in July of that year, and that the germ of *Two on a Tower* is to be found in a speculation of Maggie Tulliver's about whether astronomers necessarily hate women; he also quotes a 1905 letter to Israel Zangwill in which Hardy claims that if he had been Jewish he would have been a 'rabid zionist' and that he liked the Jews who had 'brought forth ... a young reformer who, though only in the humblest walk of life, became the most famous personage the world has ever known'. The parallel with the concerns of *Daniel Deronda* is confirmed by the comment made in the *Westminster Review* of July 1876 to the effect that Hardy was lucky that *The Hand of Ethelberta* was published in the same year as George Eliot's last novel because otherwise Ethelberta would have been considered a 'copy' of Gwendolen Harleth. Millgate also points out that George Eliot actually borrowed the term 'Wessex' (in *Daniel Deronda* of 1876) from *Far from the Madding Crowd* of 1874.[8]

In the essays of the two novelists common concerns appear; it would be very profitable to make a comparison, for instance, between George Eliot's 'Silly Novels by Lady Novelists' with Hardy's 'Candour in English Fiction'. In general, the thesis of the latter essay (written in 1890) is a plea for 'accuracy' and realism that is entirely of a piece with the theses of several reviews and essays by Eliot in the 1850s and 1860s. Thus Eliot in her review of Ruskin's *Modern Painters*, vol. 3, of April 1856:

The truth of infinite value that [Ruskin] teaches is *realism* – the doctrine that all truth and beauty are to be attained by a humble and faithful study of nature, and not by substituting vague forms, bred by imagination on the mists of feeling, in place of definite, substantial reality.[9]

And here is Hardy, thirty-five years later, on 'Candour in English Fiction':

Even imagination is the slave of stolid circumstance ... the great bulk of English fiction of the present day is characterised by its lack of sincerity ... by a sincere school of Fiction we may understand a Fiction that expresses truly the view of life prevalent in its time.[10]

Now we can switch back to Eliot: Edward Young, she came to see, after being a youthful admirer of the *Night Thoughts*, suffered from a 'radical insincerity as a poetic artist' because he did not take 'for a criterion the true qualities of the object described'.[11] Now back to Hardy: by 1890 the fiction-reading public are 'weary of puerile inventions and famishing for accuracy'.[12]

This relationship between the two writers is, of course, known but inadequately realised; my concern here is not so much to pile up more evidence for it as to establish what such forms of intellectual intertextuality *mean* and how we should treat them. Both Millgate and Gittings make the point that the comparison with George Eliot weighed with an odd heaviness on Hardy and that he tried to shake it off as though it offended him in some way. The explanation of the puzzle is, however, not far to seek. On the one hand, Hardy was obviously deeply involved in the same area of thought as George Eliot and referred in the *Life*[13] to the 'flattering' nature of the comparison with someone he admired intellectually; on the other hand, he saw Eliot as an inadequate novelist, calling her as we have seen 'not a born storyteller by any means'; the restriction of contemporary comment, therefore, to largely aesthetic and technical comparisons between the two was bound to offend the younger novelist; for Hardy *that* comparison would have been as if commentators had praised Huxley for his faithful imitation not of Darwin's ideas but merely of his literary style and technique – the comparison would be all the more painful for being, in both cases, with older colleagues admired, precisely, for their ideas. Hardy wanted to be associated with the *philosophy* of a great thinker, not with her provincialism.

Let us take it, then, that Hardy's relationship with George Eliot was an intellectual one, that he found in her writing a source for his own thought and that they can be put together as inhabitants of the same world of discourse, and with these points in mind return to the question that Hardy's violent annotation 'bosh' poses for us. Why was it against *this* excerpt that he chose to place his 'strongest comment of disapproval' on any of his notebook entries? What is so bad about the suggestion that half-belief must give way to full belief or to no belief? In considering these questions I will be circling again around the topic that I have returned to again and again in my work on Hardy, the topic of God.

At present the work of Mikhail Bakhtin is fashionable among post-poststructuralist critics and he offers us, in his concept of poly-vocality, a useful way of approaching Hardy's ambiguities on the topic of the divine. This has been explored to some extent by Deborah Collins in her recent *Thomas Hardy and His God* in which she sees Hardy as engaged with the various voices of his age, expressing a series of views of God that depend on tones, registers and themes topical in the later nineteenth century.

This is a good way of reading Hardy's insistence on the impressionistic nature of his thinking, the 'series of seemings' as he called it, the tentative provisionality he often claimed for his philo-sophy (he was, we remember from the *Life*, 'content with ten-tativeness from day to day'). Here again it is a matter of quotation, of Hardy's reading, of his listening attentively to the voices of his time. Only late in the day, in the General Preface to the 1912 edition of the works, countering the endlessly repeated accusation of pessimism, does he try to assert that his views are The Truth:

> It might be obvious that there is a higher characteristic of philo-sophy than pessimism, or than meliorism, or even than the optimism of these critics – which is truth.[14]

This is a rare voice in Hardy. Normally he is more aware of the relative and the impermanent in discourse.

Just like George Eliot, Hardy starts attending to the voice of the Bible, then of Comtean Positivism ('Catholicism minus Christianity' as T. H. Huxley called it), then of Darwinist Agnosticism, then of a non-supernatural Christianity; what he does NOT do is to invent a new discourse or somehow transcend, from some deep connection with the Wessex earth perhaps, all the voices around him. Let us beware of assuming unthinkingly that there exists a Truth which the Great Writer is somehow automatically plugged in to and which he has only to exteriorise through the neutral medium of art. Hardy himself is as post-structuralist, or as Bakhtinian, as anyone could be and certainly did not wish to claim to be a builder of a temple of truth – he is, rather, in the position of the postmodernist author, playing among the ruins, toying with the ideas available in the discourse of his age. Under these circumstances it is not surprising that he reacted so violently against the suggestion that the future would believe either less or more; the one thing of which he was normally certain, like Samuel Butler who in his notebooks coins the unoriginal aphorism that nothing is certain except that nothing is certain, was that dogmatic assertions of the Truth (whether of God's existence or the opposite) were the least likely of all propositions to command assent in a future of many voices and mixed discourses.

As an example of these theological ideas let us consider Hardy and, *en passant*, George Eliot, on the subject of Compensation. This matter, which today is likely to arouse ideas of large sums of money being awarded by courts to the victims of industrial accidents or miscarriages of justice, has, when given a capital letter, a specific theological meaning of great importance to the nineteenth century. Compensation is the doctrine that seeks to overcome the Problem of Pain by asserting that the suffering undergone in this life by those who don't deserve it will be made up to them in the next life by a divine balancing mechanism which will not merely compensate for suffering but give the just their reward a hundred-fold. Equally the wicked, however triumphant they may appear in this life, will be punished in the next. Now, obviously enough, this scheme was somewhat rearranged by Puritanism and Evangelicalism to include the present life rather more satisfactorily and it is clear that success in this world could be taken, by Mr Brocklehurst in *Jane Eyre*, for instance, or by Mr Bulstrode in *Middlemarch*, as evidence of divine approval such that it could be said that the saints were getting some of their reward here and now. Neither of these options was open to Hardy or George Eliot.

In a letter of 1856 George Eliot claimed 'I have long wanted to fire away at the doctrine of Compensation, which I detest, considered as a theory of life.'[15] She had been thinking of offering her publisher friend Chapman a book on 'The Idea of a Future Life' and clearly at this stage she was much exercised about the relationship between morality and reward in the absence of a divine guarantor. As we know she told F. W. H. Myers in her famous conversation with him that the idea of God and that of Immortality were respectively 'inconceivable' and 'unbelievable' but that the requirements of Duty remained 'absolute'. Duty, then, was on its own, something to be done without Compensation. On the other hand, as the qualification George Eliot added to her mention of 'detesting' Compensation in her letter makes clear, she was not without sympathy for the notion conceived in some other terms. She wrote that she detested it 'considered as a theory of life', implying that, considered in some other way, she might be able to think a little better of Compensation. It is not difficult to see what this alternative view might be. As a thinker famously sympathetic to the lot of suffering humanity Eliot clearly felt, as Hardy would do after her, that reward or compensation were not in themselves *bad* ideas, on the contrary it is evident that, like Hardy, she believed that nobody deserved any less, in the way of reward, than this world offered them; the only trouble with Compensation as a theory of life was that it was not true and therefore not worth betting your life on in the absence of God and Immortality.

And in 1874 Hardy was reading the abbreviated edition of G. H. Lewes's monumental *Life and Works of Goethe*. This shortened version, entitled *The Story of Goethe's Life*, which had come out in 1873, was a more manageable rescension of Lewes's magnum opus of 1855 so, as nearly as we can judge it, Hardy came, twenty years later (but then he was George Eliot's junior by twenty years) to the precise point that Eliot had been at in the 1850s, for I need not remind you of the relationship between Eliot and Lewes that persisted from the mid-1850s until her death in 1880. Hardy's first annotation, from p. 16 of Lewes's shorter version of his biography, reads: 'Goethe's religion was all taken out of him by the Lisbon earthquake'. The significance of this, under the circumstances, must be that this was the point at which Hardy saw, via Lewes via Goethe, that compensation did not work. People are swept away by natural disasters regardless of their virtuousness. Once again we notice the deeply *read* nature of Hardy's mental development: he worked hard on texts such as Lewes's biography, annotated them, extracted from them, rearranged his notes and kept them for rereading. The fact that it was *Goethe* who lost his faith in the way mentioned does nothing to diminish Hardy's interest in the matter – quite the contrary.

It will have been noticed that, in my enthusiasm for putting Hardy and Eliot together in these matters, I have allowed myself a slide from Compensation as meaning reward in the next life to compensation meaning reward in this (as in the Puritan gloss on the matter mentioned earlier). This is not altogether a mistake on my part. Hardy and Eliot certainly considered this watered-down version of compensation too – it was, after all, one of the main structures of the fiction of their century, as witness Miss Prism's comment on her novel in *The Importance of Being Earnest* from the very end of the century (1899): 'The good ended happily, and the bad unhappily – that is what Fiction means.' But it was Hardy's contention, and Eliot's, that this sort of rose-tinted optimism was just what thinking moderns could no longer indulge in; as Hardy put it in 'Candour in English Fiction': 'Life being a physiological fact, its honest portrayal must be largely concerned with, for one thing, the relations of the sexes, and the substitution for such catastrophes as favour the false colouring best expressed by the regulation finish that "they married and were happy ever after," of catastrophes based upon sexual relations as it is.'[16] The grammar here may not be too wonderful but the sentiment is clear at least: when it comes to catastrophes in the technical sense Hardy prefers catastrophes in the more colloquial sense. He had toyed, of course, with happy endings in *Under the Greenwood Tree* and *Far from the Madding Crowd*; Dick Dewy and Gabriel Oak get their compensation for having suffered at the hands of Eros, but even in these early novels there is a sizeable question-mark accompanying the 'happy ever after' pattern. What is of more significance, however, is that there is no attribution of serious moral blame in Hardy – he has no villains – so neither reward nor punishment can be seen as correlated to moral worth. It is perhaps hard to see Sergeant Troy as being as good as Gabriel Oak but he *is* as good, certainly in relation to his heredity and environment; our assumption that one is a hero and the other a villain only comes about because we are looking at the matter through conventional spectacles – or should I say Prisms?

Besides happy endings in the novels themselves, Hardy also toyed with another kind of Compensation – one familiar to readers of *The Dynasts* which ends, it will be recalled, with the hint that 'a stirring thrills the air' and that 'the rages / Of the ages / Shall be cancelled, and deliverance offered from the darts that were, / Consciousness the Will informing, till It fashion all things fair!'[17] This

Hardy called 'the Great Adjustment', the awakening of the 'All-mover' whose heart will become aware, whose 'Inadvertent Mind' will advert itself to the sufferings of Earth's inhabitants and who will then set about 'Promptly tending / To Its mending/In a genial germing purpose, and for loving-kindness' sake'.[18]

This evolutionary optimism is a mythicised version of meliorism. All Hardy scholars know that he protested often enough that he was, rather than a pessimist or an optimist, a meliorist. This meant that he claimed that things were not of themselves inherently bad or good but that, however bad they were, they could be improved by human effort. After all, the one example of consciousness that the Immanent Will had produced to date was human consciousness and man was capable of kindness; man was thus a model for what God might become if only he, too, would become conscious – loving-kindness might become the attribute of the Most High – but meanwhile we conscious beings had the opportunity to make things better gradually. Here we have yet another kind of Compensation, which we might call Darwinist Compensation; we have met its strong version which involves the All-mover in waking up and taking things into his own, by then benevolent, hands; now in its weaker version it involves humanity taking responsibility for making things better. It is often said that Hardy lost his faith in meliorism when he had fully realised the nature of the First World War, but in the *Life* he does not quite say this, he only claims to have lost faith in the stronger version of the meliorist creed saying that 'the war gave the *coup de grâce* to any conception he may have nourished of a fundamental ultimate Wisdom at the back of things'.[19] God will not wake up, and might as well, therefore, not exist for human purposes, but Hardy does not seem to have lost faith in the weaker version of the idea and he obviously continued to believe in human loving-kindness to the end of his life.

Which means that he was, once again, in the precise position of George Eliot. The term 'meliorism' was coined, exactly as one might expect, in 1858. Not, admittedly, by Eliot herself, but when she picks up the term in 1877 she is able to claim 'I don't know that I ever heard anybody use the word "meliorist" except myself' (see *OED*: 'meliorist'). She, like Darwin and Hardy, needed a term that would rescue humanity from the swamps of an absolute moral hopelessness; Hardy *read* it and used it. Here is Darwin's version of the matter from his *Autobiography* (a passage that reveals, incidentally, how much he, too, had been reading): 'If [a man] acts for the good of others, he will receive the approbation of his fellow men and gain the love of those with whom he lives; and this latter gain undoubtedly is the highest pleasure on this earth.'[20] The reassertion of a naturalised Christianity of this sort is one of the great themes of the nineteenth century, to be found in John Stuart Mill, for whom Utilitarianism turns out to have a Christian heart, in Darwin as we have just seen, in Arnold and Mrs Humphry Ward, and also in George Eliot and in Angel Clare's agnostic professions to Tess. What holds these writers together is that they are all wrestling, as we all must, with the discourse of their time: the question on the agnostic agenda is 'What compensation?' and everyone is obliged to produce an answer.

Now we can see why Hardy thought the notion of believing either more or less was 'bosh'. Given the question posed by nineteenth-century discourse, given, as it were, the nature of the terms set, it was obvious, with that obviousness that *at the time* seems to be for all time, that God and Immortality were impossible but Duty peremptory, that evolution might produce another form of self-consciousness (since it would certainly produce something) but that for the present loving-kindness was the only solution, that meliorism was the only hope, that we could not *know*. We cannot, under these circumstances, believe more, for the foundations of belief have been shaken; equally, we cannot believe less, for that would mean being able to step outside our historical situation and speak a language that did not exist – Compensation is an example of the language to which Eliot and Hardy were condemned; for them it cannot *not* be a problem.

My themes are resumed in some of the detail of Hardy's last few days on earth. According to the *Life*, on Boxing Day 1927 'he said that he had been thinking of the Nativity and of the Massacre of the Innocents, and his wife read to him the gospel accounts, and also articles in the *Encyclopaedia Biblica*. He remarked that there was not a grain of evidence that the gospel story was true in any detail.'[21] On 10 January 1928 Hardy asked Florence to read him the whole of Browning's 'Rabbi Ben Ezra', which she did.[22] Some days earlier he had dictated what Gittings calls 'two virulent, inept, and unworthy satirical jingles on two most hated critics, George

Moore, and G. K. Chesterton'.[23] On January 11 he asked Florence
to read from *Omar Khayyám* and stopped her after she had read
one quatrain. Gittings comments 'It was his last gesture towards
the Prime Mover.'[24]

First of all we notice that Hardy lived his last days through books
– his reading (or, in his condition, reading to him by others) occupied his thoughts – the Christmas Story *as story*; the meaning of it
(and, characteristically, of a massacre of babies to go along with the
birth of a baby) as interpreted by the *Encyclopaedia*; poems by his
older contemporaries, Browning and Fitzgerald, two other wrestlers
with the intellectual conditions of the nineteenth century; then the
epitaphs for two literary opponents, two writers who had criticised
his writing.

Second, we notice that nearly all of this has to do with the religion
that Hardy had supposedly abandoned and, what is more, is a
reflection on the matter of Compensation in its various forms. The
epitaphs are for two writers who were still alive – Moore died in
1933 and Chesterton in 1936. It obviously seemed important to the
dying Hardy to get the last word in, to settle the score with these
enemies. As for the Prime Mover, Rabbi Ben Ezra is clear that Compensation is the result of a planned deal, a contract between God
and Man; the aged Rabbi contemplates how his death will in some
sort make the circle complete:

> All I could never be,
> All, men ignored in me,
> This, I was worth to God, whose wheel the pitcher shaped.

> Ay, note that Potter's wheel,
> That metaphor! and feel
> Why time spins fast, why passive lies our clay, –
> Thou, to whom fools propound,
> When the wine makes its round,
> 'Since life fleets, all is change; the Past gone, seize to-day!'

> Fool! All that is, at all,
> Lasts ever, past recall;
> Earth changes, but thy soul and God stand sure:
> What entered into thee,
> *That* was, is, and shall be:
> Time's wheel runs back or stops: Potter and clay endure.

There is not space to quote all of the stanzas that conclude the poem; the point is that they establish the terms of the contract and insist on the balance that God has struck over man's youth and age, life and death. The message is that there is no need for compensation, or, better, that compensation is built into the nature of things. In the final two stanzas of the poem the Rabbi addresses God directly:

> But I need, now as then,
> Thee, God, who mouldest men;
> And since, not even while the whirl was worst,
> Did I, – to the wheel of life
> With shapes and colours rife,
> Bound dizzily, – mistake my end, to slake Thy thirst:
>
> So, take and use Thy work:
> Amend what flaws may lurk,
> What strain o' the stuff, what warpings past the aim!
> My times be in Thy hand!
> Perfect the cup as planned!
> Let age approve of youth, and death complete the same!

The tone is partly reverential but also challenging; the sentiment is that God must now, will now, complete the pattern and make these odds all even.

It must have been all this cup-and-potter stuff that made Hardy think, the next day, of their source in *Omar Khayyám*. (Browning's poem was composed in 1862, three years after the publication of the first edition of the *Rubáiyát* in 1859.) Fitzgerald, although writing first, offers a gloss on Browning's misty version of Compensation – 'Some laugh at us for leaning all awry', point out *his* cups, 'What then, did the hand of the Potter slip?' Under the circumstances of human suffering the Compensation, we discover, must go the other way – let God forgive man, by all means, but let man also forgive God for making so poor a world. The stanza Florence read to Hardy has a precise theological background and neatly presents the position in which we can believe neither less nor more; it also addresses God directly:

> Oh, Thou, who Man of baser Earth didst make,
> And ev'n with Paradise devise the Snake:

For all the Sin wherewith the Face of Man
Is blacken'd – Man's forgiveness give – and take!

As Florence puts it in the *Life*, 'He indicated that he wished no more to be read'.[25]

And finally, it is intriguing that the earlier epitaph on George Moore, the last thing Hardy ever wrote besides a cheque, has George Eliot at its origin – for the antagonism between the two writers, though greatly exacerbated by some very ill-tempered comments Moore made about Hardy's writing in his *Conversations in Ebury Street* of 1924, went back to his earlier *Confessions of a Young Man* of 1886 in which he had described *Far from the Madding Crowd* as 'but one of George Eliot's miscarriages'.[26]

Notes

1. Deborah L. Collins, *Thomas Hardy and His God: A Liturgy of Unbelief* (London: Macmillan, 1990) p. 33.
2. *Tess of the d'Urbervilles* (London: Macmillan, New Wessex Edition, 1974) paperback, Ch. 4, p. 59.
3. *The Literary Notes of Thomas Hardy*, ed. Lennart Björk, vol. 1 (Gothenburg: Acta Universitatis Gothoburgensis, 1974) p. 160.
4. Lance St John Butler, *Victorian Doubt: Literary and Cultural Discourses* (London: Harvester Wheatsheaf, 1990).
5. *Literary Notes*, p. 157.
6. Ibid., p. 375.
7. Florence Emily Hardy, *The Life of Thomas Hardy 1840–1928* (London: Macmillan, 1962) p. 98. (Cited hereafter as *Life*.)
8. Michael Millgate, *Thomas Hardy: A Biography* (Oxford: Oxford University Press, 1982) pp. 111, 181, 225n. There are many other small points of intersection that show how Hardy and Eliot inhabited the same world; might the younger novelist have been influenced by the older in his choice of titles, for instance? 'The Sad Fortunes of the Rev. Amos Barton' certainly has a Hardyesque ring to it. Then again, here is that other Unbeliever, William Hale White, protesting in the *Athenaeum* of 28 November 1885 that the 'official' biography of George Eliot by John Walter Cross was too respectable: [George Eliot has been] 'removed from the class – the great and noble church, if I may so call it, of the Insurgents, to one more genteel'. Hardy, of course, had *Hearts Insurgent* as an early title for *Jude the Obscure*. One might even wonder whether the characterisation of Sue Bridehead owed something to George Eliot. How many other models were available to Hardy of a free-thinking and intellectual woman prepared to live unmarried with a man? Eliot had lived in a species of *ménage à*

quatre with the publisher John Chapman, his wife and his mistress in the early 1850s; she may have been Herbert Spencer's mistress and she certainly was not married to G. H. Lewes. In John Chapman's Diary for 1851 we get a flavour of the intellectual concerns of the household which Eliot had entered on January 8 that year:

> Saturday 5 July 1851.... Read the articles in the Westminster Review on the Enfranchisement of Women, and on the Extinction of Slavery; neither of which are striking. The former is said to be by J. S. Mill.

(Cf. Gordon S. Haight, *George Eliot and John Chapman* (Yale University Press, 1969) p. 189.) Here, surely, is the true intellectual matrix from which Sue Bridehead derived, however much she may have differed from George Eliot physically and emotionally.

9. Quoted in A. S. Byatt, *Passions of the Mind* (London: Chatto & Windus, 1991) p. 85.
10. Harold Orel (ed.), *Thomas Hardy's Personal Writings* (Lawrence: University of Kansas Press, 1966; London: Macmillan, 1967) p. 125ff.
11. Byatt, *Passions*, p. 85.
12. Orel, *Writings*, p. 127.
13. *Life*, p. 98.
14. General Preface to the Novels and Poems in Macmillan's Wessex Edition, 1912. Reprinted in Orel, *Writings*, pp. 44–50.
15. George Eliot, *Letters*, ed. Gordon S. Haight (London: Oxford University Press, 1954) vol. 2, p. 258.
16. Orel, *Writings*, p. 127.
17. *The Dynasts* (Macmillan, New Wessex Edition, 1978) Pt. Third, After Scene, p. 707.
18. Ibid., pp. 705–6.
19. *Life*, p. 368.
20. Collins, *Thomas Hardy*, p. 168.
21. *Life*, p. 445.
22. Ibid.
23. Robert Gittings, *The Older Hardy* (London: Heinemann, 1978) p. 211.
24. Ibid.
25. *Life*, p. 446.
26. *The Personal Notebooks of Thomas Hardy*, ed. Richard H. Taylor (London: Macmillan, 1978) p. 79.

7

'Good Faith, You do Talk!': Some Features of Hardy's Dialogue

RAYMOND CHAPMAN

It was the conversation at Warren's Malthouse which eventually moved Gabriel Oak to the exclamation, 'Good faith, you do talk!' His feeling has been shared by generations of readers who have been impressed, sometimes overwhelmed, by the rich variety of what Hardy's characters say to one another. Hardy is more powerful in this respect than many novelists: his fiction continually presents people who are talking vigorously about themselves and their affairs, or about the state of things in general. His people are highly articulate, so much so that some critics have thought that their words go beyond what their supposed situations make credible. The reviewer in the *Athenaeum* of *The Return of the Native* thought that the characters 'talk as no people ever talked before, or perhaps we should rather say as no people ever talk now' and continued, 'the language of his peasants may be Elizabethan, but it can hardly be Victorian'. Hardy's reply, not dealing strictly with the charge of stilted diction, showed his awareness of the problem of getting speech on to the printed page:

An author may be said to fairly convey the spirit of intelligent peasant talk if he retains the idiom, compass, and characteristic expressions, although he may not encumber the page with obsolete pronunciations of the purely English words, and with mispronunciations of those derived from Latin and Greek. In the printing of standard speech hardly any phonetic principle at all is observed; and if a writer attempts to exhibit on paper the precise accents of a rustic speaker he disturbs the proper balance of a true

117

representation by unduly insisting upon the grotesque element; thus directing attention to a point of inferior interest, and diverting it from the speaker's meaning.[1]

Throughout his career, critical opinions of Hardy's use of rustic speech were variable. Andrew Lang took a poor view of dialect in *Far from the Madding Crowd*: 'Shepherds may talk in this way: we hope not; but if they do, it is a revelation; and if they don't, it is nonsense, and not very amusing nonsense.' A distinctly backhanded compliment was paid to *The Mayor of Casterbridge*: 'the dialect of the agricultural labourers ... forms the most, if not the only, amusing portion of the book'. J. M. Barrie thought that in *The Woodlanders* 'there is now a tendency to spoil the rustics by putting clever sayings into their mouths'. However, Edmund Gosse wrote in his largely hostile review of *Jude the Obscure*, 'we are never more happy than when he allows us to overhear the primitive Wessex speech'.[2]

We recall that Alice, looking at her sister's book, thought that it was a dull book, without pictures or conversations. Pictures are not so much in fashion for novels today, but we should feel deprived without the conversations. Speech in the novel is a vital part of its contact with the real world of which it is a microcosm. It is a way of forming that relationship with the characters which is a dimension of the relationships which they form among themselves. Such at least is the way in which the Victorian novelists and their readers approached their art; some modern criticism would repudiate any attempt to frame the novel in reality or to find in characters anything more than words generated by the text. Such reaction against Bradleyan excesses which sometimes obscured both drama and prose fiction can be useful but it has to be suspended when we come to Hardy and his contemporaries.

What does not change in any period is the basic problem of using visual means to convey auditory experience. The author does not perfectly reproduce that experience for the reader, but it is necessary to confront the discrepancy between what is possible in speech and in writing. Many nuances of speech are lost on the printed page and have to be supplied by authorial comment or by stretching resources of spelling and typography to suggest such things as stress, intonation and dialect pronunciation. Even apart from these things, the words which purport to be spoken are vital in the creation of character, and particularly of that development of personal relationships which is one of the features distinguishing the novel proper from plain prose narrative. Dialogue also advances the plot, and allows the expression of authorial ideas in a form more concealed than that of expository prose inserted into the story. This last function is often a snare for novelists, particularly of the nineteenth century, and can result in a temporary or more lasting loss of character credibility.

Despite all weaknesses and infelicities, the vast range of Victorian fiction offers through its dialogue insights into the time that are not otherwise accessible. Most of what we know about Victorian speech comes from its fiction, which is true indeed for speech through almost all the literate centuries of history. Among the major Victorian novelists, Hardy is not the leader in every aspect of dialogue. Dickens is supreme in the comic idiolects which instantly identify his characters and become part of his imaginative world. George Eliot has a fine ear for the tone and quality of voices, for the phonational element which the early phonetic studies of her time had not scientifically explored. Trollope, by the testimony of contemporary reviewers, produces dialogue which has the true ring of conversation. Hardy does things which are different from any of these but which make him at least their equal.

It may be as well, before coming to his particular excellence, to spend a moment on the criticisms that have been made of his dialogue. No writer is perfect all the time, and there are certainly lapses in Hardy's conversational as well as in his narrative style. Sometimes his speakers seem impossibly artificial and stilted; the same can be said of all the Victorian novelists at some point, and it is worth remembering that speech in the nineteenth century was often more formal than it has since become, especially among strangers and slight acquaintances. It is certainly hard to credit the observations which are supposed to accompany a ride through the woods in *A Laodicean*:[3]

Abner Power was quite sentimental that day. 'In such places as these', he said, as he rode alongside Mrs Goodman, 'nature's powers in the multiplication of one type strike me as much as the grandeur of the mass.'

Mrs Goodman agreed with him, and Paula said, 'The foliage forms the roof of an interminable green crypt, the pillars being the trunks, and the vault the interlacing boughs.'   (Bk Fifth, Ch. 2)

There are also the theatrical outbursts which seem more appropriate to the stage of melodrama than to the novel. For instance, Eustacia Vye in *The Return of the Native*:

> O, the cruelty of putting me into this ill-conceived world! I was capable of much; but I have been injured and blighted and crushed by things beyond my control! O, how hard it is of Heaven to devise such tortures for me, who have done no harm to Heaven at all! (Bk Fifth, Ch. 7)

Of such passages – and there are a number in Hardy's fiction – more should be said. The accents of melodrama are frequent in Victorian novels, part of the collusion between author and reader which is necessary in any literary form and which in this particular genre often subverts the claims to realism. In a society where legitimate drama was still fighting its way back from the centuries of monopolistic control, a dramatic element in fiction was welcome. Consider, as just one example, how Dickens makes Nicholas Nickleby speak when he defends Smike against Squeers:

> 'Wretch', rejoined Nicholas, fiercely, 'touch him at your peril! I will not stand by and see it done; my blood is up, and I have the strength of ten such men as you. Look to yourself, for by Heaven I will not spare you if you drive me on!' (*Nicholas Nickleby*, Ch. 13)

Hardy knew what he was about; he usually gives such speeches to histrionic characters like Eustacia, and he has an illuminating comment in *The Woodlanders* which may confirm the experience of his contemporary readers:

> At moments there was something theatrical in the delivery of Fitzpiers's effusion; yet it would have been inexact to say that it was intrinsically theatrical. It often happens that in situations of unrestraint, where there is no thought of the eye of criticism, real feeling glides into a mode of manifestation not easily distinguishable from rodomontade. (Ch. 18)

Sometimes Hardy seems to be using his characters as mouthpieces for his own sentiments, as when Sue gives her views on marriage to Phillotson: 'domestic laws should be made according to temperaments, which should be classified. If people are at all peculiar in character they have to suffer from the very rules that produce comfort in others!' (*Jude the Obscure*, Pt Fourth, Ch. 3). But Hardy, unlike many lesser novelists, never keeps up expository dialogue for long. Further, he has an almost disconcerting way of surprising the reader by subverting his own characters. In the same novel, Jude is insufferable about Christminster:

> It is a unique centre of thought and religion – the intellectual and spiritual granary of this country. All that silence and absence of goings-on is the stillness of infinite motion – the sleep of the spinning-top, to borrow the simile of a well-known writer.

The immediate reply is not authorial comment but the voice of a villager coming in like Bottom reducing fairy music to the tongs and bones:

> O, well, it med be all that, or it med not. As I say, I didn't see nothing of it the hour or two I was there; so I sent in and had a pot o' beer, and a penny loaf, and a ha'porth o' cheese, and waited till it was time to come along home.   (Pt Second, Ch. 6)

We may now turn to the qualities of dialogue in which Hardy excels. One is the representation of the different levels of speech according to situation and relationship. What is known as *register* in speech is familiar to all of us. We do not use our language in the same way all the time, but vary it according to whether we are speaking to a member of the family, a close friend, a stranger or a child. We associate certain forms of language with professions and circumstances. Register is more clearly marked grammatically in languages like French where the choice of second person singular or plural accords with the relationship between the speakers; and some, like Japanese, have a wide range of difference for polite forms. English has to depend mainly on choice of vocabulary, accompanied by intonation and non-verbal signs, but variation in address is still clearly marked. It was much more apparent in the nineteenth century when the social code emphasised differences which are now lost or diminished. In *The Trumpet-Major* there is a splendid piece of register shift from the melodramatic style previously discussed when Festus Derriman is speaking about Anne Garland:

'Ask her to alter her cruel, cruel resolves against me, on the score of – of my consuming passion for her. In short,' continued Festus, dropping his parlour language in his warmth, 'I'll tell thee what, Dame Loveday, I want the maid, and must have her.'   (Ch. 36)

The same novel has some amusing examples of language influenced by the character's occupation. John Loveday has memorised army regulations:

And, by the orders of the War Office, I am to exert over them (that's the government word) – exert over them full authority; and if any one behaves towards me with the least impropriety, or neglects my orders, he is to be confined and reported.   (Ch. 11)

His sailor brother Bob speaks in the tradition of earlier seafaring heroes in fiction and drama. 'Let me pilot 'ee down over those stones', he says to Anne; and again, 'I … admired you as a sweet little craft' and of refined women, 'any little vulgar action unreaves their nerves like a marline-spike' (Ch. 19). Longways in *The Mayor of Casterbridge* has a garbled memory of an official citation: 'Your mother was a very good woman – I can mind her. She were rewarded by the Agricultural Society for having begot the greatest number of healthy children without parish assistance, and other virtuous marvels' (Ch. 13).

The style of formal religion, founded on the Book of Common Prayer and the Authorised Version of the Bible, was more familiar to ordinary people. The milkmaid Marian in *Tess of the d'Urbervilles* is so embarrassed by arriving late at church 'that I hardly cool down again till we get into the That-it-may-please-Thees', that is the Litany which followed Mattins (Ch. 23). In the same episode, Izz Huett, who admits to having 'a' ear at church for pretty verses' saucily reminds Tess that there is 'A time to embrace, and a time to refrain from embracing' – quoting from Ecclesiastes. The reference to the Litany reminds us of another allusion in *The Woodlanders* where Creedle observes of Mrs Charmond that she will 'tell off your hear-us-good-Lords as pat as a business-man counting money' (Ch. 4). Religious echoes can be sardonic, as when Dare in *A Laodicean* refers to the Book of Job and tells his father that he comes, 'From going to and fro in the earth, and walking up and down in it, as Satan said to his Maker' (Bk Second, Ch. 5). There is a moment which is both moving and ironic when Sue Bridehead after the death of her children says that people are talking about her – '"We are made a spectacle unto the world, and to angels, and to men!"'. Jude replies, 'No – they are not talking of us…. They are two clergymen of different views, arguing about the eastward position' (*Jude the Obscure*, Pt Sixth, Ch. 2).

Victorian fiction frequently reflects the social concern about proper and improper words. While the influence of public opinion and the circulating libraries generally caused elision or paraphrase of oaths and sexual references, popular slang was put into the mouths of characters. The effect is sometimes to place social status, sometimes to show the independence of the younger generation, using modish slang which shocks their elders. Angel Clare startles his family by remarking that 'that mead was a drop of pretty tipple' and has to explain, 'blushing', that it was 'an expression they use down at Talbothays' (*Tess of the d'Urbervilles*, Ch. 25). His brothers, university men, should not have been surprised: the same word is used by the eponymous hero of *Tom Brown at Oxford*. The ambivalent young Dare, already quoted, grossly but effectively mixes registers when he says, 'My dinner to-day will unfortunately be one of herbs, for want of the needful. I have come to my last stiver' (Bk. Third, Ch. 4). Sue Bridehead, in one of her frequent emotional outbursts, drops suddenly and rather endearingly into a piece of almost schoolgirl slang: 'I suppose I ought not to have asked you to bring me in here. O I oughtn't! I see it now. My curiosity to hunt up a new sensation always leads me into these scrapes' (Pt Third, Ch. 7).

Such delicate points of lexis help to build up the character who uses them. Other aspects of register reveal social and personal relationships, often in a subtle way which the modern reader may overlook. The society which Hardy knew in his youth was moving from the almost feudal structure of the pre-industrial age towards the modern state. Relationships were still more formal than they were later to become, a formality not occasioned only by differences of rank. A great deal could be expressed by the giving or withholding of titles and the progress of an acquaintance could be charted by its linguistic record.

Class differences were strongly marked. If we examine the unhappy affairs of Tess, we find that Alec feels free to address her by her Christian name from their first meeting, while she calls him 'sir'. Even after she has borne his child, she still instinctively exclaims, 'O no, sir – no!' when he confronts her with a marriage licence and when he later offers to help her family. Angel Clare calls her 'Tessy' but she addresses him as 'Mr Clare' even though they are sharing in the same dairy work. Crick the dairyman, ostensibly Angel's employer, honours his social position as a clergyman's son with 'sir'. When Tess returns after her marriage, Marian is uncertain what to call her – 'Tess – Mrs Clare – the dear wife of dear he!' (Ch. 42).

Hardy was acutely sensitive to the rural hierarchy with its relative positions which more sophisticated society would not have noticed. In *The Woodlanders* Giles calls Marty South by her Christian name while she calls him 'Mr Winterborne'. Grace Melbury, however, reflects that the girls she had known at her finishing school were those 'whose parents Giles would have addressed with a deferential Sir or Madam' (Ch. 6). Similarly, Diggory Venn honours Thomasin as 'Mrs Wildeve' while she continues to call him 'Diggory'. Old John Smith in *A Pair of Blue Eyes* finds himself saying 'sir' to his son and exclaims, '"Sir", says I to my own son! but ye've gone up so, Stephen' (Ch. 23).

Hardy charts the progress of romance by attempted or permitted changes in styles of address. With our modern free use of Christian names – really a very recent phenomenon – we may find it hard to grasp the full implications of what we read. When Gabriel Oak starts boldly, 'Well, then, Bathsheba', he is cut short: '"Miss Everdene, you mean," she said with dignity' (*Far from the Madding Crowd*, Ch. 20). The little boy Johnny, too young for serious flirtation, is similarly rebuked for his 'Yes, Eustacia' with 'Miss Vye, sir' and replies confusedly 'Miss Vy-stacia' (*The Return of the Native*, Bk First, Ch. 6). When Boldwood has fallen into disgrace, Gabriel can call Bathsheba by her Christian name without rebuke, and refer to his former rival as plain 'Boldwood', while previously he had called him 'sir'. Perhaps we have lost in delicacy of understanding where we have gained in informality. A modern Elizabeth-Jane would not say to Lucetta, 'You called my father "Michael" as if you knew him well' (*The Mayor of Casterbridge*, Ch. 27), and surely two young people would not have the exchange, 'Why, Elfie' – 'Not Elfie to you, Mr Knight' (*A Pair of Blue Eyes*, Ch. 20). Familiarity is pressed even closer in *A Laodicean*:

'May I call you Paula?'
'Yes, occasionally.'
'Dear Paula! may I call you that?'

'Oh no – not yet.'   (Bk First, Ch. 15)

Later Paula says, 'Now, George – you see I say George and not Mr Somerset, and you may draw your own inference' (Bk Third, Ch. 11). The Victorians knew some excitements that we do not.

A second way in which Hardy excels is in the use of dialect to show relationships and relative positions. This is an extension of the register pointers which we have been considering, and also a part of his achievement in using regional speech to build up the country of the mind which he calls 'Wessex'. One feature of speech in the nineteenth-century novel is the use of dialect to do more than create passing local reference or to increase the comicality of minor characters. Scott had shown the way; Gaskell and Eliot had carried it into the new style of the novel. Neither has such an acute ear as Hardy for the subtleties of the rural hierarchy, to which he had become sensitive in his childhood, poised between the 'workfolk' and the lower gentry of small farmers. There is surely an echo of his mother in Mrs Dewy's rebuke to her husband, 'talking about "taties" with Michael in such a work-folk way. Well, 'tis what I was never brought up to! With our family 'twas never less than "taters", and very often "pertatoes" outright' (*Under the Greenwood Tree*, Pt First, Ch. 8).

Hardy used dialect to good effect, partly from personal experience and partly through his respect for its antiquity. He never forgot what he learned from Barnes, in whose obituary he wrote:

> In the systematic study of his native dialect ... he has shown the world that far from being, as popularly supposed, a corruption of correct English, it is a distinct branch of Teutonic speech, regular in declension and conjugation, and richer in many classes of words than any other tongue known to him.[4]

Later, in a preface to Barnes's poems, he described the Dorset dialect as 'a tongue, and not a corruption'. With this understanding, he was able to show in his representations of dialect that it could express not only the semantic needs of the community that used it, but also the pragmatic, that is to say, the effect on an utterance of its whole context, personal and social. This is true of all languages and language varieties but its importance is often overlooked. Hardy's dialect shows far more than the locality of its speakers. Nor, unlike Barnes, was he trying to come close to a phonemic transcription of

Dorset speech. He seldom uses such devices, puzzling to the reader, as diaereses and doubled vowels. How closely Hardy reproduces the auditory experience of listening to dialect is a separate matter, and an interesting one. The present concern is with the way in which dialect adds to the strength of his fiction.

During his lifetime, the tendency to uniformity of language was steadily increasing. There was as yet little erosion of dialect speech itself, but better communications, and in the later part of the century general state education, were making people aware of standard English not only as a written but also as a spoken realisation. Hardy makes use of contacts, and sometimes tensions, between different varieties of English. His comment on Tess is well known, and exemplifies what is linguistically known as *diglossia*: the coexistence of two varieties of language within a speech community, each having its own functional range:

> Mrs Durbeyfield habitually spoke the dialect; her daughter, who had passed the Sixth Standard in the National School under a London-trained mistress, spoke two languages; the dialect at home, more or less; ordinary English abroad and to persons of quality.   (Ch. 3)

Those who could not switch codes so easily could get into difficulties in an unfamiliar social situation, lexically or phonically. Gwendoline Chickerel is unable to obtain *chippols* in London, and her more sophisticated sister has to explain, 'they call them young onions here' (*The Hand of Ethelberta*, Ch. 23).[5] The church choir in *Two on a Tower* are a trial to their educated incumbent when they sing:

> 'The Lard looked down vrom Heav'n's high tower!'
> 'Ah, that's where we are so defective – the pronunciation,' interrupted the parson. 'Now repeat after me: "The Lord look'd down from Heav'n's high tower."' The choir repeated like an exaggerative echo: 'The Lawd look'd daown from Heav'n's high towah!'   (Ch. 2)

These are pleasant: and how long will some readers and critics fail to honour Hardy as a great humorous novelist as well as a tragic one? There is a more sombre comment on the tensions of Victorian upward mobility in Henchard's anger with Elizabeth-Jane:

'"Bide where you be",' he echoed sharply. 'Good God, are you
only fit to carry wash to a pig-trough, that ye use such words as
those?'
She reddened with shame and sadness.
'I meant, "Stay where you are," father', she said in a low, humble
voice. 'I ought to have been more careful.'

(The Mayor of Casterbridge, Ch. 20)

Henchard's own ambivalent social status is shown not only by his
violent objection to dialect but also by his use of *ye* in his rebuke.
A notable tragicomic instance of the transition from dialect to
standard appears in the poem 'The Ruined Maid':

> – 'At home in the barton you said "thee" and "thou",
> And "thik oon", and "theäs oon", and "t'other"; but now
> Your talking quite fits 'ee for high compa-ny!' –
> 'Some polish is gained with one's ruin,' said she.

The use of linguistic pointers as well as those of fashion and
outward appearance here is brilliant.

The spoken use of what was later to be called Received Standard
English, and eventually Received Pronunciation, is not confined by
Hardy to the formally educated or the newly affected. He uses
dialect pragmatically to show the differences in local status. In *The
Mayor of Casterbridge*, the richest of the novels in usage of dialect, the
magistrate Grower argues with Stubberd the constable. Now
Grower would certainly have sounded to a fashionable London ear
as a regional speaker, but his use of standard speech on the printed
page gives the required effect of his relative position and power to
command. Stubberd's helpless anxiety is emphasised by deviant
syntax, dialect lexis and malapropism – the literary mark of the local
constable ever since Shakespeare's Dogberry and Elbow.

> 'What can we two poor lammigers do against such a multi-
> tude!' expostulated Stubberd, in answer to Mr Grower's chiding.
> '"Tis tempting 'em to commit *felo de se* upon us, and that would
> be the death of the perpetrator; and we wouldn't be the cause of a
> fellow-creature's death on no account, not we!'
> 'Get some help, then! Here, I'll come with you. We'll see what a
> few words of authority can do.'   (Ch. 39)

Similar is the way in which Sue and Jude normally speak without trace of dialect while those around them, such as Mrs Edlin and the old shepherd in whose cottage they take refuge, are broad dialect speakers. The difference here will also owe something to the convention of Victorian fiction that major characters of intelligence and virtue speak better than their associates: Dickens's Oliver Twist and Lizzie Hexam are well-known examples. Gabriel Oak, in the Malthouse conversation from which I quoted at the beginning, is more of a standard speaker than the rest, to a degree not to be explained simply by the fact of his slightly superior status as an independent shepherd. Dialect pointers are also dropped among those of equal status and importance when they talk intimately and informally together. Henchard's returned wife and supposed daughter domestically show little of the dialect by which Elizabeth-Jane later annoys him. Thomasin and Diggory Venn talk together in a different manner from the minor characters of Egdon Heath. Tess and the other milkmaids are similarly scarcely marked in their conversation.

Such a convention is useful not only when it is observed but also when it is deliberately broken. In the earlier, serial version of the novel, the use of dialect by Tess is said to be 'only when excited by joy, surprise, or grief'. This appears when she returns home after her marriage and exclaims to her mother, 'That's where my misery do lie! But I thought he could get rid o' me by law if he were determined not to overlook it' (Ch. 38). Stronger dialect often signals emotional upheaval; a point which can be considered psychologically sound as indicating reversion under pressure to the more basic instinct, but which is also highly effective in heightening dramatic tension. Gabriel Oak comes closer to peasant speech when he is vexed with Bathsheba, foregrounding their difference in status and also his agitated state of mind:

> If wild heat had to do wi' it, making ye long to overcome the awkwardness about your husband's vanishing, it mid be wrong; but a cold-hearted agreement to oblige a man seems different, somehow. The real sin, ma'am, in my mind, lies in thinking of ever wedding wi' a man you don't love honest and true.
>
> (*Far from the Madding Crowd*, Ch. 51)

To turn for a moment from Wessex to Scottish speech, Farfrae uses scarcely any regional forms after he has been established as a Scot on his first appearance. But even in private conversation with Lucetta, his later speech signals distress:

> I couldna sing to-night! It's Henchard – he hates me ... I would understand why there should be a wee bit envy; but I cannet see a reason for the whole intensity of what he feels. (*The Mayor of Casterbridge*, Ch. 34)

A sudden change from dialect can be immensely effective. There is a fine example in *The Mayor of Casterbridge* when Henchard as a magistrate is confronted by the furmity woman who had witnessed the sale of his wife. She is brought in as a vigorous dialect speaker, calling the constable 'old turmit-head', but when she starts to accuse Henchard she loses most of her non-standard speech features and takes on a more choric role, as an avenger from the past: 'A man and a woman with a little child came into my tent.... They sat down and had a basin apiece' (Ch. 28).

The furmity woman brings me to Hardy's third area of excellence in dialogue, and this is the speech of his minor characters. I would say that one of the tests of literary greatness in drama and fiction is the ability to sustain characterisation beyond the chief protagonists and to give individuality to those who appear less prominently. If their part in the action is significant and not merely a mechanical adjunct to the plot, we are brought more deeply into that sense of 'felt life' which Henry James said was an essential quality for the novel. We think of the masters in this respect: of the way in which Shakespeare brings a character to life in a few words. Macmorris the eternal Irishman rising to the bait – 'My nation? Who talks of my nation?' – or Justice Silence having drink taken – 'I am not so well as I might be, but I'll ne'er out.' Dickens has the same capacity, using the broader exaggeration of caricature, a word I use in no derogatory sense. One thinks of the clothes-dealer who frightens David Copperfield, 'Oh, my eyes and limbs – goroo! – don't ask for money', or Mr F's Aunt, 'He has a proud stomach this chap.... Give him a meal of chaff.'

Hardy at his best can stand in this company, though his method is different. He does not rely so much on the repeated phrase for identification, but he has his own way of making minor characters live through their words. The furmity woman is an example of a character, convincing in her own right, who takes on a choric function. There are several such in *Jude the Obscure*, mostly sinister figures who act as agents in Jude's increasing doom, but who are at the same time living their own lives without giving him much thought. There is Challow the pig-killer who arrives too late to prevent Jude's messy performance; his voice breaks into the action, 'Well done, young married volk! I couldn't have carried it out much better myself, cuss me if I could!' (Pt First, Ch. 10). His well-meaning words are bitterly ironical in the context of what 'married' means for the couple and for all the principal actors in the story, and he compounds the irony by going on to speak of 'the delicate state, too, that you be in at present, ma'am', a state which both Jude and Arabella know was a deception. The mixed company of drinkers at Christminster who incite Jude to say the Creed in Latin represent the classes he is trying to cross, from artisan to undergraduate. They can meet only in the temporary fellowship of a sordid tavern. The idiom of each group is brilliantly displayed in a few sentences as they press upon Jude. The mason 'Uncle Joe' says, 'If you are such a scholar as to pitch yer hopes so high as that, why not give us a specimen of your scholarship? Canst say the Creed in Latin, man? That was how they once put it to a chap down in my country.' One of the undergraduates repeats the challenge in the idiom of his class, 'The gentleman in the corner is going to rehearse the Articles of his Belief, in the Latin tongue, for the edification of the company' (Pt Second, Ch. 7).

Some choric minor characters are less intrusive and more sympathetic. Like a Greek chorus they comment on what has passed and relate it to the destiny of mankind. Mother Cuxsom, well established through her breathless, gossiping idiolect, rises to dignity when she speaks of the death of Susan Henchard: 'all her shining keys will be took from her, and her cupboards opened; and little things a' didn't wish seen, anybody will see; and her wishes and ways will all be as nothing!' (*The Mayor of Casterbridge*, Ch. 18). This is splendid, for the speaker maintains her non-standard pattern of speech with a new cadence and a closing alliteration which is elegiac but unforced. Robert Creedle in *The Woodlanders* is a broad dialect speaker and a figure of fun throughout the book; his relationship with his employer Giles Winterborne is intimate and continually fraught with exasperation at his mistakes. When Giles is dead, Creedle voices the universal sense of mortality, without any modification in his dialect speech or any word or thought that seems unconvincing for him: 'I've knowed him from table-high; I knowed his father – used to bide about upon two sticks in the sun afore he died! – and now I've seen the end of the family, which we can ill afford to lose, wi' such a scanty lot of good folk in Hintock as we've got. And now Robert Creedle will be nailed up in parish boards 'a b'lieve; and nobody will glutch down a sigh for he!' (Ch. 43).

The term 'rustic chorus' has been applied to scenes in Hardy when a number of such minor rural characters come together and comment on the affairs of their village and of the world in general. There is the company in Warren's Malthouse, with which we began, the dispossessed church choir in *Under the Greenwood Tree* and those who gather to light the fire on Egdon Heath in *The Return of the Native*. It would take too long to recall these extended conversations, but the careful reader will easily see how the speakers are differentiated by phraseology and cadence. One feature that can be noticed is the warmth and kindness which a simple character will sometimes verbalise. The sentiment may be commonplace or even verging on the comic, but there are characters whose speech is the opposite of the cynical and damaging choric type. Hardy, having exacted a good look at the worst, continually reminds us through dialogue that there is a way to the better. There is basic human goodness – I am not embarrassed to use the phrase in this cynical age – when Jacob offers Gabriel some bread and bacon with the warning, 'Don't ye chaw quite close, shepherd, for I let the bacon fall in the road outside as I was bringing it along, and may be 'tis rather gritty. There, 'tis clane dirt; and we all know what that is, as you say' (*Far from the Madding Crowd*, Ch. 8). In the story 'The Three Strangers' when the shepherd Fennel's wife protests to him about the amount the unknown man is drinking, he replies in the Wessex idiom but in the voice of the hospitality of the poor through all history: 'He's in the house, my honey; and 'tis a wet night, and a christening. Daze it, what's a cup of mead more or less? There'll be plenty more next bee-burning.' The universal human voice may be heard also from Captain Jacobs in *Desperate Remedies* persuading a passenger that the paddle-steamer should wait for the hurrying man believed to be Cytherea's brother. He is an unwitting agent in the unfolding story, for the man proves to be not her brother but Springrove, but he is also the voice of human empathy and compassion, though his speech is rough and non-standard: 'Suppose, now, you were a young woman, as might be, and had a brother, like this one, and you stood of an evening upon this here wild lonely shore, like her, why you'd want us to wait too, wouldn't you, sir? I think you would' (Ch. 2, pt 4). There are moments like this in Hardy which it is not excessive to call Shakespearean.

Finally, I want to draw attention to some of the women's voices in Hardy. There has been a good deal of feminist criticism of his work in recent years, some of it very illuminating. I do not intend to embark on this controversial area but only to suggest that Hardy is outstanding among male Victorian novelists in rendering the speech of women. It is not easy to detect specifically feminine characteristics in fictional dialogue of the time, apart from matters of content. There is more talk of domestic affairs, of the family, of love and marriage. There is an interesting preoccupation with the masculine woman, sometimes sympathetic like Marian in *The Woman in White*, often comic or disagreeable like Sally Brass in *The Old Curiosity Shop*. Such woman are characterised by using more abrupt and aggressive speech, with a higher incidence of slang and familiar forms of address. Their presence says something about the insights and anxieties of the male authors who created them.

Hardy shows a different sensitivity to the tensions of his time. Many of his leading women are self-divided. They are more intelligent, perhaps more educated, than most of the men around them; they have strong wills, sometimes devious in getting their own way. At the same time they lack ultimate confidence, because society does not give it to them. They are vacillating, uncertain of their emotion, easily swayed by the man who can match them in cunning or intelligence. 'Tremulous' is a word which Hardy often applies to their voices and manner: Tess tells Angel Clare that 'There are very few women's lives that are not – tremulous' (Ch. 29). Such in their different ways are Fancy Day, Eustacia, Lady Constantine, Paula Power, Lucetta, Grace Melbury, and above all Sue Bridehead. We might add Bathsheba and Tess, less formally educated though they are; Tess suffers from not being devious or ruthless enough until events force her into her final tragedy. Only in Hardy's last published novel do these characteristics move to the male side with the lifelong indeterminacy of Pierston.

Sue Bridehead voices the direct protest which was becoming more forceful by the end of the century. Her position as a 'New Woman' asserting feminine rights has often been noticed. Hardy wonderfully verbalises her feelings, the bold claims which have a faltering tongue because the time for them has not yet fully come, her reticence in speaking about sex and the half-apology for her boldness. She is arguing with Phillotson after she has fled from their bedroom:

> 'What is the use of thinking of laws and ordinances,' she burst
> out, 'if they make you miserable when you know you are commit-
> ting no sin?'
>   'But you are committing a sin in not liking me.'
>   'I *do* like you! But I didn't reflect it would be – that it would be
> so much more than that…. For a man and woman to live on inti-
> mate terms when one feels as I do is adultery, in any circum-
> stances, however legal. There – I've said it! … Will you let me,
> Richard?'   (*Jude the Obscure*, Pt Fourth, Ch. 3)

This has the ring of truth, while it also expresses the dilemma that
would seem portentous if it were stated objectively in narrative.

Wives who are emotionally in tension with their husbands
generally have less sense than Sue of universal principles but no less
poignancy. Hardy forms their speech so that their real grievances
and distress are mingled with the fear of finally alienating their
husbands; the weakness of their condition continually subverts the
strength of their personalities. For example, we have Bathsheba and
Troy:

> 'Can you jest when I am so wretchedly in earnest? Tell me the
> truth, Frank. I am not a fool, you know, although I am a woman,
> and have my woman's moments. Come! treat me fairly,' she said,
> looking honestly and fearlessly into his face. 'I don't want much;
> bare justice – that's all! Ah! once I felt I could be content with
> nothing less than the highest homage from the husband I should
> choose. Now, anything short of cruelty will content me.'
>   (*Far from the Madding Crowd*, Ch. 41)

I do not think that any other male novelist of the last century can
surpass this; few of them looked so deeply into the marriage
relationship. Sometimes the woman's voice is more acquiescent and
resigned, the tones of those who can fight no longer against the way
things are. Tess accepts her dismissal:

> I don't complain, Angel. I – I think it best. What you said has quite
> convinced me. Yes, though nobody else should reproach me if we
> should stay together, yet somewhen, years hence, you might get
> angry with me for any ordinary matter, and knowing what you

do of my bygones you yourself might be tempted to say words, and they might be overheard, perhaps by my own children. O, what only hurts now would torture and kill me then! I will go – to-morrow.   (Ch. 36)

This pathetic tone is one that Hardy catches throughout his fiction. It is often heard in his poetry too, where the constraints of verse form do not destroy the sense of spoken words. It appears in 'The Going of the Battery':

> O it was sad enough, weak enough, mad enough –
> Light in their loving as soldiers can be –
> First to risk choosing them, leave alone losing them
> Now, in far battle, beyond the South Sea! ...

and in the voice of the mother who narrates 'A Sunday Morning Tragedy':

> No voice replied. I went within –
> O women! scourged the worst are we...
> I shrieked. The others hastened in
> And saw the stroke there dealt on me.

Of course, not all Hardy's women are tremulous and resigned. He can also create the peremptory voice of those who are determined to be obeyed. It is heard through the whole range of his novels, from Mrs Dewy to Arabella, whose colloquial tone when she is scheming to get Jude to remarry her contains the deadly efficiency of a Medea or Lady Macbeth:

We must keep plenty of good liquor going in the house these next few days. I know his nature, and if he once gets into that fearfully low state that he does get into sometimes, he'll never do the honourable thing by me in this world, and I shall be left in the lurch. He must be kept cheerful. He has a little money in the savings-bank, and he has given me his purse to pay for anything necessary. Well, that will be the license; for I must have that ready at hand, to catch him the moment he's in the humour.

(*Jude the Obscure*, Pt Sixth, Ch. 7)

Men have heard women speaking in their company; they have

not been able to listen to women talking alone together. Hardy gives us many such opportunities of eavesdropping, when character emerges through speech. Ethelberta is talking with her sister Picotee; the difference between them is made more clear in dialogue than by any description. Ethelberta, the widow drawn into sophisticated society by circumstance and ambition, has the modulated sentences and figures of speech which befit her role as a professional storyteller. Picotee knows little of the world and feels the uncertainty of first love. Ethelberta speaks first:

> 'Love from a stranger is mostly worthless as a speculation; and it is certainly dangerous as a game. Well, Picotee, has any one paid you any real attentions yet?'
> 'No – that is – '
> 'There is something going on.'
> 'Only a wee bit.'
> 'I thought so. There was a dishonesty about your dear eyes which has never been there before, and love-making and dishonesty are inseparable as coupled hounds. Up comes man, and away goes innocence. Are you going to tell me anything about him?'
> 'I would rather not, Ethelberta; because it is hardly anything.'
> 'Well be careful. And mind this, never tell him what you feel.'
> 'But then he will never know it.'
> 'Nor must he. He must think it only. The difference between his thinking and knowing is often the difference between your winning and losing.'   (*The Hand of Ethelberta*, Ch. 6)

I have said that Hardy more perhaps than any novelist defies claims that fictional character in the traditional sense is no longer a viable concept. We are not being naively lacking in critical sense or respect for the self-containment of the text when we admit that we associate his people with specific places, and that the voices of his Wessex do not always fade back into the printed page when we close the book. It is not only of the few names in the poem 'Voices from Things Growing in a Churchyard' of whom we may feel:

> – And so these maskers breathe to each
> > Sir or Madam
> Who lingers there, and their lively speech
> Affords an interpreter much to teach,

As their murmurous accents seem to come
Thence hitheraround in a radiant hum,
    All day cheerily,
    All night eerily!

Notes

1. The review appeared in the *Athenaeum*, 23 November 1878; Hardy's
    reply was in the next number, 30 November 1878. The former is
    reprinted in R. G. Cox (ed.), *Thomas Hardy: The Critical Heritage*
    (London: Routledge, 1970) pp. 46–7, and the latter in H. Orel (ed.),
    Thomas Hardy's Personal Writings (London: Macmillan, 1967) p. 91.
2. *Academy*, 1875, vii; *Saturday Review*, 1886, lxi; *Contemporary Review*,
    1889, lvi; *Cosmopolis*, 1896, i. All are reprinted in Cox, *Critical Heritage*.
3. Quotations from Hardy's novels are taken from the New Wessex Edi-
    tion, published by Macmillan, London in 1974–5. Chapter references
    are given in parenthesis following quotations.
4. The obituary appeared in the *Athenaeum*, 16 October 1886; it is
    reprinted in *Personal Writings*.
5. The linguistic interest of this dialect word is discussed by Desmond
    Hawkins, 'Knowing One's Onions', *Thomas Hardy Journal* vi, 1; further
    note by Raymond Chapman, ibid., vi, 2.

8

'A Bewildered Child and his Conjurors': Hardy and the Ideas of his Time

TIMOTHY HANDS

'I have no philosophy', Hardy recorded in the *Life*, '... merely what I have often explained to be only a confused heap of impressions, like those of a bewildered child at a conjuring show'.[1] Few critics have believed Hardy – it has of course been academically convenient not to. But then Hardy himself could on other occasions be specific and informative about the influences on him. 'My pages', he confessed to Ernest Brennecke in June 1924, 'show harmony of view with Darwin, Huxley, Spencer, Comte, Hume, Mill, and others (all of whom, as a matter of fact, I used to read more than Sch[openhauer].'[2] These contrasting quotations, the one deflective and denying, the other informative and analytical, epitomise Hardy's bifurcated approach to the ideas of his time. He is knowing and unknowing, simultaneously intellectual and instinctive, derivative and original. This paper hopes ultimately to get at the first trait of mind by way of an analysis of the second, with particular reference to the writers Hardy mentioned above. A tailor-made phrenology provides as five headings for this analysis the religious, the scientific, the free-thinking, the pessimist, and the meliorist.

'Religion is the great business of life, I sometimes begin to think the only business,' remarks a character in *Lothair*, Disraeli's *roman-à-clef* of 1870 in which a namesake and close relation of the vicar of Stinsford appears.[3] The Victorians were determined to Christianise the nation. But, split as they were into deep divisions of dissenting versus established churches, and, within the latter, factions of High, Broad, and Low, they were bitterly divided about how to approach

137

the task. 'There never was a time in England in which there was more of religious controversy than at present', R. S. Smith, father of Hardy's friend Reginald Bosworth Smith, and vicar of the parish neighbouring Stinsford, pronounced.[4] Hardly anywhere could this controversy be avoided. In Westminster Abbey, at Palmerston's funeral service, which Hardy attended on 27 October 1865, all looked impressive and serene: 'I think I was never so much impressed with a ceremony in my life before,' Hardy wrote to his sister Mary.[5] But only the year before, Pusey, on behalf of the High Church faction, had written to A. P. Stanley, the Broad Church Dean of Westminster whom Hardy saw in charge of this service, in highly inhospitable tones: 'I believe the present to be a struggle for the life or death of the English church, and what you believe to be for life I believe to be for death; and you think the same reciprocally of me.'[6] Palmerston might have relished the set-to.

Hardy's religious life reflected the divided nature of his times, as indeed of his native county. For though nineteenth-century Dorset was one of the most Evangelical regions in the country, Stinsford was an isolated stronghold of remarkably advanced High Church practice, presided over by a vicar, Arthur Shirley, who had been at Oxford in the formative years of the High Church Tractarian movement. Much has been made of the symbolic significance of Matthew Arnold's baptism, with his father, champion of the Broad Church, standing beside his friend John Keble, chosen as godparent despite his High Church antipathy to Arnold's liberal views. Hardy's baptism contains a symbolism no less potent, both in social and religious terms. Initiated into the Church by a great believer in that Church's authority, Hardy was given the name of the Christian religion's archetypal exponent of doubt. The tension was always to remain with him.

That Hardy was for many years an earnest Christian has never been doubted. He himself recorded that he was 'churchy; not in an intellectual sense, but in so far as instincts and emotions ruled. As a child, to be a parson had been his dream.... He himself had frequently read the church-lessons, and had at one time as a young man begun reading for Cambridge with a view to taking Orders.'[7] Though nothing more has proved discoverable about Hardy's ordination plans, it is possible from various sources to ascertain more of his religious sympathies, in particular of his troubled involvement with the Baptists through his fellow apprentice Bastow, and of what seems to have been an Evangelical conversion experience. The latter, datable from a Bible marking to 'Wednesday night April 17th/61, $\frac{1}{4}$ to 11', appears to have been brought about by Hardy's contacts with the Moule family, and with a nationwide Revival of remarkable potency which affected Dorchester in the early 1860s – according to the Archbishop of Canterbury of the day, nothing since the Day of Pentecost could justifiably be compared to it.

The twin pulls of Stinsford and Dorchester, High Church and Low, are remarkable for their apparent simultaneity, and produce a distinctive effect. They explain how Hardy could, paradoxically, find a sense of isolation or individuality by identification with communal values, and arrive at well-informed catholicity by the experience of contrary ideological extremes. In the poems these effects find a remarkably powerful literary expression, in such much-anthologised pieces as 'The Oxen', 'A Sign-Seeker', 'The Impercipient', 'Afternoon Service at Mellstock' and 'The Darkling Thrush', the latter a kind of parody of a poem Hardy noted in his copy of Keble's *The Christian Year*. Such poems derive their effect not only from their stark contrasts of faith and doubt, tradition and innovation, individual and community, but also, more particularly, from the poignant and understated balance with which such opposites are retained in a closely felt and understood perspective. It was not only about Emma and her rivals that Hardy could write so effectively from the heart.

In the novels the religious effects are simultaneously easier and more difficult to analyse. On a literal level, it has long been realised that incidents from Hardy's religious youth provide a quarry for incidents in the novels – Shirley's superannuation of the Stinsford choir for *Under the Greenwood Tree*, for example, and the dispute over paedobaptism with Bastow for the opening of *A Laodicean*. But much less emphasis has been placed on the way in which Hardy's religious understanding influences the characterisation of his novels. 'Who will deny', Walter Pater questioned in a famous review of 1888, 'that to trace the influence of religion upon human character is one of the legitimate functions of the novel?',[8] and Chapter 3 of my *Thomas Hardy: Distracted Preacher?* explores the way in which religious stereotypes help shape a character typology for Hardy's fiction. More strikingly, in the final novels, Hardy's religious experiences seem at times to be providing the animus for his writing, *Tess* providing an exorcism of his Evangelical, as *Jude* of his Tractarian past. *Tess* reads like a parody of the Evangelical tract, in particular the most famous of them, Legh Richmond's *The Dairyman's Daughter*, sales of which reached two million. A pure minded country girl of humble origins, Tess's initial character and circumstances have much in common with those of Richmond's Betsy; but, whereas Betsy is saved by her chance encounter with a preacher, an itinerant clergyman who 'held strange notions',[9] Tess is corrupted rather than redeemed by her contacts with the outside world. A parody of the Evangelical cautionary tale, Tess depicts not a young girl saved by Evangelicalism, but a heroine destroyed by exponents of it. Likewise Jude apes the High Church Alter Christus tradition, in which the believer becomes gradually more like Christ, as St Francis had. 'Yes, Christminster shall be my Alma Mater; and I'll be her beloved son, in whom she shall be well pleased', Jude announces (Pt I, Ch. vi). But this modern day Jerusalem offers only rejection. Christ and minster ironically cannot be linked at this location.

Almost as influential perhaps on Hardy's cast of mind as religious matters was scientific thought and advance. In Beatrice Webb's opinion 'The belief in science and the scientific method ... was certainly the most salient element of the mid-Victorian Time-Spirit'.[10] Hardy's contact with the scientific thought of the nineteenth century, by which is meant principally geological and more particularly evolutionary studies, was of course non-specialised, but so too in a way were those studies themselves, modern works of science being then, as they are not now, generally accessible to the general reader. The two principal men of the scientific movement were, for Hardy, Darwin and Huxley, the one formidable as an amasser and original interpreter of evidence, and the other a lecturer and polemicist of exceptional ability.

Scientific advance has a threefold effect on Hardy. Gone for the Victorians was the easy-minded if precisely calculated theorem of Bishop Lightfoot that Man was created by the Trinity on 23 October, 4004 BC, at nine o'clock in the morning. Victorian chronological perspectives were lengthier. According to Darwin, in Chapter ix of *The Origin of Species*, Sir Charles Lyell (1797–1875), was the scientist who brought about this 'revolution in natural science', Lyell's *Principles of Geology* stressing 'how incomprehensibly vast have been the past periods of time'.[11] In this, as in another respect, Hardy could not have lived at a more fortunate time. For the discoveries of science were happily at one with his own temperament, eager as it was to remind the infinitesimal of its larger context, and encouraged by the reading of formative years (not to mention interest in the fossil-chipping activities of the Dorset Natural History and Antiquarian Field Club and all Roman-searching spadework in the Max Gate shrubbery) to stress a sense of perspective. 'If it be possible to compress into a sentence all that a man learns between 20 & 40,' the *Life* reports, 'it is that all things merge in one another – good into evil ... the year into the ages, the world into the universe. With this in view the evolution of species seems but a minute process in the same movement.'[12] Novels and poems are accordingly, from the earliest, full of such contexts: the 'roll of the world eastward' as seen from that 'shape approaching the indestructible' Norcombe Hill in Chapter 2 of *Far from the Madding Crowd*, and the confrontation of Knight and the trilobite in the cliff scene of *A Pair of Blue Eyes*. Egdon, at the middle of the Wessex topography, occupies a similar centrality in terms of the fusion it provides for the author's chosen specialities: local knowledge, temperamental colouring and scientific background. The heath's vegetation seemed to belong to 'the ancient world of the carboniferous period', and even the landscape's 'trifling irregularities were not caused by pickaxe, plough, or spade, but remained as the very finger-touches of the last geological change'. All these things, the narrator tells us, 'gave ballast to the mind adrift on change, and harassed by the irrepressible New' (Bk I, Ch. 1).

Secondly, scientific discoveries radically altered human perception of the ethos of the natural world. William Paley, in his *Natural Theology* of 1803, a textbook for Tennyson at Cambridge, and indeed one well into the twentieth century, ended an account of a country walk with the conclusion that 'It is a happy world after all. The air, the earth, the water, teem with delighted existence. In a spring noon or a summer evening, on whichever side I turn my eyes, myriads of happy beings crowd my view'.[13] Darwin's world picture was a different one. 'We behold the face of nature bright with gladness,' he remarks in *The Origin of Species*, but 'We forget that the birds which are idly singing round us mostly live on insects or seeds, and are thus constantly destroying life; or we forget how largely these songsters, or their eggs, or their nestlings, are destroyed by birds and beasts of prey.'[14] Again this aspect of scientific change accorded with Hardy's temperamental disposition, the Anglo-Saxon gloominess of his natural demeanour. Arthur Symons, with typical

poetic insight, justly remarked that Hardy was a writer who was
'sorry for Nature, who feels the earth and the roots, as if he has sap
in his veins instead of blood, and could get closer than any other
man to the things of the Earth'.[15] With such very early memories as
the half frozen fieldfare, starved and then stoned, still vividly recall-
able in his last year,[16] it came easily to Hardy to see life in Darwinian terms as a struggle for survival, and novels and poems are
packed pat with such Darwinian perspectives. 'In a Wood'
miniaturises the canvas of *The Woodlanders* as

> Great growths and small
> Show them to men akin –
> Combatants all!
> Sycamore shoulders oak,
> Bines the slim sapling yoke,
> Ivy-spun halters choke
> Elms stout and tall.

By the time of *Jude* the idea of the struggle for survival, of the extent
to which the fittest are prepared to survive at the expense of the
defenceless, has become a guiding structural principle. As though
contributing to some operatic quartet, each of the principal characters is in turn provided with a soundbite on the subject. 'Cruelty is
the law pervading all nature and society', Phillotson remarks with
schoolmasterly fervour and preciseness (Pt v, Ch. VIII). 'Why should
Nature's law be mutual butchery?' Sue expostulates after the sale of
her two pet pigeons 'all alive and plump' (Pt v, Ch. VI). For the
young Jude, employment as a bird scarer is an unwelcome education in the gap between the welfare of God's birds and the welfare of
God's gardener: 'Nature's logic was too horrid for him to care for'
(Pt I, Ch. II). But this is merely the matriculation ceremony in Jude's
education: graduation by pig-killing awaits him.

   Lastly, scientific advance had a considerable effect on the Victorians' tenuous grip on their belief in God. For Paley and his
eighteenth-century ilk the study of nature invariably involved a
greater respect for and understanding of God. Even Gideon
Algernon Mantell's *Wonders of Geology* (1838), leant to Hardy by his
friend Horace Moule after its appearance in the Moule household
had scandalised Moule's clergyman father and suggested the arrival
of the free-thinking volume in Chapter 18 of *Tess*, tamely declared
that 'every physical phenomenon which has taken place from first

to last has emanated from the will of the deity'.[17] Only three-quarters of a century later, Hardy's friend Edward Clodd, chronicling recent scientific developments in his *Pioneers of Evolution* (1902) would reach exactly the opposite conclusion: 'There is no possible reconciliation between Evolution and Theology', he felt able to conclude.[18] This change, of course, affected Hardy, but it was far from having a great effect upon him. It challenged his beliefs far less, for example, than did the group of thinkers to be dealt with next.

Free-thinkers are the third kind of magician present at Hardy's figurative conjuring show. The label is loose but the cast of mind distinctive. According to Hastings's *Encyclopaedia of Religion and Ethics*, a copy of which Hardy owned, nineteenth-century philosophy, like nineteenth-century politics and the nineteenth-century novel, distinguishes itself by a concern with the concept of political and social freedom, the right of the individual to develop and discover his own identity unhindered. Thus John Stuart Mill was for Hardy 'one of the profoundest thinkers of the last century' and *On Liberty* one of Hardy's most treasured texts – on 1 July 1868 he specified the 'Individuality' section in the book as one of his three 'cures for despair'.[19]

Hardy's free-thinkers are to be identified not only by this concern with the rights and distinctiveness of the individual but also by the courage with which they challenge all aspects of the ideological status quo. To quote a phrase from a passage of Matthew Arnold's 'Heine' much studied by Hardy, they are 'Dissolvents of the old European system of dominant ideas'.[20] Their cast of mind was empirical, questioning, agnostic, with all the implications of that word employed by its coiner T. H. Huxley:

Agnosticism, in fact, is not a creed, but a method, the essence of which lies in the rigorous application of a single principle. That principle is of great antiquity; it is as old as Socrates; as old as the writer who said, 'Try all things; hold fast by that which is good;' it is the foundation of the Reformation, which simply illustrated the axiom that every man should be able to give a reason for the faith that is in him; it is the great principle of Descartes; it is the fundamental axiom of modern science. Positively the principle may

be expressed: In matters of the intellect follow your reason as far
as it will take you, without regard to any other consideration. And
negatively: In matters of the intellect do not pretend that matters
are certain which are not demonstrated or demonstrable.[21]

The free-thinkers influenced Hardy's ideas, and especially his religious and philosophical ideas, in a number of ways. First, they were,
as regards Christianity, iconoclastic. Leslie Stephen can perhaps be
taken as the chief influence here – Hardy described Stephen as the
man 'whose philosophy was to influence his own for many years,
indeed, more than that of any other contemporary'.[22] Hardy's poem
'The Schreckhorn' likens Stephen to that Alpine peak 'in its quaint
glooms, keen lights, and rugged trim'. Perhaps more concretely
informative are Stephen's *Essays on Free Thinking and Plain Speaking*
(1873) and *Agnostic's Apology* (1876) both from the period when
Hardy was associated with him as editor. 'The one duty which at the
present moment seems to be of paramount importance, is the duty of
perfect intellectual sincerity', Stephen declares in the first of the
Essays.[23] That duty involves a renunciation of orthodox Christianity,
and a resulting pleasure in new-found intellectual freedom: 'Let us
think freely and speak plainly, and we shall have the highest satis-
faction that man can enjoy.'[24] For Stephen the loss of orthodox views
was not so much 'an abandonment of beliefs seriously held and
firmly implanted in the mind, but a gradual recognition of the truth
that you never really held them'. He perhaps encouraged Hardy to
feel the same when, rather startlingly, he invited him to witness his
renunciation of Holy Orders on 23 March 1875.

Hardy's free-thinkers replaced orthodox Christianity with agnosticism. We commonly misunderstand agnosticism today as something passive and unaffirming, whereas for the Victorian it had a
more positive and militant quality. Certainty and not doubt was the
hallmark of many Victorian agnostics. As we have seen, for Huxley
agnosticism was 'the rigorous application of a single principle': 'In
matters of the intellect do not pretend that conclusions are certain
which are not demonstrated or demonstrable.' If Huxley was an
agnostic, Hardy might more aptly and literally be described as a
'not-knower': it is indeed significant that Hardy struck out the draft
title 'The Agnostic' for one of his most famous religious poems, and
replaced it with 'The Impercipient'. For there is nothing organised
about Hardy's not-knowing as there is about Huxley's agnosticism.
Huxley felt certain about what he could believe, but Hardy experi-

enced no certainty at all. Commanding a lucid intellect and a scientist's habit of marshalling his ideas, Huxley was able to set clearly defined limits to his beliefs and doubts. Hardy, more artist than thinker, could not. Where there were no limits to his possible beliefs, there were equally no limits to his doubts. Although there were few things which he could not believe, there were likewise few things that he could.

A crucial influence on Hardy here may well have been Herbert Spencer. Long before Spencer's death, let alone Hardy's, Spencer had become an unfashionable and much ridiculed figure, 'the most immeasurable ass in Christendom', as Carlyle proclaimed him.[25] Biographically, however, Spencer and Hardy had much in common: an underprivileged background leading to radical sympathies, a technical training, and an autodidacticism leading to varying degrees of literalness of mind. Thus Hardy faithfully remained Spencer's champion, referring to Spencer's much discredited *First Principles* (in much the way that he referred to Mill's *On Liberty*) as 'a book which acts, or used to act, upon me as a sort of patent expander when I had been particularly narrowed down by the events of life'.[26] An aspect of *First Principles* that particularly appealed to Hardy seems significantly to have been its concept of 'the Unknowable', a profound yet unexplainable mystery at the back of the universe, from which all things proceed. Hardy was upset by attempts to discredit the idea: 'I am utterly bewildered to understand how the doctrine that, beyond the knowable, there must always be an unknown, can be displaced', he complained.[27]

And this significant difference from the free-thinkers with regard to agnosticism entails a further significant difference from them with regard to the miraculous and supernatural. Miracles were a totem to the Victorian controversialists. 'Miracle is to our time what the law was to the early Christians', the hero of Mary Augusta Ward's bestselling novel *Robert Elsmere* remarks: 'We *must* make up our minds about it one way or the other.'[28] But make up their minds about it the Victorians corporately – or indeed individually – could not. On the one hand the author's uncle Matthew Arnold could declare in italic in *Literature and Dogma*, that '*miracles do not happen*', yet on the other Hardy could find him guilty (in a triumph of mixed metaphor) of balancing dogma on its feet by hair-splitting.[29]

Here the significance of Hume, the only eighteenth-century figure on Hardy's list, becomes apparent. For Hardy seems to have valued Hume not as an empiricist philosopher *per se*, but rather for a small

part of his philosophical discourse, his scepticism about the miraculous. As Hardy's poem 'Drinking Song' puts it

> Then rose one Hume, who could not see ...
>   Required were much
> To prove no miracles could be:
>   'Better believe
>   The eyes deceive
> Than that God's clockwork jolts,' said he.

The source is 'Of Miracles' in Hume's *Inquiry Concerning Human
Understanding*, which later goes on to assert that 'no testimony for
any kind of miracle has ever amounted to a probability, much less to
a proof'.[30] But for all that Hardy may have revered Hume's sceptical
intellect, the attitude was not one that he slavishly followed.
Hardy's imagination is heavily reliant on the interference of the
supernatural, whether it be through portentous coincidence or
disconcerting appearance. 'I am most anxious', Hardy once told
William Archer, 'to believe in what, roughly speaking, we may call
the supernatural – but I find no evidence for it!' He would willingly
give ten years of his life to see a ghost, he remarked, but then
eighteen years later claimed actually to have observed one, an
eighteenth-century-clad gent fond of Stinsford church and in favour
of a green Christmas.[31] 'When a man falls he lies', 'A Sign-Seeker'
regrets; yet at the same time Hardy's poetry peoples villages, towns,
houses, cliff-tops, and, for preference, churchyards with multitudes
of the still-speaking dead. There are, indeed, at least nine of them
murmuring mildly throughout 'Friends Beyond'. 'How long halt ye
between two opinions?' Hardy had pencilled in his 1861 Bible. But
for Hardy the final choice between Humean scepticism and human
gullibility always remained avoidable.

Hardy's free-thinkers also encouraged him to see the Christian
religion as but one amongst many religions, and far from necessarily pre-eminent amongst them. More than any other factor
anxiety about the Christian religion's claims about its own
exclusiveness seem to have been responsible for Hardy's doubt
Hardy's markings in his religious books, so informative about the
shades of his belief, appear at first remarkably unforthcoming about
the reasons for his doubt. *At first*, that is, because in fact a marking
that relates with remarkable particularity to the onset of Hardy's
doubts was later erased by him with such zeal that much of the

paper surface has been removed, and only forgery detection techniques have been able to reclaim the original marking. This is a single word, 'doubt', and a date, 11 September 1864, against an otherwise still extant marking of Isaiah 45:5.

This text, with its exclusive claim that 'I am the Lord, and there is none else, there is no God beside me' appears much to have troubled Hardy, and with good reason. According to Stephen in the *Agnostic's Apology*, 'the one thing certain is, that all creeds have perished'.[32] Everywhere in the free-thinking writers, as well as very prominently in the poetry of his revered Swinburne, Hardy could observe attempts to place Christianity and other religions, especially Hellenic ones, side by side, and to indulge in comparative evaluation. '"Pagan self-assertion" is one of the elements of human worth, as well as "Christian self-denial"', Mill's *On Liberty* declared, in a passage which Hardy marked in his copy of the text.[33] Hardy's writings follow suit, and with increasing virulence. The barn scene in Chapter 22 of *Far from the Madding Crowd* deliberately develops a correspondence between Weatherbury's church and its barn, thus emphasising a natural religion which rivals the traditions of ecclesiastical Christianity. The barn expresses not a 'worn-out religious creed' which is 'founded on a mistake' but practices which have suffered 'no mutilation at the hands of time'. Not surprisingly, the editing Leslie Stephen found the scene 'excellent'.[34] Later novels, emboldened, employ a contrast between Hebraic and Hellenic religion as a founding structural and ideological principle. Thus Clym's repressive Hebraism triumphs over the more joyful Hellenism of Eustacia; Angel has 'been so unlucky as to say to his father, in a moment of irritation, that it might have resulted far better for mankind if Greece had been the source of the religion of modern civilization, and not Palestine' (*Tess*, Ch. 25), and *Jude* constantly reverts to struggles between Christian self-denial and pagan self-assertion, not least in the scene where Sue reveres her pagan statuary to the accompaniment of readings from Swinburne and others.

On Egdon pagan impulses seem 'in some way or other [to have] survived mediaeval doctrine' (*Return of the Native*, Bk VI, Ch. 1), whilst in *The Woodlanders* we are reminded of Marty South's 'ancestral goddess' Sif, and of the 'ante-mundane Ginnung-Gap believed in by her Teuton forefathers' (Ch. 3). As Hardy's sense of Wessex develops, so does his sense that it might possibly be a region somehow miraculously as yet untouched by the emissaries of Augustine.

Having dealt with the twin oppositions of faith and doubt, it is necessary to turn to the inevitable opposition of pessimism and optimism, or meliorism, as it is probably better to call it. *The Times* for 12 January 1928 had no doubt in acclaiming Hardy as 'the greatest writer of his time'. It was equally clear about the character and antecedents of his philosophy:

> His philosophy, no abstract or *dilettante* theorizing, but an energetic conviction permeating his work from first to last, was too stern and melancholy to arouse flippant applause. He had embraced with sad-eyed acquiescence the metaphysical doctrine of SCHOPENHAUER and VON HARTMANN, that the life of man is the product and the wind-driven derelict of a blind Will, immanent in the Universe, but careless, because unconscious, of human happiness or human progress. It is a form of pessimism less than any other likely to tempt the cheerful genius of these islanders... . HARDY nevertheless succeeded, not in converting many to his view of life, but in extorting respect for his interpretation of it, and he succeeded by virtue of a personal quality in himself, remote from cynicism or pedantry.

Accuracy and inaccuracy are both usefully prominent here. That Hardy had a single philosophy permeating his work from first to last, and that this philosophy was almost imitatively derived from pessimistic German sources, are assertions which nowadays command little support. Quite apart from Hardy's own disclaimers on the subject, of which we may properly be wary, there is the simple fact that Hardy knew little German, that an English translation of Schopenhauer's *World as Will and Idea* was not published until 1883, and that Hardy's notes on this German pessimistic school date from the late 1880s and early 1890s by which time his career as a novelist was all but over. *The Times* reveals itself as just that: belonging in its assessment to a generation of readers accustomed to Hardy as active only as a poet, and more generous in its estimation of *The Dynasts* than subsequent generations have allowed. For the enthusiast of *The Dynasts*, however, and of those poems (sometimes perhaps of dubious merit) which develop its schema (e.g. 'The Subalterns'), this obituary offers with succinct clarity a summary of the salient features of the philosophy in question: a blind will, immanent in the universe, and unconscious of human affairs or progress. Even more usefully, however, the obituary recognises that Hardy's 'personal quality' was essential for the successful modification and transmission of the ideas of his time. The obituary thus gives us an interesting historical and critical document: a one-sided view of Hardy from a particular period and viewpoint; and, at the same time, and in more concealed form, an essentially right-minded and more lasting assessment of Hardy's literary personality.

For Hardy's pessimism has in the end a far more Anglo-Saxon and emotional than Germanic and philosophical quality. 'The ideas which have animated Mr Hardy's books were already present in his mind and conversation, and were the result of temperament and observation, rather than of "influence"', Gosse correctly told the troublesome F. A. Hedgcock in 1909.[35] In the final analysis, there is but a very short difference in effect between the more thoroughly worked through perceptions of the German school, and the more thoroughly lived through early influence of Jemima and her relations. In a sense Hardy progresses little beyond the early notebook *aperçu*: 'Mother's notion, & also mine: that a figure stands in our van with arm uplifted, to knock us back from any pleasant prospect we indulge in as probable',[36] for here indeed is a notion of a frustrating will imaginatively far more potent than anything to be found in philosophical translations. Hardy's pessimism, at first a heady influence, and at one stage perhaps a Germanic affectation, slackens finally into a debilitating cast of mind. 'I, who could go anywhere, at any time of the year, go nowhere' he wrote with a touch of pride to one correspondent in 1906.[37] The attitude took its toll on Florence, for all that she occasionally managed to make light of it in correspondence. 'He is now – this afternoon – writing a poem with great spirit: always a sign of well-being with him', Florence told Cockerell in December 1920. 'Needless to say', she added, 'it is an intensely dismal poem.'[38] Certainly, Hardy's gloomy cast of mind reduced Max Gate conversations, if not Max Gate poetry, to a minimum:

FH: It's 12 days since you spoke to anyone outside the house.
TH (*triumphantly*): I have spoken to someone.
FH (*surprised*): Who was it?
TH: The man who drove the manure cart.
FH (*much impressed*): What did you say?
TH: Good morning.[39]

Reasons for Hardy's pessimism, quite apart from the influence of the German philosophers, are not hard to find. *Tess* refers to 'the chronic melancholy which is taking hold of the civilized races with the decline of belief in a beneficent power' (Ch. 18): 'We are the generation who have had to see "the spring shine out of an empty heaven, to light up a soulless earth"', the mathematician and philosopher W. K. Clifford pronounced; 'we have felt with utter loneliness that the Great Companion is dead'.[40] In the last analysis, one has to admit that there were ample grounds for gloom in what Hardy had inherited, read, lived through – some might add lived with – and that he was by providence provided with a temperament adequately blessed, when the occasion arose, for the exploitation of them all.

This is however no excuse for avoiding the more optimistic side of Hardy's ideology, his belief in progress, which, partly because less understood, receives less attention. Perhaps in later years nothing made Hardy look quite so old fashioned as his belief in advance. This is not temperamental but circumstantial, and has two chief origins.

Scientific advance, and in particular the theory of evolution, naturally entailed optimism about man's future: 'Onward and ever onward, mightier and forever mightier, rolls this wondrous tide of discovery' G. H. Lewes enthused in his *History of Philosophy*: with George Eliot to contend with across the breakfast table few can have begrudged him the stimulus.[41] To some minds, even the vigorous and well informed, it appeared that science might be able altogether to abolish human misery. Thus 'A time will come when science will transform [the world]', wrote Winwood Reade in *The Martyrdom of Man* (1872), 'Disease will be extirpated; the causes of decay will be removed; immortality will be invented. Man will then be perfect.'[42]

There was also a philosophical background to this belief in progress. For Hardy, this existed principally in his familiarity with the theories of Auguste Comte, the founder of Positivism, or the religion of humanity. Positivism saw itself as succeeding theology, and replacing the catholic and revolutionary spirits. Comte held that 'The highest progress of man and of society consists in gradual increase of our mastery over all our defects, especially the defects of our moral nature.'[43] To encourage this he envisaged the creation of a Positivist liturgy and calendar, which would introduce Positive ceremonies for birth, marriage and death and opportunities for the worship of great men of different ages and cultures, especially Caesar, St Paul and Charlemagne. He also suggested the foundation, under his leadership, of a Western European republic, for which he proposed an international coinage and for which he designed a flag, which would have Positivism's scientific motto *Order and Progress* on one side and its moral and aesthetic motto *Live for Others* on the reverse. Comte was clearly not blessed with a pictorial imagination. But in the nineteenth century, his ideas enjoyed a substantial following. Hardy's mentors, especially Stephen and Moule, were much interested in Comte, and the precedent was powerful. 'No person of serious thought in these times could be said to stand aloof from Positivist teaching & ideals', Hardy told one correspondent, and added in the *Life*, 'If Comte had introduced Christ among the worthies in his calendar it would have made Positivism tolerable to thousands who, from position, family connection, or early education, now decry what in their heart of hearts they hold to contain the germs of a true system.'[44]

Though Hardy stopped short of card-carrying Comteism, he retained many of its ideas. In 1876, he had copied well over a hundred quotations from Comte into his notebook, and the influence shows in *The Return of the Native* where Clym, 'acquainted with ethical systems popular at the time' of his stay in Paris (Bk III, Ch. ii), attempts to convert the Egdon masses, not least in his final, highly Positivist, sermon, which Hardy characteristically surrounds with much irony. In *Tess*, Angel, arguing with his father, reels off the Positivist clichés. Religion must be reconstructed: humanity, not God, should be the focus of reverence and attention. No wonder that Hardy's friend Frederic Harrison, leader of the English Positivists, and therefore perhaps not the most impartial of critics, should tell the author that 'To me it reads like a Positivist allegory or sermon.'[45] But again the irony, which the partisan Harrison was perhaps not the party most suited to notice, is all pervasive. Positivism prided itself on its practicality, and it is the untheorising Tess who more strongly represents the Positivist motto of *Live for others*, especially in the course of her relationship with Clare. 'Her mood of long-suffering made his way easy for him, and she herself was his best advocate' (Ch. 37): the ideological Angel triumphs at the expense of his more deserving partner.

Just as poetry was of special importance to Comte, so too it is in Hardy's poetry that the influences of Positivism are most apparent. Comte held that nineteenth-century poets must now 'adequately portray the new man in his relation to the new God'.[46] Two poems in *Satires of Circumstance*, 'A Plaint to Man' and 'God's Funeral' do

just this. Following significantly after Hardy's elegy on Swinburne
they mark the death of orthodox religion and look forward to

> The fact of life with dependence placed
> On the human heart's resource alone,
> In brotherhood bonded close and graced
>
> With loving-kindness fully blown,
> And visioned help unsought, unknown.

Proposing that poetry should be used extensively in Positivist
solemnities, Comte looked to artists 'to construct types of the
noblest kind, by the contemplation of which our feelings and
thoughts may be elevated'.[47] Here too Hardy conformed, offering
types of the noblest kind (albeit unexpected ones) in order to elevate
thoughts and feelings in a quasi liturgical manner. 'The Blinded
Bird' obliges in exemplary fashion:

> Who hath charity? This bird.
> Who suffereth long and is kind,
> Is not provoked, though blind
> And alive ensepulchred?
> Who hopeth, endureth all things?
> Who thinketh no evil, but sings?
> Who is divine? This bird.

Lastly, more than a hint of Positivism can be found in that other
rara avis, as it were, Hardy commenting extensively on the nature of
his art in the remarkably undiffident Apology prefixed to *Late Lyrics
and Earlier*. In a sentence where the earnestness is responsible well
nigh for the evanition of syntax, Hardy's philosophy of 'evolutionary meliorism' is expounded. Pain should everywhere 'be kept
down to a minimum by loving-kindness, operating through
scientific knowledge', remarks, ironically, the only poet to share a
birthday with the Marquis de Sade. Having assimilated scientific
advance, religion and reason may perhaps now be reconciled
through 'the interfusing effect of poetry': the Comtean goals of
order, progress, altruism, and the perfection of the moral nature are
amongst the implied benefits resulting. The thought processes here
are thoroughly Positivist, and not for nothing are both Harrison and
Comte amongst the authorities cited.

The First World War, as Hardy knew even at the time of writing this dying-swan like Apology, called all such prospects in question. Its aftermath brought an altered *zeitgeist*. 'The mould in which the Victorian age cast its hopes is broken. There is no law of progress', Dean Inge could declare in his *Outspoken Essays*, favoured reading with the Hardys in the 1920s.[48] Though even the Apology had to admit that a new Dark Age threatened, Hardy certainly remained full of sympathy, if not also minor hope. To quote 'God's Funeral' out of context, 'I did not forget / That what was mourned for, I, too, long had prized'.

For the ideas of his time, then, Hardy directed principally to Darwin, Huxley, Spencer, Comte, Hume, Mill, Schopenhauer and others. Cataloguing alternatively by subject, this lecture has laid these and associated intellectual influences out as religious, scientific, free-thinking, pessimistic and meliorist. Where finally does the bewildered child stand in relation to this analysed conjuring show?

Hardy might have approved of pursuing the matter by reference to story and to art. Determined to build up the identity and respectability of the school, a distinguished mid-century Headmaster of the school at which I now teach decided to produce a prospectus. 'Some Typical Old Boys' he titled the last page, and began the list with St Anselm. At the same time, he decided to woo Maugham and Walpole for their money, and succeeded in getting from Maugham his library and from Walpole his collection of manuscripts – Yeats's first poem, two Scott novels, and, lest the bequest be thought entirely altruistic, two large portraits of Walpole himself. One of these, by an unknown artist, now hangs in the school assembly hall, and the other, by Augustus John, in a far removed classroom. The portrayal of Walpole in the hall shows him in front of his books; John's portrayal, in front of a totally black background, unmistakably emphasises his sexual aggression. Clearly it was unsuitable for mass youth consumption. John's sketch for his far more famous portrait of Hardy shows the writer, à la Walpole, against a blank background. But the final oil shows a change of mind, for there as a backdrop are the Max Gate bookcases. In the finished portrait, John seems magnificently to have sensed, and to wish to draw our attention to, Hardy's relationship with his reading. The subject is closely interested in those books – they are pictorially *and* intellectually his background – but at the same time the lighting stresses that he is also completely independent of them: interested (of course), amused (because worldly-wise), sometimes bad tempered (because that reading can be so misleading) but most of all detached, somehow altogether transcendent.

In the end, I prefer taking John's assessment of Hardy's reading to Hardy's own. The bewildered child image is a creation of Hardy's modesty, and indeed of his wry sense of humour, which John puts firmly in perspective. Hardy was no intellectual innocent. Bemused he may have been, but ignorant or clueless he was not. Hardy asked to be remembered as the observer of a conjuring show. Rather, this collection of essays recalls him as the superb presenter of them.

Notes

1. *The Life and Work of Thomas Hardy*, by Thomas Hardy, edited by Michael Millgate (London, 1984) p. 441 (cited hereafter as *Life*).
2. *The Collected Letters of Thomas Hardy*, ed. R. L. Purdy and M. Millgate (Oxford, 1987) vol. VI, p. 259.
3. B. Disraeli, *Lothair*, ed. Vernon Bogdanor (London, 1975) p. 47.
4. *Impressions on Revisiting the Churches of Belgium and Rhenish Prussia* (London, [1875]) p. xi.
5. *Life*, p. 506.
6. Cited in David L. Edwards, *Leaders of the Church of England* (London, 1971) Ch. 5.
7. *Life*, p. 407.
8. 'Robert Elsmere. By Mrs Humphrey Ward', *Guardian*, 28 March 1888, p. 469.
9. *The Dairyman's Daughter* (Otley, 1817 [1816?]) p. 29.
10. B. Webb, *My Apprenticeship*, 2nd edn (London, n.d.) p. 123.
11. Penguin edition, ed. J. W. Burrow (Harmondsworth, 1968) p. 293.
12. *Life*, p. 114.
13. Cited by Darwin, p. 116.
14. Darwin, *The Origin of Species*, p. 116.
15. A. Symons, *A Study of Thomas Hardy* (London, 1927) p. 58.
16. *Life*, p. 479.
17. G. A. Mantell, *Wonders of Geology* (London, 1838) p. 679.
18. E. Clodd, *Pioneers of Evolution* (London, 1902) p. 93.
19. *Life*, pp. 355, 59.
20. *The Literary Notebooks of Thomas Hardy*, ed. Lennart A Björk (London, 1985) entry 1017.
21. T. H. Huxley, *Science and Christian Tradition* (London, 1894) pp. 245–6.
22. *Life*, p. 102.
23. L. Stephen, *Essays on Free Thinking and Plain Speaking* (London, 1873) p. 32.
24. Ibid., p. 362.

25.   *Oxford Companion to English Literature*, 4th edn (Oxford: Clarendon) p. 774.
26.   M. Millgate, *Thomas Hardy: A Biography* (Oxford, 1982) p. 246.
27.   *Life*, p. 400.
28.   M. A. Ward, *Robert Elsmere* (London, [1907]) p. 575.
29.   *Life*, p. 224 .
30.   D. Hume, *An Inquiry Concerning Human Understanding*, ed. Antony Flew (London, 1962) p. 132.
31.   W. Archer, *Real Conversations* (London, 1904) p. 37; Meynell, *Friends of a Lifetime* (London, 1940) p. 305.
32.   Stephen, *An Agnostic's Apology* (London, 1893) p. 343.
33.   Taken from TH's copy, People's Edition (London, 1867) p. 36.
34.   Letter to Hardy, 17 February 1874, Hardy Memorial Collection, Dorset County Museum.
35.   Millgate, *Thomas Hardy*, p. 199.
36.   Quoted by R. Gittings, *Young Thomas Hardy* (London, 1975) p. 146.
37.   Letter to Clodd, 12 February 1906, *Collected Letters*, vol. III, p. 197.
38.   Meynell, *Friends*, p. 307.
39.   Ibid., pp. 309–10.
40.   Cited by Walter E. Houghton, *The Victorian Frame of Mind* (New Haven, 1957) p. 85.
41.   Cited in Webb, *My Apprenticeship*, p. 115.
42.   Ibid., p. 114.
43.   A. Comte, *A General View of Positivism*, trans J. H. Bridges (London, n.d.) p. 241.
44.   *Collected Letters*, vol. III, p. 53; *Life*, pp. 150–1.
45.   Letter to TH, 29 December 1891, Hardy Memorial Collection.
46.   Comte, *A General View*, p. 252.
47.   Ibid., p. 209.
48.   Dean Inge, *Outspoken Essays*, Second Series (London, 1922) p. 179.

9

Conscious Artistry in *The Mayor of Casterbridge*

CRAIG RAINE

In *The Autobiography of Alice B. Toklas*, Gertrude Stein recorded this magisterial dismissal of Ezra Pound: he was, she wrote, 'a village explainer' and she appended the following carefully expository snub, 'excellent if you were a village, but if you were not, not'.[1] When G. K. Chesterton anathematised Hardy as 'a sort of village atheist brooding and blaspheming over the village idiot',[2] his epigram contained an additional objection to the primary theological distaste for the cosmic pessimist that the Roman Catholic Chesterton shared with the Anglo-Catholic T. S. Eliot. This secondary objection, mining the first, is to Hardy's provincialism and is related closely to Gertrude Stein's put-down of Ezra Pound. In *After Strange Gods*, Eliot's theological orthodoxy is, we can see, underpinned by a similar social orthodoxy: 'the work of the late Thomas Hardy represents', wrote Eliot, 'an interesting example of a powerful personality uncurbed by any institutional attachment or by submission to any objective beliefs'.[3] In 1933, of course, when Eliot delivered these words as part of the Page-Barbour lectures at the University of Virginia, he had submitted his own powerful personality to the curb of institutional attachment by becoming a convert. However, in 1920, long before religion was a major consideration, Eliot had written of another metaphysical maverick: 'we have the same respect for Blake's philosophy (and perhaps for that of Samuel Butler) that we have for an ingenious piece of home-made furniture: we admire the man who has put it together out of the odds and ends about the house. England has produced a fair number of these resourceful Robinson Crusoes.'[4] Not the discipline of philosophy, then, but the make-do of *bricolage*, the improvisation of the amateur. The condescension is confident of its mental manners, unapologetic, and educated to its fingertips. It would be utterly unmoved by Saul Bellow's description of the novel, in his Nobel Prize acceptance speech, as 'a latterday lean-to, a hovel in which the spirit takes shelter'.[5] In 1920, and earlier, the consensus was opposed to both the 'village explainer' and the 'village atheist' – the force of each retort lying in the shared epithet, *village*.

In *The Mayor of Casterbridge*, as in the other Wessex novels, Hardy the autodidact wears his learning uneasily and overinsistently. At the same time, he is as defiantly provincial in his subject matter as Patrick Kavanagh is in his poem 'Epic'[6], where he recalls a land dispute over 'half a rood of rock' between the Duffys and old McCabe in 'the year of the Munich bother', 1938. 'Which,' asks Kavanagh,

> Was more important? I inclined
> To lose my faith in Ballyrush and Gortin
> Till Homer's ghost came whispering to my mind.
> He said: I made the Iliad from such
> A local row. Gods make their own importance.

Yet how defiant is this defiance? Kavanagh's provincialism here is exactly the same as Hardy's – confident, but ultimately dependent on an appeal to the unassailable classic author and text, Homer and his *Iliad*. *The Mayor of Casterbridge* is shored and decorated with a similar display of sophisticated allusion and reference, designed to ward off that one blighting word, 'village'.

On the one hand, there is Hardy's easy expertise with dialect words: 'wimble' (a gimlet), 'furmity', 'keacorn' (windpipe), 'swipes' (poor-quality beer), 'to plim' (to swell), 'rummers' (large drinking glasses), 'lammigers' (cripples), 'bruckle' (fragile), 'twanking' (whining), 'diment' (diamond), 'stunpoll' (fool), 'voot' (foot), 'varden' (farthing), 'dumbledore' (bee), 'leery' (famished), 'greggle' (wild hyacinth), 'zwailing' (swaying), 'larry' (a loud but indistinct noise), and 'hontish' (haughty). On the other hand, there is an anxious show of learning which, by its very anxiety, lends support to Chesterton's and Eliot's insinuation of intellectual narrowness. The Seven Sleepers from the *Koran*; Terpsichore, the Greek muse of dance; the Jewish historian, Josephus; the Scandinavian race of giants, the Jotuns; the education of Achilles by Chiron; Laocoön; Baruch, the author of Biblical apocrypha; Titian; Corregio; Novalis; Carlyle on *Faust*; Bellerophon; Alastor; Tennyson's Princess Ida; *Julius Caesar* and *As You Like It*; *Comus*; 'The Revolt of Islam' and 'Prometheus Unbound'; *Diana Multimammia* and the maxims of La Rochefoucauld: these are some of the pre-emptive names not so

much dropped by Hardy as affixed to his text like rosettes. Or like
testimonials to his reading.

The suggestion left by this list is of an author unprepared to leave
the assessment of his sophistication to chance. And yet, that last
allusion – to La Rochefoucauld – embodies Hardy's novelistic pre-
cept and practice. He believed in 'the art that conceals art', hence his
allusion to La Rochefoucauld's 289th maxim: 'Simplicity put on is a
delicate imposition.'[7] As readers, we should not be deceived by
either brand of coarse simplicity so obviously on offer – neither by
the strenuous learning which puts us in mind of Larkin's celebrated
undergraduate invention, the 'Yorkshire scholar' ('Had tea wi' t'
Dean on Sunday – I showed him I'd been reading his book'[8]), nor by
the provincial folk wisdom to be found in the back bar of the Three
Mariners. Genuine aspects of Hardy, both are nevertheless products
of a single source, despite their apparent differences. That source is
Hardy's reading. The rustic chorus, often compared to Greek drama,
is in fact drawn less from life than recycled from *Henry IV*, *Much Ado*
and *Measure for Measure*. The rude mechanical policeman, Stubberd,
gives evidence like Elbow and conducts himself like Dogberry and
Verges. He is a literary figure and the remainder are characters in
their anecdotage, indulged by their author rather than ironised for
their exaggerations, as they are in *Silas Marner*. Only Mother
Cuxsom's drily accurate account of Susan Henchard's deathbed
instructions and her subsequent tender elegy transcend the overall
tendency to overacting:

'"Yes," says she, "when I'm gone, and my last breath's blowed,
look in the top drawer o' the chest in the back room by the window,
and you'll find all my coffin-clothes; a piece of flannel – that's to
put under me, and the little piece is to put under my head; and my
new stockings for my feet – they are folded alongside, and all my
other things. And there's four ounce pennies, the heaviest I could
find, a-tied up in bits of linen, for weights – two for my right eye
and two for my left," she said…. Well, poor soul; she's helpless to
hinder that or anything now,' answered Mother Cuxsom. 'And all
her shining keys will be took from her, and her cupboards opened;
and little things 'a didn't wish seen, anybody will see; and her
wishes and ways will all be as nothing!'[9]

It is a beautifully judged piece of writing and, as we shall see,
Hardy's success here encourages him, at a more crucial moment in

the narrative, to prefer reportive speech to direct portrayal. Hardy understood, perhaps from Greek drama, the advantages that telling can have over showing.

The apparent simplicity of Mother Cuxsom's account is exactly what La Rochefoucauld meant by a 'delicate imposition'. Despite its air of wordiness, it is in fact much more laconic in its means than a full-scale deathbed scene could possibly be. It concentrates on Susan herself by concentrating on the laying-out of the corpse and coffin clothes. It resists the temptation to sentimentality by choosing a narrator with the least susceptible attitude – namely, the corpse-washer, whose sentiment, when it comes, is therefore both impersonal and pure. There is nothing simple in this simple narration.

Hardy's true gift, as here, is for a simplicity, an apparent simplicity, a 'delicate imposition', which is actually intensely sophisticated both in its strategic grasp of structural necessity and in its cunning local tactics. Consider, for instance, the last two chapters. Structurally, *The Mayor of Casterbridge* depends on the idea of crime and punishment – on Henchard's sense of appropriate penalties and on Hardy's presentation of key analogies. Tactically, Hardy's problem in the final chapters is how to make Henchard a sympathetic and, therefore, tragic figure, when, for so much of the novel, he has been portrayed as bullying, irascible, moody, headstrong, misguided, vengeful, egotistical and mendacious.

Of course, these negative qualities are held in balance, if only just, by Henchard's positive qualities: his honourable behaviour during his bankruptcy; his refusal, when wrestling, to press home his murderous advantage over the prone Farfrae; his merciful decision to return to Lucetta her compromising correspondence; his rejection of the ploy to reveal Elizabeth-Jane's illegitimacy as a way of blighting Farfrae's revived amorous interest. These are long-term considerations. More constant as well as more double-edged is Henchard's demanding, passionate temperament – his imperious gift for love with its all-or-nothing fervour. In his strange, rambling meditation on Hardy's novels, D. H. Lawrence has little to say about *The Mayor of Casterbridge* since it appears not to fit into the pattern Lawrence identifies – 'the first and chiefest factor is the struggle into love and the struggle with love: by love, meaning the love of a man for a woman and a woman for a man'.[10] But Lawrence's preoccupation with the sexual makes him unresponsive to the accuracy of his diagnosis as applied to *The Mayor of Casterbridge* – which is a novel about Henchard's 'struggle into love and the struggle with love', first with

Farfrae and then with Elizabeth-Jane. His two sexual partners, Lucetta and Susan, represent responsibility rather than passion, except in so far as rivalry with Farfrae exacerbates his interest. Lawrence divides Hardy's characters into rebels and conformists, without seeing how his formulation equally applies to *The Mayor of Casterbridge*. 'This is the theme of novel after novel,' writes Lawrence; 'remain quite within the convention, and you are good, safe, and happy in the long run, though you never have the vivid pang of sympathy on your side.'[11] Henchard is demanding and vulnerable but with a real capacity for love, which we come to appreciate partly as we observe it taming his pride and his impulsiveness – and partly as Hardy contrasts his suffering and fidelity with the less profound emotions of the other characters.

Farfrae, for instance, can be heard at his wedding 'giving strong expression to a song of his dear native country that he loved so well as never to have revisited it'.[12] Henchard, the uninvited guest, has by contrast 'washed his hands at the riverside'[13] after a three-day journey back to his heart's magnet in Casterbridge. In the subsequent search for Henchard, Farfrae is shown to be financially mean ('that will make a hole in a sovereign,'[14] he says when faced with the prospect of camping out for the night) and emotionally inadequate: 'Dear me – is that so!'[15] is his response to the account of Henchard's demise. As readers we may feel that Hardy's finger is in the scales, particularly when Newson's newly acquired sense of paternity is revealed to be equally shallow: 'the contiguity of salt water proved to be such a necessity of his existence that he preferred Budmouth as a place of residence, notwithstanding the society of his daughter in the other town'.[16] Newson's character, however, has already been called into question more subtly by Hardy when the sailor contributes a sovereign towards the skimmity ride *after* learning that it is to ridicule marital irregularity. Nor is Newson's untroubled decision to give up his daughter in the first place ever satisfactorily explained: Susan's latterday disquiet is hardly a sufficient reason for a father to part with his only child. Newson's shallowness is on a par with Farfrae's early-established transfer of love from Elizabeth-Jane to Lucetta – not to mention Hardy's entirely plausible analysis of Farfrae's emotions after the burial of Lucetta.

> Time, 'in his own grey style', taught Farfrae how to estimate his experience of Lucetta – all that it was, and all that it was not. There are men whose hearts insist on a dogged fidelity to some

image or cause, thrown by chance into their keeping, long after their judgment has pronounced it no rarity – even the reverse, indeed; and without them the band of the worthy is incomplete. But Farfrae was not of those. It was inevitable that the insight, briskness, and rapidity of his nature should take him out of the dead blank which his loss threw about him. He could not but perceive that by the death of Lucetta he had exchanged a looming misery for a simple sorrow.[17]

The full force of this judgement on Farfrae is not clear until the final chapter of the novel, when Hardy risks his boldest stroke of demotion. Henchard's death has established him as one without whom 'the band of the worthy is incomplete', as one whose heart has insisted 'on a dogged fidelity to some image or cause, thrown by chance into their keeping, long after their judgment has pronounced it no rarity'.

For this to be true, Elizabeth-Jane, the object of Henchard's abject devotion, must be quietly but firmly demoted by Hardy: 'all was over at last, even her regrets for having misunderstood him on his last visit, for not having searched him out sooner, though these were deep and sharp for a good while'.[18] How finely judged this is – not a denial of feeling and remorse, merely a denial of their durability, whereas Henchard was destroyed by his feelings and his remorse.

As well as these tactical demotions, Hardy's presentation of Henchard in the last two chapters is a model of novelistic cunning. For instance, the pathos of Henchard's exile from Casterbridge is increased by Hardy's treatment of time. After Newson's displacement of Henchard, Henchard's journey to Weydon Priors is described in detail. The presumably short time between Newson's enquiry about the wedding and its actual occurrence is deliberately lengthened by Hardy's shift in narrative gear. The pure preterite is replaced by a continuous or habitual past tense: 'And then he would say of himself, "O you fool! All this about a daughter who is no daughter of thine!"'[19] Again: 'Very often, as his hay-knife crunched down among the sweet-smelling grassy stems, he would survey mankind'.[20]

But Hardy's greatest coup is to avoid direct description of Henchard's death, choosing instead, for the second time in the novel, the faltering, digressive, but entirely economical narrative testimony of a rustic – this time, Abel Whittle, whose report skirts the indecorous in order to plunge the reader into the vividly tragic detail. 'O sir – Mr Henchet! Didn't ye know it? He's just gone – about half-an-hour ago, by the sun; for I've got no watch to my name.'[21] This heart-breaking pedantry continues in Whittle's remembrance that the sea-coal sent to his mother by Henchard had 'hardly any ashes from it at all' – and in the additional 'taties' that Whittle recalls, and in the name of 'Grey's Bridge', and in his remembrance of 'the blue o' the morning, when 'twas hardly day', and in the disclosure that the corpse is to be measured, and in the confession of illiteracy which brings us to Henchard's will and its pair of spelling mistakes that risk the comic – as Whittle's whole speech has done – in order to pierce us not by rhetorical heightening but by its opposite, a calculated lowering into dialect.

This decision of Hardy's – to entrust the narrative to a simpleton – isn't only a local decision. It is also a structural requirement of the novel. Whittle's Christian name is Abel and on several occasions Henchard compares himself to Cain, most notably when he leaves Casterbridge immediately prior to Elizabeth-Jane's encounter with her real father: 'I – Cain – go alone as I deserve – an outcast and a vagabond. But my punishment is *not* greater than I can bear!'[22] The difference between Henchard and the Biblical Cain is that, in Genesis 4:13, Cain, after slaying his brother, declares to God, 'My punishment is greater than I can bear.' The similarity between Henchard and Cain is that both have committed crimes against the family – Henchard by selling his wife for five guineas at Weydon Priors.

Henchard's willingness to accept punishment, indeed his expectation of punishment, solves retrospectively at least one numinous and apparently inexplicable moment in the novel – namely the powerful confrontation of the suicidal Henchard and his image in the water of Ten Hatches. It is a scene one instinctively pairs with Diggory Venn's dicing against Wildeve by the light of glow-worms, or with Troy's sword practice in *Far from the Madding Crowd* – as one of the inexplicable 'moments of vision', as Virginia Woolf called them, even as she added the critical codicil that they were 'succeeded by long stretches of plain daylight'.[23] We know what she means: certain episodes have an iconic force comparable, say, to the still of the nurse's blood and broken spectacles in Eisenstein's *Battleship Potemkin*, or Robert Capa's photograph of a Spanish republican infantryman at the moment of death on the Cordoba front. But whereas these two images are, by their nature, serendipitous – snapshots that hold us, and life, between their

teeth – Hardy's scenes are deliberate contraventions of average reality. They are consciously miraculous. They are aware of the effect
they are making and we readers accept them as we accept the *bons
mots* in a comedy of Wilde or Congreve. They are the narrative equivalent of the perfect epigram: both know their own memorability.
Which is, of course, a long way from Virginia Woolf's idea of Hardy
as an 'unconscious' writer, like Dickens and Scott, at the mercy of
the inspirational wave which lifts and then 'sinks and they cannot
say what has happened or why.'[24]

In fact, Hardy was no more an unconscious writer than Dickens,
and in the case of Ten Hatches his guile is everywhere in evidence,
most particularly in the way he separates the actual incident from
the instructions, so to speak, which tell us how to interpret what he
shows us. Two hundred pages lie between the first, crucial account
of the Schwarzwasser of Casterbridge and Henchard's later suicidal
inclination there. After Susan's death, Henchard opens her letter
which tells him that Elizabeth-Jane is not his daughter but
Newson's. His reaction is not only stoical ('Misery taught him
nothing more than defiant endurance of it'[25]) but mistakenly inter-
pretative: 'Henchard, like all his kind, was superstitious, and he
could not help thinking that the concatenation of events this
evening had produced was the scheme of some sinister intelligence
bent on punishing him. Yet they had developed naturally. If he had
not revealed his past history to Elizabeth he would not have
searched the drawer for papers, and so on.'[26] By the time of the harvest disaster, following Henchard's loss of faith in Wide-Oh, the
weather prophet, this superstition has hardened: 'At this turn of the
scales he remained silent. The movements of his mind seemed to
tend to the thought that some power was working against him.'[27]
The significant phrase here is *'at this turn of the scales'* which suggests the idea of justice, not merely supernatural malignancy. On the
night Henchard discovers the true parentage of Elizabeth-Jane, he
goes to the Schwarzwasser where the water roars down the back-
hatch 'like the voice of desolation'. At this juncture, Hardy imparts a
crucial piece of information without which it is impossible to interpret the later suicide-averting effigy scene. We are told that this is
where public executions took place and that there is a square mass
which is 'like a pedestal lacking its statue'. Hardy continues: 'This
missing feature, without which the design remained incomplete,
was, in truth, the corpse of a man; for the square mass formed the
base of the gallows, the extensive buildings at the back being the

county gaol.'[28] In this topographical digression, Hardy secretes an essential structural fact – the idea that, for Henchard, there is a *design* which requires the corpse of a man for its completion. Moreover, the design comes with the accoutrements of justice and legality – gallows and scales.

One of Hardy's finest touches occurs in the first chapter, just after Susan has left with Newson, somewhat to Henchard's surprise. Henchard's instinct is to blame not himself but his wife: 'If she's up to such vagaries she must suffer for 'em.'[29] And the next morning finds Henchard remorseful enough to take a vow of abstinence, yet still inclined to deflect the blame on to his wife. 'Seize her, why didn't she know better than bring me into this disgrace'.[30] At this early moment, Hardy inaugurates the shift on which Henchard's behaviour will depend. He comments: 'there was something fetichistic in this man's beliefs'.[31] With this observation, Hardy sets in train the movement in Henchard from blaming his wife to his own full acceptance of his crime and, if necessary, the punishment of death.

Immediately after his lie to Newson, Henchard, expecting the sailor's rapid return on discovering his daughter still lives, goes to Ten Hatches: 'There would remain nobody for him to be proud of, nobody to fortify him; for Elizabeth-Jane would soon be but as a stranger, and worse. Susan, Farfrae, Lucetta, Elizabeth – all had gone from him, one after one, either by his fault or by his misfortune.'[32] Henchard's attempts to reconstitute a family, to replace the one he so foolishly and, in his own eyes, criminally destroyed, have been in vain. And it is worth noting here that Hardy is careful to assimilate Farfrae to the theme of family – and not simply friendship. Even before Henchard has persuaded Farfrae to stay on as his manager, he remarks enigmatically: 'Your forehead, Farfrae, is something like my poor brother's – now dead and gone; and the nose, too, isn't unlike his.'[33] Hardy doesn't labour the point. Rather it is presented as improvised, somewhat makeshift causation for the depth of Henchard's impulsive response to a stranger. It is, however, not simply a demonstration of Henchard's groping psychology. It is part of the novel's concealed structural armature – as is Henchard's equally irrational decision, on Farfrae's first morning, to kindle an unnecessary fire: 'let's make a blaze – there's nothing I hate like a black grate, even in September'.[34] The implicitly mild month tells us that oblique tribute is being paid to Hestia, goddess of hearth and family.

Farfrae, then, is a significant item in Henchard's accountancy at
Ten Hatches. There Henchard sees 'not a man somewhat resembling
him, but one in all respects his counterpart, his actual double'.[35] The
earlier prophecy is, therefore, fulfilled in a sense. Two hundred
pages earlier, at this very spot, Henchard imagined that 'some
sinister intelligence [was] bent on punishing him', but that this
design 'remained incomplete' without 'the corpse of a man'.[36] The
effigy from the skimmity ride is read by Henchard as a sign that his
persecution is over: 'the sense of the supernatural was strong in this
unhappy man, and he turned away as one might have done in the
actual presence of an appalling miracle'.[37] And the chapter closes
with Henchard's scorched avowal of salvation: 'Who is such a
reprobate as I! And yet it seems that even I be in Somebody's hand!'

Immediately prior to Henchard's sighting of the effigy, Hardy
reverts to an aspect of Henchard's character that is more symbolic
than plausible. When Henchard's oath of abstention reaches its term
in Chapter 33, he compels the choir to sing the 109th Psalm in the
Three Mariners – intending the comminatory verses for Farfrae,
though in the event their prophecy forms the substance of his own
will. After the singing, he says: 'Don't you blame David.... He knew
what he was about when he wrote that! ... If I could afford it, be
hanged if I wouldn't keep a church choir at my own expense to play
and sing to me at these low, dark times of my life. But the bitter
thing is, that when I was rich I didn't need what I could have, and
now I be poor I can't have what I need!'[38] A moment's reflection will
show that this regret of Henchard's scarcely makes plausible sense.
In what way is music a consolation only available to the rich? What
is preventing Henchard from attending church and listening to the
choir there? Nevertheless, at Ten Hatches the thought recurs: in
place of Susan, Farfrae, Lucetta, Elizabeth, 'he had no interest,
hobby, or desire. If he could have summoned music to his aid his
existence might even now have been borne; for with Henchard
music was of regal power. The merest trumpet or organ tone was
enough to move him, and high harmonies transubstantiated him.
But hard fate had ordained that he should be unable to call up this
Divine spirit in his need.'[39] One explanation is that Henchard himself cannot play an instrument, or sing – but this isn't adequate as a
gloss on a paragraph which suggests that music itself is forbidden
him.

It is succeeded, too, by a paragraph of anti-music coming from
Ten Hatches:

The wanderer in this direction, who should stand still for a few moments on a quiet night, might hear singular symphonies from these waters, as from a lampless orchestra, all playing in their sundry tones, from near and far parts of the moor. At a hole in a rotten weir they executed a recitative; where a tributary brook fell over a stone breastwork they trilled cheerily; under an arch they performed a metallic cymballing; and at Durnover Hole they hissed. The spot at which their instrumentation rose loudest was a place called Ten Hatches, whence during high springs there proceeded a very fugue of sounds.[40]

Of course, the regal power of music over Henchard can be partially accounted for by the way in which the story of Saul and David, in I Samuel, ghosts the relationship of Henchard and Farfrae. Shortly after David is anointed by Samuel, he is commanded to the court of Saul as one whose harp-playing can drive away the monarch's depression: 'And it came to pass, when the evil spirit from God was upon Saul, that David took an harp, and played with his hand: so Saul was refreshed, and was well, and the evil spirit departed from him.'[41] The most obvious parallels between Hardy's novel and the story in Samuel are Saul's visit to the witch of En-dor to call up the ghost of Samuel (which is followed closely in Henchard's visit to Wide-Oh, the weather prophet) and the competition for popularity between Henchard and Farfrae: 'And the women answered one another as they played, and said, Saul hath slain his thousands, and David his ten thousands.'[42] The most thorough analysis of these correspondences can be found in Julian Moynahan's tenaciously argued essay in *PMLA* (1956).[43]

As with Farfrae's striking, and strikingly fleeting, resemblance to Henchard's dead brother, Henchard's love of music and his apparently absolute banishment from its consolations doesn't make sense in any obvious, literal way. When are we ever shown Henchard's mayoral musical evenings? When are we *shown* any musical interest in Henchard at all before Hardy visits on his readers these press releases about his character's musical susceptibilities? The answer is once only – when Henchard hears the young Farfrae's voice through the heart-shaped holes in the shutters of the Three Mariners:

After leaving the Three Mariners he had sauntered up and down the empty High Street, passing and repassing the inn in his promenade. When the Scotchman sang, his voice had reached Henchard's ears through the heart-shaped holes in the window-shutters, and had led him to pause outside them a long while. 'To be sure, to be sure, how that fellow does draw me!' he had said to himself. 'I suppose 'tis because I'm so lonely. I'd have given him a third share in the business to have stayed!'[44]

The connection between love and music could hardly be made clearer by Hardy. And it is this identification of the two which makes sense of Henchard's otherwise enigmatic remarks about music. They are really remarks about love – the heart-shaped holes in Henchard's life. When he had love, he threw it away – selling Susan, jealously quarrelling with Farfrae, snubbing Lucetta on her first arrival, rejecting Elizabeth-Jane when she proves not to be his daughter. Substitute 'love' for 'music' and Henchard's bitter regret in the Three Mariners makes sense at last: 'when I was rich I didn't need what I could have, and now I be poor I can't have what I need!' The nearest analogue is Antony's comment on the death of his estranged wife, Fulvia:

> She's good being gone.
> The hand could pluck her back that shoved her on.[45]

The equation of love with music and harmony is consistent throughout *The Mayor of Casterbridge* and extraordinarily detailed – hence the anti-music of Ten Hatches at Henchard's lowest point emotionally; hence, too, the 'dead songster', the caged goldfinch at Elizabeth-Jane's wedding, where Farfrae has engaged a string band from Budmouth as a 'reserve of harmony';[46] hence, too, the 'trite old evening song' sung by a 'weak bird' as the Henchard family trudge into sight with their atmosphere of 'stale familiarity';[47] hence, lastly, the disharmony of the skimmity ride: 'the din of cleavers, tongs, tambourines, kits, crouds, humstrums, serpents, rams'-horns, and other historical kinds of music.'[48] This doesn't exhaust the list of examples by any means, but I want to examine more closely those 'heart-shaped holes' in the shutters of the Three Mariners, through which the equation of music with love is first made.

As with the two episodes at Ten Hatches, Hardy similarly staggers his explanation and his demonstration. It is easy enough to make the association between love and musical harmony, given the heart-shaped holes through which Henchard hears the music, but in point of fact Hardy's instructions to the reader are more complicated than that. Twenty pages earlier, Hardy has imparted vital information: 'the bay window projecting into the street, whose interior was so popular among the frequenters of the inn, was closed with shutters, in each of which appeared a heart-shaped aperture, somewhat more attenuated in the right and left ventricles than is seen in Nature'.[49] The hearts, then, are the usual idealised hearts found symmetrically decorating valentine cards, rather than the authentic item of biology. In telling us this, Hardy tells us, too, that Henchard joins the other fatally idealistic characters of Tess and Jude. Their tendency and Henchard's are linked by a shared image – that of the halo. Just as the real Christminster differs radically from the haloed Christminster Jude sees in the distance, so Lucetta acquires a spurious value in Henchard's eyes when he tumbles to Farfrae's amorous interest: 'they sat stiffly side by side at the darkening table, like some Tuscan painting of the two disciples supping at Emmaus. Lucetta, forming the third and haloed figure, was opposite them'.[50] Even to non-Christians there is something laboured and tasteless in this comparison of Lucetta with the risen Christ. It is followed by an incident improbable enough to match this image – the struggle over a slice of bread by Henchard and Farfrae. All the same, the halo is significant in general terms, even if it is a local failure. It shows us that the strengths of Henchard's emotions are also their weaknesses.

Hardy demonstrates this best in his account of the deterioration in their relationship when Henchard discovers he isn't Elizabeth-Jane's true father. The heart-shape has to be perfect. Nothing else will do. And Hardy is clearly an expert in moods and maps out the terrain of Henchard's sudden irritable coldness like a writer who knows the emotional landscape intimately. It is not pleasant reading, nor has it the theatrical force of the Ten Hatches confrontation, but it is written by someone who knows intimately both the undisclosed motive and its unceasing hurtful manifestations – the perpetual soreness within causing a perpetual infliction of pain without.

The Hardy so often recommended to us by enthusiasts is an instinctive writer. Yet he seems to me a novelist with the control of James or Flaubert, the two writers with whom Virginia Woolf chooses to contrast Hardy. For instance, buildings are carefully presented in *The Mayor of Casterbridge*, from the leering mask over the side-door of High Place Hall to the construction of Priory Cottage from 'scraps of tracery, moulded window-jambs, and arch-labels' taken from the 'long-dismantled Priory'.[51] Henchard, who lodges there, dresses not as the hay-trusser he has once more become, but in 'the remains of an old blue cloth suit of his gentlemanly times, a rusty silk hat, and a once black satin stock, soiled and shabby'.[52] Casterbridge is presented as a town haunted by history. The Ring has its own bloody legends: 'old people said that at certain moments in the summer time, in broad daylight, persons sitting with a book or dozing in the arena had, on lifting their eyes, beheld the slopes lined with a gazing legion of Hadrian's soldiery as if watching the gladitorial combat'.[53] As Casterbridge, so Henchard: when he sees Newson through his telescope, it is no exaggeration of Hardy to write that Henchard 'lived a lifetime the moment he saw it'.[54] It is no accident either that Hardy's local urchins call the returned Susan by the nickname of 'the Ghost'.[55] Nor is it chance that, when Susan and Elizabeth-Jane first enter Casterbridge, Hardy should devote a paragraph to the clocks of Casterbridge. If the paragraph is picturesque, it is also pertinent: 'Other clocks struck eight from time to time – one gloomily from the gaol, another from the gable of an almshouse, with a preparative creak of machinery, more audible than the note of the bell; a row of tall, varnished case-clocks from the interior of a clock-maker's shop joined in one after another just as the shutters were enclosing them, like a row of actors delivering their final speeches before the fall of the curtain; then chimes were heard stammering out the Sicilian Mariners' Hymn; so that chronologists of the advanced school were appreciably on their way to the next hour before the whole business of the old one was satisfactorily wound up.'[56] The word play in the last two words – wound up – should alert us to the symbolic possibilities of the passage. Henchard, too, is appreciably on his way to the next hour before the whole business of the old one has been satisfactorily wound up. Like the artist of the Three Mariners inn sign, he perceives Newson as a person of two dimensions – 'a half-invisible film upon the reality of the grain, and knots, and nails ...'.[57] Hardy wastes very little.

Notes

This essay first appeared as the introduction to the Everyman's Library Edition of *The Mayor of Casterbridge*. All subsequent references to Hardy's text are to that edition.

170   *New Perspectives on Thomas Hardy*

1.   Gertrude Stein, *The Autobiography of Alice B. Toklas* (Penguin, 1966) p. 217.
2.   G. K. Chesterton, *The Victorian Age in Literature* (Williams & Norgate, 1913) Ch. ii, p. 143.
3.   T. S. Eliot, *After Strange Gods* (Faber, 1934) p. 54.
4.   T. S. Eliot, *Selected Essays* (Faber, 1956) p. 321.
5.   Saul Bellow, Noble Prize speech quoted in *Saul Bellow and the Latterday Lean-to*, a Radio 3 documentary edited by Philip French (1976).
6.   Patrick Kavanagh, *Collected Poems* (Martin Brian & O'Keefe, 1972) p. 136.
7.   La Rochefoucauld, *Maxims* (Penguin, 1959) p. 75.
8.   Philip Larkin, *Jill* (Faber, 1975) Introduction, p. 13.
9.   *The Mayor of Casterbridge*, Ch. xviii, pp. 126–7.
10. D. H. Lawrence, *Selected Literary Criticism*, ed. Anthony Beal (Heinemann, 1967) p. 167.
11. Ibid., p. 168.
12. *The Mayor of Casterbridge*, Ch. xliv, p. 343.
13. Ibid., Ch. xliv, p. 342.
14. Ibid., Ch. xlv, p. 350.
15. Ibid., Ch. xlv, p. 352.
16. Ibid., Ch. xlv, p. 347.
17. Ibid., Ch. xlii, pp. 319–20.
18. Ibid., Ch. xlv, p. 353.
19. Ibid., Ch. xliv, p. 338.
20. Ibid., Ch. xliv, p. 339.
21. Ibid., Ch. xlv, p. 351.
22. Ibid., Ch. xliii, p. 331.
23. Virginia Woolf, *Collected Essays*, vol. i (Chatto & Windus, 1966) p. 258.
24. Ibid., p. 258.
25. *The Mayor of Casterbridge*, Ch. xix, p. 133.
26. Ibid., p. 133.
27. Ibid., Ch. xxvii, p. 201.
28. Ibid., Ch. xix, p. 134.
29. Ibid., Ch. i, p. 13.
30. Ibid., Ch. ii, p. 16.
31. Ibid., Ch. ii, p. 16.
32. Ibid., Ch. xli, p. 314.
33. Ibid., Ch. vii, p. 50.
34. Ibid., Ch. xii, p. 81.
35. Ibid., Ch. xli, p. 315.
36. Ibid., Ch. xix, pp. 133–4.
37. Ibid., Ch. xli, p. 315.
38. Ibid., Ch. xxxiii, p. 247.
39. Ibid., Ch. xli, p. 314.
40. Ibid., Ch. xli, p. 314.
41. I Samuel 16 : 23.
42. I Samuel 18 : 7.

43. Julian Moynahan, '*The Mayor of Casterbridge* and the Old Testament's
     First Book of Samuel: A Study in Some Literary Relationships',
     (*PMLA*, 71, 1956).
44. *The Mayor of Casterbridge*, Ch. VIII, p. 59.
45. *Antony and Cleopatra*, I. ii. 135–6.
46. *The Mayor of Casterbridge*, Ch. XLIV, p. 341.
47. Ibid., Ch. I, pp. 2–3.
48. Ibid., Ch. XXXIX, p. 297.
49. Ibid., Ch. VI, p. 42.
50. Ibid., Ch. XXVI, p. 192.
51. Ibid., Ch. XXXI, p. 234.
52. Ibid., Ch. XXXII, p. 242.
53. Ibid., Ch. XI, p. 76.
54. Ibid., Ch. XLIII, p. 328.
55. Ibid., Ch. XIII, p. 87.
56. Ibid., Ch. IV, p. 30.
57. Ibid., Ch. VI, p. 43.

10

Hardy's Vision of the Individual in *Tess of the d'Urbervilles*

CHARLES P. C. PETTIT

Among the notebook entries which Hardy selected for inclusion in his *Life* are a number which can be seen to contain the germ of a later novel or poem. Sometimes Hardy himself draws attention to their significance, as in the famous note of 28 April 1888: 'A short story of a young man – "who could not go to Oxford" – His struggles and ultimate failure. Suicide. [Probably the germ of *Jude the Obscure*.]'.[1] The bracketed annotation is Hardy's own, not Florence Hardy's, as Michael Millgate's edition makes clear. In other instances there is no authorial pointer, but the reference is so specific that the connection of note and later work can hardly be missed, an example being the note of 30 September 1888 which identifies ' "The Valley of the Great Dairies" – Froom' and laments the 'decline and fall of the Hardys'.[2] Here some of Hardy's preoccupations as he began composition of *Tess of the d'Urbervilles* are unmistakably signalled. Whatever his strictures on biographical intrusions, Hardy clearly felt that the search for the genesis of a novel or poem was a legitimate literary enquiry, and was happy to give a helping hand.

However, the pages of the *Life* also reveal a number of other notes which have an equally significant relationship to a later novel or poem but which, for whatever reason, have not been signposted by Hardy. A note of March 1888, shortly before Hardy started work on *Tess*, seems to me to go straight to the heart of one of that novel's most fundamental qualities. The note runs:

People who to one's-self are transient singularities are to themselves the permanent condition, the inevitable, the normal, the rest of mankind being to them the singularity. Think, that those (to us) strange transitory phenomena, their personalities, are with them always, at their going to bed, at their uprising![3]

Here is the germ (or at least *a* germ) of the novel's explorations of the nature of individuality, the 'otherness' of other people and the relationships between individuals which build into the network called society or community. For in his later fiction Hardy is constantly probing beneath the conventional narrative level of Victorian fiction, and in *Tess* this results in a vision of individuals and their interrelationships which is one of its most distinctive, if least ostentatious, achievements. It is this achievement which I propose to explore in this paper.

On the surface, Hardy fulfils conventional expectations in his portrayal of the individual at the centre of radiating circles of relationships with family, lovers, friends, local community and work community, and it is worth noting the skill with which Hardy achieves this. He convincingly depicts the Durbeyfield family's dynamics in the uneasy scenes in which Tess and her parents decide whether or not she should go to Trantridge to claim kin. Tess's relationships with her younger brothers and sisters are memorably shown during the christening of baby Sorrow in which the depiction of Tess as a larger than life figure in the eyes of the younger children also adds a further dimension to the reader's view of Tess. With scenes as effective as these, only a small number are needed to create a convincing picture of Tess as a member of her immediate family. Though showing Tess ill at ease in the beery conviviality of Rolliver's, Hardy sketches in her relationships with her old school fellows on her return from Trantridge (when their visit 'revived Tess's spirits'[4]) and with her 'female companions' on their way back from harvesting, deliberately contrasting the feeling of community at Marlott with its lack at Trantridge where the 'community of fowls' is, ironically, all that remains (Ch. 9). At Talbothays as at Marlott, Hardy presents a real community in which Tess can become involved, particularly with her fellow milkmaids and the Cricks. With superb economy and minimal narratorial comment Hardy creates a real feeling of Tess as a member of her family and friends, and through her circle of friends and working companions, as a member of the wider community.

Yet this is of course not *Under the Greenwood Tree* or *Far from the Madding Crowd*: as the later stages of *Tess* make clear, the community is not stable but disintegrating, and disintegrating fast. It is here that

Hardy does feel the need to reinforce his narrative by an ostentatious narratorial commentary, reusing material from his essay
'The Dorsetshire Labourer' (1883). The power of this presentation of
the break-up of the rural community has often been noted, and is
indeed so powerful that it has misled at least one critic into
believing that *Tess* was '"about" the destruction of the peasantry'.[5]
The resulting vulnerability and isolation of the individual can
hardly be missed, whether in the 'fever of mobility' as the field-folk
move to new homes on Old Lady-Day (Ch. 51) or in the Flintcomb-
Ash scenes in which rootless individuals are shown forced to work
for minimal wages for a bullying farmer and an itinerant traction
engine, with no sense of belonging to either farm or community, and
with no personal interest in the future of either. Despite the narratorial commentary it is through Tess that we are primarily shown
the disintegrating community: Tess traipsing along the roads of
Wessex looking for work, Tess swede-grubbing, swede-trimming
and reed-drawing at Flintcomb-Ash, Tess moving with her family
out of Marlott and searching desperately for somewhere to stay,
Tess at the mercy of the monied Alec throughout. We are undoubtedly shown the community through the individual, but our main
focus is the individual and the vulnerability of the individual as the
community disintegrates all around.

It may appear that Hardy is presenting a simple juxtaposition of
an ideal rural community at Marlott (a late surviving equivalent of a
Mellstock or a Weatherbury), and a catastrophic destruction of community elsewhere, with the causes identified as the mechanisation
of agriculture, rural depopulation and the disappearance of an
'interesting and better-informed class' in villages (Ch. 51). To a large
extent this is clearly so, and the use of the personal essay 'The
Dorsetshire Labourer' as a quarry shows that we are here concerned
with a conscious authorial input, not simply a narratorial stance.
But the contrast is not really so simple.

There is a powerful sense in which any individual in *Tess* is alone,
and this is as true of Tess herself as of many less fully realised characters, and as true when Tess is seen in the midst of lovers, family,
friends and the village community as when she is alone on the roads
of Wessex. In words reminiscent of that germ of the novel in the *Life*,
the narrator comments: 'She was not an existence, an experience, a
passion, a structure of sensations, to anybody but herself. To all
humankind besides Tess was only a passing thought' (Ch. 14).
Unlike some of the narrator's comments on the characters, this is

both powerfully stated (with an effectively insistent rhythm) and an assessment that seems genuinely to grow out of the situation described. The importance of this concept to Hardy is shown by its repetition in very similar language some hundred pages later: 'Upon her sensations the whole world depended, to Tess: through her existence all her fellow-creatures existed, to her. The universe itself only came into being for Tess on the particular day in the particular year in which she was born' (Ch. 25; strictly, though rather unconvincingly, these thoughts are given to Angel).

This concept is evident throughout the novel, even in those parts which superficially show those radiating circles of relationships characteristic of a stable community. When she leaves for Talbothays, Tess reflects: 'Her kindred dwelling there [in Marlott] would probably continue their daily lives as heretofore, with no great diminution of pleasure in their consciousness, although she would be far off and they deprived of her smile. In a few days the children would engage in their games as merrily as ever, without the sense of any gap left by her departure' (Ch. 16). Tess's mother perceptively remarks to Angel at a later stage that 'I have never really known her' (Ch. 54). Tess belongs, but yet she is separate.

This perception is very noticeable in the portrayal of the relationship between Tess and Angel. Yes, there are plenty of obvious barriers to a real intimacy between the two in their courtship at Talbothays; as the narrator comments: 'neither having the clue to the other's secret, they were respectively puzzled at what each revealed' (Ch. 19). There are other secrets besides the obvious one of Tess's sexual experiences, these including Tess's d'Urberville ancestry and Angel's own sexual adventure in London, but the distance between them is due to much more than mere hidden information. Nor is it simply a difference of social class, though this does create another barrier. Beneath these surmountable obstacles, Hardy emphasises Angel's inability to see the real Tess behind the whole host of stereotypes into which he tries to fit her: 'She was no longer the milkmaid, but a visionary essence of woman – a whole sex condensed into one typical form. He called her Artemis, Demeter, and other fanciful names, half-teasingly – which she did not like because she did not understand them' (Ch. 20). But would 'the milkmaid' be much better than Artemis? It is another stereotype, associated with some sort of pastoral vision, as becomes horribly clear after Tess's confession when Angel complains: 'I thought – any man would have thought – that by giving up all ambition to win a wife with social standing, with fortune, with knowledge of the world, I should secure rustic innocence, as surely as I should secure pink cheeks' (Ch. 36). Hardy clearly demonstrates Angel's inability to think in anything other than stereotypes: in his eagerness to get hold of this specimen of pink-cheeked rustic maidenhood and transform her by a 'few months' travel and reading' (Ch. 38) into someone worthy of introduction into Society, this forerunner of Shaw's Professor Henry Higgins[6] genuinely seems to have no conception of the real individual at all. Hardy is remarkably effective in allowing Angel to condemn himself out of his own mouth, the series of stereotypes coming from a man who can congratulate himself for recognising that 'the typical and unvarying Hodge [had] ceased to exist' (Ch. 18).

Tess on the other hand does accept Angel as an individual even though she is fully aware that there are things she does not know about him: 'Having begun to love you, I love you for ever – in all changes, in all disgraces, because you are yourself' (Ch. 35). Yet even this does not mean that she completely understands him; his 'hard logical deposit' (Ch. 36) of conventional morality is shown to be a real shock. Even in those magic days of reconciliation after the murder of Alec there is some distance between them: 'Each clasping the other round the waist they promenaded over the dry bed of fir-needles, thrown into a vague intoxicating atmosphere at the consciousness of being together at last, with no living soul between them; ignoring that there was a corpse' (Ch. 57) – a remarkably barbed narrative comment. In the deserted house where they live for five days: 'By tacit consent they hardly once spoke of any incident of the past subsequent to their wedding-day' (Ch. 58). In other words, union is achieved by deliberate avoidance of problem areas.

The cumulative effect of all this is to make clear, not that the love of Tess and Angel is lacking in substance or depth, but that if these particular hindrances were not there, then there would be something else. Even in the closest relationship, we are shown, and despite the most intense love, there is some sort of distance, some barrier, some sense in which each individual is beyond the reach and understanding of the other. It is not that Hardy is intending this feeling of the separateness of individuals to undercut the positive portrayal of the power of love which comes through so strongly in *Tess*; it is rather than he is trying to go deeper into the nature of individuality and of relationships between individuals than was customary in the Victorian novel. Perhaps, *pace* Donne, there is a sense in which every man *is* an island.

   How does Hardy convey this vision? His most important tool in this portrayal of the individual and society is his use of many different points of view in his narration. By points of view, I mean literally the imagined visual angle on a scene – the eyes through which it is seen. As many critics have noted, it is no accident that Hardy sometimes seems obsessed with eyes. Tess's own eyes are described in amazing detail: 'the ever-varying pupils, with their radiating fibrils of blue, and black, and grey, and violet' (Ch. 27) is only one example of many detailed descriptions, while even the natural world seems to be watching her: 'The trees have inquisitive eyes, haven't they?' she says to Angel at Talbothays (Ch. 19). These points of view are constantly changing: we modulate unostentatiously from the eyes of one character to those of another character, and on to those of an unspecified observer who is yet fixed as firmly in time and space as one of the characters. This constant modulation gives the text a richness that would simply not be possible if the novel were either presented by an omniscient narrator or seen entirely through Tess's eyes. The reward of this approach is to combine the involvement and intensity of a first-person narration with the ability of a third-person narration to see the wider perspectives. With his flexible approach, Hardy avoids the abrupt shifts of narrative perspective shown by Dickens in *Bleak House*, in which, with similar objectives to Hardy's, whole chapters are presented either by the narrator or by Esther Summerson. The technique and vision will later reach their culmination in *The Dynasts*, but if *The Dynasts* is an obvious reference point, it is also different in its very self-consciousness. In *Tess* the techniques are less ostentatious and, rather, subtle and probing – they grow out of the novel rather than being an overt part of its structure. Artistically they are effective in terms of that art of concealing art of which Hardy wrote so approvingly.[7]

   The basic range of viewpoints can be seen in the scene describing the death of Prince, the Durbeyfields' horse (Ch. 4). This episode starts off in the typical, detached Victorian narrative mode:

   Her mother at length agreed to this arrangement. Little Abraham was aroused from his deep sleep in a corner of the same apartment, and made to put on his clothes while still mentally in the other world.... His sister became abruptly still, and lapsed into a pondering silence.... Tess was not skilful in the management of a horse, but she thought she could take upon herself the entire conduct of the load for the present ...

The narrator has knowledge of Tess's thoughts as well as of her words and actions, and relates all this with effortless omniscience. The narrative and hence the reader are objective, detached, uninvolved. But in order to feel the full horror of the accident to Prince we imperceptibly modulate into Tess's own viewpoint:

> The mute procession past her shoulders of trees and hedges became attached to fantastic scenes outside reality, and the occasional heave of the wind became the sigh of some immense sad soul, conterminous with the universe in space, and with history in time [Tess, not the narrator, is having these fantasies] .... A sudden jerk shook her in her seat, and Tess awoke from the sleep into which she, too, had fallen.
>
> They were a long way further on than when she had lost consciousness, and the waggon had stopped. A hollow groan, unlike anything she had ever heard in her life, came from the front, followed by a shout of 'Hoi, there!'
>
> The lantern hanging at her waggon had gone out, but another was shining in her face – much brighter than her own had been. Something terrible had happened.

Though nominally written in the third person, this is in fact seen through Tess's eyes and rudely awakened consciousness: we piece together what has happened just as Tess does, bit by bit: where is she? (further on); what is happening? (they have stopped); there is a noise (hollow groan); there is a light shining in her face: 'Something terrible had happened.' (What an effective short sentence this is for conveying the power of the blow on Tess.) How much more impact this scene has on the reader than an objective narration could ever have, because the reader has in effect lived through the experience with Tess. Then, with equal ease, we are back with an objective view of the scene, hearing the explanation of the accident from the narrator, and watching Tess and the mail-cart man coping with the practical consequences. Finally, we stand back to look at the aftermath of the accident almost as if it were a tableau:

> The atmosphere turned pale, the birds shook themselves in the hedges, arose, and twittered: the lane showed all its white

features, and Tess showed hers, still whiter. The huge pool of blood in front of her was already assuming the iridescence of coagulation; and when the sun rose a hundred prismatic hues were reflected from it.

There is a feeling of a real observer there, seeing and listening. There are so many complementary dimensions in this dramatic scene: Tess's personal experience of the accident, an impersonal narration showing the interplay of the two characters and their practical actions, and finally that marvellous word-picture from the observer-narrator watching the figure in the landscape and that terribly beautiful image of the red pool of blood against the white of the lane and Tess's face, colour-images which are of course used recurrently in this novel.

This technique, of sliding into and out of Tess's consciousness and vision, is used again and again, and plays a significant part in creating that intimacy between Tess and the reader which is such a remarkable feature of the novel, for it is Tess's eyes which predominate. Leaving aside qualitative measures of the power of her presentation, it is clear enough from bare statistics: out of 59 chapters in the novel there are only eight in which Tess does not appear in person. A few instances will show the variety of ways in which Hardy uses Tess's viewpoint.

On some occasions the objective seems to be simply the striking visual angle designed to catch the reader's attention. It is a way of looking at things captured memorably in a note from 1891 quoted in the *Life* : 'If I were a painter I would paint a picture of a room as viewed by a mouse from a chink under the skirting.'[8] On their removal from Marlott to Kingsbere the Durbeyfields stop briefly for refreshments at a roadside inn: 'During the halt Tess's eyes fell upon a three-pint blue mug, which was ascending and descending through the air to and from the feminine section of a household.... She followed one of the mug's journeys upward, and perceived it to be clasped by hands whose owner she well knew. Tess went towards the waggon. "Marian, and Izz!" she cried...' (Ch. 52). This touch certainly brings visual immediacy and catches the reader's attention by creating momentary suspense, but it serves no purpose beyond this localised narrative effect.

More frequently, Hardy's aim is also to gain sympathy for the main character by seeing things through her eyes, rather than simply exploiting unusual visual angles for their own sake. For example, when Tess first meets the religious sign painter (Ch. 12) we hear him coming up behind Tess as she does, and try to work out with her who he is: 'As she walked, however, some footsteps approached behind her, the footsteps of a man; and owing to the briskness of his advance he was close at her heels and had said "Good morning" before she had been long aware of his propinquity. He appeared to be an artizan of some sort, and carried a tin pot of red paint in his hand.' We are following Tess's thought processes, trying to work out who the man is, and the narrator refuses to show us anything that Tess herself cannot see. The objective is to make the reader experience the scene with Tess, so sharing her emotion on the memorable morning of her return from Trantridge to Marlott.

When Tess is returning to Marlott on another occasion, having been sent for from Flintcomb-Ash because of her mother's illness, we re-enter the village with her, seeing everything not just through her eyes but also with her memory and imagination:

> At three she … entered Marlott, passing the field in which, as a club-girl, she had first seen Angel Clare, when he had not danced with her: the sense of disappointment remained with her yet…. As soon as she could discern the outline of the house … it had all its old effect upon Tess's imagination. Part of her body and life it ever seemed to be…. A stupefaction had come into these features, to her regard; it meant the illness of her mother.   (Ch. 50)

Hardy simultaneously reminds the reader of the earlier incidents in the story, shows us the impressibility of Tess, and involves us with her concern for her mother; a number of objectives are achieved in one short passage.

These different levels are perhaps most striking in the frequently analysed garden scene at Talbothays in which Tess listens entranced to Angel's harp-playing (Ch. 19). Here we move from the objective narrator who states 'To speak absolutely, both instrument and execution were poor' into Tess's fascinated spirit as she is 'conscious of neither time nor space' and undulates upon the notes of the harp. However, while we can feel Tess's emotion, we are also made subtly aware of the damp of the grass, the 'offensive smells' of the weeds, and the sticky blights on the apple tree trunks. In scenes like this we are beyond the visual and even beyond Tess's conscious thought-processes, feeling things as they seem to her emotions and to her subconscious. With the same effortless sliding into and out of an individual's views seen in the visual angles, we see the objective viewpoint and then how things are perceived by the individual concerned: to use Hardy's terminology from the confession scene, we move from the substance (thin notes of a badly played harp) to the essence (? the harmony of the spheres).

After hearing the story of Jack Dollop from Dairyman Crick:

> The evening sun was now ugly to her, like a great inflamed wound in the sky. Only a solitary cracked-voiced reed-sparrow greeted her from the bushes by the river, in a sad, machine-made tone, resembling that of a past friend whose friendship she had outworn.   (Ch. 21)

When overwrought after Angel has been pressing her to marry him, Tess retreats to a 'thicket of pollard willows at the lower side of the barton':

> At half-past six the sun settled down upon the levels, with the aspect of a great forge in the heavens, and presently a monstrous pumpkin-like moon arose on the other hand. The pollard willows, tortured out of their natural shape by incessant choppings, became spiny-haired monsters as they stood up against it.   (Ch. 28)

As Tess looks down over Emminster the church tower 'had a severe look in her eyes' (Ch. 44). The marvellous imagery in many of these passages is one of the joys of the novel, but it is not a mere *tour de force* of evocative writing: much of our understanding of and sympathy with Tess comes from Hardy's success in involving the reader in her sensibility and imagination, particularly in these personifications of the natural world which are so striking a demonstration of the pathetic fallacy.

Although this close association with Tess may be the most frequent narrative mode, it is by no means the only one. The narrative slides into and out of other characters' viewpoints with equal ease, though less frequently. Hardy makes most use of Angel Clare's perspective. As he stares at the log fire at Talbothays, having just been looking through some music scores, the flame 'seemed to jig to his inward tune' (Ch. 18) – how different, incidentally, from the fire the couple look into at Wellbridge, though in both cases the fire is of course an objective correlative for the characters' feelings. The church tower at Emminster that seems so severe to Tess has a different, if equally unsettling look to Angel: 'the tower of the church rose into the evening sky in a manner of inquiry as to why he had come' (Ch. 39). As Angel returns to Talbothays from a visit to his parents in Emminster, we ride back with him 'an up-hill and down-dale ride of twenty-odd miles' (Ch. 27) and enter the house with him: *hearing* the sounds as he does: 'Sustained snores came from the cart-house, where some of the men were lying down; the grunt and squeal of sweltering pigs arose from the still further distance'; and *seeing* Tess with him as she comes down the stairs: 'he saw the red interior of her mouth as if it had been a snake's'; and then *feeling* Tess with him as he holds her: 'Tess's excitable heart beat against his by way of reply…. Having been lying down in her clothes she was warm as a sunned cat.'

This is exactly the same technique used in the scenes featuring Tess's perspective, but by varying the viewpoint from Tess to Angel, Hardy achieves a number of objectives. Firstly, he helps to create some badly-needed sympathy for Angel, building on the instinctive empathy the reader feels with the character through whose eyes the action is seen. Secondly, he introduces variety into the narrative and creates dramatic suspense in situations in which Tess's viewpoint would not provide it so effectively, if at all. And lastly, and perhaps most important of all, he shows us Tess from the outside: a personality and a body seen by someone else. We are made aware again of the divergence between how we see ourselves and how others see us. Moreover by showing us Angel's reactions to Tess we are invited to, as it were, share his feelings of love for Tess. This lover's view of Tess as someone to look at and to hold, adds immeasurably to the reader's feelings for her in a way that would not be possible if the narrative had been either impersonal or seen through Tess's own eyes. Tess becomes a person to whom we can relate as well as someone whom we know from the inside. Much play has been made of the narrator's erotic fascination with Tess, and the erotic charge of the passage quoted above is unmistakable, but it is worth emphasising that in passages like this Hardy is quite explicitly showing us Tess through her lover's eyes, not through the narrator's.

This use of limited visual or perceptual viewpoints is not restricted to Tess and Angel. Hardy will on occasion use even the most minor character's viewpoint, with a similar range of objectives. In addition these perspectives give a view of the major charac-

ters as they appear to others – a visual equivalent of the gossip
about Bathsheba and her lovers by the regulars in Warren's Malthouse in *Far from the Madding Crowd*, about Henchard, Farfrae and
Lucetta by the inhabitants of Mixen Lane in *The Mayor of Casterbridge*, or about Tess and Alec by the harvesters at Marlott: 'A little
more than persuading had to do wi' the coming o't [the baby], I
reckon. There were they that heard a sobbing one night last year in
The Chase; and it mid ha' gone hard wi' a certain party if folks had
come along' (Ch. 14).[9]

The most striking instance in the novel is the discovery by Mrs
Brooks, the landlady of The Herons, of the murder of Alec. After
Angel's departure Tess returns upstairs, and for all the crucial following section we see everything through the eyes of Mrs Brooks as
she softly climbs the stairs, listens at the door and looks through the
keyhole. We see exactly and only what Mrs Brooks sees: it is that
mouse's-eye view used to brilliant effect:

> The landlady looked through the keyhole. Only a small space
> of the room inside was visible, but within that space came a
> corner of the breakfast-table, which was already spread for the
> meal; and also a chair beside it. Over the seat of the chair Tess's
> face was bowed.... Then a man's voice from the adjoining
> bedroom ...   (Ch. 56)

The quarrel between Tess and Alec starts, and Mrs Brooks 'thinking
that the speaker was coming to rush out of the door, hastily
retreated down the stairs'. We then hear with her somebody moving
about overhead and see Tess leave the house; later we see with Mrs
Brooks the tell-tale blood stain appearing on the ceiling, and learn of
the murder when a man she has called in to help goes into the
upstairs room and finds Alec. This consistent use of Mrs Brooks's
viewpoint gives the scene its suspense and dramatic impact, while
avoiding the melodrama and the diminution of sympathy for Tess
which might have occurred had we been shown the murder directly.
It also gives the reactions of the outside world as a counterbalance
to the following chapters in which the intensity of Tess and Angel's
love swamps normal moral judgements; it is a forewarning of the
'Justice' which is to come at the very end of the novel.

Mrs Brooks is definitely one of the characters in the novel, albeit a
minor one. However some of the visual angles used in *Tess* belong
to people who can barely be called characters: they have no name

and serve no function other than to give one particular viewpoint in one scene. Here, for instance, is Alec d'Urberville approaching Flint-comb-Ash:

> For hours nothing relieved the joyless monotony of things. Then, far beyond the ploughing-teams, a black speck was seen; it had come from the corner of a fence, where there was a gap, and its tendency was up the incline, towards the swede-cutters. From the proportions of a mere point it advanced to the shape of a ninepin, and was soon perceived to be a man in black, arriving from the direction of Flintcomb-Ash.   (Ch. 46)

How Hardy loves these perspectives of people advancing or receding along a road or across a field. We might expect that it is Tess who is watching his advance, but no: 'The man at the slicer, having nothing else to do with his eyes, continually observed the comer, but Tess, who was occupied, did not perceive him till her companion directed her attention to his approach.' Even though the man at the turnip-slicer is not named, is not individually distinguished in any way and is not referred to again, there is still that feeling of immediacy which comes from seeing through an individual's eyes. Why did Hardy not use Tess's eyes? I would suggest that it is because he is emphasising that continuous hard work which she has to endure at Flintcomb-Ash and which lowers her resistance to Alec's renewed advances: she is working so hard and is so exhausted that she cannot guard herself against him, and in this particular instance literally cannot see him coming. Again, we move from a visual angle to an image, or a symbol.

As another example, there is the unnamed individual who sees Tess and Angel walking sadly across the meadows at Wellbridge after the wedding night confessions:

> It was said afterwards that a cottager of Wellbridge, who went out late that night for a doctor, met two lovers in the pastures, walking very slowly, without converse, one behind the other, as in a funeral procession; and the glimpse that he obtained of their faces seemed to denote that they were anxious and sad. Returning later he passed them again in the same field, progressing just as slowly, and as regardless of the hour and of the cheerless night as before.   (Ch. 35)

This is a marvellous vignette whose remarkable resonance comes both from the quality of the language and the decision to use this personalised witness.

A further example is the caretaker through whose eyes we see Tess and Angel asleep in the deserted mansion near the end of the book: 'A stream of morning light through the shutter-chink fell upon the faces of the pair wrapped in profound slumber, Tess's lips being parted like a half-opened flower near his cheek' (Ch. 58). Again, it is not just the visual angle, effective though this is; the imagery of light and flower reflects the quality of the union eventually achieved by Tess and Angel.

Probably no two of these examples are exactly the same in their function: some are purely visual, some combine the visual with an implied consciousness, some are explicit commentary on what is seen or what has been seen by others. Cumulatively, however, they play no small part in the novel. From one perspective they emphasise that individuality of the individual which is so crucial to Hardy's vision: the more viewpoints we are shown, the more we are made conscious of a world of individuals rather than a unified society. But at the same time, they also build up a sense of a community which is more threatening than reassuring: the less attractive side of that sense of community shown so positively at Talbothays. Wherever Tess goes it seems that the eyes and ears of all are upon her, and the pressure of all these watchers hems her in, constrains her freedom and limits the expression of her individuality.

Even in her most intimate crises, whether in The Chase with Alec or at Wellbridge or in the deserted mansion with Angel, the eyes of the community are watching her. Moreover, Tess is very conscious of these watching eyes, so that one of the attractions of the move to Talbothays for her is: 'the sense of being amid new scenes where there were no invidious eyes upon her' (Ch. 16). But escape from watching eyes is not so simple, and Tess is soon being watched by Angel Clare: 'having a consciousness that Clare was regarding her [she] began to trace imaginary patterns on the tablecloth with her forefinger, with the constraint of a domestic animal that perceives itself to be watched' (Ch. 18). On the road to Flintcomb-Ash she practically and symbolically cuts off her eyebrows and covers half her face to guard herself from troublesome admirers, but even then she cannot escape attention: Marian asks why her face is tied up like that – 'Anybody been beating 'ee? Not *he*!' (Ch. 42).

This constant feeling of being watched is deliberately accentuated by the reappearance of the same pairs of eyes, bringing their knowledge of the past from which Tess is trying so hard to escape: these reappearing onlookers include the man with the red paintpot, the Amazonian sisters Car and Nancy Darch, and most striking of all, Farmer Groby who reappears in both Casterbridge and Flintcomb-Ash to remind Tess of her Trantridge days. These hostile onlookers make credible Tess's despairing feeling that 'Bygones would never be complete bygones till she was a bygone herself' (Ch. 45). It is no wonder that Tess can occasionally feel eyes where there are none, like the eyes in the trees, or in the scene at Talbothays when the Cricks return unexpectedly and surprise Tess and Angel: 'But I wasn't really sitting on his knee, though it might ha' seemed as if I was, almost!' exclaims Tess, to which Crick placidly replies: 'Well – if so be you hadn't told us, I am sure we shouldn't ha' noticed that ye had been sitting anywhere at all, in this light' (Ch. 31). Even in the novel's lightest moments Hardy emphasises the watching eyes and their effect on Tess.

The whole moral/ethical/religious debate about purity, sexual relationships and marriage constantly emphasises the distinction between an individual's actions (the 'substance of things', observable by others) and motivation, thought and feeling (the 'essence' of the individual which outsiders cannot comprehend); individual moral standards are set against the conventional standards of the community. These constant watching eyes, listening ears and gossiping or opinionated mouths are Hardy's method of giving substance to the narrator's assessments of the powerful influence of society's dictates on Tess. The moral codes which she breaks (or is forced to break) are not mere abstractions, but views strongly held by most of those around her: this is why it is so difficult for her to ignore them and why she even begins to share them herself. When John Durbeyfield hears of Tess's return from her wedding: 'the intrinsic quality of the event moved his touchy sensitiveness less than its conjectured effect upon the minds of others' (Ch. 38), and it may seem that Hardy is simply exposing Durbeyfield's weakness by showing that he is more concerned about the village gossips than about his daughter. Yet clearly he had good reason to be worried: at the first opportunity after his death the family is turned out of their house, primarily on the grounds of the family's lack of respectability. The Marlott vicar, for all his assurance to Tess that her baby will not suffer because of the improvised christening, refuses to give the child a Christian burial although, he says, 'I would willingly do so if only we two were concerned' (Ch. 14); one suspects that the guardians of village morals have more influence on his decision than either theological conviction or deference to the Church hierarchy.

There is a feeling that although society is self-evidently a collection of individuals, it also has a corporate identity which is not simply the sum of its constituent individuals but is something alien and admonitory. Hardy describes Tess pondering why she could not return to Talbothays after the wedding:

> She could not have borne their pity, and their whispered remarks to one another upon her strange situation; though she would almost have faced a knowledge of her circumstances by every individual there, so long as her story had remained isolated in the mind of each. It was the interchange of ideas about her that made her sensitiveness wince. Tess could not account for this distinction; she simply knew that she felt it.   (Ch. 41)

Wisely, Hardy avoids trying to define the distinction himself, but for the reader it is one more strand in the novel's search for an understanding of the nature of the individual and of his or her place in society.

All the viewpoints examined so far are of imagined characters, however minor a role they may have in the novel. However there is a stage beyond this, for Hardy will often use a precise visual angle even though no actual observer is created. One example has already been cited, in the passage describing the death of Prince: you feel that in that final word-picture there is an implied observer in a particular spot looking at the scene. There is another example in the first description of the Vale of Blackmoor:

> The traveller from the coast who, after plodding northward for a score of miles over calcareous downs and cornlands, suddenly reaches the verge of one of these escarpments, is surprised and delighted to behold, extended like a map beneath him, a country differing absolutely from that which he has passed through.   (Ch. 2)

This traveller is not one of the characters in the novel, not even in the sense that the anonymous cottager at Wellbridge is: he is more in the nature of an extended metaphor, but this viewing of the scene from a precise viewpoint by one who is 'surprised' and 'delighted' with the view has an immense vitality which simply could not have been achieved by straight description.

More frequently, the viewpoint zooms in and out with no mention of an observer. As Tess climbs to the top of Egdon Heath she gets her first view of the Valley of Great Dairies and we see the 'bird's-eye perspective' which Tess sees, share her feeling of harmony with the 'cheering' natural scene, and then follow her down the slope into the valley. But then suddenly and very effectively, we are in one of those aerial perspectives used so frequently in *The Dynasts*: 'Tess stood still upon the hemmed expanse of verdant flatness, like a fly on a billiard-table of indefinite length, and of no more consequence to the surroundings than that fly' (Ch. 16). One minute we are sharing the scene with the individual; the next that individual is merely a fly. It is a stunningly effective narrative technique, keeping the reader constantly on the alert and making us readjust our impressions, building up a view of life from hosts of different perspectives, contrasts and connections, as a pointillist picture or a newspaper photograph is made up of countless dots.

'Thus Tess walks on; a figure which is part of the landscape' (Ch. 42) writes the narrator as Tess journeys towards Flintcomb-Ash, and so she is, from one perspective, whether harvesting at Marlott, milking cows at Talbothays, toiling on the upland fields at Flintcomb-Ash, or as here, and so often, walking along the endless roads of Wessex: a figure in a landscape, or a fly on a billiard table. But she is also a unique individual whose vision of the landscape depends crucially upon her own consciousness: to Tess the natural world can condemn her guilt, reflect her despair or enhance her joy; as Tess walks later along another road, far from being a figure in the landscape, she is so absorbed in her mental world that she can hardly see the landscape and is in danger of losing her way (Ch. 44): the landscape exists only through the individual or, in the narrator's words: 'the world is only a psychological phenomenon' (Ch. 13). In less skilful hands this might have resulted in a confusion of conflicting perspectives. In *Tess* Hardy succeeds in using the very tension and interplay between the two perspectives to create his own vision, enriching the novel's perceptions further through the use of a wide variety of complementary visual angles.

The vision is not unique to *Tess*, and can be seen in less developed form in Hardy's other fiction. The use of varied visual perspectives is notable in *Far from the Madding Crowd*, for example, but one would hesitate to argue that they form a major structural tool. The germ of *Two on a Tower* is a similar interplay of contrasting but complementary perspectives, but the novel fails to fulfil the promise of its preface: 'This slightly-built romance was the outcome of a wish to set the emotional history of two infinitesimal lives against the stupendous background of the stellar universe, and to impart to readers the sentiment that of these contrasting magnitudes the smaller might be the greater to them as men.' In *Tess*, however, the vision does permeate the whole novel, and is used as the central vehicle for conveying Hardy's concept of a woman who retains inner purity despite the outward events of her life.

Two major threads, therefore, seem to me to run through Hardy's vision of the individual in *Tess*. Firstly there is an insistence upon the unique nature of each individual and an appreciation that society is both a group of individuals and something quite other. Secondly, despite the overt 'purpose' directing the novel (apparent from the subtitle, Preface to the Fifth Edition and much narrative commentary) there is a refusal to take the simple option of a single narrative perspective using Tess's eyes, and a determination instead to use a variety of perspectives to show both the 'substance' and the 'essence' of individuals in a perspective which encompasses both. Hardy, in effect, forces the reader to make that effort of the imagination to feel both the individuality and the otherness of others which is evident in that germ of the novel quoted in the *Life*: 'Think, that those (to us) strange transitory phenomena, their personalities, are with them always.' Because of Hardy's wealth of narrative strategies, however, the multifaceted perspectives of the novel eventually defy expository summary, and there is at the deepest level an affinity with Keats's 'negative capability': 'that is when man is capable of being in uncertainties, Mysteries, doubts, without any irritable reaching after fact and reason'.[10] Or, as Hardy writes in his Preface to the novel's Fifth Edition: 'a novel is an impression, not an argument'.

Notes

This paper, which was the reserve lecture for the Hardy Conference, is based on a lecture given to the Thomas Hardy Society in Sturminster Newton on 6 April 1991.

1. *The Life and Work of Thomas Hardy, by Thomas Hardy*, ed. Michael Millgate (London: Macmillan, 1984) p. 216. Subsequently cited as *Life*. Other examples of Hardy drawing attention to germs of later works concern *The Well-Beloved* (*Life*, p. 226) and *The Dynasts* (*Life*, pp. 109–10: 'In this same month of 1875, it may be interesting to note, occurs the first mention in Hardy's memoranda of the idea of an epic on the war with Napoleon – carried out so many years later in *The Dynasts*').

2. *Life*, pp. 223–4.

3. *Life*, p. 215. In Florence Emily Hardy's edition (London: Macmillan, 1962) p. 206, the balance of the second sentence is marginally affected by the italicisation of '*their*' [personalities].

4. *Tess of the d'Urbervilles*, Chapter 13. Quotations are taken from the Clarendon Press edition, edited by Juliet Grindle and Simon Gatrell (Oxford: Oxford University Press, 1983; corrected reprint 1986). Chapter references for subsequent quotations given in parentheses in text.

5. Arnold Kettle, modifying his earlier views wrote: 'A few years back I described *Tess* as being "about" the destruction of the peasantry rather than about a pure woman. I would not put it quite that way any longer', *Hardy the Novelist: A Reconsideration* (University College of Swansea, 1966).

6. George Bernard Shaw, *Pygmalion*, first performed in 1913.

7. *Life*, p. 323: 'That the author loved the art of concealing art was undiscerned.'

8. *Life*, p. 246.

9. This passage was a late insertion, for the Fifth Edition of 1892, showing Hardy's continuing concern for the reader's perception of Tess as a 'pure woman'; perhaps it was the hostility of some press reviews which determined him to emphasise in this way the allocation of blame for the scene in The Chase.

10. John Keats, letter to his brothers G. and T. Keats, 21 December 1817. Quoted in Chris Baldick, *The Concise Oxford Dictionary of Literary Terms* (Oxford: Oxford University Press, 1990).

11

Questions Arising from Hardy's Visits to Cornwall

F. B. PINION

Some uncertainty must remain on the number of times Hardy visited Cornwall. In his later years he remembered, and recorded in his *Life*, eight visits, two of them after the death of Emma. These two became the final one in 'The Seven Times', a poem written when he was an 'eighty-years long plodder', 'shrunken with old age'. It appeared for the first time in 1922, in *Late Lyrics and Earlier*, and is undoubtedly based solely on the visits recalled in his *Life*, which had progressed as far as the year 1895 by 1918. When he read his wife's *Some Recollections* soon after her death late in November 1912, Hardy added a footnote in pencil: 'the second visit being by invitation of Mr Holder, the third and fourth professional, and the later ones entirely personal'. Like his architect employer Crickmay, he was absent when the restored church at St Juliot was opened on 11 April 1872. Emma remembered it as a 'brilliant occasion', and states that from that time Hardy came 'two or three times a year' to see her. It will be seen that this recollection implies an improbable number of subsequent visits, and it is surprising perhaps that the statement elicited no comment from Hardy. Naturally his memory was not altogether trustworthy in old age. Besides the eight visits which he recorded in his *Life*, there was at least one other he had forgotten, though it lasted three weeks. This was in October 1871, as his letters at the time disclose.

Chronologically and in context, the visits for which evidence exists are as follows:

1.   Hardy set out for Lyonnesse early on the frosty morning of 7 March 1870, and it was dark in the evening when he reached St Juliot rectory, where he was received by Emma Gifford. In 'The Seven Times' he remembered that life for him was clogged with care. His whole career was at stake: he wished to renounce

191

architecture, but his first novel *The Poor Man and the Lady* had been rejected, and his hopes of *Desperate Remedies*, which he had sensationalised and just sent off, all but the last three or four chapters, to Macmillan, could not have been high. His anxiety on that score can be gauged from the words of Hamlet against which he wrote 'December 15, 1870', after sending the complete work for publication to Tinsley Brothers, 'thou wouldst not think how ill all's here about my heart: but it is no matter'. In March he had visited St Juliot to plan the restoration of the church; he prolonged his stay to spend more time with Emma Gifford, and went home with the lovelight in his eyes.

2.   In August that year he returned as the guest of the Holders, who drove him to picturesque spots along the wild rugged Atlantic coast, including Tintagel Castle. The season was unusually dry, and Hardy realised from press cuttings which his friend Horace Moule sent that he and Emma had sat reading Tennyson in the rectory garden while the bloody battle of Gravelotte was being fought in the Franco-Prussian war. At the time he noticed an old horse harrowing in a field below, in the Valency valley, an incident he distinctly remembered when he wrote 'In Time of "The Breaking of Nations" ' more than forty years later, during a bloodier war against Germany. Just when the August drought was broken is not clear; on the 22nd Hardy and Emma were caught in the rain while he was sketching her with Beeny Cliff in the background.

3.   Soon after his August stay with the Holders, the tower and the northern aisle and transept were demolished. At the end of May 1871, when Hardy made his third visit (of which little is known except that it was professional), rebuilding was under way, after Emma had laid the foundation stone. The poem 'Love the Monopolist', which was begun in 1871, probably recalls the sight of her in blue as his train left Launceston. At Exeter station he was chagrined to find the three volumes of *Desperate Remedies* listed at half-a-crown in W. H. Smith's remainder catalogue.

4.   The following October he combined another professional visit with a holiday of about three weeks, during which he still hoped that Macmillan would publish *Under the Greenwood Tree*, and informed Tinsley that he had begun the novel which was published as *A Pair of Blue Eyes*. He was not yet in a position to abandon architecture.

5. His next return to Cornwall as far as is known was at least ten months later, four months after the reopening of St Juliot church. After sending the first instalment of *A Pair of Blue Eyes* for publication in *Tinsleys' Magazine*, with instructions to send the proofs to Kirland House (near Bodmin), where Emma's father lived, he sailed on 7 August 1872 for Plymouth from London, where he had been helping Professor Smith to prepare designs for London schools, the Education Act of 1870 having made elementary education obligatory for all children of eligible age who were not pupils. At the end of the month he and Emma were at St Juliot, after staying with her friends the Sergeants at St Benet's Abbey, Lanivet, not far from Kirland.

6. Early in 1873, after completing *A Pair of Blue Eyes*, he made 'a flying visit' to St Juliot rectory.

7. From 'The Seven Times' and his *Life* it seems evident that the last time Hardy saw Emma Gifford in Cornwall was at the end of 1873. Their 'tryst' before his 'journey's end' suggests she was staying, as she had often done, with her cousins at Launceston, and that she and Hardy travelled for a short stay with her sister and brother-in-law, probably at Christmas. (In the early summer he had spent a few days with her in Bath, before taking her to see Tintern Abbey. Since then he had been busy writing *Far from the Madding Crowd*, the first instalment of which he found given pride of place at the beginning of *The Cornhill Magazine* when he reached Plymouth on his way home on New Year's Eve.)

8. Not until after Emma's death almost forty years later did Hardy revisit St Juliot and neighbouring places which had brought him so much happiness from 1870 to the end of 1873. He set off with his brother Henry on 6 March 1913, intending to see the rectory the next day, the anniversary of his first visit. Florence Dugdale, whom he married less than a year later, stayed at Max Gate, a loaded revolver in her bedroom as a safeguard against any night marauder in such an isolated place.[1] In Plymouth, on the return journey, after calling on Emma's cousins at Launceston, he made arrangements for a tablet in memory of her to be placed in St Juliot church. Revivification of a happy past with inevitable reflections on the cruel irony of its unfortunate sequel had proved to be such a painful experience that he wondered what had possessed him to make such a visit.

9. The last visit took place in September 1916, when Hardy and Florence, after calling on the cousins at Launceston, travelled to St Juliot to ensure that all was satisfactory with the design, inscription, and erection of the memorial tablet. A visit to Tintagel sowed the seed from which another memorial to Emma, *The Famous Tragedy of the Queen of Cornwall*, ultimately grew, after an early start that autumn.

Emma's statement that Hardy came two or three times a year after April 1872 must be misleading; in its context it seems to imply visits to St Juliot for a considerable period. His inscription on the tablet to her memory makes it clear that she lived at the rectory from 1868 to 1873. He remembered only three visits to St Juliot after the reopening of the church, the last at the end of 1873. The question arises where she lived from then until their wedding in September 1874, when the success of *Far from the Madding Crowd* seemed to have made his literary career assured. She had no income, and was entirely dependent. When Hardy last met her in Cornwall she was at Launceston with her cousins. She probably spent some time with them (and may have already moved there), possibly also with the Sergeants at Lanivet. Her father's favourite daughter, she could have spent much time with her parents at Kirland House. Not long before her marriage she stayed with her brother Walter in Maida Vale. As will be seen, it is reasonable to deduce that Hardy in 1873 would not be eager to revisit John Attersoll Gifford. The gap of at least ten months between his fourth and fifth visits to Cornwall seems long enough to warrant the question whether one may have been overlooked, but by and large the indicators suggest that the seven pre-marriage ones can have little margin of error. How much more on this, and questions of greater moment, would be known if, very late in her life, in one of her fits of rage and resentment, Emma had not burned all Hardy's love-letters, and insisted on the return of hers, which were also consigned to the flames. They were, he told his second wife, quite as good as the Browning letters, and might have been published.[2]

The questions which follow arise from poems by Hardy relative to his Cornish visits, and from passages and details in *A Pair of Blue Eyes*. Some may be regarded as unanswerable; some suggest that accepted biographical 'facts' are wrong, less often that Hardy was deceived by memory long after the experience under consideration.

Reference has already been made to Hardy's sketching of Emma with Beeny Cliff in the background when they were caught in the rain. He drew the scene afresh from his old stained copy, and wrote the caption below it with the date, 22 August 1870, and lines from 'The Figure in the Scene'. Like 'Why did I sketch?', its companion piece in *Moments of Vision*, this poem was written from an old note. Their content shows that the two poems were composed after Emma's death, and it is a reasonable inference that Hardy's new pen-and-ink sketch of Beeny Cliff with the cloaked and hooded figure in the foreground was made about the same time. In his *Life* he associates these poems with a third, 'It never looks like summer'. The result may be an inclination to link such a comment by Emma with the summer of 1870, though Hardy states that these poems, 'with doubtless many others, are known to be … memories of the present and later sojourns … in this vague romantic land of "Lyonnesse" '. He refers, however, to the 'August drought' of 1870 in 'Quid Hic Agis'; in 'It never looks like summer', written at Boscastle on 8 March 1913, he recalls how dreary Emma thought the scene:

> 'It never looks like summer here
>   On Beeny by the sea.'
> But though she saw its look as drear,
>   Summer it seemed to me.

The continuation –

> It never looks like summer now
>   Whatever weather's there;
> But ah, it cannot anyhow,
>   On Beeny or elsewhere!

– tells how Hardy felt after Emma's death. 'Drear' though it had looked to her on Beeny, it seemed summer to him; the summer was in his heart. It is almost certain that her memorable complaint was made in the summer of 1870, for Hardy seems to be harking back to it, specially for her, in the novel on which he was engaged: 'a wild hill that had no name, beside a barren down where it never looked like summer'.[3] Despite the August drought, the temperature was rarely high, and there may have been many days in the Boscastle area when the sky was disappointingly overcast. (August 1872 has no special claim for consideration, as it was almost as rainless as August 1870.)[4]

'When I set out for Lyonnesse' shows that Hardy had fallen in
love with Emma during his first visit; he returned to Bockhampton
with 'magic' in his eyes. The poem 'certainly' refers to his first
visit, he wrote in his *Life*. He was not sure whether 'At the Word
"Farewell"' applied to the end of his first or second. Like 'Near
Lanivet, 1872' and 'Why did I sketch?', it was published after
Emma's death in *Moments of Vision*. Some weeks later Hardy
informed Mrs Henniker that he liked such poems because they
were 'literally true'. That being so, it is clear from the bare boughs
of the trees beyond the rectory lawn that it was his first visit in
March 1870, not the second in August, which ended cheek-to-
cheek:

> 'I am leaving you…. Farewell!' I said
>   As I followed her on
> By an alley bare boughs overspread;
>   'I soon must be gone!'
> Even then the scale might have been turned
>   Against love by a feather,
> – But crimson one cheek of hers burned
>   When we came in together.

Had Hardy referred to the poem when he wrote more than forty
years later, his uncertainty would have vanished.

The second visit poses a number of questions, among which two
call for comment at this stage. When, at the end of 1870, Hardy
learned that a deposit of £75 was required for the publication of
Desperate Remedies, he realised the risk he was running with 'only
£123 in the world, beyond what he might have obtained from his
father – which was not much', when he was 'virtually if not distinctly engaged to be married to a girl with no money except in
reversion after the death of relatives'. This engagement must have
been at the heart of the discussion which is hinted at in 'By the
Runic Stone'. Much has been written on this monolith and its
whereabouts by Evelyn Hardy; unconvincingly, I thought, after considering all the evidence historically and *in situ*. I remembered the
sketch of a round-headed pillar by Hardy which had impressed me
in the New York Public Library. Obviously it had a special significance for him, and a copy showed that it was the Celtic cross
which stands just within the churchyard at St Juliot, on the southern
side near steps down a small but steep bank above a meadow slop-

ing down towards the Valency valley. I referred the question, with all the relative evidence, to Mary Henderson, the authority on ancient crosses in Cornwall; and she wrote immediately to say (this was in 1975) that she had not the slightest doubt that this was the monolith of Hardy's poem. Only recently she had received an inquiry from a Cornish writer who referred to one of those wheel-headed crosses as 'a Runic stone'. The poem shows that all sense of time was lost as the lovers sat when the 'die' was cast 'in such a place' (that is, by the ruinous church which had brought them together). This must have happened in the summer, for Hardy was white-hatted, and they sat there for hours in the breeze. Emma wore her old brown dress; they were not far from the rectory. When he first met her that August she was dressed in summer blue, which suited her complexion better, he thought. The happiness of that holiday led to the relatively carefree idyllicism of *Under the Greenwood Tree*, where the heroine appears in blue to play the new church organ, just as Emma in blue had been observed at the harmonium by Hardy during Mr Holder's services. The Holders had done their best to promote her engagement; she had disappointed a young farmer ('rather dumb of expression', she writes in *Some Recollections*), who lit the candles at the evening service which took place on 14 August, as Hardy noted on the manuscript of 'The Young Churchwarden', in Mr Holder's other church at Lesnewth. Hardy undoubtedly provided Emma with what she must have regarded as a heaven-sent opportunity to escape the dullness of a life in a remote part of the country where people were 'slow of speech and ideas'. Writing more transcendentally towards the end of her life, she claimed that she had kept herself free until the intended one arrived.

The manuscript of 'In the Vaulted Way' bears the date '1870'. Its detail suggests autobiographical verisimilitude. If this is so, the poem indicates that Hardy had been hurt by a light-tongued remark the previous evening, and that Emma yearned for reconciliation, and looked beseechingly at him, as they were about to part:

> In the vaulted way, where the passage turned
> To the shadowy corner that none could see,
> You paused for our parting, – plaintively;
> Though overnight had come words that burned
> My fond frail happiness out of me.

He whose 'one long aim' (so it must have seemed to him, an ardent lover, if the incident took place at the end of his summer visit) had been to 'serve' her, whose happiness had suddenly seemed frail (Hardy characteristically taking nothing for granted), kissed her, and all was well, though he left puzzled by her remark. (Even at this time Emma was capable of sudden inconsequential comments.) At one time I wondered whether the parting took place in a subway leading from one platform to another at Launceston station, but a friend who lives near assured me there had never been one, and undertook research in Launceston and elsewhere in Cornwall, after I had listed a few possibilities. He conducted this very thoroughly over a long period, and concluded, as I had done, that Launceston offered the most convincing solution. He and the local historian agreed that the most likely spot was either a dark alley called San-ford Timeswell Lane, which runs its crooked way below Castle Mound 'down to the High Street very near to the Temperance Hotel, from where the waggonette left for the station', or the Market House, built in 1840, which had 'vaults', a basement or lower floor which was reached by a flight of stone steps and where wet fish were sold. The former title of the poem was 'In the Crypted Way', and, as I think Hardy would use his architectural term exactly rather than figuratively, I prefer the second location, remembering from *Some Recollections* the delight which Emma found in visiting markets with their 'display of vegetables, flowers, dairy produce, and meat'. I assume that she and Hardy had stayed overnight at least with her cousins, and that she had shopping to do before she returned while he made his way to the station. (Other alternatives were the butter market, demolished early this century, and the main part of the Market House, which had a vaulted roof and, I was assured, a 'shadowy corner that none could see'.)

We turn next to the question when Hardy first met Emma's parents. It has been generally agreed, as far as I know, that this was not before August 1872; there are reasons for thinking it must have been earlier. His instruction to send proofs of the first instalment of *A Pair of Blue Eyes* to Kirland House, c/o John Gifford Esq., was designed, biographers say, to create a favourable impression of his prospects at a time when he wished 'to make a formal request for Emma's hand'. I can find no ground for either of these assumptions. Hardy was diffident, and could never have spoken at this period with any assurance of his career. After losing money on *Desperate Remedies* and selling *Under the Greenwood Tree* with the copyright for only £30, he was finding it necessary to work as an architectural assistant. He could not be certain that his new novel, for which he was being paid £15 per instalment, would be a success in any way; for both serialisation and the three-volume edition he was to receive only £200. Nor is it likely that Emma's father had been kept ignorant of her engagement for two years. There was no question of an imminent marriage, and no evidence exists that there was any opposition to it. In 'The Seven Times' Hardy recalled this August visit as 'The best and rarest ... of the rare'.

For evidence that he and Mr Gifford were no strangers at this time we turn to the early chapters of *A Pair of Blue Eyes*, which show no important change of substance from the first instalment in *Tinsleys' Magazine*. A short fictional proem has been discarded as an irrelevance. The most significant change had taken place at the proof-stage, when lines sung by Elfride –

> For his bride a soldier sought her,
> And a winning tongue had he

– were replaced by Shelley's verse

> O Love, who bewailest
> The frailty of all things here,
> Why choose you the frailest
> For your cradle, your home, and your bier!

The title first proposed for the novel had been 'A Winning Tongue Had He'; this theme was to find expression in Hardy's next novel, *Far from the Madding Crowd*. The introduction of the death-note, the first of a series of overtones leading to the tragic finale, shows that the decision to change the theme was made when Hardy returned to Cornwall in August 1872. Not surprisingly, when questioned on this only a few months before his death, he could not remember having had 'A Winning Tongue Had He' in mind for the title, and failed to see its relevance to *A Pair of Blue Eyes*.[5] For our present purpose the fact that no important changes have been made in the first five chapters since they were revised (presumably at Kirland House) is crucial.

Evidence that Hardy already knew Emma's father is to be found in the character of the heroine's father and in the description of Lord Luxellian's home. Mr Swancourt reveals John Attersoll Gifford's snobbishness and his habit of quoting Latin (noted by Emma in *Some Recollections*). These notable characteristics were to be sustained in the chapters Hardy wrote immediately after finishing his first proofs; and the first hero's sense of his class inferiority (like his author, he is the architect son of a humble master-mason) becomes such a cardinal issue that Emma, who would have been eager to assist by making an extra copy of Hardy's work then or later, must certainly, it can fairly be assumed, have known something of his family background. Neither would wish to prejudice her father by disclosing the truth at this juncture. The original of Lord Luxellian's mansion was Lanhydrock House, as Hardy hinted in the 1912 postscript to the preface of his novel, and admitted in June 1920. From his presentation of the 'ancient gateway of dun-coloured stone, spanned by the high-shouldered Tudor arch', and the gallery portraits, it is clear that Hardy had already visited it. For two and a half centuries it had belonged to the Robartes family. In August 1870 Emma told him a story of Miss R ——, an aristocratic lady living at Tintagel with whom she had stayed when her sister was in service there as the lady's companion. Emma was recovering from an illness at the time, and the 'eccentric old lady of county family' sent her a pony, the one she had at St Juliot, when she returned to Kirland. If, as is generally thought, she was a Robartes, the Gifford girls probably heard a great deal of Lanhydrock House, which Emma may have visited when staying near, with her parents or with the Sergeants at Lanivet. She (Emma) could have introduced Hardy to her father in the summer of 1870 or in October 1871, and, while at Kirland House, would have done everything possible to satisfy his interest in architecture and paintings by ensuring that he visited this stately home with its striking barbican and its gallery of portraits.

Hardy had to press on with *A Pair of Blue Eyes*, and it must have been a relief – his subject being so inextricably linked with his own situation at the time – to leave Kirland House and stay with Emma's friends, Captain Charles Sergeant and his wife, at St Benet's Abbey, Lanivet. There he could write with greater freedom and detachment. He and Emma were on their way back to St Benet's, after a long walk, possibly including a visit to Lanhydrock House, when she tiredly sought the support of a handpost, extending her arms along two of its direction signs as if she were crucified, an ill omen he thought in retrospect, as he recorded in the poem 'Near Lanivet, 1872' after her death. They probably stayed with the Sergeants a week or two, for according to the family tradition a good deal of the novel was written in their summer house.[6] Hardy may have written rapidly, and revised assiduously later on. The serial shows care at all stages. All that is known is that he thought he was comfortably ahead of schedule, for he was touring in Devon before the end of the month, when he was at St Juliot (where he could not remember writing any of his fiction, he told his second wife).[7] He must have found that more revision was necessary than expected; on 30 August he assured William Tinsley that the October instalment was ready, though he wished to keep it several days longer. He stayed until 10 September. Sufficient copy at least for the November number was posted from Bockhampton at the end of the month. Hardy had given up working in London to concentrate on his novel.

With his letter of 30 August Hardy sent the names and addresses of friends who had promised to order *Tinsleys' Magazine* if he presented them 'with the first number of the story'. He would be surety for six of them. It would be surprising if the Sergeants, the Holders, and the Giffords were not among these six. If, as may be supposed, John Gifford, who set so much store on social status, followed the next instalments, his suspicions may have led him to question Emma when she paid her parents a visit. The poem 'I rose and went to Rou'tor Town' (Bodmin, not far from Rough Tor, a moorland height) relates how she set out 'With gaiety and good heart', to be made unhappy soon after her arrival by 'The evil wrought ... On him I'd loved so true'. On the vexed question which Hardy had been fictionalising, she had previously argued, I believe, as Elfride does with Stephen Smith:

Why should papa object? An architect in London is an architect in London. Who inquires there? Nobody. We shall live there, shall we not? Why need we be so alarmed?

At the time Emma ignored social differences; she was 'The woman whom I loved so, and who loyally loved me', Hardy remembered after her death, though, at her worst, when the Gifford sense of superiority asserted itself, she had wounded him more than once in their later years by referring to his 'peasant' stock. By the time he had won success and fame with the publication of *Far from the Madding Crowd*, her father must have been reconciled to their marriage; he was already there to greet them when they arrived at their first home after honeymooning in Paris. How much later it was that he referred to Hardy in a letter as a 'low-born churl' who had 'presumed to marry into' his family is not known;[8] probably in one of those maudlin moods when, reminded perhaps that she had not yet settled comfortably and respectably in a house of her own (which did not happen until 1876), he had been drinking heavily, as he habitually did to find solace for the loss or ill-fortune of one of his dear ones.

I omit the topographical autobiography in *A Pair of Blue Eyes*, and keep to the story a little longer. Emma was no weak, vacillating Elfride, and Hardy, I am sure, was a more restrained lover than the unbashful Stephen Smith. The chess games in which the latter shows an autodidact's ignorance of etiquette seem very convincingly autobiographical; it is certain from *Some Recollections* that Emma had learned tactics and moves from her youngest brother, a proficient at the age of five who gave other members of the family no rest until they played with him. One might assume, as one biographer does, from Elfride's behaviour while Stephen sketches inside the church, that Emma ascended the pulpit while Hardy was preparing restoration plans for Crickmay, though we cannot be expected to believe from what immediately follows that she wrote the rector's sermons, as Elfride, leaning over the front of the pulpit, tells Smith she did. I think Hardy took the trouble to be exact, however, when he wrote in the serial version:

> Has the reader ever seen a winsome girl in a pulpit? Perhaps not. Nor has the writer; but he knows somebody who has, and who can never forget that sight.[9]

This is a mere detail. Much more important is the way the story develops when extreme jealousy strangles the love which had arisen between the second hero and Elfride. I believe the cruelly rigorous form it took originated when Hardy had time to reflect on the jealousy he had felt on discovering that Emma had become almost engaged to the young farmer he saw lighting the candles in Lesnewth church. He remembered the words 'Jealousy is cruel as the grave' in the Song of Solomon, and they led him to write the improbable fiction of 'The Face at the Casement' in *Satires of Circumstance*.

A manuscript note shows that 'The Young Churchwarden' was prompted after Emma's death by what Hardy observed at the Lesnewth evening service on 14 August 1870. After ushering them to their pew, the churchwarden lit candles for them, and Hardy noticed the light fall on his hand, and how it trembled as he scanned them with a vanquished air. Years later, 'When Love's viol was unstrung', Hardy had grievous reason to wish that

> the hand that shook
> Had been mine that shared her book
> While that evening hymn was sung,
> His the victor's, as he lit
> Candles where he had bidden us sit
> With vanquished look.

It was the ninth Sunday after Trinity, and the reading or lesson 'decreed' was the nineteenth chapter of the First Book of Kings on Elijah and the still small voice, as Hardy recalled during the 1914–18 war in the poem 'Quid Hic Agis?' ('What doest thou here?'):

> [When I] heard read out
> During August drought
> That chapter from Kings
> Harvest-time brings;
> – How the prophet, broken
> By griefs unspoken,
> Went heavily away
> To fast and to pray,
> And, while waiting to die,
> The Lord passed by,
> And a whirlwind and fire
> Drew nigher and nigher,
> And a small voice anon
> Bade him up and be gone, –
> I did not apprehend
> As I sat to the end
> And watched for her smile
> Across the sunned aisle …

There is, it is worth noting, a curious discrepancy in the above two poems about where Emma sat that evening. If, as I have supposed, she sat across the aisle from Hardy when she played the harmonium, how is it they shared the same book to sing the hymn in 'The Young Churchwarden'?

'Quid Hic Agis?' is structured on three readings of the Elijah story, the third of which took place on 20 August 1916, the day after the poem's appearance in the *Spectator*, not long before Hardy and his second wife made their visit to see the tablet commemorating Emma's links with St Juliot church. In the final section, after thinking of this memorial, he feels the 'wind and earthquake' of the prolonged war against Germany, with its mad shelling and unending toll of lives, and he hears distinctly the voice 'What doest thou here?'. Like Elijah, he is 'waiting to die'.

In the second section he recalls how he himself read 'At the lectern there' (i.e., at Lesnewth) 'The selfsame words / As the lesson decreed'. Here, we must conclude, Hardy's memory deceived him. In his *Life* he tells us how the death of Mr Holder reminded him 'sadly of the pleasure he used to find in reading the lessons in the ancient church when his brother-in-law was not in vigour'. As the church was too ruinous to be used for public worship several years before its partial restoration was completed for its reopening in April 1872, Hardy could not have read any lesson there before the following August, after a period at Kirland House and St Benet's Abbey. At no time, there or at Lesnewth, to judge by all the available evidence, could he have read the decreed Elijah lesson. 1873 seems to be out of the question; Hardy saw Emma three times that year, and there can be little doubt that at the time the 'lesson decreed' was read, on 10 August, he was busy preparing *Far from the Madding Crowd* at Bockhampton. In 1872 it was read on 28 July, ten days before Hardy left London. The lesson was a favourite with him; he had heard it often, and knew it so well that he must have imagined hearing parts of it when he made Knight its reader (with Elfride at the organ) in *A Pair of Blue Eyes*.[10] Perhaps this, and its inevitable association with St Juliot church, led him to think forty-four years later that he had read it there, all the more so because he had sometimes thought of himself and Emma in the development of Elfride's relationship with Knight, who is about the author's age. At one point in their conversation (shortly after the Elijah reading) she uses a passage from one of Emma's letters to Hardy, as we know from one of his notebooks.[11] It is a fair guess also, judging from photographs of the author, that the heroine's observations of Knight's round-shoulderedness and incipient baldness were a pleasant acknowledgement of some comment Emma had made on him.[12] It is difficult to believe Hardy fictionalised the second section of 'Quid Hic Agis?' for poetical gain. The poem might, in fact, have been more effective had he restricted himself to the subject of its first and third parts, providing the kind of life-and-death contrast he gives in 'Beeny Cliff', one of the poems which resulted from his penultimate visit to Cornwall forty-three years after his first.

For our final question we turn from biographical issues to the interpretation of this poem. My concern is with the Virgilian purples attributed to 'Beeny Cliff' by Donald Davie in an article published in the spring-summer 1972 number of *Agenda*. The 'bloom of dark purple cast' that, as we read in the 1895 preface to *A Pair of Blue Eyes*, 'seems to exhale from the shoreward precipices' leads him to claim that the purple of the poem is not only visual but, 'in terms of what Beeny does to its ambience of sea and sky and land and the people who move there', spiritual also – 'a seeming, a floating off, an exhalation; something which may at times inspire terror'; the 'purples which prink the main ... are the spiritual light of sexual love – as indeed we should have guessed, for what but sexual passion is so likely to terrify and irradiate alternately or at the one time?' Confirmation for this stupendous claim is found in 'the purple light' which illumines Stephen Smith when Elfride appears, looking 'so intensely *living* and full of movement'.[13] This light originates, we are told, from the sixth book of Virgil's *Aeneid*, where it is a feature of the underworld abode of the blessed. Support for this is conveniently, but not convincingly, found in the 'Veteris vestigia flammae' epigraph of 'Poems of 1912–13', taken from the fourth book of the *Aeneid*, when, after hearing the story of his sufferings and setbacks, the widow Dido feels that Aeneas has reawakened love in her. The phrase is then related to Dante's repetition of it in Canto xxx of the *Purgatorio*. These transitions lead to a conclusion that Hardy's meeting with Emma's ghost, before dawn breaks in 'After a Journey', subsumes the meeting of Aeneas and the dead Dido (in the underworld) and that of Dante and the dead, transfigured Beatrice. (There is a *non sequitur* here: Dido is a distressed ghost, not one of the happy souls in Virgil's Elysium. I forbear to discuss the Beatrice association; the divine love which she transmits at the end of the *Purgatorio* inspires some of the most ecstatic lyricism in T. S. Eliot's poetry, but is non-existent in Hardy.) Lengthy passages follow from a Dante critic, with much on other poems by Hardy, all of which has hardly any relevance to what 'Beeny Cliff' meant to its author. The early part of the essay, summarised above, is brilliantly presented, and undoubtedly has spell-binding qualities, but, far from being a feat of perceptive

integration, it is an intoxicating *tour de force* founded on false
assumptions.

First, there is nothing in 'Beeny Cliff' which suggests sexual
passion or the terror which it may inspire. The first part was based
on Hardy's note for 10 March 1870: 'Went with E. L. G. to Beeny
Cliff. She on horseback.... On the cliff ... "The tender grace of a
day", etc.'. 'The tender grace' – it would be rash to associate this
Tennysonian reminder with passion, and much nearer the mark to
equate it with Keats's 'tender eye-dawn of aurorean love'. The only
March 1870 feeling expressed in the poem is happiness, 'As we
laughed light-heartedly aloft on that clear-sunned March day.' This
was less than three days after Emma and Hardy first met. 'The
woman whom I loved so, and who loyally loved me' clearly refers
to the love that followed and lasted for years.

Next, the purples that 'prinked the main' are out at sea, not in the
sky or on the land or around 'the people who move there'; they are
not an exhalation from the cliff. Many Hardy enthusiasts must have
sat or stood high up, where Hardy sketched Beeny when Emma and
he were caught in a shower, and seen such colourful reflections on
the ocean waters to the left. In the poem they have no overtones:
'the Atlantic dyed its levels with a dull misfeatured stain' as a low
rain-cloud passed over, 'And then the sun burst out again, and purples prinked the main.' Hardy refers to this actuality in the poem 'If
you had known', where, writing in 1920, exactly fifty years later, he
remembers how Emma and he were caught in the rain as they
listened to 'the far-down moan / Of the white-selvaged and
empurpled sea'.

In the third place, it seems very unlikely that Hardy, who had
recently turned again and again to the secret diaries which Emma
had kept for about twenty years, could imagine her in the abode of
the blessed, however much he recalled their old love. They regis-
tered the envy, jealousies, spite, and resentments of a tormented
spirit, the split personality of this regrettable record on the one hand
and of the happy memories in *Some Recollections* on the other. If we
are to pursue the Virgilian parallel seriously, Emma's tormented
spirit would be with Dido's rather than in the Elysian fields.

The claim that 'the purple light' which illumines Smith when he
falls in love originates from Virgil is a major flaw in the Virgilian
purples case. Hardy's first published novel *Desperate Remedies*
shows that he had probably read the whole of the *Aeneid* in the
Dryden translation copy of Virgil's works which his mother gave

him when he was young; whether he remembered the 'purple' detail on which so much significance has been laid (it is comprised in a single word) is another matter. Infinitely more appealing and memorable were many of the poems in the copy of *The Golden Treasury* which his friend Horace Moule gave him; he read from it continually. Its effect can be seen in *Desperate Remedies*, which reveals the origin of the 'purple light' in a passage on the 'supremely happy moment' when hero and heroine first kiss:

> The 'bloom' and the 'purple light' were strong on the lineaments of both. Their hearts could hardly believe the evidence of their lips.
> 'I love you, and you love me, Cytherea!' he whispered.
> She did not deny it.... [14]

Hardy's 'bloom' clearly proves that his 'purple light' originates from a line in 'The Progress of Poesy' by Thomas Gray, 'The bloom of young Desire and purple light of Love'.

Despite Dryden's retention of 'purple' for the Elysian light, Hardy by 1913, if not much earlier, would know that the Latin adjective meant varying shades of red; there is no reason to think that he did not know it could also mean 'bright', as John Conington indicated for the Elysian lines in his 1884 commentary on the *Aeneid*. All these meanings, and others, appear in the 1894 edition of Lewis and Short's Latin dictionary. He would realise that Gray's 'light of love' was purple in the classical, not the English, sense. Gray acknowledged that his line derived from the Athenian poet Phrynichus, 'and on his rose-red cheeks there gleams the light of love', a translation which makes excellent sense, I suggest, of 'the purple light' that illumines Smith in *A Pair of Blue Eyes*. No light of human love invests Virgil's Elysium. Nor is it purple; it is exceptionally bright,[15] the sheen of a superhuman beneficence.

Finally, the design of 'Beeny Cliff' precludes the hypothetical link with Virgil. Like the two stanzas of another Beeny poem, 'It never looks like summer' (already quoted), it depends on the sharpness of contrast; it is a 'satire of circumstance'. In the first part, which concludes with the purples out at sea, there are no hints of death or overtones of mourning – no suggestion of anything in Virgil's underworld. Its happiness (a vivid recollection of 10 March 1870) is unqualified, and quite antithetical to the climactic March 1913 section, which reads:

– Still in all its chasmal beauty bulks old Beeny to the sky,
And shall she and I not go there once again now March is nigh,
And the sweet things said in that March say anew there by and
    by?

What if still in chasmal beauty looms that wild weird western shore,
The woman now is – elsewhere – whom the ambling pony bore,
And nor knows nor cares for Beeny, and will laugh there nevermore.

Notes

1.   Florence Dugdale to Edward Clodd, 7 March 1913, Brotherton
Collection, Leeds University Library.
2.   Florence Hardy to Howard Bliss, 10 January 1931, Princeton University
Library.
3.   *Desperate Remedies*, Ch. xv, 3.
4.   The records of the National Meteorological Library and Archive for
this period consist of local notes which are too brief to be useful. The
detailed register kept by Dr J. Merrifield of the Navigation School,
Plymouth (daily for 1872), is the best for the area, and I am grateful to
J. H. Goldie for sending me all the available details.
5.   Florence Hardy to Howard Bliss, 17 September 1927, Princeton
University Library.
6.   According to the writer of 'Whispers and Echoes' in the *Cornish
Guardian* of Thursday, 19 January 1928 (three days after Hardy's
burial), the Sergeants' son Colonel Sir William stated that 'a considerable number of instalments' were written at St Benet's. Wildly
exaggerated as this report must be, it suggests that Hardy wrote
busily for several days at least. I am indebted to J. H. Goldie for a copy
of the above.
7.   Reference as for note 5.
8.   Reference as for note 1.
9.   Compare *A Pair of Blue Eyes*, Ch. iv.
10.   *A Pair of Blue Eyes*, Ch. xix.
11.   For Emma's letter (24 October 1870) see Evelyn Hardy's edition of
Thomas Hardy's Notebooks (Hogarth Press, 1955), pp. 31–2, or R. H.
Taylor's *The Personal Notebooks of Thomas Hardy* (Macmillan, 1978) p. 6.
12.   *A Pair of Blue Eyes*, Ch. xviii.
13.   See note 9.
14.   *Desperate Remedies*, Ch. iii, 2.
15.   See Roger Lonsdale's edition of the poems of Gray, Collins, and
Goldsmith (Longmans, 1969) p. 166. J. W. Mackail in his edition of the
Aeneid (1930) gives 'brilliantly luminous' for 'lumine purpureo', and
Cecil Day Lewis in his translation (1952) gives '[clothing the vales in]
dazzling light'.

Index